THE LESS YEAR

C.K. OLDFIELD

PART I

BEFORE

He could smell them burning. It wasn't a familiar smell, but it didn't have to be. Deep down, some part of him just knew what it was. It embraced him as he snapped awake, buried under the mingled scents of torched wood and heavy smoke. All around him, the house was ablaze. He screamed.

Dry and ragged, his prepubescent shriek was more cough than cry. He hacked into the air, young lungs pining for whatever last gasps of oxygen could be found. Hungry orange flames consumed the timber walls of the cabin in a gluttonous frenzy. The room was more smoke than not, his saving grace the simple fact that he had fallen asleep on the floor. He blinked back the ashy haze, his vision dappled and fluttering as he crawled toward the kitchen. The flames hadn't reached there yet, shades of glowing onyx tucked away from the growing fire. He made it a dozen feet before stopping.

Where is everyone? Where is Rachel?

Then he remembered the smell. It was meat. It was *people*.

"Rach!?" he cried. "Rachel!?"

His shouts were hoarse and muffled, the inferno claiming

the noise for its own. He dragged himself back into the den, the silky soot smudging his hands and wrists as he crawled. He followed the light upward as the fire cracked and huffed, caressing the ceiling with its thin tendrils of concentrated heat. The Boy, hardly past his eleventh birthday, whimpered as he pushed deeper into the scalding smoke, every inch an expedition.

Finally, he saw her leg sticking out from under the table. The wood was scorched and freshly aflame.

"Rachel!"

The worn soles of her boots glimmered in the vagueness. Scrambling toward her, he pulled his shirt over his face, desperate for unspoiled air. He tucked his chin as he shimmied over the floorboards. They were warm to the touch and dark. Delicate black-grey flakes trickled down like hot rain, painting the wood as it reflected the light. He reached out to grab his sister's leg, slapping at the flames, pulling her towards him.

But her leg wasn't there. It was just a charred and fragile shell of nothingness. His hand pressed straight through.

The Boy screamed.

He screamed as he grasped at her torso, but she was hot and empty, her melted flesh sticking to him as desperately as he flailed for it. Its gelatinous grip bored into his hands, burning his skin. He was still screaming when the last bits of her ruined body seared into his forearm.

She was on fire, what was left of her. The Boy was too. But he didn't want to let go. He couldn't. So he held her ashes as they burned together and let the darkness take them.

1

Six years later.

It was a fever. Hardly past sunrise, a cloudless sky loomed bright and clear above the tired homestead. The formless cobalt ceiling conjured heat, cooking the world into a prolonged stupor as a dry wind blew east off the lake, the water's grey-glass surface stale and timeless. A hundred acres of gaunt, half-plowed fields and anorexic woodlands greeted Magnus as he stepped out into the morning, all of it brown and wilting.

Skirting past the skeletal orchard and its matchstick trees, he headed straight for the barn, a late breakfast of hard bread hastily stuffed into his mouth. Within minutes, and not even a few hundred yards from his front door, Magnus could taste sweat. He could feel it birthing under his arms. It was on his lips, tickling his beard. After he swallowed, he spat.

"Bastards," he grumbled, cursing those who came before.

Because all Magnus could remember was hot. Fifty-some years of holding on with calloused hands, and all he could remember was the crunch of parched earth and the stench of a summer that never truly ended. The season was like a stubborn fire that just wouldn't go out, its embers gobbling up every last scrap of kindling within reach.

"Bastards," he repeated, rolling his shoulder. The joint was perpetually stiff, courtesy of a cracked bone that had never set. With a yawn, he rolled it again, remembering one fire in particular as he lumbered toward the dilapidated shed. It was the fire that changed everything.

He counted the years, padding his fingertips as he edged his way around the fragile garden. "Six years..."

For a long moment, he was back in that fire. Searching for his children. Choking on smoke. Breathing in bodies.

"Oh, um, morning, da'," his son interrupted. Magnus blinked into the light, spotting the startled Boy in the crooked shade of the barn, tucked away beside a heap of mulch. A book was propped open in his lap, his greasy hair sweat-damp and pushed off his forehead. Beside him, leaning against the weathered wood, stood a rusty hoe. Its metal blade was recently sharpened. And clean.

"I take it yer done?" Magnus probed, his tone prickly, knowing full well the kid hadn't even started his chores.

The Boy shook his head. "I'm...still digesting. I'll start soon. It's goin—"

"Best start now cuz it's gonna b—"

"...going to be hot, I know," his son echoed, closing his book with a sigh. Dusting himself off, and tucking the book into his pocket, the Boy grabbed the weathered implement and plodded off toward the garden, a straw hat crowning his dark mop of hair.

Magnus floundered as his son passed. "What...ah...what book you readin'?"

The Boy stopped, peeking out from the brim of his tattered sunhat, and flashed the paper manuscript.

"*The Tales of Sarris Gamling*? That one for the exams?"

Magnus knew the answer but he didn't know what else to say. Ever since the fire, he and the Boy had found themselves on shaky ground. He knew he didn't have much in common with his son—the Boy was much more like Mar—but Rachel had always been around to bridge the gap between them. With her gone, that distance had only widened.

And it's only going to get worse when he finds out...

"Not much else to read up here," his son shrugged, kicking at a stone in the dirt.

"Hm. I suppose not, eh." He and Mar had been prodding the kid to take the exams for a couple seasons now, though the Boy was reluctant. He didn't much like spending time in Hope. But he couldn't be a recluse forever, and the exams were the first step toward getting a position at the school and, if all went well, with the village council as a clerk.

"Why don't—"

"Well, I—

His son stopped, letting Magnus continue. "Why don't I poke around Mayor Haakan's office tom—...the next time I'm in for council? See if he's got some other books you can borrow."

The Boy bounced his head, a brooding tight-lipped smile his only reply.

"Alrighty, well, best get to it," Magnus huffed, clapping a hand against his leg.

Before he took two paces, someone whistled. Mag followed the sound toward the Luddstows' farmhouse. A few hundred yards off, Tom and Saira Luddstow's small cabin rested on the largest of the little knolls that made up their semi-shared plot of land. Beyond the Luddstows' paltry back garden, Tom's kid waved, swinging a stick into a thistle patch.

How old is Tom's kid now? Nine? Ten? Too young for a Year...

Magnus realized his son was staring at him.

"Yeah, yeah, go see what he wants," Magnus conceded. "But

keep 'er quick. You got chores, and so does the little one, and I want these carrots dug today."

The Boy nodded, darting across the bone-dry garden. He edged along the palisade that fenced in their backyard before crossing the drizzle of a creek in a single bound. The two boys talked for a moment before they started ravenously hacking away at a thistle patch.

"That was nice of you," a voice flitted in over his shoulder. Stepping out of the cool shade of the barn, his wife leaned against its doorframe, chewing at the gristle of a misshapen crab apple. "What's the occasion?"

Magnus ignored her playful snipe and watched the boys hack away for another minute before finally replying, his voice weighted with a sudden seriousness.

"It's coming, Mar."

Mariam stopped chewing. He could tell she wasn't surprised, but her body language shifted, her hand brushing against the knife on her hip.

"That explains the fingerprints on the case," she finally replied. "The lock had been opened too, I saw. I was hoping it was just you being paranoid."

Magnus smiled. Of course she noticed that he had opened the trunk. They hadn't opened it in years. Hadn't even so much as talked about it.

But now...

"You sure?" she prodded, crossing her arms, her long limbs tanned and glistening, the dirt under her nails dark and thick.

Magnus nodded. It was coming. Even after its long absence, he could feel it in the air. The subtle doom of it, like a coming eclipse, casting its long shadow over everything they had worked so hard to build.

"Did Haakan say anything?" his wife continued. "Or Ax?"

Magnus spat a fresh round of sweat off his lips. "How old is Tom's boy now?"

"Eight," his wife replied without missing a beat.

"Hm." Magnus drifted back to his early Years, remembering. "Maybe he won't remember much." He knew that was wishful thinking. He was younger than eight during his first Year. And while not all Less Years were bad or bloody, some were. And he remembered.

"Does Rhys know too?" Mariam pried. "Viktoria must, I'd wager. That old hag has her fingers in every pie."

Magnus shrugged. "Runner will be by today with a summons. I saw the papers."

Mariam grabbed her hat and stepped out into the light, lobbing the apple core into the field. "Poor Haakan," she grinned. "Shit time to be mayor."

Mag grinned too. But then his wife's tone shifted back to seriousness.

"Why didn't you tell me sooner? You must have known for... three days now at least? Since the council meeting?"

Back across the field, the Luddstow boy was throwing rocks up into the air and trying to bat them as Magnus' son read aloud from the Sarris Gamling book.

Because I wanted us to have a few more normal days before the world ends.

"Kid shoulda been trainin' since the fire," Magnus said instead. "We wasted time pushin' him toward the exams. He shoulda been learning the real stuff."

His wife rubbed her dirt-stained hands on her pants as she paced in the shade. He could smell the garden on her as she neared. Shucked corn, vine tomatoes. Mint and nettles and purslane.

"Better late than never, I s'pose," he added, albeit half-heartedly.

With a long, slow pull, Mariam freed her knife from its sheath, letting the thin blade fall to her side. The tip grazed the barn wood as she walked. Every few paces, she poked the metal into the old planks and timbers.

Magnus eyed her knife. "Think you still got it?"

His wife smirked, twirling the blade, tracing circles in the air. "Why don't you go open that trunk, get your tools, and find out?" She feigned a few quick thrusts in his direction, agile and quick as ever. Magnus pawed at her with lazy, unhurried jabs. He had been thinking about the trunk—and his tools—all morning.

"We should have kept up with it," he asserted. "His training, I mean. Even after the fire…"

Magnus had taken pride in the training he gave Rach and the Boy before the fire. Winter swims, throwing knives, wrestling. Kids or not, he wanted them ready for the worst of it. But while it all came naturally to his daughter, for the Boy, well, it just wasn't his wheelhouse.

Especially after the fire…

Mariam lowered her knife, slipping it back into its sheath. "We were building something new. Something better."

From her vest pocket she plucked out a couple small cherry tomatoes and popped them into her mouth. She handed Mag a few as the pair watched the boys play in the distant field. They were trying—and failing—to do handstands in the tall grass beside a brittle tuft of dried-out raspberry bushes.

"And they said it was over," she added. "That the Years were over. That we could move on. Rebuild."

"And we believed them," Magnus scoffed, his stomach tightening.

His wife grabbed his arm, no doubt sensing the blossoming rage that seeded his gut. "Our kids got a peaceful childhood. Something we never got. No Years of worry or famine or bloodshed. Just years as *kids*. That's a gift, Mag. Fire or no, that's priceless."

Magnus crossed his arms, in no mood to argue. Not that he could outmaneuver his wife anyway.

"We have plenty of time to prepare now," she continued. "So let's tell the Boy and be out with it. We can all go into Hope for the announcement."

Magnus pivoted to face her, eyebrow raised. "You don't wanna skip the announcement?"

Mariam shook her head, chewing on the red and orange flesh of the wrinkled fruits. "He's seventeen. He needs to see what's coming. Not read about it in one of his books, not be told about it. He needs to see it for himself. Needs to feel it."

Before Magnus could reply, raised voices floated in from the Luddstow homestead. Somewhere out of sight, Tom was chewing out his wife. But half a heartbeat later, Saira volleyed back with just as much gusto. In the grass, the Boy and Tom's kid stopped playing, gawking at the house where the argument was mounting.

"We'll need to talk about them," Magnus muttered, nodding toward the Luddstow house. He was about to whistle and wave the Boy back over, but his wife stopped him.

"Let him have the day, Mag. You know how hard change is on him. Just give him one last day."

Magnus pressed his teeth together, watching his son and the Luddstow boy play, oblivious to the uncertainty that was about to engulf them all.

It should be Rachel here...

Mag stamped out the guilty thoughts before they took root. "He can have the day."

In the distance, the kids roamed further into the field, away from the arguing that was slow to die down. His son was reading as they went but didn't make it a dozen feet before tripping over a divot in the garden and dropping his book.

Magnus bit his tongue and looked away, avoiding his wife's disapproving stare. Because in the back of his mind, blood and bones and hope, all fighting for a place at the table, swirled like a maelstrom. Graves long buried were coming undone.

We never should have stopped testing him. He's not going to be ready.

"He'll be ready," his wife assured him, as if reading his mind. "Question is, husband, do you think *we'll* be ready? It's been a lifetime." She leaned in, resting her warm head against his bad shoulder. "Do you remember what needs doing?"

Magnus scratched at his beard, pondering. Not only were they both out of practice—*and old*, he thought to himself—but they had someone to protect now. That changed everything.

"It has been a minute," he conceded, remembering Years past. The blood and violence. The isolation. His hands hinted at a quiver, so he rolled his shoulder, embellishing a grimace as he kneaded the muscle.

Because for the first time in almost twenty years—long, good, quiet years—Magnus was afraid.

"But some things," he added, looping his thumbs into his pockets, "you just don't forget." Then he smiled and kissed his wife. Because for the first time in almost twenty years, he also felt alive.

2

It was raining bones. Again. The hypnotic *pitter-patter* was almost soothing. Like the warm caress of summer rain or the soft lapping of the great lake against the ragged curves of its weathered shore. Dry and white, the alabaster chunks tumbled from the sky like hard snow.

Then the pieces grew.

Fingers into femurs, toes into skulls and spines. Every moment loosed larger fragments from the oily sky. They plunged into the water and shattered against the dirt, kicking up a shroud of dust as they flattened fields of faded wheat. The bones whistled their opus, a high-pitched hymn sacred and foreboding.

Standing alone in the field, the Boy watched the godless heavens spill their history. The hail danced at his feet, kissing the air around him. It covered the earth, flooding the horizon with an ocean of skeletons.

Then the bodies came.

Naked and fragile, the corpses crashed around him like thin stones thrown from great heights, splashing red over the jagged white sea of bones. Some were afire, falling embers enveloped

in wind-whipped flames. No voices. No screams. Just color on
canvas. It swirled around him, a boundless depth of horror.
Bodies on bones, night after night after—

Magnus' son shot up, gasping for air. Subdued grey light
enveloped him as his chest rattled calm. Overcast sky washed
his room in daylight as a half-hearted breeze misted tiny
droplets of water against the window. No blood, no bones. Just
delicate spheres of clear water perched on old glass. He flopped
back down in his bed. The sun was well up, its frail glow
pressing through the speckles to cut a smooth line across the
room. The familiar embrace of warm, fresh bread wafted from
the kitchen below.

He waited for the bodies to come crashing through the ceiling, for a storm to rip his house to kindling and drown him in
an ocean of shattered bones. For better or worse, nothing came.

Pushing back his scruffy mop of greasy hair, the Boy rubbed
his eyes, bringing himself to life. The soft pink of his faded
scars reflected the morning in stark contrast to his farmer's tan.
He looked around the bedroom, shaking off the cobwebs of
another restless night.

The room was narrow and cramped, boxed in by a sloping
ceiling that angled over his headboard. On his nightstand, two
books were folded open, their handwritten pages battered and
well read. Half a dozen other books were stacked on his dresser,
a bulky piece that had been in the family for generations. It was
sturdy and made of dark wood, a remnant from a time when
dark wood still existed. Two windows invited light and heat
into the room, their dirty glass fragile and timeworn, blurred by
brown stains and wandering cracks.

His sister's bed sat perpendicular to his across the room. Its
wooden frame rested under the other window, dust dancing
along its edges. The blankets were long since folded and left to
age, their purpose lost.

He traced his fingers over his scars, a familiar prelude to his day. Before gloomy thoughts of what could have been took root, he jumped into his trousers, grabbed a dirty shirt from the crumpled pile on the floor, and headed downstairs for breakfast.

Like most kids his age, the Boy didn't have a name. In a tradition dating back generations, children went unnamed until they survived their first Year. Or, like his sister, survived part of a Year—something she had never ceased to remind him of. It was a mechanism parents used to distance themselves from those who would not come of age...for one bitter reason or another.

Almost twenty years since the last Year, it had become an unwieldy tradition in what was now the largest gap of Less Years since their reinception over a century ago. With the Years thought ended, most folk let their children take a name when they turned 18—something Magnus' son had been dreading.

Beats having to earn one, though, he thought to himself.

"Morning," his mother beamed, interrupting his tired thoughts.

"Mornin'," he mumbled, slipping into his chair at the kitchen table. Mariam slid a jug of lukewarm water his way, but he ignored it, entranced by the waves of steam rising off the crusty loaf and the pot of nettle tea beside it. Still staring, he tore off a chunk of bread, letting it sit in his hand. It was piping hot. He let the heat rise for a few long moments before shoving it into his mouth and quenching it with a gulp of water.

"You were shoutin' again," his father grumbled, not bothering to look up from the crinkled paper he was scribbling chicken-scratch notes upon.

The Boy stopped chewing. He didn't look up either. The wheaty mush in his mouth softened into paste as he eyed the cup in front of him. Carved into its side, in crude misshapen letters, it read RACHEL.

"We thought to wake you," his mother chimed in, "but, you

know, doc said to just leave you be." She passed him a plate colored by dollops of jam and honey, which he accepted, smearing a hunk of bread against them.

"It's fine," he lied. "Was just a dream."

"Was it a—"

"—a fire?" he cut in, letting his mother off the hook. "No. Not really." He clicked his tongue, remembering the dream. "Not this time."

His father nodded, gently rapping his dull pencil against the blemished wood of the dining table. The Boy wondered if he, too, had nightmares. If he ever fought the urge to relive the night their world turned to cinder. He didn't ask—he never could—so he let the conversation die, pressing his toes into the floor, curling them into tight balls until his muscles fatigued. He knew the fire wasn't his fault. He knew it. But what he knew and what he felt were two very separate things.

"We're goin' into Hope today," Magnus stated, setting down the pencil.

The Boy shrugged into his breakfast. "Okay."

"You're comin' too."

There was a tension in his father's voice. A hesitancy. Magnus' son looked up. "What? Why?"

His parents exchanged looks.

"Why?" he asked again. "If it's for the exam, I said I'm not ready. I'll do it when I wa—"

"It ain't for the exam," his father insisted. "Just get ready after chores."

The Boy looked to his mother for support but she offered only a conciliatory nod. In the silence that lingered, a creeping vine of anxiety curled itself around him. He wasn't a fan of going into the village, not since the fire, but there was no point in saying no either. His father wasn't a man to argue with.

Pushing himself back from the table, the Boy stuffed another piece of bread into his mouth and stalked back upstairs without a word. He was almost out of earshot, shuffling up the creaking stairs, when he heard his father mutter.

"He's too soft, Mar. Kid's gotta toughen up."

Swallowing the lump in his throat, he plodded into his room and picked up a book, knowing full well his father was right.

MAGNUS FINISHED his meal in silence, scraping the dregs of oats from his bowl. The drizzle outside, long overdue, hummed a frail tune in the background.

He regretted snapping at the Boy. He had meant to offer some assurance about what was to come, but the words refused to leave his throat. They choked him, suffocating his mind as they stumbled over one another, leaving him to brood in his own wayward thoughts.

He looked to his wife for some intangible sense of comfort, but she too was equally lost in thought, her slender neck and its myriad scars craned toward the window. Like him, she was no doubt ruminating on the past. For better or for worse.

Likely worse, Magnus thought.

Both he and Mar were familiar with worse. They had lived it. Had drank and bathed and bled it. But their boy? He was soft.

The whole damn world has gone soft...

Beyond the fire, their son had never seen real terror. Had never smelled it, never felt it clawing at the back of his eyes or gnawing at his guts.

But Magnus had. And he had learned from it. It was time the Boy learn too.

3

_____

There will be a Less Year. The mayor didn't say the words—not exactly, anyway. The Boy knew he couldn't; they were banished words. Forgotten words. Words tied to a dark and unenlightened past. Instead, the mayor danced around them, desperate and drowning. But the Boy knew what he was saying. They all did.

He whispered the syllables himself, tonguing their dread. "There will be a Less Year."

It was the first such announcement in some twenty years, and it left the people of Hope gutshot. Murmurs surged as the crowd realized the axe had fallen. Whispers of confusion butted against the din, rising into shouts and curses. It was an announcement they were told would never again be made, and it hung in the air like a noxious fume, suffocating and corrupt.

"We don't need the Year here!" someone shouted.

"Southern whoresons!" another spat. More curses followed.

Like most everyone in Hope, the Boy was hearing this announcement for the first time. The words rattled around in his head, distracting him and leaving him lost. He forgot how sweaty his back was, how the sun was cooking the nape of his neck on account of him having forgotten his hat. The pickled stench of unwashed bodies was gone too, paved over by the mayor's worrisome declaration. A delicate silence bloomed in the space of skipped heartbeats, waiting for a miracle to deliver them safely from their new fate.

The Boy mouthed the words again, a spoiled mantra left to rot in the sun. *There will be a Less Year. There will be a Less Year. There will be a Less Year...*

He looked to his father for a cue. Magnus was scratching at the tangled and greying beard he'd been growing all summer, his face unsurprised and unimpressed by the news. Meaty shoulders, momentarily shrugged, folded themselves against a chest made broad by a lifetime of hard labor on hard land. An uninspired glower, one the Boy was abundantly familiar with, bore down on the podium.

In the morning light, his father's age was noticeable, wrinkles and scars alike. While taller than his father, Magnus' son's own frame and patchy stubble offered little comparison. The man was mumbling to himself so the Boy looked away, surveying the gathered crowd instead.

Miners and builders and survivors, the people of Hope were hardy folk. Tucked away at the edge of the world, they had to be. But as the young mayor, pushing back the diminishing wisps of his sweat-soaked hair, mustered his resolve and clarified the official details, the Boy realized the limits of that hardiness. He watched as the few hundred people of Hope were consumed, moment by moment, drawn and quartered by circumstance.

Come the Year, there would be no trade with other settlements. Caravans and wagon trains, market days and holiday festivals would be prohibited. The road between settlements would no longer be safeguarded by rangers and militiamen; laws would still apply, though the Boy wasn't sure if people would be around to enforce them. Come the Year, every village and town would isolate. Those who could get by would get by. And those who couldn't wouldn't. From Hunter's Point in the north to Fort Bastion in the south, progress would be slowed. The world was too frail, too sickly. It needed respite. No new fields would be plowed, no new buildings constructed or trees felled. The world would be left to heal.

Lacking the patience and skill to untangle the anxious web of gloom that bubbled to the surface of his mind, the Boy looked to the towering statue in the distance. The triumphant iron and bronze colossus loomed over the harbor, the chiseled form of Sarris Gamling pointing to the horizon.

Hope, like all the towns along the Great Lakecoast, owed Sarris their freedom. He delivered them from the Years. He built Freed City as a haven from the Less Year, and for generations his people drifted up the coast, establishing new settlements, creating a free society beyond the yoke of less. Settlements like Hope.

But then the Years returned. And—after almost a twenty-year absence—returned again.

Overwhelmed by the growing jeers of the crowd, the Boy focused on the nearby creaking of the mill instead, its slow and steady grind a familiar comfort. As he listened, eyes closed, his mother reached out and tucked her arm around his. A few strands of her wiry black hair stuck to his sweat as she leaned in, her long fingers and calloused hands wrapping around his bicep and forearm. They pressed into the ruinous scars that stained his skin, into the patchwork of pink lines that spilled past his elbow.

"You okay?" she mouthed.

The Boy nodded slowly, eyes fixed on the podium. "So much for the exam..."

Pulling him closer, he felt her tap a message against his arm in Morse. It helped. But not much.

Because he had read about Years past. Had learned of their

viciousness, their corrosiveness. Things, he realized, were about to change. Again.

It's another fire...

The thought was suffocating. Like smoke in the lungs, it slowed him. His mind stuttered. The thousand carefree futures he had daydreamed for himself—a quiet life on the farm reading books, maybe even doing some teaching or writing of his own—were already fading into irrelevance or impossibility. Probably both. Instead of picking a name next year, he was going to have to earn one.

Because less was coming. It was coming for all of them.

4

"Is this yours?" the Boy asked, staring into the open trunk.

"No," his father replied with a smile. "It's your mother's."

His mother flashed him a wink as she lit another candle. He never knew his parents owned a gun. Never even suspected. Even back before the fire, when his parents made him train with his sister—archery, wrestling, knife throwing, making traps—he had no idea there was a rifle in the house.

Like the dirty and damaged trunk, the gun had seen better days. The stock was marked with a handful of dents and chips along its butt, and the metal lever showed its age, the texture of it porous and speckled. But it shone in the night, long and welcome.

He suspected now, weighing the solemn stares his parents gave the weapon, that this was no ornament. Perhaps they even practiced when he was away at school. Questions waylaid him as his mind wandered off in a dozen different directions.

"When...I mean...how...?" He reached out to touch the weapon.

"I've had it since I was younger than you are now," his mother replied. "It was a gift from my father. For one of my first Years." Her sly grin drooped as memories flittered in. "It's one of the last ones ever made, I think."

"For the best," Magnus mumbled.

Like most of the village, his family were farmers and laborers, not hunters or keepers of livestock. Without animals to hunt or protect, there was no real need for a firearm. Wolves and coyotes were more or less extinct, and there hadn't been any brigands in the area since he was a child. Rangers protected the road, and the militia kept the peace. Things were safe.

Of course, he had seen his mother shoot at the fair, but he thought little of it at the time. In truth, as he stared at the polished and dated firearm, he realized he knew very little about such weapons. He knew there hadn't been any built in some sixty or seventy years and that only a few people in the village owned them. Though, with his parents' secret revealed, he couldn't help but wonder who else in Hope held secrets close.

He looked back to the open trunk. It was dark and long and layered with dust; his father's fingers left fresh prints along its exterior. The case was beat-up and old, full of nicks and scratches. A hefty padlock rested on the table, loosed from a rusted iron latch too dark to catch the flickering candlelight.

He never knew his father to be overly graceful, yet there was a delicacy to how the man lifted the weapon, gently resting the rifle in his lap. Slow, measured movements belied history. Intimacy.

A metallic *click* brought him back to the moment. The rifle clinked again as his father fed the weapon, slipping rounds into its chamber. The Boy plucked a bullet from a bag in the trunk, feeling its weight, watching its casing glint in the shifting dim. Bullets, too, were rare, though the Boy spied fifty or more in the case and its pouches. He scooped a handful up, rolling them between his fingers.

Suddenly, with frightening and practiced speed, his father cocked the weapon, priming the tool with a grinding pump of its lever. At the same time, he spun the rifle forward, springing to his feet.

The Boy jolted. Bullets slipped from his palm and scattered onto the hardwood. His mother didn't even flinch. That's when the Boy saw his father—truly saw him—for the first time in his life. There was a violence in his eyes. A wildness Magnus' son had ever only caught glimpses of. It was frightening.

Silent, he picked up the rounds he had dropped, giving himself an excuse to step away. To look away. Peering up from the floor, and still unsure of what to say, the Boy let his eyes wander. They quickly fell upon the next item in the trunk: an old carpenter's tool belt. It was creased and worn, the leather pockmarked by an untold number of faded scrapes. The belt had been laid flat under the weapon, spread out against the padded cloth of the chest's interior.

On each side sat an adjustable metal stirrup. In each stirrup was a hammer. They were old—much older than the rifle—and chipped and splattered with rust.

After passing the rifle to Mariam, who coddled it while attaching a sling, his father took the belt out and dusted it off. He worked it around his waist until it settled on his hips. Adjusting the belt, his fingertips brushed the tops of each old hammer. These were more than just some tools, that much was clear. They were heirlooms. They were treasure.

His father reached out and offered him a tool. The Boy took it, holding the hammer up to the light. The wooden shaft was smooth at the bottom, the head solid metal and dotted with rust. Covering the handle were dozens of carved notches.

"What are the notches for?"

He tallied them quickly. Some were worn, others more

recent. He stopped counting at fifty-two, looking to his mother for a reply. Her lips were tight and unmoving. Turning his gaze back to the hammer, he picked at the rust that coated it, dragging his nail over the metal as he looked to his father for a reply. It was then, in the liquid embers of the evening fire, the Boy realized it wasn't rust that colored the tool.

He knew what the notches meant, then. Knew what they tallied. They were the price of a name.

The thought made his stomach churn, so he handed the hammer back, shoving it into his father's hands. But his father didn't put it away. He set the hammer down on the table, leaving it to taunt the Boy with untold tales of horrors past. And horrors yet to come.

5

A few days after his introduction to the family's secret weapons, the ration wagon arrived. Meandering down the potholed dirt road, a rickety horse-drawn wagon bounced its way toward the homestead.

A good hour's walk from Hope, the farmhouse was a jumble of parts and pieces cobbled together over the decades. The cellar dated back to before the End, its crumbling walls made from stone and concrete long since stained and flaked.

The main floor was a mix of limestone and timber. Lengthy, dark planks of hardwood lined the den while cold, smooth stone covered part of the kitchen. The second floor was a more recent addition, crafted from thick trunks of felled trees with a roof of clay and grass.

Ahead, the lone road cut a lean swath along the coast. It was buttressed by the lake, snaking parallel along the shoreline. Like a mirror of rusted steel, the brown-grey water filled the horizon, its greatness and its name long forgotten.

From the shade of the wide porch, the Boy and his father watched the wagon near, setting down his book as the cloud of dust breezed closer. He was sweaty and running on the losing end of a few hours' sleep, the victim of another fitful rest. The sun, still low on the horizon, impressed a heat wave upon the village and its scattered surrounds, broiling the world.

Two rangers flanked the wagon on horseback. They were burly and well armed. Each wore the standard green and brown long-sleeved ranger tunic, the fabric covered by a boiled-leather jerkin. Both men carried a short sword on their hip and a bulky crossbow on their back. Their half-empty payload was driven by an older man who sat crooked at the reins. The man talked the horses to a standstill, shifting on the wooden bench as he waved. It was a familiar face.

"Good to see ya, Mag!" the old man hollered. His grey-white beard was wide and long, obscuring much of his face. It inched down to his chest like dirty snow before coiling together in a tight braid. The man gave them each a nod. Grabbing a staff, he hopped from the wagon, landing on his only foot. A wide double-sided axe rested on the cart's bench seat.

"Ax, welcome!" His father embraced the old man with a bear hug, careful not to throw him off balance. Ax turned to the Boy next, sizing him up.

"Well lookatchu, Boy! Growin' like a weed! Whaddya now? Sixteen?"

"Seventeen," Magnus' son replied.

"Seventeen? Time to move to the village then. Get yer own place away from this ol' goat!" Ax teased, prodding Magnus with his elbow. "It's good to see ya though," he added, extending a hand.

The Boy stepped in to shake it, arm outstretched. Without a word, the old-timer tugged him off balance, tripping him up with his staff and sending him spiraling to the ground. By the time he realized what was happening, a massive axe was screeching toward his chest. He winced, eyes forced shut in reflex. The blow never came.

"You'll need to be a wee faster than that, Boy!" Ax chuckled. "A wee faster indeed!"

The old man was nothing but a grin, his blade hovering over the Boy's ribs. He felt his neck flush, a warmness inching up his face as he caught his breath. After a moment, his father helped him up, hoisting him to his feet and giving him a quick dust-off.

Tossing his axe back in the wagon, Ax pointed to Magnus's tool belt. "You been teachin' him?"

Magnus offered a tight-lipped smile. "Soon."

"Best be," Ax said, turning to the Boy. "Wasn't my looks that got me through the Years, if ya take my meanin'!" The old-timer flashed a half-toothless smirk, continuing, "Maybe he'll be an axe man like me. Ladies do love a man with a big axe!" He gave the Boy a friendly slap on the arm as he chuckled. "Lads too," he winked.

"Ya can have mine, if ya can lift it," Ax continued. "'Bout time I give it up, anyway," Ax sighed. "Don't think I got another Year in me."

As the Boy eyed the polished and sharpened blade, his father spoke up. "I reckon you'll manage just fine."

"Ppfff, let's hope not," Ax scoffed. "Piss on the Year. I'm too old."

"Doesn't seem that way to me," the Boy chimed in, stumbling into the banter.

"Well, come find me when yer old man has taught ya a thing or two and we can try again. I tell ya, gettin' by's a trick when you're down to one foot and are waist-deep in bodies. HA!"

Magnus' son forced a subdued chuckle, unsure of his response. After an awkward moment, he handed Ax their ration paper.

"Right, right, yer rations. Let's get to 'er." Ax scanned the document, his lips moving as he read it over. He frowned. "Hm.

Hate'ta say it, Mag, but you won't be gettin' what's owed. A runner from down south arrived yesterday. None of us will be by the looksa things. Even us councilors are shit outta luck. Mayor too."

His father shrugged. "Not surprised."

"You know how they get down there," Ax spat. "We send 'em stones and wood and everything else under the sun, and they pinch pennies when it comes time to pay up. Bastards."

"Ain't that the way," Magnus huffed, looping his thumbs into his belt. "But we'll manage."

"Aye, no doubt about it. Though it ain't the well prepared that stir the pot. Anyway, I pity the poor fool who comes a-knockin' here," Ax joked, limping to the back of the wagon. "Alright, let's get to 'er."

The Boy began unloading their allotment while Ax reviewed the manifest. As they tallied the crates, he couldn't help but stare at the armed escort. On top of the two rangers, half a dozen militiamen equipped with swords, bows, and spears waited nearby, spying in every direction. Ax, too, looked over his shoulder every few moments, hand never far from his axe.

"I'll be back with the rest—if the rest arrives," Ax said when they had finished unloading the dozen or so crates. "You'll get papers by runner or rider. But don't hold yer breath!" Reaching back into the wagon, he pulled a handful of flowers from his rucksack. "My better half picked these. Thought Rach might like 'em. She was a sweet kid. Always helpful."

For a dragging heartbeat, the Boy was back in Ax's burning house, where the world was ended by cavalier flames. It was where Ax's world ended too, the man's own son lost to the fire that claimed a generation.

I should have woken up. They'd all still be here if I would have just woken up...

His father handed him the flowers. He kept his eyes on the

bouquet, avoiding Ax's gaze as he admired the gift, the myriad colors bright and fresh.

"Thanks, Ax," Magnus said.

The old man nodded, grabbing the reins. Brushing off the somber moment, he looked to the Boy. "Best be ready next time, son!"

Magnus' son nodded, forcing a smile.

"I'll make sure of it," his father cut in, patting him on the back as they saw the man off.

"You better! And best start thinkin' of a name, Boy!" Ax added, giving the kid a wave. The old-timer knocked his knuckles against the metal blade of his axe, grinning. "Just don't just pick the first thing that comes to mind!"

The wagon and its crew disappeared back down the road, their silhouettes swallowed by the scant wood that lined the route to Hope.

"He saved my life, once," his father said, breaking the silence. "Cut a man straight in two with that axe. *Whhhhsssssht.*" Magnus sliced his hand through the air, mimicking the blade. "Just like that. Never heard anything like it."

What does a man getting hit with an axe sound like? the Boy wondered. He kept the question to himself, summoning the courage to ask another in its place.

"How did he lose his foot?"

His father tugged at his beard, his expression blank. "A hammer."

THE LUDDSTOWS' rations arrived the next day. As with everyone in the village, they received less than expected.

"Stingy whoresons!" Tom snapped. The Boy didn't reply, keeping his head down as he helped unload the wagon. He was familiar with the man's temper, grazing his eyes over Tom's withering garden instead. The Luddstows' yard was large enough for a dense garden but not much else, owing to the poor soil and rocky slope. For that reason, Tom had become more of a farmhand than a farmer himself.

Generations past, his family had land and livestock south near New Gamling. The Boy had never been, but he had heard it was a decent place, as far as places go. While families in Hope and other settlements stopped bothering with surnames centuries ago—there just weren't enough people left to make them necessary—New Gamling kept the tradition alive. While Tom's last name may have set him apart from the rest of Hope, his allotment didn't.

"Fuckers, all of 'em! I bet they're feasting down south, the greedy shits!"

The Boy stayed quiet. In truth, he had always wondered why Tom settled for his position. He knew the man had pulled a few shifts in the militia, but his skill with a bow and knack for bushcraft could have easily seen him into the ranks of the rangers. Wandering the road between settlements, keeping it safe—it sounded much better than scything wheat or breaking up fights at the mill.

"Go on, boy, what is it?" Tom sighed as he dragged a small crate off the wagon.

"What?" the Boy replied, blinking off his thoughts.

"I know that look. Dumb-faced, eyes glossin' over. I can see the smoke comin' from yer ears. What is it?"

"Oh," he stumbled, "I was just wondering why you didn't become a ranger. They get bigger allotments and, well, you're good with the bow."

"Ain't that a fact," Tom smirked, resting his foot on one of the wagon's battered spokes. "Lemme tell ya why, 'cuz I know if I don't, you'll be hemming and hawing about it all afternoon. See, my older brother was a ranger, back when. Got to see more of the world—or, what's left of it—than most. Rockmantle, the Mills, Resolute. Even Sainte Falls before it dried up. Saw it all and then some. And yer right, it paid well. Honest pay for honest work."

Tom paused to wipe the sweat from his forehead as he looked over the wagon and the rangers who stood guard a dozen paces off. "Anyway, he got jumped by outlaws one day, just south of New Gam. He killed 'em all—all six, no less—but they got him good and he bled out on the road."

The Boy didn't know what to say, so he said nothing, tasting embarrassment on his tongue.

"It's all fine now," Tom insisted. "He took the pricks with him, and we're all better for it. He was a good man. Good as they come."

"Is his family still down south?" the Boy asked.

"His family? Oh, yeah. Yeah, they're down there. Safe and sound." There was a waver of hesitation in the man's voice, but the Boy didn't press. He knew as well as any that some thoughts weren't for sharing.

They went back to hauling boxes, though there really wasn't much to unload. In a normal year, that wouldn't be a problem. Tom could pick up extra work throughout the winter to keep his family afloat. Do some escort work for any caravans heading south, fill in at the quarry.

And as a seamstress and tutor, Saira could rummage up odd jobs to make ends meet. Worst case, Tom could head off into the Faroff or go north to Hunter's Point to forage and hunt. He was unmatched with the bow. In fact, as the Boy thought back —to the village fairs, to his time training before the fire—he realized he had never actually seen the man miss.

"I know you ain't much of a fan of all this nonsense," Tom said, his tone oddly serious, "I know you just wanna read books and be left alone to do yer own thing. I get it. Especially after..."

The Boy's stomach tightened.

"But you can't hide forever, kid," Tom continued. "A shit-storm like no other is gonna come knocking. Best to suck it up and bite the bullet. Besides," he added, looking the Boy in the eyes, "you'd make just as good a ranger as I would. Or as yer sister, bless her. A different kind of ranger, maybe. But you got heart. And brains. I s'pose that's what really matters."

The Boy nodded, not sure what to say. In the gap of thought, his mind wandered to Tom's brother, dying alone in the wilderness, bleeding out in a saddle because someone wanted his boots and his steel.

"She was a good kid, yer sister," Tom added, his voice on edge.

For a moment, the Boy was back in the fire. Choking. Burning. He looked away, unable to hold his neighbor's stare. Before his jaw began to quiver, he spoke. "Yeah. She was."

After an impromptu moment of silence, Tom switched gears, drumming his fingers on the knife strapped to his belt. "So Mag says yer gonna start training soon. Bet yer not too happy about that, eh?"

The Boy deflated. He hadn't been out training since his sister died. He was in no mood to start it all again.

"Guess he hasn't told ya, eh? Well, you didn't hear it from me. Though for what it's worth, you won't just be runnin' and swimmin' and playin' with knives. He's gonna teach ya the good stuff." Tom mimicked a banging hammer and the Boy connected the dots.

"Can't fight the rain, kid," Tom shrugged, giving him a friendly shot to the arm. "Things are gonna get ugly faster than shit through a goose. But I suspect you know that. Come the bells, survival is everything. Time to buck up and play for keeps. You've got a name to earn, after all."

With the last crate squared away, Magnus' son started to head home, his mind busy digging up old memories from when he and Rach used to train. He was never one for all that stuff and was loath to start it all again. Even with a Year knocking at the door, he'd much rather take his chances and stick to the gardens and his books.

Hardly a dozen steps from the Luddstows' porch, lost in conjured worries, he heard Tom shout. Saira's voice fired back not a moment later, their voices raised and raised again. A door slammed. Then another. And then the world was quiet.

6

_____

The nail disappeared in a single hit. Not fully, the Boy realized as he looked closer, but it was more or less buried. His father brought the tool down once more for good measure, pushing the metal deep into the plank. He lined up another nail, this time using his left hand. He gave it a slight tap so it stuck before pounding it down with a heavy blow.

"Simple," his father said, giving the hammer a quick spin before sliding it into his belt. "Your turn."

Magnus unbuckled the tool belt and offered it to him. The Boy reached for it but fumbled. A hammer slid out and onto the ground.

"S-sorry," he stuttered, plucking it up from the trampled grass.

They had set up a pair of sawhorses in the backyard, a thick beam of timber spanning the gap between them. In the grass below sat a rusted tin of nails. "There's a good fifty or so nails there," his father said. "Hit 'em all down, pry 'em back up, and then hit them again. Right hand only. That's it."

"That's it?" the Boy asked, fastening the belt around his

waist. It was lighter than he expected, not nearly as bulky as it looked. The leather was pliable, clinging to his hips at an incline. He straightened it. "No running laps around the back field? No throwing knives at scarecrows or holding my breath underwater?"

"That's it," his father nodded, collecting his hoe. "Just don't bend 'em. Those are all we have." With a nod, the man plodded off to weed what remained of the wilted garden, leaving the Boy to his task.

"Uhhhh, okay." He pulled out a hammer, letting the weight settle in his grip. It was heavy—heavier than a regular hammer. It tugged at the muscles in his forearm as he moved it around. "Just hit them down," he muttered to himself. "I can do that."

He picked up a nail, gave it a steadying tap, and eyeballed his target. The sharp *ting* of metal on metal rang when he brought the hammer down. The nail hardly moved an inch.

"Well. Shit."

His palms were blistered by the time he finished. They bubbled up on two of his fingers and on the inside of his thumb. The latter had popped early, the torn swatch of skin red and smeared with blood. His entire arm, from his wrist to his shoulder, was immobile, the limp stiffness encroaching onto his back.

An hour later, when his father returned, he was still struggling to open and close his fist, massaging the tender muscles as he absentmindedly counted the various jars and cans and preserves that lined the pantry shelves, including one particularly grubby bottle of moonshine.

"Lemme see your hand, son," his father said as he stepped into the doorframe. His face was red from the sun and creased with lines of dirt and sweat. The Boy held out his hand, blisters and all.

Magnus inspected his wounds with a nod. "Go get cleaned up."

With a yawn, Magnus' son headed out the lake for a quick swim. As he walked, he peeled a flap of skin from his hand, rolled it between his fingers, and flicked it into the dirt. He was poking at another blister when his father shouted after him.

"Oh, and don't stay up readin' your books tonight. We'll work your left arm in the mornin'."

"WHAT TH—"

The Boy shot up as ruffled feathers slapped his chest and chin. A slight pain danced down his torso. Then came the laughter. Not his—his heart was racing its way through his chest—but his parents', full and hearty. He propped himself up against his headboard, his arms sore from weeks of battering nails. A beady-eyed bird stared back at him from the edge of the bed. Apparently, his parents had bought a rooster.

He smiled, his tender shoulders easing into a soft bounce. The laughter was infectious. Cathartic. It was the first time they had really relaxed together since the announcement. It felt good.

"We bought a rooster," his mother said, leaning against his dresser.

"You don't say," he quipped, eyeing the bird as it poked around his room.

"He's got some lady friends out in the yard, too," she added.

"Must be nice," the Boy muttered, kicking himself out of bed. He peered into the yard and spied a half-dozen hens in the grass, scratching at the dirt and pecking away at anything that caught their fancy.

"What's its name?" he asked, nodding to the rooster. "And where did you get it?"

His father shrugged, a tight-lipped smirk his only reply. Livestock was rare and getting rarer by the year. Only a few people in Hope had animals.

"I suppose you won't tell me either?" he asked his mother.

"Let's just say your father has friends in far places," she winked.

The Faroff?

Beyond the villages and towns along the road, there were folks who lived in untamed places. Far-off places the world had left behind. Bordering the ruins of lands long poisoned, the Faroff was a place between worlds. A place where life stood stubborn witness to the past and its consequences.

The Boy couldn't help but wonder if his father had ventured out into the Faroff or if he just happened to meet a hermit who had come into Hope to trade. Or maybe his mother just meant *far away*, as in from one of the villages down south. He wanted to ask a thousand questions, though he knew he'd get no more than a word or two in reply.

Few people in the village—or anywhere, really—bothered with livestock. They were an inefficient use of grain and water, not to mention expensive. He hadn't a clue how his father paid for them—another question he would need to investigate. He tucked them away for later, confident he could pry the truth from his mother when they were alone. For now, he wanted to see the animals up close.

He spent the better part of an hour watching the chickens, captivated by their bobbing heads and sudden sprints and the sheen of their well-groomed feathers. He never had a pet—let alone seven of them—and he was already thinking about names for each one.

"Don't bother naming them, son," his father chimed in from the other side of the fence, as if reading his mind. "They aren't pets. They're the backup plan." Magnus didn't bother to stop, marching out to the fields with a large scythe on his shoulder.

But it was too late. The Boy had already named the rooster. Standing knee-high, the bird never seemed to stray far from his feet, content to linger in his shadow while the hens pecked about. The rooster's brown and black feathers were etched with a dark blue hue. Compared to the hens, he was an imposing specimen.

"I think I'll call you Sarris."

THE NEXT MORNING, after working his muscles into a fit with the hammers, the Boy reluctantly prepared to head into Hope with his mother. It would be the first time he went to the village since the announcement and his stomach was in knots.

"You're bringing that?" he asked, staring at his mother's weapon as she laced her boots. The gun was slung muzzle-up across her back. A narrow bandolier rested over the wampum belt on her hip.

"The rifle?" she asked without looking up.

Magnus' son clicked his tongue. "Well, it's technically a carbine. I read that rifles have longer barrels. But yeah."

His mother cocked an eyebrow, shaking her head with a smile before pushing herself to her feet and heading out the door. Shouldering a rucksack full of herbs and roots, the Boy followed her into the day.

They reached the village an hour later. Even on the outskirts, it was clear to the Boy why his mother had chosen to bring her weapon. Dozens of people were out and about, and every single one of them was armed. Knives, clubs, axes. He even saw one well-to-do young woman with a pair of rusted flintlock pistols on her waist, the wood and metal cratered and corroded.

His eyes drifted around the square as he weaved amongst the market stands and their accompanying aromas, doing his best to avoid the most crowded areas. There were crates of writhing worms in black soil and broken-winged birds flittering in small cages. Wooden jars of fresh honey, whose golden innards leaked slow lines down their smooth containers, sat idle on a hawker table. Bolts of colored cotton drooped like weary flags in the breezeless morning as dried skins of lesser rodents were flayed taut on ropes and racks, the gutsy stench of blood clouding the nearby stalls.

In Butchers Row, a crowd gathered to watch a man skin a deer, a rare find so close to Hope. It was tick-infested and riddled with brown tumors, its matted fur patchy and stained red. The creature had likely gone mad from tickrot, stumbling its way back to where hunters still roamed, its brain turned to mush by dementia. The Boy had a dreadful fear of getting tickrot—most people did—and checked himself religiously for tick bites. Few things, he wagered, were worse than losing your mind.

With a wince and a wrinkled nose, the Boy stalked off in the opposite direction. From a lane off the edge of the market, warm fruits and sweet breads enticed him. His stomach rumbled in reply but he ignored it. Peering over the lean crowd, he spotted his mother near a table of fabrics and old clothes, her carbine poking over her shoulder as she rummaged. She beckoned him with a wave, so he unenthusiastically shuffled back into the square. Someone started shouting.

"I said I was 'ere first, and I ain't gonna say it again, so fuck off!" a man spat, his baritone voice loud enough to turn heads. The Boy stopped in his tracks, looking toward the commotion.

"Don't you cuss at me, you little shit! You weren't even in line!" an older man barked, stepping in with a hard shove.

The younger of the two, heavy set and stocky, lurched backward before checking his momentum with a planted foot. Then the younger man charged forward, fists up and moving. His blows flew wide before the pair wrestled themselves into a grapple, spinning between the gaggle of onlookers.

The Boy didn't recognize either man, but that was no surprise, recluse that he was. Standing on his toes, he looked about for the sheriff or deputy, confident someone would rush in to end the fight.

As the struggle spilled onto the ground, nobody intervened. Grunting and cursing, the two men hopped back to their feet, throwing punches before they were wrapped up in one another again, their shouts more growl than curse.

While he scanned for help, he spotted a girl looking at him. Two curious and familiar eyes stared from across the semicircle, darting back to the fight when he noticed them. He smiled, staring longer than he should have. When she glanced back, he caught her eyes again. It was a face he hadn't seen in a long time. He waved.

And then he was stumbling.

"WHAA—?!"

His shout was half exhalation and all surprise as a hand on his backpack shoved him forward. Two dozen faces gawked at him as he tripped into the makeshift ring that encircled the belligerent men. He glanced back to the shelter of the crowd, red-faced and glaring at the person who pushed him: his mother. He made it two steps before she stopped him in his tracks. Staring him down with the heat of a thousand summer suns, she took a half-step forward, stonewalling him.

The warmth in his face was palpable, a strawberry flush dashing across his cheeks as his heart pounded. His hands, hanging aimless at his sides, were touched by sweat and tingling. The world was bellowing in his ear, blurs of unfocused color streaming liquid fast.

Enveloped by the chaos, the Boy did what he could to make sense of it. Stepping into the fight, he stretched out his limbs to part the flailing fists, shouldering his way between the combatants.

"Hey, stop! HEY! Please, can you...just ple—"

The embarrassed words wobbled halfway off his tongue, cut short by a misaimed punch. It rang the side of his jaw with the distinct slap-crunch of skin and bone colliding. It was by no means a knockout blow, but it dazzled and dazed him. He tasted blood.

"Mind your business, burnt boy!" the younger man growled.

The slow press of suffocating panic in the Boy's chest evaporated. So too did his embarrassment. The clamminess in his palms disappeared. Sharp lines and vibrant colors cut the world into focus. Shifting his weight, he noticed the difference in tension in his boots, his left laced tighter than his right. It bothered him. He suddenly felt how damp his back was too, the closeness of his rucksack smothering his skin. The air was dead around him, stale and hot and breezeless. He simmered in the smells of the mob and the market and the two unwashed men that bore down on him. Then, he exploded.

Magnus' son rammed his arms outward with a feral shout. Years of stacking wood and picking rocks paid their dividends as he heaved both men backward. Caught off-guard, the taller of the two—the one whose punch had caught the Boy mid-chin —stumbled backward over a bench and fell, cracking his head on the cobblestone. He didn't get up.

The younger man tripped into the nearest stall, spilling a bushel barrel of cloth as his arms tangled among some wooden hangers. Flailing his legs free, the stocky young man started to stand up, but the Boy stomped toward him, mimicking his mother's glower. Defeated, the troublemaker raised his hands in submission.

Around him, the wide-eyed crowd traded murmurs as they shuffled off, their entertainment ended. Magnus' son, chest thumping dynamite salvos against his ribs, made a break for a gap in the mob. He ignored the gawping and the hands that patted him as he passed. Eyes cast to his feet, he didn't see the younger man come up behind him, didn't sense the knife lunging his way. All he heard was the collective gasp of the crowd.

By the time he spun around, the stocky man was a foot away, knife swooping in to hook into his ribs. The blade, curved and dirty and wide, arced to take him in his exposed side.

CRACK.

The burst of sound was jarring, the unexpected *pop-cough* of explosive air overcoming the jabbering crowd. The stocky man's forehead creased like the bruised flesh of an overripe peach. The sound of metal breaking bone was lost to the echo of his mother's shot as blood leaked through the man's loosened eye socket.

Before the Boy had processed the sight, his attacker's limp body folded sideways. The man's knife bounced on the stone at his feet. The Boy didn't hear it. The world was miles away. A rush of blood drained to his toes. He didn't move. Couldn't move. His legs were stone pillars on the verge of crumbling. Eyes wide and unblinking, he shuddered.

Across the crowd, the girl he saw before was wiping blood and gunk from her cheek. Her shirt was speckled red. He knew who she was, somewhere in his mind, but everything was muted now. She was younger than he was but just as tall, her legs long and her frame scrappy. She had wide shoulders and a tangled mess of dirt-brown hair that sat in lazy curls, a few braids pulled back across the side of her head.

His brain shoveled words into his mouth but nothing came out save the quiver of his jaw and the last gasps of his old life. But he smiled at her. Tasting blood, he smiled.

MARIAM REGRETTED SHOVING her son into the mix as soon as she watched her baby boy get hit. But she also knew it was time for him to be tested. For him to see the reality that was hurtling toward them. As she waited in the sheriff's office, she grappled with her choice in silence.

"Shorryta keep ya, Mar. You'n the Boy can go," Deputy Step slurred, limping into the room. Bull-necked and barrel-chested, Step towered over Mariam by a solid foot. The carbine rested loose in the woman's hands, an offering. "All's well now. Give my best ta Magnush."

"I will," Mariam replied, wrapping her hand around the forestock. She kept the muzzle aimed at the floor of the jailhouse. "And sorry for the hassle, Step," she added, shouldering the rifle as her son picked up their bags.

She kept her glance short, eyeing a crumpled map that was half buried on Step's desk instead to ensure she didn't stare overly long at the woman's injury.

A gift of a Year long past, Step's face was bent crooked from a broken jaw that never set. The warped bone sloped to the left, drooping and jutting out at a sharp angle. Her mouth never fully closed, though it never fully opened either. Mariam tried to remember when it happened—and what had happened—but it was a memory long since buried.

"Bound'ta happen shooner or later," Step shrugged. "You know how it getsh."

"All too well," she nodded. *All too well.*

Shuffling back out into the afternoon, Mariam pressed a quick pace through the village. She was in no mood to talk about the day's events with anyone but her son. Though, out of the corner of her eye, she could see that he was in no mood to talk to anyone at all. His head was down, hands slipped tight into his pockets, no doubt a million miles away.

Did I have to push him into the fight?

She knew that it was stupid. But she also knew that the Boy needed to toughen up. That he *had* to toughen up. She just didn't expect things to go sideways.

When they were halfway home, she finally broke the silence. "Are you okay?"

"I'm fine," came the expected reply, shallow and automatic.

Mariam stopped in the road, gently grabbing her son's arm. "I know you're *fine*. But are you okay?"

The Boy nodded. "I'm fine. Really, Ma." He wouldn't look at her, glancing around the road.

"I shouldn't have pushed you into the fight. That was foolish of me." She paused, hoping the silence would coax her son into a reply. When no response came, she pressed on. "I—your father and I—know what's coming. When the road closes and things begin to run out, it's going to get ugly. Worse than most Years, I imagine. It takes..." she paused, hunting for the words, "a certain kind of person to manage in that environment. It takes—"

Her son looked her in the eyes. "A killer?"

The words, their resigned tone, were a gut punch so unexpected she could feel the pull of gravity on her shoulders. Her chest tensed as she fumbled for an excuse. For a justification. For any answer that would save her son from the truth. But there was nothing.

"Yes," she finally huffed. "And now you've seen what that means. Now you've seen the truth."

She walked on, letting her son drag his heels a few paces behind. She would leave him to his thoughts. For now. She knew he needed the space, needed time to reflect on the disastrous events that have bookended him.

By the time they saw home, evening neared the horizon, the air warm and quiet and lonesome. Breaking up the lane, the smells of the forest road—the dry pine and dying leaves and stagnant ditchwater—gave way to the honey-floral dance of the cornfield and orchard, which in turn faded into the green, grassy bouquet of the garden and its fragrant vine tomatoes.

Magnus met her on the porch, tucked away from the dying light of the day. She could hear his chair on the wood, rocking slow.

"How'd it go?" he asked.

Mariam stepped up the two small stairs to the porch, her son close behind. The Boy didn't stop, striding around her and walking straight inside. Moments later, his unhurried footsteps trudged up the stairs.

Magnus stopped his rocking. "Bit of a day?"

"Mm," she nodded. Slipping the rifle off her shoulder, she leaned it against the weathered wooden pillar beside her.

"Mind giving it a clean? I'm tired," she said.

"'Course," he replied. "You okay?"

"I'll be fine," she sighed, leaning down to kiss her husband on the top of his shaggy head.

She walked a few steps to the door before turning around, plucking a bullet from her belt. "Here." She tossed the round to her husband. "You'll need this."

Mariam dragged her weary feet up the stairs, passing her son's bedroom without slowing. Closing her bedroom door behind her, she didn't bother to light a candle, the formless dark sequestering her from the day's events. She hadn't killed anyone in years. Long years. Good years. She had almost forgotten how it felt. How good it felt.

8

_____

She had seen it coming a mile away. Patt had always been an opportunistic jerk. And sneaky too. Pulling a knife on Magnus' son—when his back was turned, no less— was precisely the kind of shit he liked to do.

But if I saw it coming, why did I freeze...?

Beckett's daughter whipped her father's knife into the target opposite her, rattling the thick circle of wood.

"Why did I hesitate?" she asked aloud, sulking across the room to pull the blade free. She replayed the day's events in her head nonetheless: the Boy, wide-eyed and nervous, tripping into the fray. Ol' Buck's head bashing against the ground after the Boy pushed him backward.

She tensed at the memory of that one. The heavy thud of Buck's skull bouncing off the cobblestone made her shiver. He was out cold after that, and she didn't see him get up.

"Poor Buck," she sighed, launching the knife again.

Then there was Patt. Beckett's daughter was glad Mariam shot him. No, not just glad. Happy. Patt deserved a bullet. And not just for what he did in the market either.

"Asshole," she grumbled. She relived the memory of Patt's

dumb head caving in one more time before sheathing her knife and slipping out of her shirt. She held it up, examining the splotches of red. The bloodstains were dry. They wouldn't be coming out.

Grabbing a new shirt from the closet, she shimmied into the loose fabric, tucking her long braid under the collar. The soft linen greedily soaked up the sweat that collected along her spine. She left a couple buttons at the bottom undone so it wasn't too tight, ensuring that her knife was accessible.

Squeezing the handle of the weapon as it rested against her belt, she pictured it buried hilt-deep in Patt's chest. She knew her father wouldn't have approved...but he wouldn't have been all that mad either.

Longing for fresh air, the Girl started for the stairs. Even with her curtain closed to block the light, her room was stifling. On the third floor and facing south over Hope, the room baked like an oven. As a kid, the space had been used solely for storage; it was too stuffy even for guests. It was the place her father had kept his odds and ends. A place for trivial things he never bothered to get rid of.

Which is exactly why Viktoria moved me here.

The spacious and sparsely decorated bedroom was borderline austere. A bed. A nightstand. A wooden target for her knife. Her father's old worktable. That was all her aunt let her have. She never bothered to put up a fuss about it; she had learned to pick her battles. And since Viktoria and her bratty brood of demon children never ventured up to the sweltering third floor, she was mostly left in peace.

A fair trade, she thought to herself as she sat down on the edge of the bed to tie her boots. The double-sized straw-and-down mattress rested on a sturdy oak frame that never squeaked or shifted. Viktoria may have disliked her, but she wouldn't let her get away with lousy posture from a poor sleep.

On the nightstand, a washed-out sketch of her father

looked out over the room. His old letters and books collected dust in its drawer. Save the knife on her hip, those were her only possessions.

The Girl closed her eyes, pushing away the world as she thought back to better days. Days with her father. His voice, his bear hugs that swallowed her up. They way he'd chase her up the lane when she was a kid, stomping like some lumbering monster from the Faroff. Days spent on the water, pretending to be adventuring in far-flung lands. Days with family. A real family.

Beckett's daughter reached for a folded paper under her mattress and gently tugged it free. It was a map, faded and bent and hand-painted. A couple misshapen brown continents filled the center, though the majority of the map was a formless, empty blue littered with sparse question marks and mysterious creatures.

She traced her finger along the waves, letting daydreams sweep her away until the heat of the room grew unbearable.

"Ugh. Just silly dreams." Beckett's daughter folded the map and tucked it away. And then she wiped her eyes.

Rolling her shoulders back and standing tall, she made her way down the spiral staircase. After the events in the market, she wasn't in the mood for criticism.

Halfway through the foyer, her aunt cornered her. "I thought I heard you mucking about up there," Viktoria chided, grabbing her by the wrist. "Let me see those hands? Tsk. So ugly. If you keep up your little hobby, you'll have ugly hands for life, you know."

The Girl didn't pull away. She didn't reply either.

"Going to the market? I need some things." The woman handed her a small note.

Beckett's daughter read the list over. "Another trunk?"

"Mmhmm."

"Are we going somewhere?"

Her aunt shrugged, feigning mystery. "Just be a dear, will you. After the incident today I suspect my visits into that rat nest of a village will be few and far between. Wretched affair. That poor Patt fellow. Did you hear? Killed by those rednecks from the outskirts. Dreadful people. I never understood why your father enjoyed their brutish company."

The Girl opened her mouth to snap back but hesitated, her voice freezing in her throat. Her aunt was never satisfied until she got in at least one jab about her father.

"Sass me and see what happens, young lady," the old woman crowed.

The Girl stayed silent, eyes down until the woman to let go of her arm.

"Off you go now. Don't tarry."

Heading to the door, Beckett's daughter passed the sitting room. On the table, she spied a fresh stack of books neatly aligned. And a map. A large one...one she had never seen before.

"A map...?"

The world wasn't a large place—not anymore. It was a clear road south, one they had traveled many times over. It was the only real road left in the world. Her aunt was certainly no adventurer. So why would she bother with a map?

She could feel Viktoria's eyes on her, so she kept up her pace out the door and toward the lane. From the bluff above Hope, she could see for miles, spying down into the village and out over the water. The sunsets were particularly pretty from the cliff's edge, though she hadn't sat down to fully enjoy one in what felt like years.

The three-story house, a mix of timber and stone from Hope's quarry, was a veritable castle compared to the cramped shacks and shanties of the village. It was the only house on the escarpment, even after all these years, something her father never intended when he built it.

Viktoria, however, very much intended to keep it that way. The woman enjoyed her privacy—and power—and refused to sever off lots to accommodate the growing populace. The steep incline of the bluff's switchbacks ensured that only those with proper business bothered to trudge their way up, insulating Viktoria and her family from the masses.

While the Girl thought her aunt selfish for refusing to share the land, truth be told, she enjoyed the extra space. She relished the ability to move unreservedly, the freedom to exist without bounds beyond the claustrophobic confines of the village. She also knew that if her aunt hadn't prided herself on being so far removed from the village, she would have been lost to the fire with all the other kids. It was precisely Viktoria's pompous distaste for Hope's destitute that had kept her separate. Separate tutors, separate chores, separate sitters. As much as the Girl hated the woman, she also accidentally owed her her life.

Kicking her feet down the track, Beckett's daughter peered out over Hope. Narrow lanes and run-down houses orbited the main square in ill-measured lines, the dust-dry alleyways and thoroughfares trampled by generations into hard-packed earth. The entire village was painted in shades of brown, save the grey stone of the village hall. Brown huts and cabins. Brown lanes. Brown leathers and tunics, brown carts and wagons and rowboats. Parched and thirsty for color. The struggling greenery had long since been pushed to the periphery, and even it was more brown than green.

In the distance, the old mill creaked its rounds in the subdued breeze, its tattered sails hanging off the vanes in dog-eared strips as the warbling din of hawkers and fishmongers cast a familiar blanket over the day.

As the village filled her ears, she looked over Viktoria's note.

Another trunk? She's got half a dozen of them already. And a wagon. What else does she need to pack?

"And why did she have a new map?" she wondered aloud as she rolled down the hill and into the outer edge of the harbor. The floating stench of a nearby latrine pushed her to keep an aimless pace. Eventually settling on the base of the village's Sarris Gamling statue, she stopped to chew on her thoughts. Viktoria had gone south to New Gamling a dozen times or more. She'd even gone as far south as Sainte Falls a few times. She wouldn't need a map for that. Nobody would—it was a straightforward jaunt down the last road.

"So why did she have a map?"

Maybe it was nothing. Maybe it was just a pile of stuff Viktoria was planning to sell before the Year. Staring into the statue's shadow, the Girl pondered. The towering Sarris Gamling stood some thirty feet tall. Axe in hand, he faced outward over the great expanse, pointing over the water whence he came.

Or where he was going...

THE BOY AWOKE with a sore jaw. Testing it, he tongued the inside of his mouth until he winced. Then he did it again.

Lying in bed, he resisted the urge to go downstairs for breakfast. He skimmed through some books instead, easing his fingers over the faded paper as his eyes feasted on stories from before the End. Before the world fell apart. A time of abundance and awe and miracles. Whether there were truly buildings that touched the sky or ships that reached the stars was a point often argued in school.

Ruminating in the jaundiced light of the new day, the Boy realized that such arguments were pointless now. Childish even. Life before the End—whatever that life entailed—was irrelevant now. Perched upon the precipice of a Year, they were simply legends given life by fanciful script. Nothing more.

"Just stupid dreams," he muttered, tossing the book aside.

Within the hour, a sudden storm blew in and kept his chores and training at bay. Drizzle and grey held the overbearing heat at an arm's length, leaving the Boy and his mind to wander. He watched the clouds darken and swirl from the den, inching toward the village like a heavy blanket slowly being pulled over his head. Beacons of light stabbed through the matte grey thunderhead only to be snuffed out as the clouds pressed onward. Electric tendrils peppered the distant horizon, slices of silver color against an oppressive backdrop.

When the forks of light slit the black, the Boy spied waterspouts raging over the white-capped lake, dancing on the surface with grace and destructive purpose.

"Are they close?" his father asked, stepping up beside him. They watched the storm through the large den window which had only been partially boarded up.

"Nah," he replied, waiting for the next flash. "Not unless the wind shifts."

The two stood in silence as the gale danced itself to death. The funnels twirled as the lightning gave up its watch, the storm fading into the impenetrable nothingness.

Glancing at his reflection, he noticed his jaw shone a soft hue of purple, the blush of color highlighting his distant gaze. He was no fighter. Never had been. Though he used to train with his sister as a kid, he'd always felt he leaned more toward his mother's diplomatic tendencies. It turns out, one punch and a bullet later, her tendencies weren't as diplomatic as he thought.

"Remember when Tom started teachin' you and Rach how to shoot?" his father asked, breaking the silence. "Said if you or Rach hit a bullseye he'd bake ya a cake—but you'd only get one arrow each."

"And a warm-up shot," the Boy corrected.

"Right—and Rach missed the target altogether with the warm-up."

"She did," the Boy nodded. "Missed by a mile."

"Not even close," his father chuckled. "But that second arrow?" Magnus traced a small circle in the fog on the window.

"Bullseye," the Boy grinned.

"Bullseye," his father echoed. "The look on Tom's face...I thought he was gonna burst."

"He cursed up a storm, I remember. To this day, I don't think I've ever eaten anything worse than that cake."

His father laughed. "It was terrible, wasn't it?"

Once more, the silence trickled in, carrying with it cradled memories. Somehow fresh and present yet so far beyond his reach they felt like dreams. He chased them through time until they caught up with him, dragging him back to the incident in the market.

"Rach woulda got a kick outta what happened in the market today," his father said. "Before the knife, anyway."

The Boy shrugged. "I suspect she would have handled it better than I did. She was made for this."

His father turned, looking at him dead on. "That's where you're wrong, son. Nobody is made for this."

Magnus gave him a pat on the shoulder and walked off, disappearing into the dark of the den. The Boy watched his father's reflection fade before turning to once more stare at his own. He relived the events in the square, remembering the sensations that prodded him. How shock bled into presence, feeding his focus, chaining him to the moment. How his muscles coiled, tightened. From his stomach to his shoulders to his hands, he remembered the power of lashing out. The power of standing over someone and watching them give up.

Staring at his own reflection, his glossy outline enmeshed with the unraveling storm, he almost didn't recognize himself.

9

Magnus breathed deep as he trudged along the uneven forest floor behind the homestead. Water sloshed around in his boots, but he paid the slight chafe no mind. The creek had flooded the ditch between his property and the Luddstows' but it wouldn't last. In a few days, the heat would be back. It was never gone for long.

"You still able to lift those things, old man?" Tom joked, prodding him with the tip of his bow.

"Why don't you shuffle off a few paces and we can find out," Magnus shot back, slapping away Tom's weapon.

"I really can't take you two anywhere, can I?" Mar chided, letting her rifle slide off her shoulder and into her folded arms. Magnus smiled as they headed toward the clearing. It had been far too long since they were all together like this. He missed it.

"Hey, don't blame me, Mar," Tom replied. "I'm just makin' sure the old-timer doesn't have a stroke once he starts whippin' those beat-up tools about."

"These 'beat-up tools' saved your life a few times over, if I recall," Magnus jabbed, stepping from the thin copse into the clearing.

Tom followed a few steps behind, chuckling to himself.

"What?" Magnus asked, turning to his friend.

"You remember that blacksmith? What's his name—"

"Ump?" Mar suggested.

"No, not Ump. Before him. The ugly guy. With the warts."

"Gareg?" Magnus answered, knowing full well where his friend was heading.

"Garrick," his wife corrected.

"Garrick! That son of a bitch. Right. Well, you 'member when we caught him stealin' that one Year? Red fuckin' handed from the storage shed behind the hall?"

"I remember," Magnus sighed, shaking his head.

"I don't," his wife cut in. "What happened?"

"Nothing," Magnus replied, waving them off as he continued across the field.

"Nothin'?" Tom objected. "That fucker pulled a revolver and shoved it right in my damn face! Funny thing is, I'd have not even noticed what he was up to if he had'a just played it cool. But nope, he pulled that beast of a gun out—the one Rhys uses now—and said he was gonna lock us in the shed."

Mar was staring at him, eyebrow raised, as Tom continued. Magnus shrugged, conceding nothing. He had never told her this story for a reason.

"So we shuffle into the shed," Tom continued, "hands in the air, and Garrick goes to shut the door and lock it. But your dear ol' husband ain't havin' any of that. He bullrushes the door and breaks it right off the damn hinges. Flattens Garrick under the whole fuckin' door!"

"Yep, and we got out safe and sound," Magnus cut in. "The end."

"We were safe and sound alright. But not before you put those tools to work."

"Oh really?" his wife interjected. "And just what exactly did my dear ol' husband do, Tom?"

Tom struggled to continue, choking on his laughter. "Well, Mag here sees that Garrick's still got the revolver in his hand. So just like that," Tom snapped his fingers for an overexaggerated effect, "he's got a hammer out. He whips it down and tears off the man's fingers. Like three of 'em, I swear. *Whffffpp*. Gone. Thing is, one of them got lodged so deep in the hammer's claw we couldn't get it out."

Tom stopped walking, leaning against his bow as he finished, his face tomato red.

"We're pullin' on the bloody thing, yankin' it this way and that but it just won't budge. Blood's everywhere. So we go to Garrick's shop and get his pliers. We make a mess of it but get the sucker free."

Magnus tucked his face into his chest, doing his best to stifle his own laughter. Tom was hysterical, gasping on his own words as he finished. "We come out and Beckett's there. He goes, 'Is Garrick in there?' Ya'know what yer husband says? Know what he says, Mar? 'Sorta'—and he tosses the finger to Beckett and just walks away."

"Magnus!" his wife scolded. "What happened to Garrick?"

"Garrick?" Tom asked, wiping a tear from his eye as he caught his breath. "That poor sucker was dead on impact. Had his brains leakin' out his damn ears!"

"I was..." Magnus started, doing his best to center himself and keep a straight face, "I was just a dumb kid. Not my finest moment."

His wife just shook her head, though a hint of a smile leaked through.

"Ya'know what, Mag?" Tom snickered. "Maybe not yer finest moment. But a damn fine moment nonetheless."

MAGNUS' son caught up to the trio in the clearing. The trees there had long since withered and rotted; the grass was low and sparse, plagued by tall thistles and knotted carpets of purslane. Tom had stabbed a handful of grey-fletched arrows into the ruined soil. Nocking a missile, he nodded out to the few trees that clung to life at the edge of the glade some hundred feet away.

"Pick a tree, kid."

The Boy gazed out over the clearing and pointed. "Uhhh, that one." He gestured to a crippled maple split down the middle by some unknown calamity, a tangled mess of exposed roots crowning its crooked base.

The arrow flew. It whistled a passing tune before slamming into the trunk. One blink later, a second arrow was in the air. It dug into the tree an inch from the first. The third hit a bit higher but only by a hair. Each arrow stabbed home at chest height, biting their metal teeth into the forlorn wood. Tom may have been a braggart, but it was justified. The man was undefeated at the annual fair, and the Boy had once seen him down a bird mid-flight. He was a marksman.

"Remember what I used to say?" Tom asked.

Magnus' son nodded. "Always take the heart."

"Exactly. Now c'mere." Tom handed him the bow. It had been years since he held it—or any bow for that matter.

"Still remember how to shoot?"

The Boy shrugged. "We'll see." Testing the draw, he shifted his stance. He looked to the target then back to his feet. He was never one for archery—that was his sister's wheelhouse. He shuffled again, delaying the inevitable as the adults looked on.

Stifling a sigh, he grabbed an arrow from the dirt, set it against the bowstring, and pulled it back toward his shoulder.

"Keep 'er level," Tom instructed. "Find yer target. Good. Aim for the heart. The chest is the biggest target. Now picture the shot before you let 'er go. Just like ya used to."

The Boy curved his aim just a little, imagining the arc of the arrow, the sound of it hitting the wood.

Always take the heart.

He let the arrow fly. It cut the air with a gentle whip before thumping into the trunk, right above the nest of roots at its base.

"Not bad, son," his father said, handing him another arrow.

The Boy checked his stance again, shuffling his feet into place—or as close to place as he thought proper. He fumbled the arrow on the string as the trio watched his every move. This time he overcorrected, arcing the arrow high and sending it through the upper branches and into the dry mess of dying leaves.

"Best go find that one, Boy!" Tom grinned. Passing the bow to his father, Magnus' son jogged out into the brush and searched around the roots and dying shrubs. He also inspected the chipped bark where Tom's shots had stabbed home. The three wounds were precisely chest height.

"Always take the heart..."

Back in position, the Boy fired off another dozen arrows. While a far cry from a failure, it was neither a deadly or precise endeavor either.

After his parents fired off a quiver each, they went about hanging wooden and woven straw targets from an old oak with a few lengths of hemp rope. The swaying discs proved no challenge to either Tom with his bow or Mariam with her carbine. Watching her hands milk violence from the weapon reminded the Boy just how tough she was.

And how alien.

He had always thought of his mother as hardy. Stubborn and strong and clear-headed. But never violent. He couldn't remember a single time she raised her voice—not at him or his sister. Yet the Boy could see now, as she eyed down the barrel of her gun, that there was more to her than he knew. There were layers, peeled back from their hidden recess, that now sat exposed, their foreignness beguiling.

When it came time to test his own skill, the Boy shouldered the carbine and loosed a half a dozen rounds toward the targets. A couple hit home, though most shot their way into the brush.

"You'll get there, son. Just need practice, is all," his father said over his shoulder. The words were echoed by Tom, who had survived almost as many years as his parents.

"Practice'll make all the difference, kid. Keep at 'er."

He wasn't sure if he found the words encouraging or frustrating, but the adults made plans to return in a week. Tom even challenged his mother to a friendly competition, the loser hosting dinner for the winner.

"Just as long as you aren't baking another cake," Mariam jabbed as she and Tom started their walk home. The Boy followed a few paces behind. Until his father called.

"Not yet, son. C'mere."

Alone in the withering meadow, he figured they would head off to pick herbs or wild blackberries while the light was good. His father pulled out his hammers instead.

ADJUSTING the tool belt on his waist, Magnus measured out ten paces, letting his fingertips stroke the edge of each hammer as his arms swayed. Their recently sharpened metal claws shone with the bright hue of fresh steel.

Settling himself, he shifted his stance, pressing his weight through the earth. He'd been here before, a thousand times over, perched on the precarious edge of necessity. The slightest of breezes tickled the stubby grass, caressing the few leaves that clung to life in the clearing. Their feeble rustle was muted by the past. It called to him, beckoning him home.

Magnus.

It was a whisper so entrenched in his mind it seemed a shout. Inescapable, like the air around him. He ignored it, fought back with movement. With habit.

His hands shot downward. Slipping the head of each tool between his thick fingers, he flicked his wrists in one fluid motion, sending each hammer into the air. They floated upward to his shoulders, hovering ever so briefly before starting their gentle descent toward the earth. It was then, hammers hanging in the ether, that he ripped them from the sky.

Cocking both his arms back, he loosed the tools with vicious speed. The feral shout that followed was felt, not heard. Fluid and barbarous, the hammers thrashed the air, spinning with a hearty whip. They hit the target blunt-face first and almost simultaneously. If there was a sound from the impact, Magnus didn't hear it. He was battling memories, remembering the first time his old man had dragged him out to train. Watching the hammers pummel the world for the first time was a frightening and beautiful thing. It still was.

He stood his ground for a lingering moment before collecting the tools from the forest floor, bits of chipped wood scattered among them. He spoke to the Boy as he walked, breaking his silent recovery.

"Your great-grandfather was a carpenter. Had a gift for it. Could build in his sleep. He built part of our house, and all the Luddstows'. Shaped wood like it was just another part of him. My old man had a knack for it, too."

He scooped up his tools and brushed the dirt off, continuing. "I can build well enough, I suppose, but not like them. They were proper craftsmen. More than a few houses in the village were put in place by them over the years. Their tools— these tools—were an extension of their will. If they could picture it, they could build it. It was a gift."

He handed the hammers to his son. "These tools worked miracles. Whether building a house or otherwise." Magnus let the words idle and sink in. He wanted to keep the Boy's attention. Wanted the notion to sit with him, unbalanced in his palm. Heavy and warm, he wanted the Boy to feel their history, their significance. The cost of their existence weighted in lives.

His son stepped in front of the target. Magnus adjusted the Boy's stance in silence, squaring his shoulders. This was a thing felt, not learned. It was breathing and seeing, not reading or writing.

Satisfied, he nodded. That was his only encouragement. Then, for the first time in his life, Magnus watched his son embrace their grizzled tradition. The Boy's throw was crooked, but it caught the target along its outer edge. The second throw had a bit more power, though it also landed far off center. He let the Boy make a dozen more throws, watched him feel his way through the process. Eventually, his son shifted his stance to throw with his left.

"Don't bother, son," Magnus interrupted, spitting out a chewed-up piece of grass. "You won't make the distance. Gotta get your strength up first. C'mere."

They stalked to the target. Magnus took it down and held the dented wooden disc at chest height. He braced himself with a planted foot. "Hit it. With your left."

The Boy dropped his right hand, positioning himself to hit the wood with the hammer in his left hand. He drew the tool back swiftly, aiming for dead center.

"Wait!" Magnus interrupted. His son startled, pausing midswing. "Don't you hit my fingers, Boy, or the Year will be the least of your problems." He narrowed his eyes, tightened his jaw. And then he smiled, shaking his head at his son who looked far too worried. "Just swing the bloody thing and hit it hard."

The hammer came down on the wood, thumping the target near center.

"Again."

His son aimed for a moment before striking, checking his stance. He let his waist connect with the blow, though his arm was tense and lacking fluidity.

"Relax. Again."

Hit.

"Again."

Hit.

"Harder."

Hit.

"Faster."

Hit.

"As fast as you can now, don't let up."

Hit. Hit. Hit. Hit. Hit. Hit.

Magnus started inching forward, slowly raising the target from chest height to head height, angling it toward the arching tool. "He's coming for you, Boy. Stop him!

Hit. Hit. Hit. Hit. Hit.

"You gotta stop him son, or he'll take it all. Don't let up. Hit 'em! HIT 'EM!"

HitHitHitHitHitHITHITHITHITHITHITHITHITHITHIT.

Magnus held the wood as his son battered it, each weary, slowing blow a reminder that they weren't ready. That he had failed.

10

"**H**ey, Boy!" Tom shouted from across the creek. "Wanna shoot a few?"

Magnus' son stopped his morning hammering mid-swing, his stomach knotting. He didn't really want to go and shoot, but he didn't really have an excuse either.

"Uh, sure," he yelled over the palisade, sheathing his tool. "Just a sec."

He slipped inside, where it wasn't much cooler, chugged a mouthful of water, and made his way toward the Luddstows'. The creek between the two homes was still wide, so the Boy kicked off his boots to cross it, sloshing through the calf-deep muck. When he paused on the other side to slip his boots back on, he heard a whistle.

Naturally, he looked up. A second later, an arrow stabbed straight into the soggy grass beside him.

"Fuc—aaah!" The Boy tumbled and splashed into the creek. Tom keeled over laughing.

Fucking asshole! Anger edged up his face, but he kept it bottled.

"Oh come on now, kid, that was funny!" Tom howled. "You gotta lighten up!"

The Boy snatched the arrow from the ground. He resisted the urge to toss it into the water. Instead, he dragged his wet feet over to where Tom waited.

"You shoulda seen your face!" his neighbor chuckled.

"Just be thankful I'm not a good shot," the Boy muttered, handing Tom the arrow before wiping the mud and grass from his pants.

"Not a good shot *yet*," Tom corrected, clapping him on the shoulder. "We'll get ya on track. You weren't so bad back when."

The Boy didn't reply, shaking more muddy water off his leg.

"Come on, don't mope. Yer sister wouldn't want ya to be all grumpy. I bet she'd be out here rippin' arrows every day."

Tom offered him the bow. He took it, shuffling a few feet so he was better aligned with the target Tom had hung near his kid's tree fort.

"That's because this all came natural to her," the Boy huffed, finding his footing.

Tom conceded the point with a smile. "She was somethin', that's a fact. She'd be a ranger by now, no doubt about it. Youngest ever, I'd bet. Sheriff eventually. Girl had a knack for it."

The Boy nodded, taking aim.

"But she trained hard too," Tom continued. "We shot every day, rain or shine. 'Member when yer old man would drag ya out to the water to swim in the cold? She'd be out there by herself sometimes, shiverin' about, puttin' in the work. She had a gift, no question. But that girl had drive too."

The Boy shivered. "I hated those swims."

"No shit! Who wouldn't? But hey, don't sell yerself short. I heard about that little scuffle in the market. You held up—and on a whim, too. Know why? 'Cuz all that training from before did ya good. It's all still in there." Tom tapped his temple. "You just gotta nudge it back to the surface."

The Boy fired off a few shots, each one hitting the target. Some out on the edges, a couple close enough to the center to not be embarrassing.

"Again," Tom mumbled as he chewed on a fingernail, handing the Boy another arrow. "Yer thinkin' too much. Turn that big brain a yers off. Don't be thinkin' about this, that, or the other thing. Just stare. Just breathe." He spat the bit of nail into the grass. "That's all this is. Shit, that's all fightin' is. Just being more *here* than the other guy."

The Boy fired off a few more shots. Maybe they were better; it was hard to say. But he felt better.

After dinner, the rhythmic echo of galloping hooves thundered up the lane. Setting his book down, the Boy rushed to the window. A young ranger on horseback slipped from his saddle as he neared the house, massaging his thighs as he strode up to the door. Sweat and dirt smeared up his neck, the greens and browns of his ranger jerkin well dusted. A few fresh bruises colored the young man's face, no doubt a product of his rough-and-tumble training.

The Boy's father welcomed the young man in. Thoughtful as always, his mother brought the messenger—who couldn't have been much older than twenty—a cup of water, offering up a chair as he chugged back the pint.

"Thank ya, ma'am. This is fer you, sir."

The young ranger-in-training pulled a handful of folded papers from his pack, rifling through them until he found the correct one. He handed it to Magnus. The paper was sealed with wax.

"From the mayor?" the Boy asked, recognizing the seal.

His father nodded, making his way to the fire to read. The Boy followed.

"Son?" his father interrupted, taking his eyes from the paper. "Take the horse to the creek then see 'em off."

The Boy sighed but nodded, leading the ranger back outside. The stars were out but only faintly, their light offset by wisps of clouds and a bright white moon.

"What's its name?" he asked as they neared the creek, giving the mare a rub.

"I dunno actually," the ranger shrugged, just as curious. "Don't think they name 'em, tell the truth."

He petted the horse as she drank from the creek, her perfume of hay and manure wafting in the evening. A moment later, the young ranger hopped back in the saddle and waved farewell, galloping off into the night. The Boy watched him disappear into the black before springing back inside. His parents were arm in arm by the fire.

"What is it?" he prodded.

"A council meeting."

"A council meeting? But it's—"

"It's early," his father replied, folding the letter and tucking it into his breast pocket. "I know."

"Too early," his mother added.

The Boy leaned into the wall, arms crossed. "When?" His brain was chasing its tail, hounding down the myriad possibilities for the summons.

"Best pack up. We leave at dawn."

HE WAS UP WELL before daybreak; his anxiety graced him with a restless sleep and an early rise. In the threshold of the back door, he waited, leaving it ajar so he could watch Sarris kick up dirt and hassle the other birds in the semi-dark. His mother, dressed and ready when she stepped into the faint light of the kitchen, had her rifle slung over her shoulder. His father wasn't far behind, tool belt snug on his hips. Neither said much as they picked at a simple breakfast of cold porridge and berries.

A lazy sunrise and a vague haze welcomed them as they stepped outside. Smoke was in the air, faint but familiar. Somewhere, the Faroff was burning. The distant forests were more tinderbox than anything else, sending a smoky ceiling over the newborn day.

The road grew busy as they neared Hope, with farmers bringing in their salvaged crops and families from the outskirts heading to market to barter. His father kept up appearances, though the Boy noticed his hands were never more than a few inches from his tools.

Every few steps, Magnus's fingers slid inward, grazing the hammers with his fingertips. At the same time, he'd scan the woods at their periphery. His shoulders were low, loose in their joints and rolled back. That's how the Boy knew he should worry: his father was relaxed. He was ready and waiting for *something.*

For anything, the Boy realized.

Looking out over the water, he spied a few boats fishing for pipe dreams and whatever meager stocks of trout and rock bass were still to be had. A small dinghy with a faded orange-yellow sail trolled just off the cliffs nearby. It was Arif's boat, *The Sunshine.* His mother waved.

"Is that Arif?" she asked with put-on curiosity.

"Yeah," the Boy nodded. "And his dad."

"You should stop in and see him sometime. I'm sure it'd be fun."

The Boy feigned a smile. "Mm. Maybe."

He'd hardly spoken to Arif since the fire and had no real intention of changing that. Arif had always been more of Rach's friend anyway.

The family walked the rest of the journey in silence. Like him, his mother looked tired. Dark circles belied sleepless nights, the amber sun showing her age to the day. While the road proved safe enough, the Boy couldn't help but look over his shoulder every dozen paces, as if the world were waiting in ambush, ready to steal him away from the darkness of his own shadow.

After dropping his father off at the village hall, he plopped himself in the shade outside the building and let his mind chew over the possibilities of the summons. He decided against walking with his mother, letting her run her errands unencumbered. Aside from her questions about Arif, they really hadn't talked since the incident in the market. The growing distance between them was uncomfortable, but he just didn't know what to say.

He sighed, rubbing his eyes. *A problem for another time.*

Pulling out a book, he settled against the village hall and waited for the world to drift away. But it didn't. It lingered. The pages turned slow, and he had to read and reread paragraphs. His focus slipped to the crowds every few moments, his attention migrating to the sounds and smells and tension in the air. That's when he saw the Girl.

———

SHE WASN'T sure she should bother him. His face was buried in a book and he was huddled well away from the rest of the people out and about. He was jumpy too, his eyes darting up every few moments to scan the crowd.

Maybe I should just leave him be...

She started backpedaling. But then she remembered the fight. She remembered the gunshot and the taste of blood and the stunned look of resignation plastered on Magnus' son's face. But most of all, she remembered his dumb smile.

"Hey, Magnus' son." It was all the nameless niece of

Viktoria Beckett could manage. The Boy looked up immediately, caught off-guard as he squinted into the light.

"Oh, hey," he replied, pushing himself to his feet.

"I saw you at the...fight the other day. How's your jaw?"

"Um, tender," he said, rubbing it reflexively. "But fine."

"Better than that asshole Patt's I bet." She could see the name didn't register. "Patt was the guy whose face your mother..." She made a gun with her fingers and pointed it at her temple. "*Kkkplatkt.*"

"Oh. Yeah."

"He was a scumbag, for what it's worth," she added.

The Boy smiled but she could tell it was forced. That he felt bad for what happened. She switched direction.

"I haven't seen you around in a while. To be honest, I was surprised you even recognized me at the fight."

"I'm not *that* much of a recluse," the Boy chuckled.

Beckett's daughter raised an eyebrow.

"Okay, maybe I am," he admitted, his sheepish grin tinged with embarrassment. "But how could I forget the person who beat me—and my sister, no less—at the fair's knife-throwing competition, back before..."

Back before the fire.

"A long time ago," she interjected.

"A lifetime," the Boy added. His fingers gently tapped on the cover of his book. Pressing into it. She remembered he used to do that when they were in school together, before Viktoria pulled her from class and hired a private tutor to teach her instead.

"Have you been keeping up with your training? Throwing knives, I mean."

The Boy shook his head. "Nah. Or, not until recently."

"We should have a rematch then. Since there's no fair this year—or next, I suppose—there won't be any competitions. What do you say?"

The Boy looked back to her. "A rematch? Like a knife-throwing rematch?"

She nodded.

"Hmmm. Okay then," the Boy agreed. "A rematch."

Without hesitating, Beckett's daughter slipped her father's knife from its sheath behind her back and flipped it into the air. It spun a few rapid rotations before she plucked it from flight and slid it home in one fluid motion. "Bring a knife with you next time, Magnus' son," she said with a wink, abruptly turning away and marching off.

Stepping from the shade, she once again felt the day's familiar heat against her face. And the unfamiliar fluttering of butterflies in her stomach.

THE MEETING WAS over within half an hour. Spying his son in the grass, Magnus knew the kid would have questions. Bad news was always brief.

The Boy hadn't seen him yet, as he was staring off into the market. He followed his son's line of sight, recognizing the girl straightaway. It was Beckett's kid. He smiled, tucking the observation away.

"It's bad, isn't it?" his son asked as he approached.

Magnus looked around before answering, making sure no one was in earshot. Then he nodded. "And it's gonna get worse."

It had been decided that no further supplies would be delivered to Hope. Any caravans that had already departed from the capital or other villages would be allowed to continue; however, the vast majority of remaining goods would not be sent. Anyone still waiting for their rations—rich or poor or otherwise—would be left to manage on their own. There was an official moratorium on mining and felling trees, and the militia would be cut back to save rations. Effective immediately. The documents declaring such were long since signed and stamped, sent by rider weeks ago. There was nothing Magnus or the council or even young Mayor Haakan could do. For all intents and purposes, the Year was starting early.

Before word could spread and rumor take root, the mayor planned to address the village. Magnus didn't envy him, though he admired the young man's dedication. It was going to be a rough crowd...rough enough that Magnus made sure he and his were watching from a distance. They waited on the far side of the square as people gathered. Word spread quickly, as it always did, and within a few minutes, half the village was there.

"I have news from the south," Mayor Haakan shouted over the crowd, holding up the paper as if it could deflect the glares that assaulted him. A few people booed.

Haakan started reading. "To protect our fragile landscape, it has been declared...it...there will be no more caravans coming. Effective today, we will also be closing the quarry and postponing all mail and exams an—"

"Closin' the quarry?" someone shouted.

"Whatcha mean no more 'vans?" another hollered. The simmering grumble of voices bubbled over as the crowd frothed. Whatever slick politicking the mayor could muster was easily overcome by a surge of jeers.

"Please...there...THERE WILL STILL BE ANOTHER CARAVAN AT THE LEAST," the mayor yelled, though his words fell on deaf ears. Angry ears.

Fists were raised as the crowd boiled over. A few stones and bits of wood were hurled toward the platform. Haakan raised his hands in defeat, retreating from the riser toward the hall. Not five feet from the door, a rock cracked into his chest, folding him over. Another drew blood on his forehead, a thin gash flashing red in the afternoon sun.

The mayor scurried from sight as a militiaman pushed

forward into the crowd. The rest of the council in attendance withdrew to the hall and barred the door, hounded by chants and screams.

Magnus watched the crowd swarm, safe on the outskirts of the market square. He could see his son was in awe of the scene.

"C'mon, son," he whistled, turning home. His wife stepped lightly to catch up. Not hearing the Boy, he looked back. His son hadn't moved. He was captivated by the wildfire crowd. Magnus paused to watch as the commotion devolved into a riot, but when he saw actual flames kick up, he knew it was time to leave.

"Son, quickly now," he insisted.

They left before the bodies fell. Before a fistfight turned to a knife fight that left both men bleeding out on the uneven stone. They left before a market stall was set ablaze, the ensuing panic knocking down a woman and her infant. They left before the trampled pair were snatched up by the heat as the adjoining shop took fire. They left before people came to their senses, scrambling to fetch water and dirt to quell the orange-black beast that fed on Hope.

They left before the crowd dispersed, soot-covered and exhausted and furious, leaving nothing behind but bloodstains and burn marks and the dying heat of autumn.

11

After the riot in the village, his parents called a meeting. There were a few scattered homesteads on the outskirts south of Hope and his father wanted to sit everyone down to discuss their situation. That left the Boy, as the oldest of the kids, to babysit while the adults gathered. He had begged to join the meeting—it was time he learned about such things, he argued—but his parents insisted he mind the other kids instead.

In a huff, he pouted his way over to the Luddstows', where the mixed brood of children was assembled. He was to spend his evening with half a dozen kids of half a dozen ages, keeping an eye—usually both—on them as he waited for news of the meeting's end.

Pushing into the house, the Boy flopped onto the worn chesterfield in the den, ignoring the adolescent chaos. The kids were already engaged in a full-on battle, howling war cries and swinging pillows to smite would-be foes. He tried to watch, tried to leave them be and enjoy the spectacle, but he couldn't stop picturing it.

It would start when a wayward blanket or misfired pillow

hit the fireplace. Embers would scatter, tumbling like lifeless fireflies. Sizzling prongs of boring color would spread. The inferno binged on them all like starving devils, famished and constant, swallowing the room in a blinding flood. He watched the Luddstow house burn from the inside out, the children blistering, their smoky screams lost to the bawling cry of reckless heat.

He snapped out of it when he heard a familiar voice.

"Everyone pile on Magnus' son!" Beckett's daughter exclaimed, throwing a pillow at him as a distraction. The kids piled on left and right, pummeling him with pillows and smothering him with blankets. He resisted until he couldn't. They poked him and battered him, tickling wherever their spidery fingers could reach. Within a handful of seconds he was hysterical, buried under the battle cries of the children who took him captive. His laughter drummed in his stomach, shaking him lax. He laughed the world away, letting the kids save him. Letting them tire themselves out as he fed on the briefest of joys, hungry as the fire in his dreams. When they eventually gave up, his face was sore from laughing so hard.

"Now skedaddle," the Girl urged, chasing the kids with outstretched arms until they dispersed. She stepped back into the fire light, flush and wide-eyed. "Hi."

The Boy peeled off some of the blankets and tossed them onto the floor, making sure they were well away from the hearth. "Hey," he said, shifting on the couch, "What brings you out this far?"

She shrugged. "I ran into your father and he mentioned that you might appreciate some help."

The Boy kept his expression blank, though he was taken aback by the gesture. His father was not the sentimental type. "Well, uh, I'm glad he did" he stuttered, tossing his book—now bent from the pile-up—onto the table in the den. "It was a boring read anyway," he lied.

The Girl scooped it up and sat beside him, peeling back the soft cover.

"Sorry about the exams by the way."

Magnus' son feigned disappointment. "I'll do them next year."

Beckett's daughter eyed him for a long moment but said nothing, looking to the book instead. As she read over the first page, he felt her settle into the sofa. After the second page, he felt her shift. It was slight. Almost imperceptible. But he could feel the weight of her intention transfer toward him. It was subtle but he couldn't not see it. Watching her eyes scan over the cursive test, he realized then that it was because of his training. Sparring with his father, hammering nails, whipping them across the yard. It had taught him balance. To sense movement and purpose. He smiled at the cruel irony, shifting his weight in response under the pretense of reading along. He felt their arms touch, warm skin ever so slightly pressed. A million ideas careened through his head as he second guessed himself.

"Not many people know that," the Girl stated, interrupting his caravan of doubt.

Magnus' son looked up, brow furrowed. "What?"

"Morse. Your fingers. You were counting in Morse."

"Oh," he replied, reflexively tucking his digits away. "Yeah. Sorry. Habit."

"I remember that from school. You tapping on the desk. You're the only person I've met who knows it. Or, the only person that isn't super old, anyway." She paused, folding the book closed in her lap "My pop taught me when I was a kid."

"My ma taught me when..." His mother had taught him after the fire, to cope and communicate when words were out of reach. When he needed to find his center. But that was not a story for sharing. "...when I was a kid, too."

Setting the book on the table, Beckett's daughter reached out and grabbed his hand. She pressed it into a fist and he let her, watching as she started tapping her fingers on the back of his hand.

"Whoa, slow down. Okay, that's good. A joke? Sure, let's hear it." He let his hand rest in her lap as she tapped away the letters. "I don't know, what do you call it?"

More tapping.

"A *scaredcrow*?" he snorted. "That's the worst joke I've ever heard."

"Well, let's hear a better one then," the Girl demanded, setting her hand on his thigh. His heart was racing now. He worked to calm it, pressing his toes into the floor.

"Alright, but I hope you're rea—" A pillow knocked him in the side of the head.

"Can we have a story now?" the young Luddstow begged, pillow firm in his grasp. The herd of children had returned, spilling into the room. Feeling eyes upon him—including Beckett's daughter's—he didn't have the heart to say no.

"A story?" Magnus' son clicked his tongue in mock ponderance. "Hmmm...nah, I don't think so," he teased, letting their disappointment hang. "But an adventure? That I can do."

The kids cheered, curling up on the floor and couch, nuzzling themselves cozy as he regurgitated *The Tale of Sarris Gamling* from memory. By the end—a happy ending of his own creation—he was on his feet, swinging an imaginary axe as he weaved his furious tale in a thundering voice. For a moment, they had all escaped. Together.

Afterward, the kids nodded off one by one, sprawled about the room like stray cats. Himself growing tired, he slipped back onto the sofa beside Beckett's daughter. She was fading like the firelight, staring at him with eyes made tired by the warmth of the crowded den. As he settled in, she nestled against his shoulder with a yawn. Unsure, he did nothing at first. But as he felt her melt into him, he relaxed. Her fingers inched their way over his arm, tracing his scars.

"Why are you afraid of Hope?" she whispered, drifting off.

The bluntness of the question left him speechless. "I...I'm not *afraid* of Hope. I just...prefer being alone, that's all. I like things quiet."

"Those aren't mutually exclusive," she yawned, eyes closed.

She was right, but he didn't want to admit it so he leaned his head against her tousled hair, letting himself melt in turn.

"You still owe me that rematch, Magnus' son,"

The Boy smiled, He tapped his fingers against her arm. *Promise.*

Magnus' son stayed awake for as long as he could, remembering the fair and the day she bested him throwing knives. That took him deeper into his childhood. He relived mock battles pitched in open fields, swinging sticks and throwing dirt. He remembered dying in the tall grass, his death throes comically over-exaggerated as his sister jabbed a wooden spear into his belly. Laughing all the way down, he tumbled to the dirt. Rach stood over him, triumphant. A crown of dandelions sat atop her head, the yellow flowers bright as little suns. She sprinkled a fistful of grass on his body in some improvised ritual. It tickled his nose but he refused to move, stifling a sneeze as he lay there dead, gazing up into the infinite.

He chased memories until the fire went out. Then, and only then, did he sleep.

12

Thunder in the night. It shook the room, rumbling him from sleep. Not thunder, he realized. Footsteps.

Footsteps?

The Boy leapt to his feet, fumbling for his bearings, arms outstretched. A nightstand. Papers and books. His books. His nightstand. Home. Sluggish memories trickled in, belated and drowsy. He remembered walking back from the Luddstows' after babysitting, vision cumbersome and blurred as he sloshed through the creek. He remembered leaving Beckett's daughter asleep on Tom's couch, curled into its worn-down curves. He remembered dreams. Good dreams.

A guttural and wordless cry brought him back to the present. It was his father raging downstairs, rattling the bones of the old farmhouse.

"AHHHHHHHHHHHHH!!"

"Ma?" Magnus' son called out, lurching into the hallway. Half blind and heart racing, he felt for the railing, forcing himself to swallow the acidic paste on his tongue. The familiar grind-click of his mother's rifle breezed past him. She was silent, a spectral siren gliding in the nebulous shadow.

He followed her, unarmed, stumbling down the steps. The shouting continued, his father's voice booming.

As he sprung into the kitchen, the Boy caught a murky glimpse of Magnus springing into the backyard. A flash of fists in the sliver of belated moonlight was all he could make out. Someone was being pummeled; it was an unmistakable sound. Fists connected to meat, a sputtering cough and ragged gasp the only rebuttal. Clandestine lungs grasped at straws before another flurry. Stillness and silence followed.

His mother spied into the blackness, rifle level. The Boy stood at her side. His mind raced as warm air tickled his exposed skin. He could smell his own sweat, feel it pooled on his back from the heat. His eyes were drawn to his mother's weapon as she scanned the dark, her relentless gaze all-seeing.

As his mind kicked free of the confusion, he darted into the den to fetch a candle, breathing life into a fragile fire. Strands of weak light illuminated the scene as his mother kept her vigil. His father was pacing just out of sight, more shape than man. He momentarily appeared in the leaking light that spilled from the kitchen, his head shaking back and forth, fists clamped white-knuckle tight. He was muttering.

"Shoulda...Shouda never came..."

The Boy crept forward to listen. To reply. His mother stopped him.

"Leave him a moment, son," she whispered. Her eyes never left the dark, rifle nestled against her shoulder, her hawkish gaze raking the stalwart shades of coal. "It's fine now. Just give him a minute."

Her tone was hardly reassuring but he let it be. Stepping back into the house, he collected more candles and spread the light about. After another minute, his mother lowered her rifle. It was over.

"Magnus, dear?" she called out. If his father heard her, he

didn't show it. His head hung low, eyes narrowed to his feet as he paced the yard.

"They can't even...you said it wouldn't..."

"Mag?" his mother called again. This time she stepped forward, walking into his line of sight, reaching out to touch his shoulder as he neared. Her touch might as well have been lightning. His eyes shot up.

"Mar?"

"Yes, dear. Are you okay?" she asked, pulling his hands up in the half-light to examine them.

"I'm fine," he insisted, shaking free of her grip. "The Boy?"

"I'm here," Magnus' son chimed in from the doorway. He approached the body that was crumpled in the grass. Beside it, a pair of burlap sacks were sprawled in the dirt. Even in the faulty light, he could tell they were moving.

"Sarris?"

Sarris and the hens had been stuffed into the sacks, their coop pried open and busted. He herded the birds back into their jailbroken shed, jamming a branch against the door to keep it closed. Equal parts nervous and curious, he shuffled back to his father and flipped the unconscious body over.

"...Fort?"

"You know him?" his mother asked, shouldering her rifle.

"Yeah," the Boy replied. "Sort of. He's a McKelsie. The oldest. Went by Fort."

The Boy tried to remember the last time he saw the McKelsies in Hope but drew a blank. It had been years at the very least. Why their mother dragged them off to homestead out past the abandoned Fort McKelsie was anyone's guess. He'd never been out that far himself but he'd heard the old military garrison was a crumbling ruin, a relic from a more prosperous time. Tucked away in a valley beyond the outskirts of Hope, it was as close to the Faroff as you want to get.

"Y'all okay over there?" Tom shouted from across the field.

Both Saira and Beckett's daughter were at his side, glowing in an orb of torchlight. Tom had his bow out.

"We're good," Magnus shouted over his shoulder, stalking off toward the palisade to meet Tom as he approached. While his father conferred with the neighbors, the Boy walked over to the toolshed, leaving his mother to watch the body. He felt around in the dark until he found some rope, binding Fort's hands and legs as best he could.

"Alright," his father sighed, stepping back from the palisade. "Let's get 'em inside."

Magnus heaved the limp body over his shoulder and carried Fort into the house. The Boy got a fire going in the den and settled in. They sat in silence, listening to the crack and sizzle hiss serpentine psalms. After half an hour, his mother creaked her way upstairs but found no rest in her empty bed. He could hear her tossing and turning for the better part of an hour. He suspected she—like him—was caught in the restless vines of their dilemma. The law was crystal clear about theft: any thieves found guilty would be hung. No exceptions.

In the morning, the family would take Fort into the village. And then they'd watch him die.

13

There was hardly a trial. In the cramped council chamber, an old stone room littered with desks and tables, folded charts and dusty books and crinkled documents needing review, his father declared the crime.

The Boy, his mother, and Tom verified the charge as witnesses. Each stepped to a podium at the center of the room and gave a brief statement, describing the event as they saw it.

In the corner, a hunched young clerk scribbled notes. Ax and the council listened indifferently from a raised platform, each man in varying stages of boredom. Off to the side, Sheriff Rhys stared out the room's only window.

A few years older than his father, Rhys had been sheriff as long as the Boy could remember. He was a grumpy old man with meaty shoulders and loose skin that drooped like ill-fit clothing. His right hand forever hovered over his revolver. A bushy grey moustache covered most of his mouth, sweeping over his lips to hide his resting scowl. He was a no-nonsense fellow, slow and deliberate and with a brusque aversion to human interaction. To the Boy, he was just a crabbier version of his father.

Fort stood opposite Rhys, flanked by two of the sheriff's militiamen. His face was swollen and blushing purple, his wrists in irons.

"Well, son, you've heard the charges. What say you?" Rhys muttered.

Fort McKelsie shrugged, sullen and silent.

"It was you who committed robbery?" the burly sheriff prodded, one hand resting on his revolver.

"Mmm," the young McKelsie coughed, clearing his throat with a nod. "It was me." He turned to look the sheriff directly in the eyes. "Only me."

Rhys rapped his knuckle twice on the table beside him. "It's a hangin' then." Tipping his hat to the council, who was already pushing up from their seats, the grumpy sheriff ambled out the door, leaving the militiamen to take Fort back to his cell.

"Wait!" Magnus interrupted. "We'll need time to let his family know."

The council was silent.

"It's the decent thing to do," his father added.

No one objected so the hanging was postponed to the following day.

When the Boy and his family returned the next morning, word had spread and most everyone from Hope had gathered —including Beckett's daughter. Her hair was pulled back in tight braids and a second knife rested on her hip. Her pants were rolled up and tucked into her boots. She looked ready for a fight. The Boy couldn't help but wonder if she knew something he didn't.

The execution grounds were in a field a couple hundred yards south of the village, set into a rutted hill past the harbor. Rounded grey and pink rock jutted out from the dirt and grass, veins of stone splitting the scarred earth. The uneven hilltop spilled toward the water, an ashen and forlorn slope.

Clinging to dregs of soil at the hill's base were a pair of

trimmed willow trees that served as the gallows. Their roots were a knotted tangle of weatherworn tentacles spilling out from the broken earth. Crude ladders scaled their trunks, platforms resting in their branches. Each was a dozen or so feet up. High enough to break a neck.

Light gusts of autumn danced the sagging willow strands, rustling the tense air. The musty perfume of the algae-spotted lake layered itself over the human concoction of sweat and squalid bodies. It smelled like any other day. But closer.

Beckett's daughter slipped through the crowd when she saw him. Her smile was brief and restrained by circumstance. He gave her a quick hug when she neared. There was no point in asking how she was. The entire crowd was feeling the same dread. It had been a long while since the last proper hanging and the Boy could tell everyone—himself included—was ill at ease. And, with his mother within earshot, he didn't want to talk about their night babysitting either.

"They sent a rider," he blurted out instead. "Just waiting for the McKelsie's to get here."

She nodded. "I heard." After a pause, she leaned in. "We can go if you want," she whispered. "We don't have to watch."

The Boy thought about the offer as he looked over the pensive crowd. His mother was behind him, carbine across her back. She smiled when their eyes met. He looked to his father next, who was chatting with Tom, stoic as always.

"Nah," he sighed. "I gave evidence at the trial. It's only fair I see it done."

The Girl squeezed his arm, letting her hand fall beside his. Before he could smile, someone hollered. The McKelsies had arrived. The disheveled bunch made their way around Hope, the five brothers unkempt and wretched looking. The runt of the lot, no older than ten or so the Boy wagered, had an unseemly arm. It was bent and crooked, as if it were attached backward. The kid was tanned dark with beady eyes that shot back and forth, rodent like. A malnourished donkey plodded behind them on a long lead. Their mother wasn't with them. The Boy couldn't decide how he felt about that.

When Fort's kin caught sight of their brother in chains they kicked up a fuss, shouting as they pushed into the crowd. Half a dozen militiamen, including the sheriff, kept a small perimeter around the hanging tree, weapons out and the will to use them fortified. The McKelsie boys reached for their own weapons, shoving the militiamen back. It was going to come to blows.

"Leave 'em be!" someone snarled.

It was Fort. His speech was slurred but firm, his resolve seemingly unflappable. The Boy saw through it though, saw the distance Fort was putting between them all. The shallow mask of acceptance, freshly painted. It was a façade he was well acquainted with.

The sheriff, making no attempt at conversation, crossed the clearing to Fort and unlocked his chains, letting him enjoy a final minute of freedom before the end. The crowd quieted, the somber mass grim and pressing. A grey sky lumbered off the coast, overcast and fretting, but the heavy clouds never managed more than a few feeble drops.

Near the hanging tree, his father inspected the rope. It was a thick noose and crude, well-worn and stained dark. Magnus had insisted he be the one to see the McKelsie boy off. He was the one that pressed the charge after all. It was only fair.

Having said his farewells, Fort climbed the makeshift ladder. Magnus followed. Once on the platform, the Boy's father slipped the rope over McKelsie's head and saw it tight. He offered the kid a hood but it was refused. Fort was given a moment to collect himself, to see himself to the finish line with at least a modicum of dignity. The Boy watched from below as his father leaned in and whispered to the doomed thief, who in turn whispered his own final words in reply.

Without looking back, Magnus turned to the ladder and

clambered down toward the lever that would send the failed thief onward. The Boy, standing in the front row of the crowd, blinked away the tension in his eyes. His jaw was clenched, shoulders taut and raised, eyes poised to close as soon as was necessary.

He never got the chance to look away.

Without warning, and not waiting for the platform to drop, Fort leapt into the air. The crowd gasped. Magnus' son braced himself for the jarring sound of breaking bone, toes pressed into the soles of his boots. But the noise never came. Maybe the branch sagged. Maybe he landed at an odd angle. Or maybe the rope wasn't tight enough. It didn't matter. He survived the drop.

Terror flashed across Fort's face as he thrashed. His eyes strained toward the crowd, wide and sharp and prying. The jagged shock bounced him ragged. Blood trickled from his mouth as he jolted and kicked, choking on wordless fear. His face washed blister red, faint-blue lips spitting white dribble and dry air. His hands, left unbound, clawed at the rope.

The Boy wanted to look away. His stomach turned. Mumbles of disgust and shock married themselves to the space between Fort's frantic convulsions. A woman behind him retched. But nobody moved as the McKelsie danced like winter rye in a gale.

Mariam, a statue until that moment, started toward Fort. Magnus got there first. The Boy's father wrapped himself around Fort's waist and jerked down with a heavy tug, sinking his mass into the carpet of hardpan at his feet. The crack was audible; Fort's neck shattered like thick glass on hard stone. He went limp.

The deed done, Magnus stepped back, leaving the body to sway like it was just another branch in the early-autumn breeze. People watched. Some sickened, some indifferent. All were frozen in tableau. Like they had awakened from some perplexing dream and didn't know what to do or what to say. So nothing was said. Nothing was done. Justice was served.

MARIAM LINGERED as the crowd shuffled back to Hope. She waited while her husband lowered the limp McKelsie boy to the ground with the help of Tom and Step. Rhys, looking uninterested, straddled the space between the living McKelsies and their dead brother. She knew, from experience, the man much preferred firing squads.

"Who's got time for all that climbin'?" he once told her, mere moments before putting a bullet in a man's chest.

She ran her fingers over her bandolier, counting the rounds. They were old, coming up to a couple decades. They'd still do the trick in a pinch—she kept them clean and dry—but sooner rather than later, a day would come when she'd have no bullets left. Even if any could still be made—and she doubted they could be—they'd be bought up before making it this far north.

She frowned at the thought, turning back to her husband. He had shouldered Fort's body onto the bare back of the McKelsie's gaunt donkey. The sagging corpse jostled and bobbed on the beast as the sullen family departed.

Maybe he's right, she thought, pondering the sheriff's words. Maybe a firing squad was a better end. No ropes. No breath-held silence as someone sputters and chokes. Just thunder and metal and a splash of red to season the finale.

"Shall we get goin'?" her husband interrupted.

"I guess so," she sighed. "Where'd our son get off to?"

"Went in with Beckett's kid," Magnus replied, glancing to Hope. "Figured that'd be fine."

She nodded, wrapping her arm around his as they made their home. The day was young and warm and she looked forward to a few hours without the Boy banging nails or bickering with Mag. Maybe she'd even fire off a couple quick shots, just to get the blood pumping.

"What are your plans for today?" she asked as they left the gallows.

"Was thinkin' I'd dig a few more traps in that fallow field. Near the trees there," he replied. "You?"

Mariam shrugged, tapping her dirty fingernails against the metal casings in her belt.

"Don't waste the bullets," Magnus said, reading her mind.

"Excuse me?" she scoffed playfully, stopping them both in the middle of the road. "We've got almost sixty left. More than enough. And after today, I think I'm entitled."

"Entitled?" her husband mocked. "And just what makes you think that?"

"Because I know your secret," she grinned.

"My secret, eh?" He gave her a good-natured stare down but she didn't budge. "Well?"

She wrapped her arm around his waist with an exaggerated sigh. "My dear, sweet Magnus. Subtlety was never your strong suit." She leaned in and gave him a kiss on the cheek, his scratchy beard tickling her nose. "Next time, don't be so obvious."

"Hmm," Magnus hummed, deflating a little. He pulled her close as they continued, his arm resting on her shoulders. "Was it that obvious?"

"Nah. I just know you too well," she teased.

Mariam let her mind drift back to the gallows. To the noose intentionally left slack. To the deceptive instructions or threats her husband whispered to the doomed McKelsie.

Truth be told, she didn't care that Mag didn't tighten the noose. Or that he tricked the kid into jumping. She knew he felt the need to send a message. To remind the world that he was not a man of half measures. To remind them all that he was a survivor.

"Well, it made an impression either way," her husband shrugged.

"It certainly did," she smiled. "It certainly did."

14

H e woke up sore every morning. Shoulders knotted, forearms tense and tender. The days blurred together as he trained. Throwing, jabbing, crushing, clawing. Fighting shadows, hitting targets. Lift. Aim. Throw. Lift. Aim. Throw. Walk and get the hammers. Walk back. Repeat. It continued for weeks, his father refusing to let him go into the village. The new announcement had changed every- thing. So, he trained. He dented targets and left gashes of skinned bark on the trees he used as dummies. Once a week he went out with the rifle or bow, resting his muscles to focus on his marksmanship. He was no natural, but he was getting better.

It wasn't until another meeting was called that his father finally let him make the trip into Hope. Sitting alone in the back row of the village hall, he listened to the councilors trade barbs and haggle over Hope's paltry options. The cavernous village hall was warmed by torchlight and the scattered bodies that filled it. A dozen long benches and a handful of stools filled the space, the stone walls mostly bare or hidden behind shelves and cabinets.

Before the End, the large building had been a place of worship. Today, it served a more practical purpose as Hope's organizational hub and seat of government. Capped by a narrow bell tower, it stood an enduring reminder of history's lost wonders. The massive windows that stretched along the upper walls had mostly been replaced, though a few works of stained glass remained. They had been boarded up, of course, their vivid colors obscured by wood and burlap.

Massaging his knotted forearms, the Boy wondered if any other colored glass remained intact elsewhere. Could it still be made? Or was it, like most things, lost to the world that came before?

As the voices droned on, he started to drift off, eyes heavy in the growing heat. Every now and then a councilmember would shout an objection and a brief spat would erupt. It would be quelled by the other councilors—including his father—before the droning continued.

Twenty-five or so villagers were sitting in the airy gallery, far less than the Boy predicted for such a significant discussion. A few rows ahead, a woman clad in dyed linens and thin furs scribbled notes as she listened, unperturbed by the tiresome warmth. She was slim and pale, her skin a far cry from the leathery brown of her neighbors. Her head bobbed raptor-like as the councilors debated, long ochre braids coiled tight against the back of her head. Her posture was immaculate.

The Boy squinted at the furs on her shoulder though he didn't recognize the creature—or creatures—they were fashioned from. He could smell her perfume though, even a few rows away. Every time he shifted in his seat, a floral bouquet both enticing and off putting teased him. He would breathe it in intentionally, only to wrinkle his nose at it when it drew up his nostrils. And then he would do it again. Her name was Viktoria Beckett.

Viktoria owned the largest plot of land in the village. It had been in her family for generations, along with sizeable chunk of land somewhere south. Maybe New Gamling, maybe further south near Rockmantle or Saviour. He supposed it didn't really matter at this point. What mattered was what she was doing here.

With no more trade coming by boat or wagon, the community was disastrously short on supplies. Unable to ship its lumber and stone, Hope's livelihood was kneecapped. It was unclear how everyone would make ends meet. Goods were currency; food was gold.

Perched high up on the bluff overlooking the village, Viktoria managed a wide expanse of plowed fields and woodland, inherited from her brother when he passed. The property still produced a decent crop too, giving the woman overwhelming leverage when it came to Hope's future.

Shifting on the uncomfortable bench, the Boy drifted into memories of when the Becketts still had cattle. Every now and then he'd trudge up the bluff to watch them plod about, chewing the dry grass to cud. They were the last herd in the whole village, though eventually they succumbed to some unknown disease like every other cow along the doomed coast.

How many cows are left in the world? he wondered, continuing his curiosity. He doubted it was many. No one had ever seen a wild one and none had been sent from the south in a decade. They were probably extinct.

It was a disappointing thought and it spoiled his fickle mood. The nail in the coffin came when the council—or at least a majority of its members—decided to remove the village's Sarris Gamling statue.

Standing tall over the harbor, the statue dated back to the founding of Hope. The iron and bronze sculpture depicted Sarris, massive axe in hand, looking out over the water, gazing into the vastness from whence he came. It was hope incarnate. But it was also metal. And Viktoria wanted the metal. She'd pay for it fairly, of course, offering food and supplies in exchange. A far more valuable trade, many agreed.

A new one can be rebuilt, they said.

It's better to save lives and support the village's coffers, they said.

It's only a statue, they said.

It all made sense to the Boy. Those were rational arguments. But he kicked himself for not speaking up when given the chance. "It isn't just a statue..."

He was tired and he knew it, realizing it was foolish for him to have come. He hadn't slept well since the hanging, his dreams dragging him back to the gallows and the McKelsie boy who swayed from its branches. While sleep eluded him at home, here in the warmth of the murmuring crowd his eyes begged for rest.

He picked himself up and shuffled outside, hoping the gentle breeze off the lake would wake him. The village wasn't quiet, but it wasn't bustling either. It was just there, dim in the early night.

"I'll miss the statue." The words were soft but they managed to startle him. "I always thought it was pretty. And worthwhile."

Victoria's niece slipped into the half-light, her brown eyes swallowing the darkness between them.

"Oh, yeah. Me too," the Boy agreed. "I always thought it was...important." He stifled a wince, too weary to confront his woefully bland reply. He stood aimless past the doorframe, lost in himself. He wanted to kiss her. To tell her things he couldn't find the words for. To share ideas he hadn't even thought of yet.

"They'll tear it down tomorrow," she continued.

"I figured," the Boy nodded, looking out toward the water.

"Do you want to go see it?" she asked, stepping out of the darkness to meet him. "One final time?"

"Now?"

Beckett's daughter smiled. "Now is all we got."

She didn't wait for his reply, leading the way down the stone path toward the lane. The Boy smiled. And then he followed.

He caught up to her as they passed the village gate and its line of burning torches. They strolled out toward the statue, which sat near the retreating shoreline. There was enough light from the sky to see the silhouette of Sarris stretching his arm out into the nothingness, pointing to everything. They walked up to its stone base, the low ebb of the lapping shore humming in the background. The Boy ran his hands over engraved words hardly visible in the growing dark. He knew them from memory.

THROUGH HARDSHIP IS THE JOURNEY. FROM LESS THERE WILL BE MORE.

Someone had already vandalized the letters, the word *MORE* scratched and slashed away. *LESS* was carved above it.

"Do you think he was real?" he asked, turning to look at her in the twilight.

She shrugged. "I doubt it. Not like the stories, anyway. But I always hoped he was."

"Yeah, me too." He listened as footsteps passed behind them, crunching the pebbled walkway before vanishing into the night. "Have you ever seen any other statues before? Like, in other villages, I mean."

"Statues? Hmm, not many. None bigger than this one, anyway. But there are much more impressive things out there than statues."

He perked up. "Really? Like what?"

"You'll have to go and see for yourself," she teased, hopping up onto the statue's stone base. "That's half the fun!" Kicking off her shoes, Beckett's daughter rubbed her bare feet against the worn limestone. It was quarried just east of the village, the last working quarry in the world.

"You know, I never really had a desire to leave here," the Boy confessed, sitting down beside her.

"I'm shocked," the Girl teased. "But aren't you curious about what's out there? About other places? Other people? There's a whole wide world to see."

"I guess," he shrugged, "but my whole life has been here. My family's here. My home. And besides, I've got books."

She slid closer to him. He could smell lavender in her hair. Her eyes devoured the night around him. "There's a world of difference between reading about something and experiencing it though, isn't there?"

The Boy's heart fluttered, her words close in his ear. But his thoughts quickly drifted to the fire. To the fight. To the Year. "A world and more," he conceded.

"My pop wanted to travel. Not just along the road but beyond. Off the map. He showed me a globe once. You know, one of those round maps? Most of it was blank. I'd love to see what's out there. Or, what's left of it. Beyond the Faroff."

"Well, maybe if we survive the Year I'll take me on a trip. I hear New Gamling is nice," the Boy chuckled.

Beckett's daughter scoffed. "New Gamling? Well, that's a start, I guess. Deal."

The pair shook hands and, side by side, gave into the silence. They listened to the fragile wavelets for quiet moments, shoulder to shoulder, close and tempting. The Boy could feel his pulse quicken but he didn't know what to do or say.

"I think we should say our farewells," Beckett's daughter suggested, breaking the silence as she slipped her shoes back on.

"Right, yeah. I should probably get back." He slipped down from the stone, brushing off his trousers. Beckett's daughter shouldered him before he managed to take a step.

"I meant say our farewells to the statue, dummy."

"Ohhh," the Boy flushed. "Right. Yeah." He looked up at the statue, then back to the girl. "Umm..."

"Why don't you say a prayer?" she suggested.

"A what?"

"A prayer. Like they used to do."

"Ah. Okay. I can do that." He put his hands on his waist, stepping back to take in the whole of the statue. "You know, it's funny. I've read that word dozens of times but I've never heard anyone actually say it aloud...or do one."

"I haven't heard one since my pop died."

The Boy stopped mid-step and hugged her. He knew the hollowness that loss leaves, the loneliness it carves out. Though he could only imagine just how much that loneliness would be amplified without anyone else to call family. To have to live with a woman who despises you, shuns you.

After holding her close, he stepped away and looked up to the statue, scratching at the budding stubble that peppered his jaw. Unsure of what to do with his arms, he let them fall idle at his side.

"Ahem. Dear Sarris Gamling, we're sorry that your statue is going to be removed and destroyed. We're, uh, very thankful—grateful, even—that you brought people here to make a new life. We're sorry that it didn't work out..." He paused, searching for the right words. "We're sorry that we let you down, and we, um, hope that you can help us make things right. Thank you."

The Girl walked up to the statue and put her hand on it, drawing her nails over the dark stone. "That was perfect."

Suddenly, muffled voices leaked from the distance as people left the hall.

"I best be off. My aunt doesn't like to be kept waiting."

The Boy nodded, hiding his disappointment. "Yeah, my da' will be waiting too."

Without missing a beat, the Girl leaned in and kissed him on the cheek.

"Thanks for the prayer, Magnus' son."

"Oh, uh, thanks for inviting me," he blushed.

As they ambled up the hill toward the hall, she wrapped

her arm around his. The Boy, his defenses shattered, let his curiosity spew out.

"Have you thought about a name? For after?"

Her reply was swift, eager, and honest. "I've thought about my name almost every day since I was a kid. You?"

He shook his head. "I don't want one, to be honest."

"Nothing feel right or...?"

The Boy stopped, an anxious thread coiling around him. "It's just too much. Too much change. Too permanent. It's stupid, I know."

Beckett's daughter leaned against him, her head on his shoulder. "Change, a wise man once said, is a bastard."

Magnus' son smiled, his tension eased. He let her keep her head on his shoulder as they stood idle on the walkway. Ahead, a group gathered around the hall entrance bidding one another farewell. "What name will you pick?"

Beckett's daughter looked at him for a moment longer than made him comfortable, her eyes like tiny black holes, consuming everything. "I'll pick my father's name."

With a wave, she walked off to greet her aunt, leaving the Boy to his thoughts. And prayers.

THE NEXT MORNING a group of men pulled the statue down. It bent and fell slow, teetering before it buckled. The impact rattled the dirt and gravel, dusting the pier and merchant stalls. The Boy didn't stay to watch them dismantle it. He had hoped it wouldn't fall or that people would change their mind once they remembered how important it is. But it fell. And so, not seeing Beckett's daughter about, he left.

He took the long way home, looping north around the village for no reason other than he felt like being alone. He followed a crumbling stone and iron fence as he ambled, the weathered limestone topped by rusted spirals and spears of chipped metal. The ancient barrier must have been a couple centuries old, maybe more. A few shaded sections of the fence were riddled by dying vines, the tangle of browns and greens webbed and knotted between the barrier's metal shafts. Beyond the fence, the grass was trampled though a few wildflowers managed to eke out a living in the sparse shade.

There were also a few dozen headstones scattered around the meadow as well. What few remained standing were crafted of stone and new, their names—earned or otherwise—carved in elegant letters. Names that would be remembered for generations. That was no small thing.

He spied the odd trinket resting in the short grass though he couldn't ever tell what they were. Maybe toys. Maybe some other keepsake. Much of the village's prominent families had plots there—including descendants of Sarris Gamling, it was said. For everyone else, a shallow backyard grave or a bonfire was the norm. Caskets and tombstones were a luxury few could afford.

Glancing across the cemetery, the Boy spied two people, mere shapes in the distant corner of the graveyard. He walked a dozen paces to get a closer look, letting his hand bounce along the fence's iron bars in tandem with his footfalls. It looked to be a parent and child. He didn't recognize who so he strolled closer. As he continued, he noticed the pair were hardly moving.

Maybe they're praying, he thought, hopping up again to peek over the fence.

A gust of warm wind blew over the grounds, scattering a few fallen leaves and pushing them around the meadow. He saw the father and child move then. They were swaying. Hanging from a stout branch, the pair twirled. One way, then the other. The ropes around their necks creaked under their shifting weight. It was a father and son. The child's face was half caved and rotted, flies and maggots feasting themselves into maturity. The father was more intact, though there was a murder of crows lurking in the branches above that would remedy that.

The Boy pressed his face against the corroded iron, staring at the signs that hung around their necks.

THIEVES. The signs said Thieves.

15

"Son, I said let me see the list."

The Boy drifted back to reality, blinking off a daydream of Beckett's daughter.

"What? Oh."

He stuffed his hand in his coat pocket and pulled out the crumpled paper. His father's chicken scratch cursive outlined half a dozen items they needed from the shop. A few other folks were already queued up waiting to be helped. The Boy had long since zoned them out, his mind a million miles away as he stared out the open door and into the tired chaos of the weathered village.

He had hoped to see Beckett's daughter during his visit; it had been a week since he saw her last and found himself thinking of her often. Every time he tapped his fingers in code he remembered her hands against his. It was an endless supply of fuel for his daydreams and he found himself drifting off more than usual. Happily so.

But he also wanted to tell her about the bodies he saw in the cemetery. Maybe she had heard what happened. Maybe she knew who they were.

He glanced around the shop, tuning back into the noises that welcomed the morning. They were in the smaller of the two general stores in town, owned by his father's friend Horse Pete. It was little more than a few cramped aisles of odds and ends. A dozen bushel barrels were stacked about, some buckets and timber piled at random. Four semi-rusted shovels and a hoe collected cobwebs in the corner. Dust-yellow light spilled in from the cracked window at the store's front, tinting the gaunt space a sandy hue. Most of the shelves were already empty.

"Mag, you sumbitch! How goes?" Horse Pete shouted from the counter, his smile wide and yellow and engulfed by a curling beard. The Boy tried not to stare at Pete's hand when the man waved; his right hand was missing a couple digits and was partially disfigured. Instead, he pondered how much it would hurt to lose a few fingers...especially the way Pete lost his.

"Lookin' for a hammer or two, eh?" Horse Pete followed up, flashing his toothy smile. "I'll give ya a good deal for the kid!"

He was chipper and chatty as always. His bulbous head, rounded out by a dense crop of brown hair, looked greasy in the grubby light. More hair, curled and dark, poked out from his collar and sleeves, covering his tanned skin. The man's remaining fingers were stubby, his hands brawny and thick. The Boy shuddered at the thought of having a horse trample his hand, picturing the doc sawing off the mangled digits off when they didn't heal properly.

More interesting than the fingers, however, was Pete's smile. Horse Pete was one of the only grown men he'd ever met not missing a single tooth. It was something Pete flaunted at every opportunity.

"Quit yer chattin', Petey. My wife'll kill me if I ain't back soon," one of the customers whinged, rapping his knuckles on the counter.

Horse Pete flipped the man a finger, flashing his yellow teeth. "It's my shop, Byorn, and I'll do what I please. So jus—"

"SHUT THE FUCK UP, ALL'YA!" someone bellowed. Everyone turned.

Elbowing into the shop were two men in long coats, the thin leather poorly stitched and weather-beaten. Their faces were masked by dark cloth and smeared dirt, their heads wrapped in fabric to keep the sun at bay. One of the men—the shorter of the two—had a milky stain in his left eye. It twitched when the Boy stared. With them came the wafting stench of sweaty horses and an odor akin to week-old compost. The maggoty kind that brought flies.

The taller of the two was long-limbed with a face that looked like it had been punched one too many times. The Boy couldn't tell if he walked with a limp or a swagger. Gripped in the man's sun-burnt knuckles was a rusty four-chamber revolver.

"None a y'all move!" the gunman roared, slamming the shop door closed. Everyone was quiet. Including Magnus. The Boy's heart galloped, the shock of adrenaline raiding his focus.

The gunman pushed his way toward the counter. When a young miner blocked his path, a quick pistol whip to the face sent the miner tumbling. The milk-eyed outlaw blocked the door, threatening the patrons with a foot-long blade. It was wide and curved and bloodied, long enough to skewer a man through with room to spare. The Boy was so focused on the knife that he didn't notice the revolver pass mere inches from his face as the gunman passed.

"Keep quiet and we'll be outta yer hair in a pinch, friends!" the gunman insisted. The revolver remained pointed at the group, ranging between customers.

"Outta my way, shopkeep!" the bandit ordered. Horse Pete, who stood, hands-raised, behind the counter, didn't flinch.

The gunslinger spat then hopped over the countertop,

knocking Pete aside with a sweeping blow from the butt of his weapon. Pete dropped. Weapon aimed once more at the crowd, the robber started filling a burlap sack with notes and money as well as some smaller items nearby. Nails, metal rods, hand tools. Anything he could reach he shoved in the sack.

For a moment, the Boy's mind outpaced his heart. He almost spoke up, catching the syllables on his tongue. It was plain stupid to steal money when there were materials here worth far more than any currency will be, come the Year.

"What you lookin' at, kid?" the gunman barked.

The Boy cast his eyes downward, holding his breath. His father shuffled half a step to cover him from the gunman's aim.

"Thought so," the man snapped. "Not a bloody word!"

With his sack full, the gunslinger gave Pete a swift kick before hopping back over the counter. "Now empty yer pockets and we'll be on our merry way!"

His voice was more direct than harsh as he aimed the weapon at each member of the crowd. His hand was steady in the act too. No shaking, no hesitation. These were not, the Boy realized, inexperienced men. The same could not be said for the store's patrons.

Aside from his father and Pete, most were younger folk who had hardly seen a Year. The sudden violence stupefied them, forcing acquiescence.

One by one, they tossed their purses and coins and pocket knives and notes into the sack. Staring at the gunman, revolver hovering mere inches from his face, his father reached into his coat for his purse, hand sliding past his tools.

His tools!

Magnus' son dared not look at his father lest he telegraph the future. Instead, he stared at the gunman. He could see the blackheads on the man's bent and hooked nose, could see where sweat and spit had stained his handkerchief. The man's neck had a few cuts and bites, their redness half hidden by a coarse and patchy beard. Hands in his pocket, the Boy waited, tapping his fingers on his leg. Counting.

His father shifted as he pulled out his promissory notes and a few coins with his left hand. His right hand, obscured by the angle, slid a hammer from its stirrup with subtle, practiced precision. Magnus reached out to offer his notes and coins to the gunman. When the robber reached for them, his father let them fall onto the floor instead. The Boy startled as the metal coins bounced off the wooden boards. The noise, small as it was, surprised the gunman. He pulled the trigger.

The Boy recoiled against the intimacy of barrage. His nostrils filled with acrid smoke. Ears ringing, he looked down to see the ruined corpse of his father. But there was no body. Only screams. Screams and carnage yet unfolding.

16

Magnus was in motion before the trigger.

As his right arm shot up, he shifted his weight, allowing the bullet to pass millimeters from the side of his head. The shot left him deaf, but alive. The men in line jolted at the opening salvo. Some even ducked or dove for cover. Magnus hardly flinched.

He jabbed the revolver-wielding ruffian in the throat with the wooden shaft of his hammer. Flipping the tool in his hand, he jabbed the man in the throat again—this time with the metal end—and bull-rushed him toward the wall. He felt the man's windpipe buckle as they toppled shelves.

Buckets of nails spilled underfoot as wooden bins and crates crashed down. Magnus paid the chaos no mind. His left hand was already swooping in, fingers lovingly entwined around his second tool. The blunt end of his hammer met the gunman's skull with a wet thud. The blow sounded like a round stone being dropped into thick muck, the man's cranium chipping like flaked rust.

Magnus' ringing ears drowned out the footsteps of the

milky-eyed thief charging in behind him but he felt the attack coming in the floorboards. He pivoted on his back foot, sweeping his right leg out as his right hand swung in tandem.

Hammer claw first, the backhanded blow connected with the robber mid-lunge. The sharpened claws of the tool caught the milk-eyed man in the face, digging into his cheek. The metal peeled skin, chipped bone. Teeth spilled onto the floor like bloodied hail, mixing with the nails. His other hammer came down hard against the thief's hand.

The man screamed, knife tumbling free. The girthy blade pierced through the outlaw's thin boot and stabbed into his foot. With his face pouring blood, the milk-eyed robber struggled to pull the weapon free. Red leaked from his wound, slicking the weapon's handle.

After a moment of struggle, the thief looked up, meeting the eyes of the gathered crowd. The men had composed themselves now, their memories refreshed. It had been a long time since a Year. They had grown soft. Grown complacent. Magnus was reminding them of their heritage. Of their inheritance.

"Pp......pweeese, shhir."

The thief's face was a battered mess, his words more blood than sound. He was on a knee, hand shattered and face torn. Pieces of his friend's skull were scattered amongst the wayward nails, splayed out like a wounded constellation. The soon-to-be-corpse swallowed blood and looked up at him.

Magnus stared back, grim and unshaken. Gore wet his beard. He could feel it trickling down his neck. He could taste it.

"Da'..." his son spoke, pressed up against the wall behind him.

Magnus didn't move. He was coiled. The darkness called.

His son shuffled forward. "It's over now."

Magnus remained still. Everybody did. A part of him tried

to coax mercy out from wherever it was hidden but those thoughts were weak and undeveloped.

Instead, two hammers sped down with traumatizing and unforgiving force. He heard the familiar sound in one ear but not the other. A final sound.

Leaving the tools bloody, Magnus slid them home. He watched, feeling the come down, as the stolen money and goods were returned to everyone in the shop. Horse Pete, having come to, walked the scene, holding a rag to the bloody gash on his head. Eyeing the broken bodies, he flashed a toothy grin.

"Better his than mine," Pete chuckled, pointing to the scattered teeth on the floor.

Magnus smiled. And then he laughed, hearty and full. Because it was either that or scream.

Among the witnesses there was little jubilation. Vacant stares gaped at the bloody scene. His son leaned against the counter, frantically tapping his fingers on its surface. The Boy was watching droplets of blood pool in the cracks of the dented floorboards. Magnus studied him. When they made eye contact his son looked away.

What few possessions were found on the thieves were given to Magnus in thanks, including the revolver and its few bullets. Magnus refused the gesture.

"You take 'er, Pete. Looks like you'll need it." He shook the gun and its rounds until his old friend reluctantly accepted. "Smells like they've got horses too if you want 'em," he joked.

"Pffff I ain't want the damn things!" Horse Pete jabbed back, waving the man off with another big smile.

Magnus took a knee and pried the knife from the dead man's boot. It was a solid blade, likely stolen from someone down the road. He wiped the blood on the outlaw's pants, rifling the sheath free. He handed the weapon to his son.

"Here," he said, arm outstretched. "Time you had a weapon of your own."

The Boy nodded but didn't reply. Accepting the knife, his son cradled the weapon against his chest, his fingers tapping on the sheath. Magnus couldn't hear the sound but he recognized the rhythm. Short-short-short-long-long-long-short-short-short. Save Our Souls.

17

It was a gruesome blade. The kind meant to solve problems. No unnecessary ornamentation, just metal and wood. Its front edge narrowed to a point that the Boy prodded into his finger. It wouldn't take much to draw blood.

Wouldn't take much to remove the whole finger, he mused, appraising the weapon. The very thought of blood and gore dragged him back to the incident at Horse Pete's the week prior. To the red monsoon his father summoned. To the violence. He shuddered.

Holding the knife in his dominant hand, pressing the worn wood into his palm, he bounced the weight in his closed grip. He couldn't help but wonder how many lives it had stolen away, how much life had leaked along its curves.

"Alright. Give 'er a go," his father instructed. Magnus was propped against the fence, hands resting on his tool belt as he barked orders. Watching. Judging. The Boy went through the motions. Sidestepping, slicing, lunging, blocking. His father shouted out a pattern and he followed through. The knife was light and balanced, a far cry from the hammers. He felt agile, quick.

"Keep your other arm back," his father cautioned. "And up. Best not see it lopped off."

The Boy took heed, curling his left hand into a fist and keeping it beside his face as a final defense. He dipped and dropped his shoulder, jabbing in from opposing angles, criss-crossing the air as he pressed forward against invisible attackers.

"Aim for the soft spots. Picture 'em."

The Boy dug a few sharp stabs forward, blows that would have spilled someone's warm guts onto the even warmer ground.

"See it happen. Right there," his father pressed, jabbing his index finger into his own forehead. "It's all up there. You wanna win? You wanna live? Make it happen up here first."

After another minute the Boy slowed. He was red in the face as he handed the blade to his father. "Can we grind it down a bit? It's a little long."

Magnus took the weapon and let his arm work a few moves before handing it back to his son. "That we can, son. That we can."

He followed his father to the shed, prickles of sweat pooling on his forehead. He wiped them away with his sleeve, though the fabric was already damp and didn't do much to help.

"Da'?" The words were out of his mouth before he realized. Before he had a chance to quiet his buoyant thoughts. His father didn't reply, managing a half step forward before turning to face him. He could tell his father knew what was coming. Knew he could never help himself when it came to questions.

"Do you think they would have surrendered? The men at the store. If you would have given them a chance, I mean?"

Magnus shrugged. "I reckon they might have."

"Do you think you could have stopped them without killing them?"

His father looped his thumbs into his belt, rocking his head back and forth, weighing the odds. "Maybe. Probably. Though truth be told I'm not as fast as I used to be, son. But to what end?" he asked. "They'da been hung either way."

"I guess."

"You don't guess, son. You know it. They'da been hung the next day, if not sooner. That's the way it is." His father barely paused a breath before continuing. "And I know you hate it. I know you wish it would be better—for everyone. I know that. We all do. Shit, we thought it was. They *said* it was. And we believed 'em, fools that we were. A better future for everyone," he scoffed. "For those of us that..."

"Survived?" the Boy interjected.

"Sure," his father conceded. "For those of us that survived. But that's not the way it is. We're all just barely holdin' on, son, and if someone comes 'round and puts that at risk then we gotta sort 'em out. No questions. No hesitations. There's just too much at stake."

"Yeah, I know," the Boy sighed. "It's just not fair, is all."

"You're right, son. It's not."

IT WAS his mother who first noticed the vessel as she chopped wood in the yard. When the rhythm of her work faltered, the Boy looked up from his book. That's when he saw it—the biggest ship he had ever seen. He couldn't help but shout, pushing up from his father's rocker to scurry down the lane for a better look.

"There's a ship coming!"

Coasting over the derelict waves was no mere fishing vessel, nor was it some merchantman on a trade route from the south. This ship was different. It was tall and broad and solid on the water. Hundreds of oars stabbed from her belly as the behemoth lumbered toward the pier like a hammer careening toward the smallest of nails.

A trio of masts formed along her spine, the stout row of ancient wood extending skyward. The ship had three levels and people shuffled about on each like fleas upon a graceless beast. It looked like the sketches of pirate ships he had seen in books. But bigger.

Magnus' son catapulted down the eroded shoreline until he was a few feet from the water. Reaching the retreating coast, he shielded his eyes from the sun as he looked onward.

"It's massive!" he exclaimed, eyes locked on the vessel. It had to be at least three-hundred-feet long. Maybe more. It dropped anchor after sailing closer to Hope, settling atop the murky water like an anvil. By then, his father had wandered his way down to join him.

"You don't look surprised," the Boy said.

Magnus shrugged. "It's *The Ark*. Comes every Year."

"For trade?"

His father shook his head.

"A refuge, then?" the Boy prodded. "Someone owns it?"

"Sorta. It's the place you go when ya got money."

"How much?" the Boy pondered aloud. He was curious, more so about the logistics than anything else.

His father scratched his beard, giving the question some thought. "I'd wager we'd need to sell our house to buy passage for the three of us."

"But the storms? How do they stay afloat during those?"

Magnus grinned. "You tell me."

The Boy ruminated on it, looking back to the floating behemoth. "Maybe they have an anchorage somewhere? Some place far enough away that nobody will bother them?"

His father nodded. "So I've heard. Nobody knows where though."

"And they...just come back after? Pretend everything is back to normal?"

His father nodded again, equally unimpressed by the notion.

The two continued watching for a few moments before the Boy piped up again. "Have you seen it up close before? It looks huge."

"Seen it? I've been on it," Magnus winked. His father gave him a pat on the back and handed him his knife. "Be back by supper."

Magnus' son smiled, fastening the sheath to his belt as he started toward Hope. He kept a brisk pace down the uneven coastline, his path clear along the dry lake bottom. Year after year, the water retreated further from shore, drying up and inching away from the coast. Coarse sand and semi-smooth pebbles were all that remained.

As he approached the village, he spied a small boat leaving the harbor. It rocked over the slender waves, rowing toward the anchored vessel. A few minutes later he saw another. They were not run-down fishing boats or small rowers either but larger merchant ships belonging to some of the village's better off. Expensive ships with expensive owners who were, as far as he could tell, making their escape.

By the time he made it to Hope the first boat was returning, its passengers relocated to *The Ark*. Jogging through the village, the Boy weaved his way to the Gamling statue—to where it used to be—and sat himself down on its empty stone base. He could hear the market in the distance, filling the air with fledgling noise. Algae and the musty fragrance of shallow water invaded his nostrils. His eyes darted from person to person, hoping to see someone coming or going from *The Ark*. He saw Beckett's daughter instead. His stomach fluttered as he perked up. For a long moment, he forgot the ship existed.

"THAT SNAKE! THAT BITCH OF A SNAKE!"

Beckett's daughter kicked a stone off the edge of the switchback before stomping halfway down the hill toward the pier. That's when she noticed Magnus' son. He was standing in the small clearing between the village and the harbor, unmoving and alone. A few folks shuffled about nearby but Magnus' son ignored them as he eyed the ship. Old hawker stalls and drying racks and more than a few boats in varying stages of disrepair littered the space around him. Rowboats, mostly, and a few small cogs that had been butchered for parts over the years. Their driftwood carcasses were piled and left to rot on the rocky beach. When the fish stocks collapsed, so too did the need for work boats.

The packed earth and trampled rocks of the harbor sloped toward the craggy coast that marked the western edge of Hope. Algae and weeds encroached from the periphery, taking back what was rightly theirs stone by stone. As the lake retreated, the pier was constantly being extended, forever chasing the drying waves. A few boats still lined its flanks, bobbing in the shallows. A couple were fishing boats but most were pleasure craft from the village's well off—including her aunt. Though even those were mostly ignored and seldom used. Until today.

On the waterlogged boardwalk, she passed a pile of luggage and weaved between hand carts as people dashed about. A hawker passed by selling eggs. They were small and speckled grey. The Girl couldn't help but wonder just what animal had laid them.

She continued along the stony muck of the waterfront, feeling the slow, clammy wetting of her soles. The wafting reek of fish guts overcame her for a long breath, soon replaced by the familiar odor of the pungent lake and the dirty bodies that moved along its spine. She came to a halt near an abandoned fisherman's stall. Pretending to fidget with her belt, she shifted her knife around. As always, she centered it at the small of her back. The way her father carried it when it was his.

She pulled the blade out, pressing the rounded end of the handle against her forehead. "She's lucky you're not here," she whispered to herself. "Boy, is she lucky."

Beckett's daughter kissed the pommel and returned it home. She felt a bit better, though her anger still radiated, a season onto itself. She was tempted to punch the wooden stall, going so far as to press her knuckles against it, but she knew it'd do more harm than good.

Up the pier, carts of food and heavy suitcases made their way to the boats docked nearby. Anyone who had goods to sell was unloading all they could to those on *The Ark*. And anyone who could get out was getting out. Including her aunt and cousins.

It all made sense, now. The extra trunk. The map. "Bitch," she muttered one last time before tucking her tangled hair into the back of her shirt.

Returning to the commotion, her eyes again drifted to Magnus' son. Now sitting on the base of the old Gamling statue, he continued to stare at nothing and everything. She started his way, doing her best to look natural and feeling mighty stupid for it. He didn't see her until she was practically standing over him.

"Come to buy a ticket?" she asked. She regretted the words immediately, sensing where the conversation might take them.

"Me? Well, I'm not much of a sailor, truth be told," he smiled. "Oh, and I don't have a secret hoard of treasure, unfortunately. Think you can smuggle me in? I can hide in your luggage."

She did her best to feign a smile but felt her façade crumbling.

"You're not going are you?" the Boy realized.

She shook her head, sitting down beside him. Against him.

"Oh. Shit. I just assumed..."

"It's fine," she shrugged. "Viktoria is taking her immediate family. But that's it."

"I...I can't believe she's leaving you."

The Girl shrugged again. "We've never really been family. Not really. I'm just a thing to her. A tool to use when she needs it. But on the plus side, I'll get the house to myself now. So there's that."

The Boy reached over and grabbed her hand, squeezing it. "That's messed up. Really. But if you end up needing anything, you're more than welcome to come out to the farm. It's not much, but it's home. We've even got chickens."

"Really?" she perked up, "I don't think I've seen a chicken in years. Where did you get them?"

"My da'—my father got them from someone but he wouldn't say who. I think it was from someone out in the Faroff."

Beckett's daughter nodded. "Hm. That makes sense. Nobody in the village has chickens. Not here, anyway. Maybe up the coast but not here."

It had been a couple years since she had left Hope, but she remembered seeing chickens—and lots of them—up in Hunter's Point. None in New Gamling, the next village south, though they still had pigs. Or, they did the last time she was there. Cute little sucklings and massive, lumbering sows. They had rabbits too.

"You should come see them," the Boy offered. "I even named one."

She tilted her head in curiosity. "And?"

"Sarris."

"Good name," she nodded, resting her head on his shoulder. "You know, I might just take you up on that. What about your name? Any thoughts?"

The Boy gave his head a quick shake. "That's a problem for next year."

The two returned to gazing out over the water, watching the grubby sparkle and dank shimmer of its surface. They listened to the waves and the market and the snippets of any conversation that drifted close.

"Do you know how long it's here for?" the Boy asked, looking at the ship.

"I heard Viktoria say two days."

"Did they…"

"They're packing now."

"Hm. Must be nice," the Boy said with a sigh. "To get away from it all."

"I doubt it. All those rich assholes in one place? I think I'll take the Year."

"You know what?" Magnus' son chuckled. "You're probably right."

They sat together for the better part of an hour, watching the comings and goings of desperate people. The Boy traced his scared fingertips over her arm, tapping secrets on her skin. It was reassuring. For the first time in a long time she felt seen.

WHEN THE TWO days came and went, the massive ship prepared for its departure. With its passengers stowed, a small and heavily armed posse made landfall in search of some final supplies. A few embittered villagers swapped insults with the mercenaries, though no blows were exchanged.

The provisions were hauled into boats and rowed back to the dreadnaught as the sun rounded out the afternoon. Practiced oars flapped against the paltry waves that swallowed the day's color. Within a few hours, under the cover of darkness, the hulking vessel would return to the deep, likely not to be seen again until the Year ended.

From the outskirts of the harbor, the Boy watched the preparations. He was far enough away that it was mostly just blurs and outlines, but as the hour passed he wandered closer. When the rickety pier slipped into view he spotted a flurry of commotion. People gathered as a fleet of boats set off from the dock. Squinting against the sunset, he closed an eye to count the moving specks, bouncing his finger from one to the other. There were at least ten small boats, maybe more. Fishing boats mostly, but some larger craft and even a couple row boats battled the languid waves. Each was alight with people as they set out into open water.

Even at that distance, he recognized one of smaller boats, its bright orange-yellow sail jostled by the meagre wind.

"*The Sunshine?*" the Boy whispered. He picked up his pace.

Why would Arif be heading out to The Ark? He doesn't have money for that...

Then it hit him. The boats weren't looking for trade. They were an armada.

"Oh no..."

He ran. Not ten seconds later, a monstrous explosion erupted from the dreadnaught. A cloud of smoke puffed into the sky, dark and fast. The concussion echoed over the water, louder than any sound he had ever heard. The shot crashed into a fishing vessel, spitting up wood and bodies. The thunder rang again. And again. And eighteen more times with clock-work precision. He could feel the blows in his chest, like a hammer on his heart, each one belching smoke and light into the dusk. If there were screams or sounds made from the shredding of the makeshift fleet, the Boy didn't hear them. Just thunder, epic and consequential.

After a pause, a second barrage shattered the air. Water plumed in wide shafts as the missiles landed. Lost in the display, he didn't notice he was walking forward. Knee-deep in the tepid, murky waters, he watched the briefest of wars.

Another chorus of noise, this time all at once. The canons erupted in unison, thrashing what was left of the flotilla, rending it to flotsam. The echo faded slow, like sand in water, sinking into place. Before long there was nothing but the pushing of waves against his knees as he dragged his feet along its shallow depths.

He continued toward the pier. The water had settled by the time he got there, the fleeting violence buried beneath the lake's surface. The bodies of those who sought to challenge the warship drifted in ruin. Some sank. Others bobbed their way to shore, ragdolls against the rocks, bent in curious ways. *The Sunshine* was nowhere to be seen.

"Arif!?" he shouted. "Arif?!"

There were no cries from survivors, no screams or shouts for help. Or maybe there were; he stopped listening after a time. All he heard was the tide rolling in, the lapping mimic a soft and supple antithesis to the uproar. Never in his wildest imaginings had he pictured a cannonade to be so dramatic, so precise. He knew then, subdued in the shallows, that all his nightmares about the Year had been far too measured. Less was coming. And he was far from ready.

18

V ague dreams of soundless thunder stalked him through the night. When he awoke at dawn, his room was thick with chill. A cold snap bowled over the late-autumn weather and dragged away the light and warmth. Kicking aside his blanket was a chore. He was hardly dressed when someone knocked.

"C'mon down when you're ready, son."

He listened to his father creak downstairs, passing the den —where he didn't stop to start a fire—before heading into the kitchen. Throwing a blanket over his shoulders, the Boy grabbed his knife and followed.

After a silent breakfast of stale bread and cold oats, the pair trudged out the front door. His father wore his tool belt and carried a thick, round target. They walked toward the lake in silence.

The ancient sprawl was dark and still. It shone like polished coal, its vast expanse married to the shore. Their divorce was slow and protracted as the thinning water clawed itself free from the coast, leaving it dry and solitary.

When they got to the eroded slope of sand, his father

launched the wooden target like a disc. It sailed a couple dozen feet before landing with a slap on the water's surface.

"Alright, take these, and get to it."

The Boy didn't bother to put up a fuss, knowing full well his father would have none of it. He peeled off his coat and shirt, grabbed a hammer and pocketed the nails, and waded out to the floating target.

The water crept up to his waist. It was cold. Not yet frigid or icy, but sharp on the skin. The lakebed sat uneven beneath his boots, the rocks and stones pressing into the mud like old bones in tired joints. When he found his footing, he started pounding the nails. Right hand, then the left. One, then the other. The wood splashed against the grey, floating this way and that as he beat metal.

He hadn't finished a dozen nails before he was shivering. Fingers white and growing numb, his grasp of the hammer was more habit than sensation. After hitting the last nail home, he started back toward the shore.

"Not yet," his father hollered, tossing the other hammer toward him. "Give me a hundred."

The Boy sighed, tensing his jaw to keep it from quivering. He took a quick breath and plunged below the surface to feel for the sunken tool, leaping from the cold as soon as he found it. Water beaded and weaved over his bumpy scars, tracing off-kilter lines from his hands past his elbow. His neck and shoulders tensed, the chill siphoning into him, sapping his breath.

With a tool in each hand, he flipped the disc and began pounding it with steady blows. Shuffling his steps as the wood floated about, he mixed up his rhythm, doubling up his hits or switching arms every other stroke. He was huffing by one-hundred but kept going, warding off the cold with lukewarm veins.

At one-hundred-fifty he stopped to catch his breath, trembling as algae buoyed and danced in stringy clumps around

him. Looking to his father, he noticed the man's gaze was elsewhere. Standing on the eroded slope above them was his
mother, rifle over her shoulder. Beside her was Beckett's
daughter.

Dragging himself and the target from the frosty depths, the
Boy hurried toward shore, tools shaking in his chilled grip. He
handed them to his father, who flashed him a raised eyebrow
and a rare smirk. Magnus' son flushed and turned away, grabbing his shirt before shuffling up the incline. He fought the
urge to jog after them, buying himself time to let his mind
adapt. To let the nervous pinch in his gut subside.

He went straight to the fire when he got in, rubbing his pale
palms in the heat. Beckett's daughter joined him, working
warmth and life back into her own hands. Her jacket was thick
and heavy, the wool speckled with glistening pinpricks of mois-
ture. It was oversized, drooping down toward her knees. The
cuffs had been folded back, a satchel resting on her hip.

"Hhhiii" he shivered, teeth chattering. She smiled, stepping
in to rub his arms. Blushing, the Boy looked away.

Across the room, his mother's ear to ear grin spoke
volumes. "I'll be outside with your father if you need anything."
Mariam turned to the Girl. "Thanks for the news."

"Ne-news?" the Boy stuttered, but his mother was already
out the door. Stepping closer to the heat, he held his arms aloft,
fending off the goosebumps that pranced over his damp skin.
"Wha-whatt news?"

"Well, I was on my way here—to bring you something—
and I overheard two militiamen talking. It looks like Mayor
Haakan and Sheriff Rhys left last night. With their families.
Step too. They took a good chunk of what was in the granary
with them. Two wagons, at least."

"Two wagons?" the Boy blurted out.

"Guards were killed too. Five in total."

"They killed them!? That's..."

"...fucked up. Yeah."

Two wagons was a monumental sum. The harvest had been a far cry from average and there wasn't more than a dozen wagons worth of food stored in the granary to begin with. Some was from trade, some from the commons. All of it needed. Every last grain.

"Ax is in charge now. But after him comes..."

"My father..." the Boy replied, mind chewing on the news.

"I'm sorry, I just thought you should know."

"No, no. Don't be sorry. I'm glad you told me. And I'm glad you came." He pulled her in close, holding her warmth against him.

"Well, I *actually* came for another reason."

She stepped back from the heat and walked over to the chesterfield. As she sat down, she opened her satchel. "When I saw these, I thought of you. Figured you might be interested in them."

She handed him three books. They were old, the pages curled and the covers worn. One of them was particularly thick. It was encased in a hard leather cover though its corners were frayed and dog-eared. Unlike most books, the thick book wasn't handwritten, the words legible and perfectly set.

"Whoa..."

The Boy had spent many an hour in school copying texts until his fingers were cramped and stiff. He never minded the task, though. Far from it. It gave him a chance to read, to explore, to think. There were only a couple thousand books left in the entire world. He felt it was his duty to appreciate them. To remember them.

"They're all from before the End," the Girl added, passing them to him. "That's when they were written, I mean. Originally."

He slipped his hands under them, his fingertips brushing

against hers for a long moment before he pulled them closer to examine them.

"They're for you. To keep," she added.

The Boy ran his hands over their covers. He was speechless. These were a rare gift. Priceless, in a way. "Did you steal these from your aunt?"

The Girl shrugged, stifling a chuckle. "She's on the boat. I figured she wouldn't mind if you borrowed them. Indefinitely."

He beamed, basking in the kindness. Books like these were treasure. They were history made tangible. Each one took hours upon hours to painstakingly copy. Printed books were a relic of the past, virtually non-existent save a few copies locked away in dusty libraries. To be appreciated but never enjoyed.

"Feel free to write me an essay on each next year if you're not too busy," the Girl joked.

"Oh, I reckon I'll have them read long before it begins," he replied, knowing full well it was the truth. He'd have them read within the next week. "This was the nicest thing that's happened in a while," he confessed, reaching out to hold her hand. "Thank you. Really."

"I heard about what happened at Horse Pete's. I figured we could use a little more *nice* these days."

After touring the homestead and feeding the hens, the two walked backed to the village and the empty house that awaited them. They spent the day together, sharing stories and secrets and questions that had no answers. They laughed together as day became evening became night.

Until laughter became whispers.

Until whispers became their bodies entwined.

Until they collapsed, together.

19

Magnus combed over the scrawny shrubs and scruff of trees that enveloped the lonely road to Hunter's Point. Watching. Listening. He had left before the Boy returned from Beckett's; he didn't want to make a big deal of the trip north.

He didn't want to wait either, refusing Ax's offer to tag along. He simply told Mar and Tom his plan and then left. The theft of two wagons was a crippling sum. Without it, a lot of people were going to starve. Time was of the essence.

He was a day and a half north of Hope following tracks that were not even partially hidden. Fresh ruts split the dust and cracked new lines in the hardpan toward the Point without even a hint of concealment. Haakan and Rhys and the rest were either careless or he was walking into a trap.

Magnus had been to the Point a handful of times over the years, though not recently. The road north wasn't much used and traveled only for trade. Tucked away in a narrow inlet surrounded by rocky shield and devastated permafrost, Hunter's Point was the last village on the road—and one that enjoyed its privacy. It was, for all intents and purposes, the end of the world. He and Mar had talked of moving there once, after the fire. For a change of scenery. A fresh start.

In his youth, he'd been as far south as south goes. Beyond the capital, even, to the barren Fort Bastion and its rolling dunes of red-gold sand. He'd seen bustling towns, the shit-ridden cesspools packed with people. He'd walked the muddy, rat-infested streets of Freed City too and saw first-hand the price of industry and progress. He wanted as little to do with that as possible. But north? To somewhere secluded like the Point? That didn't seem half bad.

He kept his hand loose on the reins as he walked the two mares onward. He wasn't much for riding, preferring to use the beasts to protect his flank from the woods. Anyone sitting on horseback was always an easy target.

Breaking tradition, two hatchets hung from the worn stir-rups on his borrowed belt. He didn't want the Boy to fuss so he left his hammers at home. The hatchets were longer and their balance dissimilar, but they would do in a pinch. And Magnus was expecting a pinch.

As he walked off the morning, he wondered how the Boy was taking his absence. Truth be told, if his son had come running up behind him he wouldn't have been surprised. He was a stubborn kid and dedicated to a fault, loyal as the day was hot. Qualities Magnus was proud of...even if he never said as much.

He fought the urge to look back. *Don't be an idiot,* he chided, turning his focus north. No one was coming. This work was his and his alone. He was overdue for some practice, anyway. Real practice.

By late afternoon the heat blistered. He pressed on, his pace unrelenting. He wanted to reach the Point by sun up to get the drop on the thieves that had betrayed them all. Dead or alive, he'd see it done.

Though why Rhys would get involved in this nonsense was

a question Magnus couldn't answer. The mayor? Sure, he was young and rash. But Step? Rhys? They had put in their time, had survived the Years. They weren't the type to scare easy.

He followed his thoughts to a Year long passed, when he had witnessed Step punch a man to death. Her heavy fists collapsed a brigand's face to mush as she threw haymakers left and right. All while her own jaw was busted and hanging loose in its socket, flapping like laundry in the wind. She was as tough as they come.

So why would she do this? What do they know?

It was a weighty question, opening doors in his mind he spent the rest of the day pondering as he made his way to the edge of the world.

CRESTING the rocky escarpment after sunrise, the sparse hamlet floated into view. And so did the swirling towers of smoke that hovered above it. Magnus' first thought was a wildfire. They were common enough and damn near impossible to stop. But as he walked the switchbacks down the slope he could see none of the surrounding brush was touched. It was scorched, but intact. Whatever happened was isolated. Intentional.

He pulled Mar's rifle from his saddlebag, rolling his shoulders loose before tying the horses to a tree in the shade. "Here we go..."

He didn't see or hear anything—or anyone—as he neared the Point. No sounds of life in the distance, no voices going about their day. It may have been a small settlement but he should have heard *something*.

As he rounded the path, edging past of a dense thicket of thorns and thistles, he smelled the first wagon. A minute later, he saw it. It was stuck in the road ahead, one of its wooden wheels shattered by a bulging stone. The two horses that had been pulling it were dead in the dust, chewed at by flies and birds and bigger things. Their skin was leathered, shriveled and dark and sundried. The animals smelled like blood and insides. He could taste the odor on his tongue so he held his breath.

The wagon itself was still half loaded with food and supplies. Whatever happened was rushed; there had been no time to empty the cart completely. Magnus let his eyes follow the tracks toward the Point, senses occupied, heart forced calm. He waited, knowing full well something was amiss. He could feel it, as real as the sun on his skin.

He let the minutes pass, choking on the noxious air until he stopped noticing it. After a quarter of an hour, he checked his rifle and continued into the silence, finger on the trigger.

The Point was empty. Whatever fires had been burning in the ruins had died out a day ago. A hazy screen of smoke hung heavy like a fog. It was in his nostrils with every breath. Almost every building had been razed. There wasn't a person to be seen.

Scanning the hamlet, he walked into the square, the hard dirt dusted by a soft layer of ash. There were no footprints in the soot. No bodies either. The village storehouse, a squat long-house crafted of wood and stone, sat in the center of the village. Magnus poked his head through the blackened threshold. It was empty.

Before he had time to wonder what happened, he heard something. Someone was sneaking up on him. Or trying to. They were doing a piss poor job of it, their footsteps crinkling the ash underfoot. He could smell them, too, even through the smoke.

He fought back the smile that forced itself onto his face. It was time for practice.

20

After tidying the attic, Mariam went about cleaning the coop in the backyard. Her son was busy digging holes in the lane. Holes that, when the Year begins, will be filled with wooden spikes. It was a bit early for the digging—the Year was still a few weeks away—but it kept him busy and out of her hair. The peace and quiet was nice.

But as the third day of Magnus' absence dragged on, worry started to get the best of her. There was only so much distraction she could rustle up to keep her mind at ease. When she started to get fidgety in the early afternoon she had her son walk her through his training. She tested the air with both the knife and hammer. The hammers, as always, felt awkward and unwieldy. The knife, though, was comfortable. She had much more experience with blades anyway.

Too much, she thought.

By late afternoon, even her son was getting antsy.

"Hey ma?"

She heard him through the open kitchen door, his voice tiptoeing on the edge of hesitant. She tilted her head to listen as he continued. "I think I might go into the village. If that's okay, I mean."

"What for?" she asked. She knew the answer, of course. It had been plastered all over his face for weeks.

"Well, I thought I'd, um, check in on Beckett's daughter? You know, just to be polite."

Mar grinned. Beckett's daughter was a good kid. She was glad the pair had hit it off. "I suppose. Just be sure you're home at a reasonable hour this time." *This time.* She smiled to herself, sensing her son's squeamishness.

Before he could reply, another noise caught her ear. From across the field she heard shouting. It was Tom, that much was clear, though whip-crack replies from Saira volleyed in response. The words were lost to the distance but their harshness was well-defined. The shouts grew louder.

"Ma?"

Mariam raised her hand in reply, shushing him as she listened. Glass broke. It sounded like a window though she couldn't be sure.

"I...I think I'll stay," he whispered.

She nodded, fixated on the argument that boiled over across the field. As the familiar voices flared, she wished that Magnus was there with her. Not because she missed him. Because she wanted her rifle.

Mariam was up early the next day. The sky spilled dull light over the landscape as warm air buffeted the shore. Fenced in by the browns of the landscape—brown dying trees, brown dying soil, brown dying crops—Mariam slipped out the front door and headed toward the road when she saw Saira. They met along the water, hidden from the homesteads by the eroded slope of the worn-down coast.

"Nice shiner," Mariam said as Saira neared. She reached

over and tilted the woman's head, examining the bruise that underlined Saira's right eye. "You okay?"

Sai nodded.

"I hope you got him back."

Saira forced a smile. "Four stitches in his leg. Stabbed him with a broken plate."

"My mom always said marriages were about give and take," Mariam sighed. "But really, are you alright?"

Saira nodded again, looking out over the water. "Tom knows I'll give as good as I get. He's just worried, is all."

"He going north? To hunt a little?" Mariam nudged.

"I've told him to but he's stubborn. You know how he gets. Besides, I'm not sure that would be enough. We're dreadfully short, Mar. Without another 'van coming..."

"I know," Mariam exhaled. "A lot of folks are short this Year. It's not going to be pretty."

The two women walked down the coast in silence, listening to the grey waves whimper their way to the pebbled shore.

"It was nice while it lasted," Saira exhaled, staring out over the water. "I enjoyed the quiet these past years."

"You think they're back for good? The Years?" Mariam asked, following her gaze.

Saira shrugged. "This one is going to be bad, mark my words, Mar. So who knows what will come after."

Mariam nodded, wrapping her arm around Saira's. "Since when were any of them good?"

"Some...had their moments," Sai countered with a wink. But then she stopped, her face fading to seriousness. "I need a favor, Mar. It's no small thing either."

Mariam stopped. She knew what her friend was about to ask but stayed silent.

"If things should take a turn for the worse, can I count on you to look after my boy?"

"If or when?" Mariam asked, eyebrow raised.

Saira shrugged. "Does it matter?"

Mariam kicked at the pebbles, dragging her eyes over the grey water. She shook her head. "I suppose not."

"Can I count on you then? You'll have enough extra for one person I suspect."

"Barely, bu—"

"Promise me, Mar," Saira interjected, grabbing her by the shoulder.

"I promise. But try to convince Tom to head north. Mag will go with him. It doesn't have to turn ugly. We can get through this."

Saira nodded, pulling her in for a hug. "I'll try, but he's stubborn as a goat. The Year has always been a game to him."

Mariam knew exactly what she meant but stayed tight-lipped.

"I best get back before he kicks up a fuss. Thanks again, Mar. Really."

"Don't mention it. Just try to get him to head north. That's your best bet—our best bet."

Saira nodded, making her way toward the slope that angled up to the road. Halfway up, she stopped and turned back to Mariam. "Mar?"

"Yeah?"

"If Tom won't go north and we get hungry, or if he starts drinking again, he might..."

Mariam waved a hand, her jaw tight. "We'll cross that bridge if we come to it."

Saira flashed a tired smile, clambering up the rest of the slope before disappearing over the ridge. Mariam turned back to the water. She plucked up a small stone and launched it into the lake, watching the ripples spread until they vanished.

When she was sure she was alone, she stepped into the cold water and kneeled in the shallows. She pushed her face beneath the surface, embracing the refreshing cold. She screamed.

21

M agnus turned and fired. No hesitation, no second guessing. He didn't care who it was sneaking up behind him; anyone with good intentions would have made themselves known.

The bullet took the man—who was soot-covered and bloody—in the stomach, right below his ribs. The round ricocheted and lodged inside him, the force of the blow doubling his attacker over. A long dagger fell into the ash. It was Mayor Haakan.

"Haakan, you idiot!" a gravelly shout echoed from behind the granary. Footsteps followed, rushing to close the distance. Magnus spun. He was too late to get another shot off so he jabbed out with the barrel of the rifle to check the lunge. It was Step, armed with a spiked cudgel. She too was dirty and, from the looks of it, wounded.

"Cowards!" Magnus roared.

Step lisped a growl in reply and reached for the rifle, tugging at it as she swung her club. Magnus ducked under the attack and let the woman yank the rifle from his grasp.

Expecting resistance, she stumbled back in surprise, the gun falling into the seared dirt at their feet.

Hands free, Magnus snapped up his hatchets and swung them out in a sweeping arc, lunging close. The hatchets curved in from opposite directions, their metal edges biting deep. They split into Step at her waist, ripping skin and fat and muscle. He felt the woman's pelvis shift, the fractured bones grinding over one another like wet rocks in a shallow pool.

Ignoring her foul shriek, Mag looked about for his next foe. He spotted the sheriff at the other end of the longhouse. Rhys' face was blackened from some previous engagement, a dirty bandage wrapped around his neck like a scarf. He was leveling his revolver.

The weapon was old and crude, its four-round cylinder partly rusted. The barrel was long, the grip made for two hands to steady against its ugly kick. It was a brute of a weapon. Magnus had seen it blow holes in men as wide as his fist. He had even fired it on a few occasions himself. It wasn't fast but it got the job done.

"Rhys!" Magnus shouted, tasting rage. Expecting the shot, he pushed Step's half-collapsed body in front of him as a shield just as the revolver burst the air. The body stopped the bullet, sending Step headlong into the soot.

Exposed, he had no choice but to whip both hatchets toward the sheriff, more distraction than proper attack. The distance was great and they both missed their mark. But Rhys flinched, sidestepping the missiles before he could take aim. It was all the time Magnus needed.

Dropping to a knee, he scooped up his wife's carbine, pumped the lever, and fired. The slim round drilled home with a short-lived puff of red mist, boring into the sheriff's jowly face. Rhys stood, immobile, for a solid count of seconds before crumbling like an avalanche of stone.

Magnus spun, guard up, in case anyone else stormed out to

greet him. He turned in slow circles, heart pounding hammer hard. When the coast was clear he waited another minute anyway, just to be sure. He hated surprises. Eventually, he lowered the gun.

"Shit," he cussed, jogging over to Rhys' body. He had been aiming for the man's shoulder, hoping to get some information from him before the end.

Instead, he collected the man's revolver and rummaged through his pockets before checking over the other two bodies. They were both dead.

"Shiiitt," Magnus cursed again, shaking his head at his bad luck. The bodies bled into the wind-blown ash, mixing the black into a paste. After scavenging the dead, he reviewed his performance.

"Room for improvement," he admitted, scratching at his beard.

He set off to explore the hamlet, finding a few tracks but not much else. Eventually, he made it to the water. That's where he found the second wagon. It was empty and the horses were gone.

Maybe everyone fled. Maybe they torched the place and sailed away or loaded up their packs and disappeared beyond the reach of the Year. Maybe some pirates crashed the place and did what they did best...

With a huff, he stalked back to the outskirts and collected his own horses. He harnessed them to the empty wagon on the rocky beach, tossing in what he salvaged from the half-looted sun-cooked wagon.

He didn't bother with the bodies. He was never the sentimental type.

22

"Hey ma! I see him!!" the Boy hollered into the house. He jumped up and leapt off the porch, skirting around the fresh pits he had dug for traps. Leading the reins of a horse, his father strode up the narrow lane, waving as he approached. Lumped on each side of the beast were bulging saddle bags. His mother's rifle poked out of one of them.

Seeing the fresh pits, his father sidestepped into the field, trampling the grass near the old orchard as he made his way up to the house. It had been the better part of a week since he left and the Boy had begun to worry.

"Hey da'," he said, reaching out to give the horse a rub. He had a million questions but knew his father wouldn't answer any of them. Not yet, anyway.

"Son," his father said with a nod, offering up the reins. "You been keepin' up with your training?"

"Twice a day," he replied, giving the horse a scratch on the neck as he took the reins from his father.

"Dug some new pits I see. Good thinkin'."

"I read about a new idea for a trap, actually." He started to elaborate but the bloodstains on his father's shirt distracted him.

"Why don't you take'er to get some water," his father cut in, "and then we can unload these supplies. We gotta send her back tomorrow."

The Boy figured it was too good to be true. Horses were getting rarer by the year and they were expensive to feed. Most belonged to the militia and the rangers.

"Can we maybe take something over to Tom?" he asked, looking over the saddlebags.

Magnus nodded. "Send over a few cans."

The Boy smiled. As he turned toward the creek, he noticed the sun reflecting off his father's shirt. Pinned to it was a star. A metal sheriff's star.

MARIAM LISTENED to her husband explain what happened as she cleaned her rifle. It felt good having it back in her hands. She missed it. As always, Mag kept his tale brief, which she could tell was bothering their son. He was bursting at the seams with questions.

Leaning back, her husband nodded. "Go on. Ask."

"Are you the new sheriff?"

"For now. That all?"

"Why would they risk leaving? What made them go north?" They were good questions. Mariam had been chewing on them all week. None of her conclusions were comforting.

"You tell me," her husband shot back. Mariam cocked her head, giving him a disapproving look. Tough love had its uses, but sometimes she wished he'd cut the kid some slack. The Boy wasn't fazed by the curt reply, though, diving into his guesses.

"Well," he hummed, "I think they knew something. Why

leave now? Why steal the wagons and kill people? They must have known something. Something involving the Point."

"And what happened to the Point, ya think?" she asked.

"Isn't it obvious?" the Boy replied. "They left. No bodies. No supplies. They went somewhere else. Probably to escape the Year. So far away from everything, I bet they know of some place safe. Someplace secret."

"Maybe," Mariam replied. "Or maybe they were taken." It was a grim notion, but it was a possibility just the same. One that seemed more and more likely as she mulled over her husband's tale.

"Taken? By who? You'd need a—the ship?!" her son exclaimed. "But why would they need more supplies? Or people, for that matter? Don't they have enough?" the Boy asked.

"Since when," Mar sighed, slipping a round into her carbine, "has anyone ever felt they had enough?"

WORD SPREAD FAST through the village, as it always did. By noon, the news had reached Beckett's daughter. She mulled it over as she stacked wood, hauling what she could into the cellar where it would be safe from prying eyes and greedy hands. As she stepped back out into the light, she saw the Boy cresting the escarpment, a horse in tow.

"I hear your old man is the sheriff now," she said as she walked out to meet him on the lane. "He going to make you a deputy?"

"I hope not," Magnus' son chuckled. "I'm not a fan of breaking up fights, if you recall."

She stepped up and gave him a kiss, wrapping her arms around him. He smelled of horses and the dried sweat of a morning spent training. But she didn't care. It was nice to be held.

"What's her name?" she asked, giving the horse a scratch on the muzzle.

The Boy shrugged. "I don't think my dad bothered to ask,"

"I'm glad he's okay. Your dad, I mean." For a heartbeat, she could feel her chest crack open, her throat tightening. The mere thought of the Boy losing his father was a kick in the chest. She knew that pain all too well.

"Me too. Thanks."

"I went down to trade a few things earlier. They're saying the Point was destroyed. All burned up?"

"That all they're saying?"

Beckett's daughter stopped petting the horse. "What do you mean?"

The Boy looked over his shoulder before speaking. "I'll tell you on the way. You should pack and come stay with us for a bit. Just until the Year settles."

"Wait, what? Is everything okay?" She wanted to ask questions, but she could see the worry etched in the Boy's face. *He's afraid.*

"No," he finally replied. "No, I don't think it is."

She listened as he told her about the Point. About the empty village, the fight. It sounded ludicrous. Rhys and Step were people she knew, people her father had been friends with. Yet for some reason, they had betrayed them all.

"Clearly, they knew something," the Girl said, stretching her legs in the grass. They had wandered to the edge of the bluff, looking out over Hope, the sun at their backs.

"The question is, what did they know? And what exactly happened to the Point?" the Boy pondered. "My ma thinks it was raided by *The Ark* for supplies. Maybe Haakan and them knew? Planned to take part and escape or something? I don't know."

"Maybe that's why she had a map," the Girl whispered.

"What?"

"My aunt, she had a map. Before she left, I saw it with her things. I thought it was strange. Who needs a map these days? There's just one road. Bu—"

"But what if there is more than one road?" the Boy cut in, sitting upright. "What if there's a secret port out there somewhere?"

"The real question," the Girl replied, "is what happens next? If the Point was raided for supplies, will more places be raided? To what end?" Deep down, she knew the answer. Because she knew her aunt.

"To the same end as always," Magnus' son shrugged. "Until there's nothing left."

23

O n the last night of the year, the Boy, his parents, and Beckett's daughter waited up together. His father had his belt draped over the chair beside him as he stared off into the dark. His mother read by candlelight in the corner, her rifle leaning against the frayed edge of the old couch. They had invited the Luddstows to join but Tom was in a mood and declined.

Curled up on the floor beside him, Beckett's daughter watched the fire. Like him, she was ill at ease and fidgety. They had told his parents about Viktoria's map. Maybe it was nothing. Maybe it was all just one ugly coincidence. There was no way to know—a fact which chewed at him as he grasped for certainty.

As his brain chased its tail, he reached out to Beckett's daughter and tapped a silent message. She nuzzled against him in response. Tired as he was, he knew he wouldn't sleep well that night. Nor the many nights to come. Staring into the flames, he picked at the edges of a callous, poking and prodding it absentmindedly.

Beckett's daughter broke the silence. "My pop always said the waiting was the worst part."

Magnus nodded. "I remember. I was with him on our first night. Our first real Year not as kids. We were on the pier when the bells rang. With Rhys and Horse Pete and a few others."

"What were you all doing?" Beckett's daughter asked.

His father scratched at his beard, smiling. "Waiting. Enjoying some finely aged beverages to ease our nerves. Beverages of your old man's making, if I recall," he chuckled. "This was back before he wisened up and became mayor of course. Tasted like piss, but we were together." His father let the silence hang before continuing. "He was a good man. A good friend."

The Boy could feel Beckett's daughter trembling so he held her tight, giving her the space to remember. He tapped out a story on her arm. A story of them traveling south together, seeing New Gamling and beyond. A story of making things better. A story of more.

"Listen," his mother cut in.

After a heartbeat, he heard it. It was as faint as a summer breeze, subdued by distance but present nonetheless. The bells were ringing.

Twelve round and hollow sounds, one for every month to come, rolled through the hungry dark, stealing the silence from Hope and its surrounds. The Boy listened to their fading echo as the black once again consumed them all with empty worry. His hand found the Girl's. He squeezed it.

The bells would stay quiet until the end of the Year, a patient sentry guarding their fragile future. Guarding their hope.

For a Less Year had begun.

PART II

BEFORE

Magnus saw the flames from the road. A vibrant orange glow, flickering and formless, pressed against the shapeless edges of October. The unfamiliar sight stopped him in his tracks, his words trailing off as he squinted into the dark. His wife stopped too, her head turning to follow his gaze. She was quick to the draw and bolted, her lean legs carrying her across the village with desperate speed. He chased after her, chest pumping fear and fury as his boots kicked up dust. He peeled off the shoulder bag that slapped against his legs as he ran, chucking it to the ground. Ahead, smoky wisps curled from a cabin. The air was shining and warm.

His wife was a few paces ahead, sprinting toward the house at breakneck speed, her tangled hair caught by the wind. She was screaming.

"Rachel?! Son?!"

She screamed again but the words were lost to the low rumble of burning wood. Magnus didn't bother to shout, didn't bother to slow down either. He bowled into the front door. He felt a bone crack but the wood cracked faster. He slammed into the house. A gust of hot air welcomed him, its searing embrace singing his exposed skin. The heat had ravaged the den's glass window, fracturing the remnants into melted continents.

Ducking through the smoke, Magnus found his son on the floor, arms strewn into the embers. Burnt and burning bodies were scattered about like ruffled blankets. His son was unconscious, entangled with a fiery corpse. The body was charred and lifeless; the flames had burned it away. Burned *her* away. He knew it as soon as he looked. His beautiful little girl.

There was nothing he could do but swallow rage. Breathing in the smoke of her, hacking as the dark air filled him, he reached down for his son, grabbing the Boy's leg and dragging him from the worst of it. His shoulder forked a lancing bolt of pain up his arm. It tingled to his fingers but faded as he held his son close. The Boy was hot to the touch, like a kettle left to boil dry, the child's exposed skin peeled back and blistered. Magnus didn't feel a heartbeat.

Blinded and wheezing, he carried his broken and burning boy to the door, lurching into the night. Mariam was on them in an instant, smothering the flames as he coughed his lungs back to life. Their boy still wasn't breathing so Mar started pumping his chest, filling his lungs with her own air until he was dragged back to life.

In the background, Saira and the others rushed about, dousing the house with buckets from a nearby well. A crowd had gathered to battle the blaze but Magnus paid them no mind, wiping stinging tears as he cradled his busted shoulder. Spitting ash from his mouth, he spied his wife wrapping a handkerchief around her face, knotting it tight as she angled toward the smoldering doorframe. She was going in after their daughter.

Magnus pushed himself up and tackled her to the ground

before she made it three paces. He held her there, cheek pressed against hers, hands squeezing her, chest hollow and shaking. He didn't speak a word. He just held her as their world burned.

24

The first month went by painstakingly slow. Training was confined to the yard and walks were allowed only within sight of the house. The family and Beckett's daughter took turns standing watch, keeping an eye on the road and the surrounding fields just in case. Nothing ever broke the horizon save a few birds, dark specks drifting in the warm winter air. One day the Boy thought he saw a coyote but it turned out to be a wild dog with tickrot.

In between chores and standing lookout, he and Beckett's daughter spent time with Sarris and the flock, watching the birds for hours while they talked and read and wondered. They were permitted to share a room so Beckett's daughter took his sister's old bed. It was awkward at first, to have someone there in his sister's space. He adjusted—he wanted her there after all —but it nagged at him, a nightly reminder of how much things had changed.

His father insisted his bedroom door be left ajar at all times as a...deterrent. It worked. At night, anyway. But there was plenty of idle time during the day when they were alone. Idle time they made not-so-idle use of.

As things settled, Magnus' son went back to training twice a day. The Girl joined in. She was fluid and quick with her knife and out threw him each and every time.

"I guess I'll stick to hammers," he joked, wiggling his knife from the slab of wood they were using as a target.

"Just be thankful you've got me to keep you safe," the Girl winked.

The winter had swung warm and they were training in bare feet, enjoying their false freedom. They had spent the morning on watch, keeping an eye on the world while Magnus and Mariam worked. The watch was divided into shifts of four hours. All day, all night. It was a schedule no one enjoyed, though Beckett's daughter took it especially poorly. He had heard her wake early a few times to get water and, occasionally, throw up. He, too, felt nauseous from the disjointed schedule, trapped in the space between sleep and restfulness.

As he walked back for another throw, his father called them into the house. He had a bag packed.

"We can go?" the Boy asked, eyebrow raised. As hesitant as he was about heading into Hope, there was something to be said about escaping his parents. Even if only for a few hours.

His father nodded. "Just drop her off, take a quick peek about, and get back. That's it."

The Boy shouldered the pack, turning to Beckett's daughter. "You sure you want to go back? I don't mind waiting a few more days."

They had talked about it half the night prior but he still felt unsure of her choice. There was likely nothing to worry about but he worried nonetheless.

"I don't want anybody poking around the house, taking what's not theirs," she replied. "My grandpa built that house. My pop looked after it, built the stockade and the stable. The barn too. Least I can do is set a few proper traps to keep it safe. Viktoria emptied the stables but she left me a good chunk of food. And I've got lots of other supplies too. I can bring them here once everything's secure."

Magnus nodded. "Alright. Don't be long, son."

The Boy fiddled with the bag's straps, ramping up his courage. "Um, shouldn't I maybe stay with her? To help out and what not?"

Before his father could reply, Mariam swooped in, peeking into the den. "I think that's an excellent idea. We need to look out for one another after all."

Magnus hooked his thumbs into his belt and leaned against the wall, clearly outgunned. "I suppose your ma's right," he conceded. "I'll come by in a couple days."

The Boy smiled, a spring in his step as he made his way to the front door. Behind him, Beckett's daughter lingered.

"I just wanted to thank you both for letting me stay here. You've been so kind and welcoming and I—"

His mother cut her off with a hug, stepping in and wrapping her arms around the Girl. "Think nothing of it. Your father was a good man and a good friend. As far as we're concerned, you're family."

The Boy's father saw them into the wind. He gave them a nod before closing—and locking—the door behind them. Exposed to the winter heat, they trekked down the lane and onto the road. By the time they reached Hope, the sky had sharpened to silver blue, its flimsy rays of subdued orange hardening bright. The air was parched.

"I'm gonna go home and wash up. Wanna take a quick look around and meet me at the house?"

"Sure," he agreed, already feeling a tinge of anxiety creeping into his gut.

Beckett's daughter gave his hand a reassuring squeeze as she leaned in for a kiss. Then she disappeared down an alley toward the bluff. For the first time in a long time, he was alone in Hope.

Adjusting the knife on his hip, and working to conjure a fragile sense of confidence, he meandered the opposite direction, eyes taking in the scene as he made his way between the houses and stalls. It was quiet, but people were about. A handful of shops were closed and boarded up, a few of them in varying states of dismantlement, but many were open too. The main hall and schoolhouse were intact and undisturbed. Boarded and locked, but undisturbed. A few militiamen wandered about, keeping the peace as they chatted. It almost felt normal.

He spent a quiet half-hour exploring, catching glimpses of people here and there. Labor and conversations peppered the background as life wafted from huts and houses. Food and piss and bodies. The usual. With nothing of note happening, he finally felt a modicum of safety. Most folks had enough supplies to get them through the winter, he wagered. Most of the folks can manage a year of isolation.

Most people will be fine.

A small weight lifted, he decided to sit in the square and eat what his father had packed for him. He flipped through one of Beckett's daughter's books as he chewed, scanning the market every few paragraphs just to be safe. He wasn't a few pages in before he heard voices. Close voices.

Shrinking behind a hawker stall, he peered around its wooden frame. A trio of men passed without looking his way, continuing into the square. There, they met a few others. The Boy studied them; their tone, their movements. Each was past their prime and carried a bag or case. The patchwork of silence that clung to Hope was ever so slowly lifted as the men revealed a handful of instruments, tuning and strumming them before settling into a cadence both familiar and imperfect. Horns filled his ears as a taut snare snapped a staccato tune. The noise blossomed into a melodic jig. With every bar, his smile grew wider, the tension in his shoulders melting. He lost all worry to the chorus, chewing open mouthed as he tapped his foot to the miracle before him.

It wasn't long before people gathered. A few kids ran and danced about, enjoying the spectacle. Young Joao, the village apothecary, donned in his finest suitcoat, rode about on a bicycle, its well-rusted frame holding together a pair of misshapen wheels that rattled more than they rolled. He sang along as the band played, circling their performance and chasing the frolicking children. He in turn was chased by a dog, yapping as it hounded the clunky contraption.

By the end, Magnus' son's face was sore from smiling. He whistled his way up the bluff, humming life into the world. His smile carried him to sleep that night, his heart an orchestra.

THREE DAYS later his father arrived. Weary pastel hues swirled and drowned out the smudgy haze of grey that loitered on the horizon. Fires burned over the Faroff as the day blossomed over the lake, baking the village.

Together, the Boy and his father walked the streets, their pace slow and deliberate and probing. Hope stirred as they explored. Oats and bread fanned from a few doors, capturing his attention with their hearty warmth. Nearby, two cats hissed in a narrow alley. Not a moment later, one scampered by clutching a dead songbird in its teeth.

Home to some hundred houses—117 households according to the last census, the Boy recalled—the village was percolating, voices rounding out the new day.

The pair walked the entire village before taking a seat in the square, setting down a knitted blanket to keep them from the dirt of the flagstones. They ate and listened, watching the town filter into daylight. The Boy had heard the music every day since he arrived but as the hour waned he began to wonder if today would be an exception.

Impatiently reading his book, his eyes darted to every sound, every shifting shadow, in anticipation. He made it a couple dozen pages before he spotted the first musician. The man wore a floppy hat of cotton over his mostly bald head, a tied chinstrap keeping it in place. Thin curls of dirty grey trailed over his ears as he shuffled into the square. His uneven gait was hobbled, his slight frame stooped. The man waved to his companions as they approached, instruments in hand.

One by one, men and women assembled, greeting each other warmly as they unpacked their instruments before the small but happy crowd. The Boy and Magnus stayed put, listening from a distance as a song took to the wind. He soaked in every note; even his father seemed to soften as the music drifted over them. Closing his eyes, Magnus' son relaxed. It was a rare moment of letting go, the weightlessness a forgotten and pristine joy.

Not long after it started, the music tripped to a stop. Instinctively, the Boy reached for his knife. He looked to his father for a cue but Magnus wasn't there.

Stepping through the crowd, his pace casual and at ease, Magnus embraced the first musician with a bear hug before shaking hands with a few others. A moment later he was handed a horn of some sort.

Questions piling on the tip of his tongue, the Boy decided to follow. He closed the distance as the band—now joined by his father—took up their instruments. A song roared up tempo, a drummer keeping time on a skin that snapped the air like crisp breaks of dry kindling. The music, like the season, warmed. Couples danced, a few kids jumped around and ran about in the square.

The Boy had never seen his father play before, never seen him so much as tap his foot or hum. Maybe he had as a child, though no real memories came back as he searched. So much had been kept hidden from him. The bad and, it seemed, the good.

After a few minutes, the song played itself out into the winter, melting like a flash of snow. Red-faced and winded, his father handed back the horn. Back pats and handshakes saw him off as he broke from the crowd, the band launching into another tune.

Suddenly, the air cracked like a loose snare. The Boy looked to the musicians. A few feet away, the man his father had just shaken hands with dropped to the ground, his grey beard dusted red. He was dead before a second bullet echoed, eyes rolled back as dark life spurted onto the flagstones.

Another sonorous crack. Another man hit, spinning from the force.

The crowd panicked, running every which way. The second body was halfway to the ground when his father plowed into him, tackling him to the stone and out of the shooter's line of sight.

Another shot. And another. Not rapid, but steady. The crack-cough of the gun had a metallic twang to it, a wheeziness that belied its age. Shouts and screams replaced the music as instruments clattered onto stone.

The Boy looked around, working to make sense of the confusion. A blur of movement caught his eye.

Charging into the square was a massive woman on horseback, screaming like a banshee. The beast that bore her was thin and roan and lacked a saddle but it carried her fast enough into the newborn fray.

Arms and legs exposed to the sun, she wore a molded top of boiled leather, amplifying her already sizable frame. A curved sword stabbed forward in one arm, her legs pressed against the ribbed sides of her underfed mount. Her hair was cropped short—too short to see its true color. Her limbs were long and thick and tanned and made the saber in her grip seem more like a knife than a proper sword.

Behind her, the rifle coughed again, a specter in the distance. It fired off shots from across the square, its marksman half-hidden behind a market stall. Careening past the shooter, another man sprung forward. He was dirty and howling, his long beard braided and flapping against his chest as he ran. Like the woman, his hair was cropped short. He too wore a boiled leather jerkin. It was bloody and glistening.

Spear in hand, the brigand sprinted toward them. His weapon was metal-tipped and long. Eight feet or more the Boy reckoned. It had two vicious-looking prongs at its tip, the steel dark and freshly used.

Without a word, his father leapt up and sprinted toward the woman. The Boy didn't move. Screams echoed hoarse over the village, a nebulous commotion out of sight. He could hear someone crying nearby but didn't dare look.

Another gunshot. They cracked the air in regular intervals, keeping time with the carnage. When a bullet pinged off the stone nearby he startled, pushed himself to his feet, and charged.

Magnus' son forced himself toward the spearman. To his left, a woman stumbled, victim of the marksman. She faltered, making it two paces before taking a knee as she clutched her chest. She collapsed a few feet ahead, forcing him to hop over her legs as she buckled. Her eyes were wide, more angry than surprised. She wasn't dead, but she'd bleed out before long, her final moments spent looking up at the wide winter sky.

A dozen paces off, his father had his hammers out, each hand wrapped around a tool as his legs carried him forward. The Boy, sprinting toward the spearman, pulled out his knife. The blade sliced the air as he pumped his arms. His hands tingled with perspiration, numb and clammy. His lungs heaved as he bounded into the gap, putting himself between the brigand and the dispersing crowd. Eyes locked on his foe, he could see the man was wearing a necklace of small bones. If it rattled, he couldn't hear it. All he could hear was his own heart pounding.

In his periphery, his father stopped running. The man planted his feet, braced himself for half a moment, then threw his hammers. His shoulders whipped the tools with enough force that his back leg kicked up, the momentum carrying him half a step forward. Metal slammed into the teeth and skull of the galloping horse a heartbeat later. The beast bucked and fell, folding face first into the stone, its rider catapulted into the air.

The woman landed hard but rolled into a lunge that caught his father off balance. Unarmed, Magnus dodged two fast swings of a sword that would have split his belly before firing a quick jab that knocked a tooth from the woman's bloodied mouth. His father used the reprieve to reach down and grab an instrument—the only thing within reach—but the woman was on him before he could lash out.

The curved steel forced him to block the downward blow with a trumpet. The power of the attack kept him low, battering him to a knee. He swung out to meet the second blow that was arching down but it was a feint. Instead, the saber came in at a lower angle than expected. Unable to block it, the sword sought out his flesh, aimed at his ribs and the tender organs they shielded.

The blow never connected.

Seeing his father forced to a knee, the Boy sprung forward and launched his knife. Weeks of practice with Beckett's daughter culminated in a single moment. The blade spun, covering the fifteen or so feet in a blink. Its arc was perfect, a slight curve tilting the weapon toward its target. He extended his follow through, watching the knife hone in. It slammed into the woman pommel first.

The handle of the blade punched the woman's cheek before

harmlessly bouncing away. It clanged against the stone, unbloodied. The mountain of a woman scowled his way, her brutish gaze capsizing his confidence.

The distraction was all his father needed.

Leaping up, Magnus bashed her head in with the rusted metal horn. She took the blows standing, her skull refusing to cave. After the fourth hit she fell, blood trickling from her ear. The Boy watched her hit the stone, watched her convulse beside his knife. Then, the spearman was on him.

Shuffling his feet, he steadied himself for the inevitable lunge. Unarmed, there was not much else he could do. When the spearman plunged the weapon toward him, the Boy side-stepped as best he could, grabbing the shaft to keep it from gutting him. He could smell the blood now. It was smeared down the man's face and neck like war paint.

The spearman growled as he stabbed forward, spittle spanning the gap between them. His arms were twice as thick as the Boy's and they pushed the weapon closer, inch by inch. The two hungry prongs gouged his shirt as he flailed backward. The spearman's stance was wide and solid, his tree trunk legs insistent. The weapon jerked and jabbed, forcing the Boy to dance and dodge as best he could.

But it was a losing battle. He couldn't outmuscle the man, couldn't escape the metal teeth that hounded him.

Necklace jangling like palmed dice, the marauder tugged his spear, hoping to rip it from the Boy's grasp. Magnus' son let him. Expecting resistance, the spearman wasn't ready for the force of his own pull. Even with his deep stance, he stumbled back, catching himself on his back leg as he prepared to thrust at the Boy once more. But the stumble was all it took.

A tool beat the air and hammered home against the spearman's exposed side. The Boy heard it coming and froze as it passed. He watched it startle the man, watched it jolt his nervous system as the spear tumbled free. The sound of his surprise was swiftly overcome by the melodic hymn of another tool. This one crashed into the man's skull. He dropped.

As if on cue, the Boy and his father turned toward the rifleman. Having stepped clearly into the square, the shooter brought his weapon to bear. The muzzle flashed.

Where the bullet went, the Boy couldn't tell. He heard it fire right as the barrel was snapped in two. A heavy axe shattered the weapon—and not a moment later, the man. Steel carved into the rifleman's hip, severing his leg at the joint. The force of the attack swept him off his feet, a second blow catching him midair. The attack dropped the sniper so hard that the blade chewed clean through his chest and into the stone below.

Even fifty paces off, the Boy heard the metal chip against the cobblestone. He watched Ax pull his namesake from the corpse a second later, waving from across the square as he did.

"It's good ta see ya, Boy," Ax hollered as he hobbled toward them. Blood dripped onto his chest as he rested the double-sided weapon over his shoulder. "In one piece, no less!"

Reaching to collect his father's tools, Magnus' son struggled to regain his composure, unable to even mutter a reply. It was shock. That much he had read about. It left him miles away yet tied to every curve of the moment, a stationary witness to himself. He tried to speak but the words lodged in his gut. He stared at the unconscious spearman at his feet, pressing his toes into the soles of his boots.

"Better late than never, old-timer," his father joked, embracing his friend.

"We stopped the rest out by the road north. Almost a dozen of 'em," Ax replied. He looked Magnus up and down with a smile. "Yer getting' old, Mag. And slow. Ha!"

"You ain't wrong on that," his father exhaled, tucking his tools back into his belt as he sucked a droplet of blood from his knuckle.

"Yer boy did well, though! Good on ya, son!" Ax slapped his

shoulder as he passed, picking up the two-pronged spear and giving it a quick look over. "You want it?"

The Boy shook his head.

"Alrighty then," Ax grinned, driving the weapon into the spearman's chest. "I'll leave 'er here!"

Magnus' son looked away. Yet everywhere he turned there were bodies and blood. He couldn't escape it. It was in the air as people rushed about checking on loved ones, tending to the wounded. His father walked back to where the corpse of the mountain woman lay. She was dead.

"Ax!" Magnus whistled, nodding to the horse. The animal was still alive, its face a ruined mess.

"I'll see to 'er. My better half'll be happy. Haven't had proper meat in a good while."

Ax hobbled over to the horse, taking to a knee to give the beast a final scratch behind the ear. "Poor thing." He gave it a few more long, slow scratches before bringing down his blade to end its suffering. With the help of some of the crowd, Ax carved up the beast right there, sharing the meat with those still standing. They left the bodies of the attackers in the sun, looting what they could and leaving the corpses to rot.

"Here, Boy!" Ax shouted, bloodied to the elbows as he worked his knife on the dead horse. He was pointing to the saber at his feet. "Best take it. I reckon yer gonna need it."

As soon as Beckett's daughter heard the third gunshot she was out the door. Knife in hand, she leapt over a razor-wire snare and weaved around the few spiked holes she had dug. The ground underfoot was hard and dry, her legs pushing full tilt. Her stomach was in knots, nausea pressing in. She ignored it. Careening down the bluff toward the square, she saw a flash of someone bowling through the market on horseback.

"What the...?"

By the time she made it from the plateau and into the square, the carnage had subsided. She slowed, taking in the scene. There were bodies—some still, some writhing—on the ground. Across the square, she spied Magnus and the Boy. There were bodies around them too. She could smell blood in the air.

"Are you okay?" she blurted out, running up and grabbing Magnus' son by the shoulders. He looked dazed, distant. She could feel him bouncing in his skin.

"Yeah," he nodded. "Yeah, I'm okay."

"He did good," Magnus said, stepping in to give his son a pat on the back. "Still needs to work on his throw, though," he winked.

Nearby, Ax was carving up a dead horse, its guts heaped on the flagstones.

"Help!"

The cry came from the edge of the square, stealing her attention. Magnus was already walking over, his head tilting to scan the market as he moved. He was steady. Confident. She knew, then and there, that the stories her pop had told her were true. That he was a man familiar with violence.

"We need to get these folks bandaged up," Magnus hollered. Bodies were sprawled all around him. "Somebody get the doc!"

"We can take them up to my place," Beckett's daughter offered. "I've got extra beds." *And I've sewn my share of wounds.*

Hearing a groan, she darted to the nearest body. It was Buck, pale as a ghost and moaning. His eyes were fluttering.

"Poor ol' Buck, she whispered, feeling his pulse slow as she pressed down on his bullet wound.

"Find a cart, son!" Magnus barked behind her. She didn't bother to look up. She just stared at the blood that swallowed her hands and watched her fingers drown in red.

WHEN ALL WAS SAID and done they had saved three people. *For now, anyway*, the Boy thought to himself. Whether those people would be alive in a week was yet to be seen.

Ax and Magnus were eating in Beckett's daughter's kitchen. He heard the duo bantering about the fight but did his best to ignore them. He didn't want to remember it. Not now.

Folded into a rather uncomfortable chair, he let his eyes ease themselves closed. He was tired. Not his body—his body was fine. His calloused hands were undamaged by the spear, his muscles unbothered by the sudden burst of violence. It was his mind that needed respite. Fear was exhausting. Always being ready, always being on the lookout. Having to help dig bullets out of guts and sew up ripped skin didn't help either. But he knew, as he heard the doc shuffling about above, that he was one of the lucky ones. The unlucky ones were the wounded, the ones stitched up and crossing their fingers.

He dug at the dried blood under his nails with the tip of his knife.

Or maybe the real lucky ones are the bodies we left out in the square.

He pushed away the thought when Beckett's daughter walked into view, her clothing wet and red and ruined.

"They're sleeping now," she sighed, unclipping her knife from her belt before collapsing onto the wide sofa near the boarded window. "Doc said they'll make it, barring infection."

Magnus' son nodded. "I hope so."

He watched her close her eyes, her hands rising and falling as they rested on her chest. She'd want to stay here now, to look after the wounded. They'd need time before they could return home, they'd need food and care. He knew she'd want to offer that. That she'd feel compelled to. He also knew his father wouldn't let him stay—not for that long anyway. A day, maybe two. But not a week. Not after today.

Out of the blue, his stomach grumbled for attention. He realized he hadn't eaten since breakfast. The thought of food was equal parts enticing and nauseating. The Girl shifted on the couch but didn't look. She must have washed her hands with soap because he could smell juniper from across the room. He tapped his fingers against his thigh, counting. His toes curled into the floor. He pressed them down harder. Anything to stop the quiver that was drilling out of his skeleton.

"I tried to kill someone today," he blurted out.

"Which one?" she asked, her voice faint.

"The woman. On horseback." He shifted in the wooden chair, feeling it creak under him. Nobody sat in this chair much, he realized. It was shiny and smooth, the paint a shade of blue so soft it was hardly blue. The chair's legs were on the fragile side of thin and there were no faded spots on the arm rests. Painted flowers covered the narrow spokes of the back-rest, weaving themselves into a crisscrossed pattern that stretched down to the flat of the seat. It was an uncomfortable chair.

"It's Viktoria's chair," the Girl said. "She never let anyone sit in it. It's decorative."

The Boy scoffed at the foreignness of the concept before his mind drifted back to the square. "My da', he's the one that killed her. But I tried."

"You did what you had to. That's nothing to be ashamed of."

"I know. It's jus—"

"It's just you feel bad that you had to kill her," the Girl interjected. "Or that you tried to, I mean. I know. I remember what it's like."

"No. No, it's not that. I don't feel bad at all, actually. But I want to. I *want* to feel upset but I just feel angry. At them. At everyone. I don't want this to be normal."

.K. OLDFIELD

"'Fraid yer a bit late on that front, Boy," Ax chimed in, hobbling into the room. "Normal went out the window long 'fore you 'n me came about."

The Boy didn't reply. He just tensed his lips and stared. A part of him wanted to stand up and bash the chair he was sitting in to pieces. Another part just wanted to curl up on the floor and sleep. He did neither.

"But no fear," Ax clapped. "Seems these shits have been raiding the road south for a while now. With them buried, things should settle down." Ax hobbled by and gave him a pat on the shoulder. "You did well, Boy," the big man added. "Yer a survivor now."

"Welp, on that note," his father cut in. "Best get back to your ma and make sure she's alright."

Before the Boy could protest his father raised a hand. "Ax said he'll stick around here until them upstairs are well enough. I'll have the doc check in once a day. When all's well, Ax will bring'er by the house."

"Shouldn't be much more'an a week or two, I'd wager," Ax added. "I'll see that the place is looked after, don't worry."

He looked to Beckett's daughter. She nodded.

"Okay," he conceded, following the adults to the door. He didn't make a big deal of the farewell, not with his father nearby. He just gave her a quick hug and a kiss and followed the two men out into the day. Halfway down the lane, his father broke the silence.

"She's a tough gal. So much like her father."

"Yeah." It was all the Boy could manage. His father stopped and looked back to the Beckett house.

Magnus' son stopped too. "What is it?"

His father turned to face him, eyebrow raised.

"What?" the Boy demanded, looking around.

"Son, for a bright kid you're awfully dense." His father

flicked his head back toward the house. "Go give'r a proper goodbye. You got two minutes."

It took half a second for the Boy to catch his father's meaning. Then he ran.

Sprinting back up the house, he weaved around the recent traps and pushed in the door, kicking up a racket.

"What? What is it?" the Girl asked, running to the door.

He grabbed her by the waist and kissed her, holding her as tight as he could. "I love you."

She smiled and kissed him back, blushing.

And then he walked over to the corner, picked up Viktoria's decorative chair, and smashed it to pieces.

25

He spent the next week training with the saber. Then the weather turned. First came snow, heavy-handed and white. Then wind. Hurricane gusts rallied on the water and battered the house. Winter storms were part and parcel of the mangled season so the family rode it out. But the superstorm worsened day by day, the gale and rain omnipresent. It forced them to bring the chickens inside. With his father's tools, the Boy crafted a crude coop in the kitchen, pushing aside the dinner table to make room for the birds. It wasn't much, but it would keep them alive.

By nightfall, the old coop was flooded. "You got lucky today, buddy," the Boy teased as he looked to Sarris, tossing a handful of oats onto the floor. Ready to curl up with a book, he made his way toward the stairs, stifling a yawn as the downpour hammered against the boarded windows. Chains of thunder rumbled close overhead.

Then, something crashed. It was a deafening noise, long and slow and tearing. He stopped, listening. His father pounded down the stairs a moment later.

"What the fuck was that?" Magnus snapped.

The Boy, eyes closed, didn't reply. He was thinking. Imagining. Playing back the noise. When he found the answer, he ran to the door and grabbed his coat from the wall, ripping out the wooden hook it rested on.

"The tree!" he blurted out, fighting his arm into his sleeves. "By Tom's."

"It must have—"

"—fallen on their house!"

"Shit!" Magnus grabbed his own jacket and wrestled it on.

Like a ghost, his mother appeared on the stairs, wide eyed and rifle in hand. "Go. I'll be ready in case someone is hurt."

The night swallowed them as they stepped into the squall. They were drenched in the span of a few steps, their pace slowed by unrelenting gusts. The Boy leaned into the wind as he pressed onward, needles of rain blinding him. He shielded his face as best he could but it was a futile gesture.

Sloshing through the snowy muck, he squinted toward the Luddstows'. There was no sense running. The half-frozen ground was slick and the mud sat heavy enough to suck his boots off his feet. He took it slow and steady until the creek, which fattened itself on the deluge. He cleared it with a leap, stumbling but staying upright.

Crossing the fallow, the gale slammed buckets of water into his eye sockets, blurring his vision until he couldn't even see the house in front of him. The thunder, now directly overhead, wreathed him in a torrent of cracked sky.

When he finally saw the house, outlined by feeble moonlight, he faltered. The wind had snapped one of the last oaks in the yard and brought it down through the Luddstows' porch. The thickest part of the trunk was sprawled across the field, stretching into the garden. Its hefty branches, however, stabbed into the farmhouse.

The Luddstows' kitchen window was smashed and the wall forced into a precarious state. A massive hole gaped into the night, leaking light into the weather. Tom and Saira were busy covering the opening with heavy sheets, struggling against the wind as rain flooded into their candle-lit home.

Magnus' son followed his father inside, dragging muck through the hall as they pushed into the kitchen. His father wasted no time, pulling out his tools to nail blankets over the gap. The Boy stood idle, staring at the crying child huddled by the stove.

"Get a saw!" his father barked. The Boy nodded, running back out into the storm toward the shed. The entire outbuilding rattled in the wind. It reminded him of the spear-man's bone necklace. But louder.

Inside the shed was pitch dark so he ran his hands over the tools on the wall, deciphering them with his fingers. He hit the teeth of the saw a moment later, nicking a small dent of flesh off his knuckle. He bolted back across the field, one hand out to slow his fall should he slip in the muck. Which he did, skidding across the grass before scrambling back to the house, saw in hand.

Once inside, he went to work drawing the mud-covered teeth over the wood as fast as he could. He pressed his weight into the effort until his shoulder burned. He switched arms, and switched back not long after. The branch was almost as wide as he was and it took time to see the job through. When it finally gave way and dropped to the wooden floor, his father slipped in beside him to hammer a quilt over the unwanted window. It was the best they could do in the weather and dark-ness. Repairs would have to wait until the storm passed. Most of the damage, it seemed, had already been done.

"Get the kid," his father ordered. "They'll bunk with us."

The Boy grabbed the Luddstow child and wrapped him in a blanket, covering him as best he could as they marched back out into the ceaseless downpour. Jumping the stream proved an awkward feat, but they made it back inside easily enough.

They had no spare bedroom so the Luddstows set themselves up in the den. He and his mother saw that they had everything they needed before retiring, leaving the family to worry themselves sick long into the sleepless night.

"Fuck those fuckin' cunts! Cuttin' us off? Whoresons!"

Magnus listened as Tom raged, wincing as his friend slammed a boot against the doorframe of his flooded kitchen. Both he and the Boy looked away, giving the man his space.

It had been a full day and a half before the storm passed, leaving a worrying amount of destruction in its wake. Under an ash-grey sky, Magnus had gone out to survey the disaster. The coop and shed would need attention, as would a good many sections of the old fence that snaked around the back field. A couple of shutters on the house would need to be replaced too. But the barn and the wire-covered palisade around the garden fared well enough. All things considered, they were lucky. The Luddstows were not.

"Just let us fuckin' be," Tom cursed. "How am I supposed to make do if those assholes won't let us trade? Where am I gonna buy food now? Fuck!"

Tom picked up a soggy, fist-sized onion and squeezed the water from it. It sprayed chunky, off-color liquid onto the waterlogged floor. With the wall half-collapsed, Tom's kitchen took in enough rain to puddle on the floor a few inches deep. That much and more leaked down into the cellar, flooding their harvest. Their cans and preserves survived, but that was just a few weeks' worth of food. A month or two at best. The garden crops—onions, potatoes, turnips, brassicas—would rot.

"Population's hardly grown, too. We don't need the Year *here*, it's those greedy fucks down south, spreading like a disease while the rest of us eat shit and die hungry. Fuck!"

"We've got extra, Tom," Magnus insisted. "Should last 'til harvest. Come spring, you'll be right as—well, you'll be good as new, anyway." He uncrossed his arms and did his best to sound positive, knowing full well it was not his strong suit. "We can hunt too. You'n me. Head to the Point—it's empty now—and see what's left. Mar and the Boy can watch over things for a few days."

"It'll take more than a few squirrels and birds, Mag. We—"

"Then we go east," Magnus snapped, cutting him off as he buried his thumbs in his belt, inching up the volume of his voice. "There's game out there."

"Yeah, three-eyed deer and mutant rodents that'll rot your insides out. It's a fuckin' wasteland and you know it."

"Then we'll figure it out!" he shouted. He gave the man a stare down before sighing himself calm. "Look, you got options. The militia could use a hand. I can talk to Ax."

Tom stayed quiet, pacing around the kitchen. He could see the man was chewing over his choices but was in no mood to talk further.

"I'll leave ya be but if you wanna head north you let me know," he offered, doing his level best to keep his temper from stewing. Tom didn't reply.

"Son!"

"Yeah, da'?" the Boy replied from the cellar.

"Take the kid. Go help him study at our place."

His son didn't say a word in response, shuffling past with his head hung low. Magnus watched them go, realizing that their problems were about to get a lot worse.

26

"That stubborn idiot," Magnus railed, pacing the kitchen. "It's all a fuckin' game to him." The situation had been weighing on him all night, prodding him toward the inevitable. With desperation knocking, it was only a matter of time before Tom did something rash.

"I take it he didn't want to head north?" Mariam asked. She was cleaning her rifle at the dinner table, the act more ritual than routine.

"'Course not," Magnus scoffed. "You know he's always liked the Year a little too much. I thought after twenty fuckin' years of normal he'd calm down. But he's angry now. And antsy for trouble."

Magnus sat down, forcing himself calm. He studied his wife's hands as they reassembled the old gun. Her nimble fingers were a far cry from his thick and stubby joints but they were just as scarred and tanned and tough. They had pulled life into the world to the sound of blood and tears and snuffed it out to the same tune. They were loving hands. But they were the hands of a survivor. That was no small thing.

His wife set the weapon down and admired her work. The

lever-action tool was older than both of them combined. It had been generations since anyone had made a new one. There likely wasn't anyone left who even knew *how* to make them.

Probably for the best, he mused.

Wrapping her fingers in her lap, Mar closed her eyes. She chewed the side of her cheek like she always did when she was thinking, no doubt mulling over their options. After a minute of quiet, she gave him an honest stare down. He met her gaze, as he always did, and let it chip away the worry that loomed in the back of his mind. The thought of his friend betraying them was an unpleasant one. But it was a realistic one just the same. Perhaps not anytime soon, but when push came to shove, Tom would do what he had to do to survive. Magnus couldn't blame the man for it. He'd do the same.

"Sai told me she was worried about him when you were away. That he might get back to drinking. But do you really think he would do something? Against us?"

Doubt trickled in. *Would Tom really try to rob us?*

"Does it matter?" he pondered aloud. "We can't take the risk, can we?"

Mariam poked at the grey in his beard, curling it around her finger. "There's no going back from this, Mag, you know that right? This is a line we can't un-cross."

Magnus didn't respond. He had hoped it wouldn't come to this, battled the options in his head a dozen times over. He was tired of the killing, tired of seeing friends die. It drained him, left him empty and weary and longing for the end. But they'd have to do something before something was done to them. Their future—their son's future—depended on it.

Magnus rested his elbows on the table and covered his ears. He pressed the silence in, shut his eyes to let the darkness swallow his sight. It was his only escape. His only peace.

In the blackness, he thought of his daughter. She'd be thriving in all this, no question. A militia captain by now, if not a ranger. She had it in her—to rise above, to push her limits. To survive. She had been his chance to build something better than himself. He hated to admit it; would never give the words life. But he couldn't help how he felt. He loved his son, there was no doubt about that. But Rachel was a gift. And she was gone.

Mar's rough hands on his neck brought him back to life, her fingertips pressing into him. She wrapped her arms around his shoulders and rested her head against his. He felt her whisper as much as he heard it.

"I can do it."

Magnus didn't reply, staring at the planks of wood that reinforced their back door.

"It will be faster," she insisted, "Cleaner."

"Nah," he huffed, shaking his head. "I have a plan. If there's no militia work—and I don't imagine there will be—then I'll see it done. I'll talk to Ax tomorrow. Maybe there's a way around this."

Mariam sighed. "Just leave their boy, Mag. Okay?"

He nodded, kissing her cheek as he rose. He walked upstairs to the dark of his room and let his mind mull over the dreadful task ahead. If push came to shove, he had no intention of letting any of the Luddstows live. There could be no loose ends. But that was a problem for another day—and a problem not for sharing.

THE NEXT MORNING, Magnus dragged his feet into Hope to see Ax. The dying wood that enveloped the village was devoid of sound, its lifelessness palpable. Hope, too, was quiet, though people were about. Most businesses were open and plenty of folks lingered around the square, chatting and bartering and playing dice. He found Ax near the hall, half naked and sopping wet.

"Mag!" the old-timer hollered. He was stripped to his waist, dragging a wooden comb through his grey mane of tangled hair. The man's torso was mapped by more scars than Magnus could count. "What brings you back to civilization? Here to play sheriff for a few hours?"

Magnus grinned at the jab, tossing Ax his shirt. "Bit cold for a swim, ain't it?"

"Keeps me young!" Ax joked. "I'll go back in if ya want. Race to the pier?"

"Rain check. Got a question though."

Ax toweled himself off with his shirt before tossing it on, wringing out his hair one last time before tying it back. "Shoot."

"It's Tom. That storm flooded his cellar and he's outta food. Or, he will be sooner rather than later."

"Well shit," Ax sighed. "Poor bugger. Gonna go north?"

Magnus shook his head. "He's not a fan of the idea. Doesn't wanna leave the fam. Was thinking maybe there was work here? Militia needs more hands. Any room in the budget to let me bring him on?"

"Militia does need more hands, no question. But we got nothin' to pay folks with—nothin' that'll be any help in the short term, anyway. Whole village is short, Mag. There's gonna be trouble, mark my words. We can't even pay you for bein' sheriff, truth be told."

Magnus nodded, tightening his jaw as he tasted the inevitable.

"Wish I could help, Mag. I do. Think he'll do somethin' stupid?"

"Unfortunately, Ax, I don't think he'll have the chance."

Magnus embraced his friend before turning home, stewing in his predicament. He was hardly past the gallows when he ran into Tom.

"Tom? What you doin' in town?"

Tom was sweating in the heat, a leather bag slung over his shoulder. His straw hat was beat-up and chewed at, a thin handkerchief tied around his forehead to keep the sweat out of his eyes. He looked tired, maybe even tense.

"Just sellin' a few odds and ends. Found a couple'a bolts I don't need—sold the crossbow years ago—so I figured I'd sell 'em. Can afford to part with some arrows too. Never run outta arrows if ya don't miss!" Tom grinned. Magnus studied his friend. He couldn't tell if the smile was forced.

"You talk to Ax?" Tom asked.

"'Fraid they ain't got much to offer."

Tom shrugged. "Figured as much."

"You wanna head north for a few days? Ain't no trouble. Hell, we can leave tomorrow."

"Nah, I'll figure somethin' out. Already got some ideas," Tom smiled again, shifting his stance.

"Oh yeah?" Magnus prodded. Something felt off.

Tom didn't look him in the eyes, his gaze drifting over the gallows. "Heck of a thing ya did, Mag. With the McKelsie kid? You got balls, I'll give ya that."

Magnus stiffened.

"You always were craftier than people gave you credit for. Secret's safe with me though," Tom winked.

"What if we ride south?" Magnus pressed, dragging the conversation back. "See what we can find?"

Tom shook his head. "Don't worry, Mag. I'll sort 'er out." He wiped the sweat from his neck on his sleeve, looking back to Hope. "Best be off. Places to go and people to see, you know the drill."

Magnus watched his friend amble into Hope before turning home. He spent the rest of his walk planning. He was going to have to kill his best friend.

THE BOY LISTENED as his parents bickered upstairs, their whispered words muffled by the distance. Tucked away in the shadows of the den, he replayed their conversation from the day prior.

Were they really going to kill Tom? What about Saira and the kid?

He questioned his train of thought, doubting what he had eavesdropped.

Should I confront them? Should I warn Tom? Why couldn't they head north?

He knew the Luddstows would starve without something being done. But the solution his parents concocted left him nauseous and anxious. He felt his skin flush and itch as he chewed on the problem.

There has to be another way. You can't just kill your friends...

He sat there for a few minutes, thinking over his options. Do nothing? Warn Tom? Confront his parents? He tripped over the choices, paralyzed by indecision.

A door slammed upstairs. His father's familiar gait creaked along the hallway above. Without thinking, the Boy leapt to his feet and tip-toed to the front door. Once outside, he ran.

———

27

He didn't bother to knock, bursting through the door as he called out. "Tom! Saira!"

The Boy rushed down the hallway toward the Luddstows' ruined kitchen, his boots smearing muddy tracks on the damp wood. He ignored the tempting aroma of fresh stew and herbs, looking to the Luddstows as they leapt up to meet him. Tom, wide-eyed and alert, already had his knife out.

"What, Boy? Speak!"

The Boy leaned against the wall, catching his breath. "My....my dad is..." He stumbled on his words, realizing he hadn't really thought his plan through. He watched Saira pull her son close, the kid gawking with glossy eyes at the sudden intrusion.

"Is what? Is he okay?" Tom demanded, putting his hand on the Boy's shoulder to steady him. It only made his task all the more difficult.

"My dad is coming. He's..." the Boy let the words trail on purpose, looking to Tom with eyes that carried his meaning. He glanced to Saira too, who caught on all too quickly. "You need to pack," he continued. "You need to pack and go."

Tom reddened. "Just wait a minute, we—"

"Tom, we should go. We should go *now*," Saira insisted. Her voice was firm, her worried tone veiled by a layer of brave necessity.

"Now look here, I'm not leaving, thi—"

"Tom, please!" the Boy pressed. He stood tall, doing his best to assert himself against the older Luddstow. "You're going to run out of food sooner rather than later. That makes you a threat. You know that. You *have* to know that. And you also know what my dad does to threats..."

Saira stood up, stepping toward her husband whose shoulders were rising and falling in a steady flurry. Tom's lips were tight, eyes narrowed, glaring past the Boy into the dreaded abyss that had just backed him into a corner. Sai wrapped her arm around her husband's waist but as far as the Boy could tell Tom didn't notice. He just stared.

The Boy turned, following Tom's gaze down the hallway. Standing at the threshold was his father. He held a bottle in his hand, his belt absent from his waist. The Boy watched him stop mid-step as their eyes met. A sudden flash of confusion plastered itself onto his father's face. He watched it contort to a disappointment so jarring the Boy had to look away.

"What did you do, son?" his father asked, the words a slow erosion.

"He did the right thing, Mag, that's what he did," Tom snapped, giving the Boy's shoulder a squeeze as. "Get my bow, Sai,"

Reaching over the table, Saira plucked the weapon and its quiver from the corner. She handed it to her husband before stepping back to her son, shielding him as she gripped a knife. Tom nocked an arrow. He kept the weapon aimed low, but ready. The Boy couldn't do much else but plant himself in the middle of the conflict he had so foolishly ignited.

"Just let them go," he pleaded to his father. "They don't want any trouble." His head bounced from one man to the other, hoping his words found purchase.

"I don't want any either, son. I just—"

"You just what? Just came to say hi? Came to offer us another spoonful of charity? Well, we're full. Thanks."

"I don't want no trouble, Tom. Just wanted to drop this off. Figured you could use it more than me, that's all." His father held the bottle to the light, shaking the clear—and no doubt potent—moonshine that the Boy had seen collecting dust in the pantry.

Did I misunderstand what he had planned? His stomach sank at the realization that he must have not heard his parents properly, and now...now he had brought things to a violent collision.

"Leave it on the porch and go," Tom ordered. Magnus complied. He set the bottle inside the front door before taking a step backward out onto the porch.

"Let's go home, son," his father insisted, waving him forward as he took another step backward.

"He stays, Mag. I'll send him home soon enough, don't you worry. But if I see you within a hundred feet of my house, so help me I'll put an arrow in ya."

Magnus frowned but nodded.

"You think I woulda done something to you and yers?" Tom asked. "After all we been through? That's cold, Mag."

The Boy's father didn't reply. He just stepped backward off the porch and into the night. Magnus' son didn't follow. Didn't move an inch. There was no point. Tom would have an arrow through his back before he made it down the hall. He was a hostage now and it was entirely his own fault.

As his father faded into the darkness, the Boy couldn't help but wonder if he'd see his parents again.

·   ·   ·

"I SAID DRINK IT ALL!" Tom roared, slapping the table. The commotion sent a wooden cup spinning off its edge. Choking down the last mouthful of 'shine, the Boy felt its fire dance along his tongue before burning its way down his throat. He stifled a cough, shuddering his eyes closed. After four drinks, the stuff wasn't tasting any better.

Or was it five...?

Tom was a drink or three ahead, his eyes as red as his glowing cheeks. He kicked at the cup to drag it back, chuckling to himself as it kept rolling out of reach. Eventually, he plucked it up, chiding the Boy with a wagging finger.

"Waste not, want not," Tom nagged. "It'll be a lonnnggg while 'fore we brew more."

The drunken Luddstow laughed to himself, though even the Boy—whose head was spinning—spied cracks in the man's façade. Tom had sent his wife and the child upstairs to bed, no doubt in case his parents came back in force.

Or in case he plans to kill me!

The thought sent him reeling. He kept his mouth shut, lips pressed awkwardly tight lest he betray himself. He dropped his left hand to the hilt of his saber, extending his fingers out with as much subtlety as he could muster. Which wasn't much. But the blade wasn't there.

"Where's my swo—?"

"What?" Tom replied, mid-sip, spilling out a few drops of the clear, heady brew.

The Boy waved him off, his brain stalled. *Where did I put my sword?*

Downing another long pull, Tom turned to him and interrupted his train of thought. "I woulda done the same, yaknow," Tom confessed. "As yer old man, I mean. I woulda..." he trailed off for a second before righting himself. "Don't feel bad. Yer a good boy, Boy. Heh." He bounced with a self-congratulatory chuckle. "Boy boy."

Tom went back to his drink, sucking the few spilled drops off the back of his hand. The bottle empty, he slid back into his chair, folding into its curves.

Magnus' son stared at the boarded-over hole in the wall, the drafts of air tickling his skin. He listened to the night, to the intimate creaks of the old home as it settled. The house felt damp, smelled damp. Like wet wood and black mold. The occasional snap from the hearth filtered in from the den as he willed himself to sober up, rubbing his eyes and holding them open to the firelight. The effect was negligible. With a sigh, he let his hands drop to his sides. His right hand bounced off the sheath of his knife before falling into his lap.

My knife!

He propped his hand on the hilt, looking to his captor to see if the gesture was noticed. Tom was mostly passed out, his body retired to a semi-conscious slumber. He didn't flinch as the Boy groped for the blade and fumbled it free. Tucking the weapon behind his arm in what he felt to be an incredible feat of deception, Magnus' son slid his chair back. Tom stirred at the wood-on-wood friction before dozing off again, his head nuzzled into his arms, his breathing easing into a drone.

The Boy stood up. The world kicked itself into a frenzy, bucking and spinning as he rose to his feet. His legs wobbled, shaky and unsure. Bracing himself against the table, he fought the urge to throw up. Tired eyes counted shadows, the spinning slow to dissipate. Not bothering to ensure they were alone, he slipped his knife into view, standing over his slack-jawed neighbor. He squeezed the handle uncomfortably tight, clenching his fist with enough force to send gentle quivers through the meat of his hand. He stood there, a looming shadow of unfortunate necessity. An assassin of his own doing.

His free hand stretched out and rested on Tom's back. Feeling out the target, lining up his thrust. His face warmed, panic dancing in his chest. Tom shuddered and snored.

They have no food. They will be a threat. They have no food. They will be a threat.

The next harvest—if there was one to be had—wouldn't be ready before the Luddstows starved. He and his parents didn't have enough to spare. Maybe they could feed one of them. But not all three. That made them a threat.

They have no food. They will be a threat. They have no food. They will be a threat.

He repeated the words over and over again until they sounded foreign. Until he realized they weren't his words. They were his parents'. They were words built for others, from a world the Boy wished he could shed. No mantra could coax him into violence. Not on a hunch. Not on an assumption of future guilt. That's not the world he wanted to live in, no matter how hard the Year tried to bend him to its will. He lowered the knife.

"Tom...? Tom?" The motion sent his head spiraling, the contents of his stomach jostling for an exit. "Tom?" he mumbled again, eyelids heavy as he poked the man in the back. "You gotta go." He shook the man again. This time, Tom opened his eyes.

"Go? But I need to tell her," the man slurred, his mouth full of spit. "Rach. She needs to know ..."

Tom slumped against the table once more, eyes rolling back into darkness. The Boy froze, the mere mention of his sister derailing him. The knife slipped from his grasp and clattered onto the soggy floorboards. He looked to his empty hands. No, not empty. His hands were never truly empty. They carried scars. They carried her.

He would have walked through a thousand fires to see her right then. To hug her and hold her close. But all he had was a fractured memory that faded year after year. Melancholic nostalgia bombarded him, stewing in an emptiness that he could only fill with a pointed rage. It flashed like a bolt of clear lightning, fast and electric.

Without thinking, he stumbled over to the sink and grabbed a wash bucket. It was full to the brim with greywater and much heavier than he anticipated. He heaved it up with both hands, pressing it against his chest as he staggered back to Tom. He dumped the entire bucket over him.

"AHH! WHAT TH—" Tom shot from his chair, babbling. His broad frame engulfed the Boy as he rose, the man's eyes glazed. But he was awake. More so than he had been, anyway. Magnus' son grabbed his knife from the floor and pointed it at the Luddstow senior.

"I don't wanna kill you, Tom, but you gotta go." He stifled a belch before continuing. "Pack your...," he pointed at the bag nearby, struggling for the words, "...things and leave. Today." He squinted out the window over Tom's shoulder, seeing blackness. "Is it night? Tonight, then. Leave tonight. Or I'll burn your house to the ground!"

He turned and marched off toward the door. The world eddied and spun but he did his best to stay upright. Tom shouted after him, a blistering fury of garbled curses that harried him down the hallway. He didn't listen, didn't look back, his focus consumed by counterfeit confidence. Bracing himself against the wall, he held his breath as he strode toward the door, fearing the sudden puncture of an arrow through his back.

He stumbled straight outside and into the night. No arrow came.

As soon as he was off the verandah, he ran. He tripped into the rocky creek bed and landed mid-stream, lurching over the slippery stones. Above, the stars dazzled against the charcoal sky while a half-hidden moon shuttered itself among the soft clouds. Blinking away the disorientation, he pushed himself forward and back onto the grass. Eyes still adjusting to the black, he never even saw the blow coming.

28

A thick and practiced fist took him hard in the gut. The air emptied from his lungs as he spewed an acidic concoction of clear liquid and partly digested food all over his attacker. He was in the dirt before he had the sense to inhale, a panicked gasp clawing at the night. He cradled his stomach, hacking up another hefty round of vomit as he coughed into the grass. The taste flared up the back of his nostrils and burned its way through his throat and mouth.

"Get up," a voice demanded, grabbing him by the arm and hauling him up. "Get inside."

It was his father.

"Noooo!" the Boy lashed out. He shoved the man, who didn't budge. "Nooooooo! Leave me alone!" Magnus' son wiped the vomit from his chin as he stumbled. "I heard you. I heard YOU. You were gonna kill him. You were gonna kill THEM! I heard it!"

His father didn't reply, shuffling to block his path.

"I did the right thing!" the Boy coughed, looking back to the Luddstow home, which was nothing but shadow on shadow in the dark. "It doesn't have to always be about killing," he howled. "There's a better way!" He pushed his father again but the man didn't move—save his hands. They were a blur too fast to track, jerking the Boy forward by the scruff of his shirt in an instant.

"You think I like this, Boy? Twenty years of peace we built, you think *this* was our plan?" The words were hot and loud in his face. He felt them as much as he heard them.

"I've washed enough blood off these hands to fill that fuckin' lake. You think I like that? You think THIS is what I want? You think this is what yer ma and me want?"

His father's helplessness lit darkness between them, a blitzkrieg of emotions.

"I've seen what happens to good people, people who try to do the right thing," Magnus continued. "Yaknow what happens to 'em, son?" He leaned in, pressing his forehead against the Boy's. "Yaknow what happens to 'em!?" He slammed his boot into the dirt. "They get buried. One way or another, they get buried!"

All of a sudden Magnus swept his legs from under him and launched him into the wet grass. The Boy bit his tongue as his head bounced off the dirt. His father was on him straightaway, pressing his face into the cold, wet earth.

"You taste that?"

The Boy, folded into a heap, sobbed as his father pushed his face into the grass. Bits of stalk itched against his skin; dirt stuck to his lips. He coughed and choked, fighting back tears. Magnus's voice, a raging wildfire, dimmed as he whispered into his son's ear, his words as soft as the crackle of kindling.

"This world is dying, son. It's been dying. We don't have the luxury of decency. Not no more. That was taken from us—from all of us—by those who came before. We fight for table scraps. That's it."

His father's voice simmered, its heat repressed once more as the man collapsed in the grass. Wiping dirt and tears and vomit from his puffy face, the Boy rolled over, looking up to the godless heavens. His chest was racing, the stars rising and falling with each ragged breath. Above, little miracles sprinkled against the black. Twinkling. Spinning.

"People went there, once," he whimpered, pointing to the sky. He tasted blood in his mouth as he formed the words. "People did mor—"

"You gotta be ALIVE to do more!" his father bellowed. "Don't you get that? A world died for you to be here. You had twenty years of peace. Twenty years of livin' without this poison in your blood. Don't you get it, son? YOU are the future. And come hell or high water yer ma and me will make sure you see the end. I don't care if you gotta use my bones as a fuckin' ladder, you're gonna climb out of this mess. No matter the cost."

For a long moment he pretended he was there. Centuries past, when the world was alive with the promise of more. More love. More beauty. More peace. Just *more*. He imagined how happy everyone must have been. He imagined how perfect it must have been.

"The cost..." he echoed, the syllables slow and gentle. He tongued the blood off his teeth and spat it into the night. Across the field, the Luddstows were shouting.

"No," he finally stuttered, pushing himself up onto wobbly legs. "We can do better, da'. We have to."

He cobbled himself together and stumbled inside, leaving his father to dream of loss and less.

29

"I said I'm fine, ma," the Boy grumbled, brushing past his mother as he limped into the kitchen. Her face was wrinkled with concern but he ignored her.

Feeling his way through the candle-lit dark, he splashed a handful of tepid water over his face, rinsing the dirt and blood and grass from his mouth. He could feel his mother watching him but he didn't turn around. He couldn't. His head was spinning. He wanted to puke. Again. He also wanted to be furious, tried to coax the anger up, to summon it.

But nothing came. It stalled behind his tired eyes. All he felt was the throbbing of his head off sync with his beating heart.

He staggered to the kitchen table, dropping heavy into one of its chairs. He was about to say something when he heard his father at the door. His mother floated down the hall, the floor's familiar creak soft under the weight of her. He could only make out the sternness of her whispered words; it hurt to focus. Instead, he folded his arms onto the table and nestled his head into the crook of his elbow, waiting for the darkness to claim him.

.   .   .

THE BOY COUGHED SO HARD he woke himself up. Around him, the world was black. He felt around, disoriented, slow to remember that he fell asleep in the kitchen. As his heart settled, he rubbed the sleep from his eyes. His neck was sore so he rolled it, easing out the kink as his teeth scraped white gunk from his tongue. His mouth was so dry he could hardly swallow.

The cup beside him was empty so he stood up. A dizzying rush of blood sent his vision spinning. He leaned into the table, steadying himself before shuffling over to the counter as his eyes adjusted. The blanket resting over his shoulders—a gift from his mother no doubt—slid to the ground. As the world seeped into focus, his eyes were drawn to the distant dancing of orange sunlight that poked through the window.

Not sunlight. Fire.

Fire?

"Fire!" he rasped, coughing the words out. He took a long sip of water, his jaw tight as he swallowed. People always assumed he was afraid of fire after the incident. He could see it when they offered him the seat furthest from the hearth or held their candles at an obvious distance. Growing up, if the fire needed to be stoked at the schoolhouse or the Luddstows', he was never asked to tend to it. Nobody ever said anything directly. But he knew.

Truth be told, fire was the least of his worries. It did its worst and he survived. He didn't blame the flames for what happened. He blamed himself. For not waking up in time. For not saving his sister.

"Fire!" he shouted again into the darkness, slamming his hands on the table. His head hurt from the effort, a budding hangover pressing its way into the nooks and crannies of his semi-drunk brain.

His parents were downstairs in a flash, armed and abrasively alert.

"What is it, son?" Mariam prodded. She was the first in the room, rifle raised as wide and tired eyes navigated the darkness. His father was behind her with a candle, silent as always. The Boy didn't need to say anything. They spotted the fire through a narrow gap in the boarded window. Woozy, he sat down while his mother peered outside.

"We should do something," he mumbled, closing his eyes to keep the dizziness at bay. "We should—"

"No," his father cut in. "You heard Tom. We get close, he'll shoot us. Can't risk it."

"You think it's a trap?" the Boy blurted out, his voice hoarse and ragged. "Their house is on FIRE!" His own volume gave him a twinge of headache as he dropped his head to his chest, eyes tight. He was too weary to shout. Too weary to fight.

"We should at least go outside and call out. Just to see," his mother asserted. Three-quarters of the way through the den they stopped in their tracks. Someone was banging on their door. It was insistent and measured, like a slow-beating drum. After four knocks, the banging stopped.

His father lit another candle and crept to the door while his mother raised her rifle and steadied herself. Their coordination was unspoken. Synchronized. Adrift in a weighty fog, the Boy fumbled for his sword in the candlelight. Hooking the scabbard to his belt was taxing, straining his concentration as he did his best to ready himself.

Magnus whipped the door open, hammer in hand. A body tumbled through the threshold. It was Saira. She was pale, muddy, and soaked. His father dragged her into the room as his mother locked the door behind them. The Boy watched, blood draining from his face.

Saira gasped. "He...I..." Her words were garbled and bloody, her teeth a cavernous shade of scarlet. An arrow jutted out through her back, poking through the side of her neck. She stared at him, arm extended. Her hands were red and wet.

"Boy..." she whispered. Droplets of blood raced down her bruised arm. Her eyes, present and all-seeing, entranced him.

"We need more light!" his mother barked. Saira's extended arm collapsed. "We need more LIGHT!"

Shaking off the cobwebs, the Boy sprung to the kitchen. Within a minute, tiny flames ate the darkness, illuminating the reality before them. Blood was everywhere. It flowed and pooled, expanding on the floor like tainted honey. Between his parents' voices, Saira gasped for air. She raised her arm again.

"Boy," she gurgled, the words sloshing around in her throat.

"I'm here," he whispered, squeezing her hand. He felt the suction of her bloodied skin against his palm. "I'm sorry," he whispered. "I—"

"Shhhhhh!" his father snapped. The Boy heard it too. It was the kid. Tom and Saira's kid. He was screaming

"Boy!" Magnus' son blurted out, realizing that's what Saira meant. *Her* boy.

He rushed into the kitchen and unbarred the backdoor. Nausea hounded his steps but he pressed onward. The night, like Saira, was dying. Dawn approached, though he still struggled in the black of it. Peering through a crack in the fence, he spied a shape in the fiery glow of the Luddstows' burning house. It was the kid. He was running.

"I'm here! At the fence!" Magnus' son bellowed. The wooden palisade was thick and topped with rusted razor and barbed wire. It would be no easy task to remove it in a hurry. Instead, he dragged over a log they had been chopping for firewood and stood on it, combing over the narrow no man's land that sat between the two houses. He couldn't see the child so he shouted again.

"Help! Help me!!" the kid sobbed in reply, a tiny shadow against the scorching haze.

"I'm at the fence," the Boy yelled again, struggling to keep his balance. His vision faltered but he blinked it off. "Hurry!"

Not three seconds later an arrow slammed into the palisade. It was off by several feet but close enough to shock the Boy and send him tumbling. Even in the dark, Tom was a killer.

Pulling himself back up, Magnus' son continued shouting to the child. Another arrow split the night, missing them both. Tom's drunkenness was their only saving grace. In response, the Boy started stripping off his clothes, throwing them onto the wire in a feeble attempt to dampen its bite. Hearing the kid near, he picked up the log, struggling with its weight before heaving it over the fence.

"Look out!"

The stump hit the ground and rolled but the kid was there in an instant, dragging it as best he could before clambering onto it. Another arrow dug into the fence.

"Hurry! I'll catch you. Just watch the wires!" The Boy was flush, unable to keep his panic at bay. Another arrow hit the wood, closer this time. He startled. Vision muddled, head pounding. On the opposite side of the barrier, the Luddstow child clawed at the wood.

"I'll catch you, just hurry!"

Magnus' son rushed to find something to stand on but nothing was within reach. Out of ideas, he yanked out his saber and used it to pry up some of the wires. The metal cables hardly budged. Muffled sobs and panting seeped in from the other side. The young Luddstow was leaping up, struggling to grab the edge of the fence. Eventually his small fingers found fragile purchase.

"Yes, you can do it! Pull! Pull! Pull!!"

The Boy pried the wires up as best he could. His muscles burned. He held the sword with both hands until quivers became spasms. The child scaled up the uneven fence and shimmied over the top, slithering under the wires head first. The metal bit at his clothing, tearing it, but the child was determined. He was fighting for his life.

Another arrow hit the palisade. And the kid.

The Luddstow child's shriek was shrill and torn from his throat, a garbling of panicked syllables. The Boy shivered as a few strands of metal slipped astray. The kid's leg was pinned to the fence, an arrow through the child's calf.

"Grab my hand!" Magnus' son shouted, holding his saber high with his right arm. He yanked at the kid with his left, hoping to tug the wounded child free. It would shred the kid's leg but it was his only option.

The young Luddstow reached out as the Boy jumped to grab his extended hand. He squeezed as tight as he could, dragging the child over. His grip on the saber slipped, his focus solely on the screaming child. Another arrow slammed into the fence. He pulled the child harder, feeling the flesh give way. After a moment, it ripped.

The Boy fell backward as the child flipped end over end off the lip of the palisade. The loosened mess of metal caught the kid as he fell, slowing his descent. A coil of rusted steel dug into the child's neck as piercing barbs nipped at his limbs. The child screamed as chunks of flesh were plucked by the metal spurs as his momentum carried him forward. Like a viscous net, the steel suspended the child in midair. It drank his blood; the razor wire was soaked within a breath, the rusted coil a terminal collar.

The Boy jumped to his feet, blinking back the stars that twinkled in his periphery. Grabbing the gasping child, he tried to ease the tension in the wire. He pushed the kid up higher, but the hungry steel had dug in. Gasps became gurgles, soft and growing distant. The child flailed but his limbs were equally entwined in the thirsty cables. The blood, warm and plentiful, followed the Boy's curves, rolling down his forearm to his elbow. Some of it dripped to the ground, some of it streamed to his armpit, tickling him. Taunting him.

He pushed the kid as high as he could, hoping the tension

in the wire would ease. It didn't. Frantic spasms surrendered to a gentle sway. Shudders eased to stillness. Breath became a memory. But the blood kept pumping. Little arteries clung to their purpose. Carrying on. Spilling color. All the Boy could do was stand there, holding the child aloft. He was still warm. Slippery, but warm. As if he could wake up any moment. As if they could both wake up at any moment.

He waited for another thud but the arrow never came. In the distance, the fire chewed through timbers, collapsing the Luddstows' home. He couldn't see it through the palisade, though the sky above glowed like an ill-timed sunrise, unsure and out of place. He could smell smoke, carried overhead by delicate winds.

"Son!" his father shouted, stepping into the dark. His hammer was raised. The Boy listened to him walk toward the mess, his footsteps tentative. Soaked in red, Magnus' son refused to let go of the half-suspended child. Blood seeped through his pants. It dripped from his armpit down over his ribs. His father cast a grim ward over the scene, his shadow lost to the darkness. There was something in his look the Boy recognized. Something peculiar even the blackness couldn't hide. He held his father's gaze, deciphering the man's silence. His muscles burned but he refused to let go of the child, holding the corpse high, an offering to something ancient and godless.

"Was this your plan?" the Boy rasped. "To get him so drunk he'd do something stupid? To get him so drunk his guard would be down and you could kill them all? Was that your plan all along?!"

His father didn't say a word. The Boy held his stare, hot blood and fresh disgust on his tongue.

"Well," the Boy continued, "looks like he saved you the trouble." He pushed the dead Luddstow child forward. "You wanted us to survive and we survived. Come take your trophy, father. You've earned it."

Magnus turned and walked back inside.

Soaked by a crimson sea, the Boy continued his vigil. He held the child close, whispering dreams of more as he cradled their calamity. As he hoped.

30

Saira and her child shared a grave. There was no coffin; the bodies were placed side by side in the dirt. Mariam spread a thin sheet over the corpses, one with an embroidered rose in each corner. The trio made sure to look about regularly. Tom was still around after all. They needed to be vigilant.

Her husband, never one for words, hardly paused a breath before shoveling on the earth. The faded threads of red were the last bits of color to disappear beneath the bone-dry soil. The resting place was capped by a few stones her son had shouldered from a windbreak. The rocks had collected over the years, appearing in the fields like weeds every time the earth was plowed. They'd get pushed up as the ground contracted and expanded every winter. For a farmer, picking rocks was an endless task. Though, as the winters warmed and warmed again, Mariam reckoned there would soon be a time when farmers didn't have to haul rocks from their fields. But by then, she wagered, rocks would be the least of their concerns.

After seeing to the bodies, she and Mag left to scavenge the Luddstow ruins. She thought about staying behind, to say something, but what was there to say? What do you say to someone who died so you could live? Whose child died because of your inaction?

Damn you, Magnus. Things could have been different. They could have at least saved the child.

"I'm sorry, Sai," she whispered. "I'm so sorry."

Dragging her feet through the singed and dying grass, Mariam kept a watchful eye on the forest's edge. Ahead, her husband was busy salvaging what he could, poking through the debris, pausing every so often to scan the area. There was nothing they could do about Tom now. He was a better tracker than either of them. A better hunter too. Chasing him would be a death sentence. They could only wait and hope he never returned. And that he wasn't watching.

While Mag raided the toolshed, Mariam approached her son, who was pacing the burnt-out ruins. They hadn't said a word to one another all day. She knew her son meant well by warning the Luddstows but bridging the gap between his good intentions and the dead child she had held in her arms was a titan's chore.

"Son?"

The Boy was staring off into the distance, lost in thought. After a long moment, he turned, avoiding her eyes. He stared at her boots when he spoke.

"It didn't have to be like that, ma."

Mariam looked her son over. He stood a fistful of inches taller, his frame sturdy from his training. His arms were tanned, his shoulders—while still not as wide as his father's—were thick from hammering. He looked almost unrecognizable from the boy he was a year ago.

"I told him I would do it," she finally confessed. Her words were halting, stopping almost as soon as they started. Her son fidgeted as she continued. "Tom would have never even seen it coming."

The Boy must have sensed her crumbling under the burden of each syllable because he looked away, his fingers tapping against his leg. "He wasn't just going to kill Tom, though," her son replied, eyes adrift. "You know that, right? He just wanted Tom drunk so he could do the job without him interfering. He was going to kill them all."

Mariam didn't reply.

"Sure, maybe we could have fed Saira and the kid," the Boy continued, simmering. "Maybe just the kid. But do you really think he'd take that risk?"

She let her son get the anger out of his system, biting her lip lest her jaw quiver.

"He didn't want you to murder your friends. I get that. But what he did...what he set in motion...that's not okay, ma. We didn't have to kill them. Any of them. Not your way, and definitely not his. They could have moved. We could have warned them...sent them off. We didn't have to kill them. We—"

"But we did, son," she finally cut in. "They would have starved twice as fast in the wild. And when the worst of it came, if they lived that long, they would do whatever they had to do to survive. Because they are survivors. You don't make it this far, don't survive *this*," she gestured toward the emptiness around them, toward the nightmare that had swallowed them whole, "if you're not willing to do what it takes. And Tom is willing. But we're willing too, your father and me. We learned the hard way, more times than once. But we learned. And you'll have to learn, too."

"But it doesn't have to be this way," her son pouted.

Mariam shrugged. "Maybe there was a day when it didn't. Maybe there will be a day when it doesn't. I don't know. But I'm a parent. My job is to keep you safe. Your father's job is to keep you safe." She looked out toward the horizon, scanning the backdrop. "If that means we have to kill our friends, then we will. If that means we have to burn down the whole village, we will. Because you're all we have now. And we won't let anyone take that away from us."

She didn't wait for his flustered rebuttal, striding off toward the blackened house and the ruins of their past.

IN NO MOOD TO LINGER, the Boy set off in the opposite direction. He needed space. Needed quiet. Before the Year, he would often walk the woods or stroll by the water. It gave him time to collect his thoughts, to daydream.

Since the Year was announced, those thoughts had cascaded into a jumbled mess, colliding into one another, entangled and asphyxiating. He needed a space to think, to let his brain pick up some of the fractured pieces it had hemorrhaged.

"It doesn't have to be this way," he insisted, grumbling to himself as he walked. He didn't bother letting his parents know where he was heading. He was in no mood to argue with either of them.

Instead, he cut across the Luddstows' front field and meandered into the thin wood. He kept his pace slow, in no rush to get anywhere but away. The rhythmic crunch of the forest floor was hypnotic, luring him deeper into the brush and down toward the road.

Ahead was nothing but trees. If he kept on, eventually he'd snake his way to New Gamling and Ranger Lake. Beyond them were the other dozen villages and settlements that made up their patchwork country. Dragging his heels, he hummed to himself. It took him a moment to realize what song it was, that it was a tune he and his sister used to sing when they were in school. Halfway through the second pass, he started singing.

Rockmantle, Saviour, Mer-cy Hills.

Res-o-lute, then the Laurent spills.
Its river splits before Sainte Falls.
New Hudson next, and The Mills.
Sarris Sound, Oneida Springs.
Then comes Cardinal where birds did sing.
Last and most is the city first freed,
Its beacon of hope a crown that gleams..."

From Hope to Freed City was a solid two-month journey on foot. The rocky hills and bedridden boreal forests of the Boy's home would eventually give way to flat farmlands and the ruins of civilization long since picked clean. The road south was well-trodden, linking Hope to the last gasps of humanity that clung to the coast. It was safe enough when times were good—it had to be. It was the lifeline that linked the known world, the single thread that connected it all.

But now the road was empty. Perhaps less safe as well, but it was quiet. That was all the Boy cared about. He basked in its solitude. Devoured it. It was in that space, that seclusion, where he built a second life, reconstructing broken bits of history into hopes and dreams. He breathed life into them, undoing the past and all that it saw burned. It was there, in the vast expanse of his mind, where a better world was made. Brick by brick, dream by dream.

He came to a stop when he heard birds. They weren't singing or chirping, just fluttering in the sparse canopy.

"...where the birds did sing," he hummed again, coming to a stop.

Dappled light broke uneven along his path, shaping the shade and shadows around him. He sat down against the base of one of the few beech trees still clinging to life, its branches a gnarled collection of thick fingers reaching upward.

He leaned into its gentle curve as he propped himself between the exposed roots. He couldn't help but sigh as he collapsed, letting the forest fill his lungs. His chest felt heavy and pressed by the weight of his thoughts. Thoughts he couldn't shake. Whatever one-dimensional notions he had before the Year were long gone. The messy reality of living in a desperate time provided ceaseless pushback against his meagre steps forward. Like having your lungs in a vice, each breath was a battle. Sometimes it felt as if his chest were itching from the inside out. Like a tangle of knotted roots had grown about him, pressing his ribs and stealing his air.

He fought it back each day, buried the anxiety where people bury the things they can't carry. But he could only dig a shallow grave. All too often, the gnawing worry chewed itself free.

The Boy pressed his palms into the dirt, digging into the leaves as he rested his head against the disfigured trunk. He was tired. Tired in a way so complete and unrelenting it was almost a part of him, like a shadow or a reflection.

He closed his eyes. He listened. Half-hidden chirps. Creaking branches. The colossal hush of the dying wood was unconditional. It was a tactile and submissive state. Like being underwater. He could finally hear himself. Feel himself. The world gifted him an unabridged moment of arrant solitude. He closed his eyes and accepted it, letting it drown the rising urge he felt to scream and cry and bash his fists into tanned bark. He fell asleep to its whispers. To its prayers.

Minutes passed. Then dozens more. Then, a sound. Distant, but familiar.

People were coming.

31

"How many?" Magnus asked. He was donning his belt, stomping toward the front door as his son caught his breath.

"A couple dozen at least," the Boy huffed, winded from his sprint. "I didn't get a count, but they were loud. They also had a wagon. I could hear the wheels."

His son gulped another mouthful of water from the wooden pitcher as Mar followed up.

"Weapons?" she asked.

The Boy shrugged. "I ran as soon as I heard them. Sorry."

Magnus bit his tongue. A part of him wanted to chide the Boy for rushing home without a proper look. Information was everything. He kept his mouth shut though. The kid was still sulking over the Luddstows.

And rightly so, he supposed.

Opening the front door, Magnus stared out toward the road. It was half hidden by the slope that rolled its way to the coast. Winter crops and the long-dead orchard blocked most of his view. He stared nonetheless. Listening. Thinking.

Mar stepped in close behind him. "They'll be passing here

before sunset," she whispered. "It'll be dark by the time they reach the village."

"Unless they decide to stop along the way," he muttered.

"They could just be traders," his son cut in. "Or people fleeing north. We—"

Magnus cut him off almost immediately, not bothering to turn around and face his son as he spoke. "They're not traders, son. Not the kind you're thinking of, anyway." His mind drifted to Hunter's Point and to the brutal facts of recent history.

If the Luddstows were around the families could have mounted an ambush. But they were gone, something Magnus was still coming to grips with. He knew he messed up, knew Mar's plan would have been the better choice. He told her as much too. Even thought of telling the Boy. But it was too little, too late.

"Without a horse, there's no time to warn the village but the militia should see 'em coming," he added, stepping back into the house.

"But, wh—"

"Nobody goes outside," he growled, cutting his son off. "No fire or candles. We'll take watch from the attic. Someone at the front door and someone at the back at all times," he ordered. "We'll rotate every hour. Be ready."

Magnus trudged upstairs, steadying himself. Less had arrived.

His wife was on watch when the siege began. Furious orange plumes danced on the horizon over Hope. The evening was alight, gifting a haze of heat that leaned into the black like a soft sunrise. His son had fallen asleep in the den after dinner. Magnus second guessed waking him—the Boy would likely want to do something rash—but his son needed to learn.

"There's trouble in the village," he whispered, shaking his son awake.

"In the village?" the Boy coughed, the syllables stuck on the corners of his dry mouth. "We need to go, we need to get—"

"It's too late for that," he insisted. For a moment, he thought he heard thunder. "C'mon."

The pair went upstairs and climbed the ladder to the attic. Mariam was crouching by the lone window. There wasn't enough room to stand, leaving the trio to sit or squat by the open frame. Colors flickered in the distance. Familiar colors. Ruinous colors. Light flashed over the water.

"It's not just a fire," his son realized.

"No. No it's not," Mar murmured, reaching out to him.

"The posse from the road?" the Boy asked.

"Mm," Magnus nodded, his eyes staring out across the distance. "The posse and more."

His son started shuffling toward the ladder. "I—I need to go."

"You can't, son," he replied, keeping his words firm. "It's too late."

"No, da', I have to go. She—"

"She's a smart girl. She's safe," his wife interjected. "Think about it. She's on the bluff so she's had time to get away. Her house isn't on the way to the mill or the granary or the market." She let go of his arm but continued. "Think, son," Mar insisted, "She's hiding. And she'll come here when it's safe."

"No, ma," the Boy sighed, a lonesome quiver in his voice, "she's not hiding. She's fighting. And we should be too."

His son scurried down the ladder, rushing back downstairs. Magnus followed. He watched his son leap to the door and jump into his boots, frantically knotting the thin leather laces. The Boy patted his knife, tightening his belt so his saber stayed put. When he reached for the door, Magnus spoke.

"What happened last time you acted on a whim, son?"

The Boy stopped.

"Go on," Magnus continued. "Tell me. What happened last time you rushed out the door tryin' to save the world?"

"That...that's not fair," his son quaked.

"It sure as fuck ain't. And neither is this. So suck it up."

Magnus started down the stairs, one at a time. His son faltered.

"You've already figured it out anyway. At a dead sprint you'd need, what? Thirty minutes to make it to the village? Maybe twenty, if ya pushed it? But then you'd be too winded to do anything but die. And even if all three of us went, Tom is still out there somewhere. Maybe nearby, maybe not. You willin' to risk that?" Magnus stood over him now. "I said are you willin' to risk that?"

His son held his ground. The Boy was silent, his face red. Fists clenched. Maybe there was some spine in the kid after all.

"You want a fight, son?" he asked. "This is the fight. *Surviving* is the fight. Not just when the bullets are flyin'. Not just when there are knives out. Every damn minute of your life is the fight!" His blood was flowing now, the violence in his gut lured into wakefulness. "You wanna play hero?" He jabbed the Boy in the chest. "Tell me, what do you think is gonna happen?"

His son stayed quiet.

"Really, tell me. What do you think is gonna happen, Boy?" Magnus pushed past his son and opened the door. "Go on. Go play hero. And when the worms are diggin' through your eyes, maybe then you'll learn the damn lesson."

"Magnus!" Mar shouted, stomping down the steps. "Leave him be!"

Magnus could taste the rage now, feel it billow. He grasped at it, curled his soul around it like a hot stone on a cold night. "No, not this time, Mar," he spat. "This time he needs to learn. He needs to grow up. This ain't one of his stories."

His son was unmoving, tapping on his leg. The Boy knew it

was pointless, that there was nothing he could do now. Magnus watched the realization crush the kid. It was heartbreaking. And it was necessary.

"Sure, *Magnus*," his son finally replied. "I'll grow up. But I hope I grow up to be nothing like you."

The Boy shouldered past and stomped upstairs. He didn't look at his mother. Didn't acknowledge her outstretched hand as he passed. He just walked to his room, and slammed the door.

Magnus turned to his wife, whose face was as flushed as his.

"What if he would have gone?" she asked.

Magnus sighed, shoveling dirt on his fury until it calmed. "Then we would have followed him, Mar. He's our boy."

32

E ven after rinsing her mouth out she could still taste the vomit. "Ugh."

Beckett's daughter rested her head against her arm, curled over the wooden bucket between her legs.

Another dinner wasted, she thought as she took a sip of water, waiting for her stomach to settle. With the house empty and the wounded sent home, she finally had the space to throw up freely. Without trying to be quiet. Without questions. She forced a smile.

It's the little things.

After catching her breath, she set the pail down, walking away from its unfriendly odor to splash some water on her face. It was lukewarm but still felt nice. She rested her eyes as she leaned over the sink, embracing the momentary darkness. It had been a long two weeks since the incident in the market. She was tired.

Candle in hand, she shuffled over to the kitchen table where its fourteen chairs sat empty. Her list was there, more or less complete. The food was packed, as were some books, and she had a bag of clothes prepped too. Whatever she couldn't carry—from extra food to clothing to firewood—would be left to Ax and his partner. They'd be by in the morning to escort her to Magnus and Mariam's place and that would be that. All that was left to do was to set the tripwires and say her farewells.

She looked across the empty room. In the corner, pieces of her aunt's busted chair were littered on the floor. She smiled. Her father would have gotten a kick out of that.

A gunshot startled her. Another followed. And another. For the span of slow moments there was silence. Then, screams. They were muted by distance but still uncomfortably close. For a second she thought she heard an explosion.

Slinging her backpack over her shoulder, she bolted to the door. She didn't bother setting the last traps. Didn't bother grabbing her jacket from the wall. She just ran into the evening, sprinting toward the tall grass beyond the stable.

Below, Hope was on fire. From the bluff, she could see the flames spreading. People were running as thunder echoed over the water. Lights poked through the darkness, bobbing in the harbor. Boats were coming. People were coming.

She jogged another hundred feet, far from the lane but close enough that she could see if anyone neared. The evening glowed as the fires grew. Panic and shouts filled the gaps between screams and volleys. Some were fleeing, some point-lessly trying to douse the mounting flames. A handful bounded toward the road south where a skirmish had kicked off, torches dancing in the chaos. A larger group ran toward the pier where a raiding party was landing. Hope was under siege.

"Oh no..." In a frenzy, she slammed her bag into the grass, rifling a second knife from her pack. And a third. She fastened them to her belt and aimed herself toward the pier.

But then she froze. Just like at the market when Patt tried to kill Magnus' son. Just like a thousand other times when Viktoria chewed her out and smacked her around. Her throat tightened, her mouth tasting bile. Fear tunneled into her chest.

At the bottom of the bluff, the fighting persisted. Gunfire. The intimate screams of hand-to-hand violence. People were dying.

She ran.

The incline rocketed her toward the dock. She swerved right and angled away from the village, turning toward the water. The pungent stench of dirty water was overwhelmed by a smokey fume that umbrellaed itself above her. Weaving between stalls and carts and boats dragged aground, the Girl flanked the invaders as they came ashore. She studied the violence. Saw familiar faces bloodied. Heard familiar voices scream unfamiliar cries. She charged.

She got the drop on one of the pirates, stabbing him twice the back before ducking behind a run-down hawker stall. When a man was pushed and stumbled her way, she slipped back into the light, pumping her blade into his ribs three times, holding him steady as she dug in. He fell before seeing her face.

By then, the marauders had pressed forward and were making their way up the boardwalk. What little resistance Hope offered had been overpowered. Save one. A lone figure, standing on the stone foundation of the old Gamling statue, held the invaders at bay. It was Ax.

She recognized his bellows, watched his weapon work brutal magic in the twilight. He was surrounded, conjuring fountains of blood from the bodies that piled around him. She hesitated joining him. A part of her was tempted to stay hidden, to slink off into the shadows and run straight to the Boy's place on the outskirts. The temptation was so powerful it kept her cemented in place. She looked down at the blood-soaked weapons in her hands. To her father's knife.

"Fuck!"

Her feet moved. They carried her from the shadows into the growing sphere of light. She closed the gap, whipping a knife into the first man she saw. A second knife followed, stabbing into another pirate. She barreled into a third, tackling his legs out from under him. She didn't have time to pull a weapon so she punched and screamed and clawed at him. He threw punches in reply but she held on, ripping at his ear, feeling the skin tear as she tugged at it, biting his face as he lunged upward, tasting blood and wet flesh. Finally, she freed her knife.

Something cracked into the back of the head. It sputtered her vision, flickering her sight. She tumbled into the dirt, semi-conscious. Her mouth was slick and warm with blood. She couldn't feel her hands, didn't know if they were moving. The world was slipping dark. Somehow it felt like she was floating. Like she was being whisked off into the air, far away from the violence that had engulfed her.

Her very last thought was of her father. She hoped he was proud.

33

The Boy was alone on watch in the attic when someone broke from the tree line.

"Someone's coming!" he shouted, spilling his breakfast as he bolted upright. Sludgy clumps of porridge slopped onto his pants and shirt as he shifted for a better view. He slapped the food away, wiping his hands clean before scrambling for the ladder. He didn't bother with the rungs, heaving his body through the hatch.

"Someone's coming!" he shouted again.

He was barreling down the stairs by the time his parents had the door open, his father leading the way. Magnus had his hammers out while Mariam leveled her rifle toward the trees. The Boy pulled his saber.

"It's Ax!" his mother yelled. The big man was dirty and soot-covered, hauling a wooden sled behind him. As he staggered closer, the Boy could see the sled was occupied.

He sheathed his blade and sprang forward. He couldn't tell if his parents followed, the sound of his footsteps and his racing heart blocking out the world. But the closer he got, the more details came into focus. And the more his heart began to sink.

The old man dug his axe into the ground as a crutch with each hurried and hobbled step. With his free hand, Ax hauled the stretcher, the makeshift sledge bouncing along the uneven field. His beard was bloody, his face was bloody. In fact, as the Boy stared he realized that most of the man was covered in a frightening amount of blood.

Magnus' son stopped in the middle of the field, searching for signs of movement in the distance. He scanned toward the road, teasing out the details of the landscape. By then, Ax had closed the gap. The old man's grizzled wheezes were ragged, his massive chest heaving as he neared.

"Boy!" Ax yelled as he slowed, flashing a smile before crumbling to the ground like a broken mountain. "We're bein' followed," he panted. "Buncha fuckers comin'."

The Boy looked to the tree line but saw nothing. Ax gasped a few more hoarse breaths before continuing. "Fuck, I think I might be old!"

With his view unobstructed, Magnus' son could finally see who Ax was pulling on the stretcher. What was left of his heart stopped then and there. It was Beckett's daughter.

He rushed to her side. She smelled burnt. Burnt hair. Burnt leather. Burnt skin. Blood pooled around one of her eyes, rolling down her cheek. He checked her pulse. She was alive. Barely.

"She did good," Ax huffed, pulling her knife from his belt and handing it to the Boy. "Her old man'd be proud."

The Boy turned to yell for help before realizing his parents were right behind him. His mother stood over them, rifle raised, patiently waiting to claim life. His father took a knee beside the Girl. He looked her over, feeling out her wounds before hauling her straight up and over his shoulder.

"We'll hide out in the house," Magnus declared. "Son, get Ax."

He nodded, stepping toward the winded man as he panted in the flattened grass.

"Leave me, Boy. Let me breathe."

"My da' said—"

The whip of an arrow whispered in his ear for half a second before flashing in his periphery. His father sidestepped in the nick of time. The crack-cough of his mother's rifle replied.

"Bastards are quick!" Ax coughed.

"Too quick," his mother growled, rifle level. "I think that was Tom!"

"Tom?" Ax replied, confused.

"Down!" his mother shouted. They hit the dirt as another arrow zipped past. Magnus' son looked to the forest's edge. He saw nothing.

"Here! They're over here!" a voice hollered from the brush. It sounded like Tom but he couldn't be sure.

"Get to the house, the both of ya!" Ax snapped. Beads of sweat carved fresh lines along the old man's weathered face as he forced himself to stand. The Boy raised his sword, though it did little good. He didn't see anyone, nor did his mother as she scanned the greens and browns for a target.

Another arrow honed in. The trio ducked reflexively as it soared high. A rebuttal from the rifle replied, his mother firing from a knee, eyes narrowed on the brush.

"Go! The rest'll be comin' along soon. I'll see 'em slowed to a proper tune!" the big man laughed, finding his balance. "Go on, now. Mar, be a gem and collect yer boy."

Ax gave his weapon a quick kick with his peg leg, knocking off the dirt and grass that clung to the blood on its edge. "Earn that name, Boy," Ax winked. With a grunt, the big man pushed himself forward, limping toward the trees.

"Ma?"

"Go." Her words were quiet. Distant. She was hunting, eyes piercing the trees ahead. But she was stepping backward too.

One foot. Then the other. The Boy did the same as Ax limped toward the forest.

Not half a minute later an arrow split the green and stabbed into the big man's good leg, sending a shudder through the man and stopping him in his tracks. Another arrow soared high, this time toward the Boy and his mother, a thin arc against the blue.

"Run!" Mariam shouted, springing toward the house.

The Boy didn't move. The missile screeched in his ear before stabbing the dirt beside him. He remained still—as he had done a hundred times over in his dreams. In his nightmares of bones and endings, of porcelain and pale life picked clean. Alabaster rain clinked and whistled in his ears. *Pitter-patter. Pitter-patter.*

If any other arrows fell nearby he didn't notice. His eyes were on Ax. He watched the man cleave someone in two, splaying flesh with a feral cry. The sharpened blade demolished the brigand's torso as it slid through skin and sinew to burst out the other side in a spray of gore and guts.

It wasn't a breath later that a man on horseback exploded through the greenery, a banshee growl to rival Ax's. More shouts followed from the trees, loud and close. One outlaw rushed forward and stumbled into a snare. The man's leg bent below the knee as sharpened sticks stabbed through his foot and calf. His high-pitched shriek lasted uncomfortable seconds before being overcome by the shouting man on horseback. The rider, shirtless and covered in ash, leveled a crossbow. Ax took the bolt in the chest but it hardly slowed his momentum. The sharpened metal of his axe met the beast head on. The veteran blade removed the entire muzzle from the horse as Ax sidestepped the charge, cleaving the beast's face in one fell swoop. The rider flew from his mount and folded in the dirt, crossbow lost to the tall grass.

Ax was slow to get to him, limping across the field to finish the job. Pushing himself to his feet, the rider pulled a knife and lunged. The blade met skin but the force of it was lacking; Ax had interrupted the attack with a powerful downswing that parted the man's chest. The colossal blade spewed a mist of red as Ax yanked the weapon loose. He twirled it, dirt and blood spinning free, before continuing toward the brush.

A moment later, a cacophony of screams erupted from the greenery.

"Come on!" his mother yelled, tugging his arm. He had been standing still in the open field, lost to the onslaught. He looked at his feet. Eight arrows poked from the dirt around him. He ran.

His father was waiting for them at the door. Magnus took the rifle and stood watch on the verandah while Mariam rushed to Beckett's daughter. Her practiced fingers searched for lacerations to be sewn and burns to be dressed.

The Boy stood idle. His mother didn't need his help—nor would he be much of it in his state. He could only watch as she pulled her knife from her belt and cut a jagged line down the Girl's singed shirt. She was still unconscious, her skin tanned where it wasn't burned or bloody. Blisters and burn marks danced along her collar and chest. A few small cuts shaped dirty red smears along her softened belly.

"Pack up, son," his father barked from the door. "We need to leave."

"Wait, what?" the Boy replied. He was still staring at his mother, red faced and lost.

"They'll be comin' any minute now. We can't risk staying. Pack a bag. I'll pack up some food and we'll be on our way."

His father was marching to the pantry when the Boy spoke up once more.

"We can't leave her, da'." The words clung to the back of his tongue but he spat them out as best he could, grappling with the syllables.

"We can't take her either. She can hide i—"

"She's pregnant, Mag," Mariam interrupted.

All eyes were on the Boy now. Nobody spoke. The shallow breaths of the injured girl floated faintly between them, patient and ragged.

He opened his mouth but the words lumped in his throat. Questions fired, forcing him to sort through the mess in his mind. "I...we...I wasn't sure of it before," he confessed. "But she's been sick often. In the mornings. And evenings too. And she'd gained weight. I...we can't leave her."

His memory dragged him back to the dying Luddstow child, the kid shivering in his arms as life fled from him by the pint. As his muscles kicked their final ode to life.

There has to be more. There has to be hope.

That much he knew, deep down. It was his true north. They'd all keep running in circles without it. A violent and pointless circumnavigation of desperate acts. That couldn't be all there was—he refused to let it be so. Sarris Gamling was right. From less there would be more.

He didn't wait for his parents to reply. He simply stepped back into the den, dragging his saber free. "I won't leave her."

His parents exchanged a long and telling glance. No words were spoken.

"Alright," his father agreed. He stepped toward Mariam and planted a kiss on her forehead. "If they come, they come."

"If they come, they come," the Boy repeated. His hands were shaking.

34

Magnus waited. Hands on his tools, he watched the group approach. The sun was shining bright as spring eased itself into place. The heat remained at arm's length, softened by a handful of off-white clouds nudged about by a lazy breeze. He could smell the lake if he focused, the familiar waft of algae and weeds a base layer to his senses. He looked to the water but there was nothing to see but grey.

Rolling the tension from his shoulders, he let his focus narrow. To the temperate wood in his grip. To the wisps of dancing grass that bent to the weather. He could hear his heart beat, feel it pumping. The skin of his stomach pressed into his trousers as he sucked in air.

The posse neared. He counted eight, though whether more were flanking in from the trees or waiting back, he couldn't say.

He rolled his shoulders again. "One problem at a time."

They were within range, now. Not his—he only had his tools—but Mar's. Perched on the rooftop, she could no doubt pick a couple of the bastards off before they got too close. But then they would scatter, hide, and smoke the family out.

Anything worth defending was worth stealing. He'd seen it done time and time again. He'd done it himself.

A part of him was tempted to drift back to Years past. To bore into old horrors and buried memory. But habit wouldn't have it. He shifted his weight instead, adding a hint of bend to his knees as he settled. He looked to the brigands, cobbling together his plan as they stalked across the field.

They were an unimposing crew save the hulking brute that led the way. The man had a beard that drooped down to his chest and cradled a spiked club as wide as Magnus's thigh. It had to be close to four-feet long. The brute no doubt swung it with gluttonous abandon too. Nobody carries a weapon that big unless they enjoy using it.

Letting his eyes continue, Magnus noticed the big man's left arm—or lack thereof. It was severed at the forearm. A lengthy metal tip sat where his hand should've been. The crude spear was a foot long or more, fastened to the outlaw's arm with leather straps.

Magnus couldn't help but smile, knowing full well that Mariam would drop the bruiser first. Bastard might even take two bullets. The thought gave him comfort as he looked over the brawny mountain of a man once more. In truth, some part of him wished they could go toe to toe. It would be a proper fight, no question. Maybe if he were younger he'd have risked it. Maybe.

He let the posse near. A cloud of sweat and blood and piss preceded their arrival, the pungent stench of a terrible campaign cologned upon them. As expected, they fanned out, walking a crescent line toward him. All of them—Magnus included—were quiet.

Ignoring the leader, he kept his eyes on the archers. Mariam would take them next, though he couldn't help but worry just how many shots would be loosed his way before she finished her work.

One of the archers wore a maille coat over his shirt. It was dark and metal and, Magnus wagered, uncomfortable. He was never much a fan of armor.

"Fuckin' archers," he sighed, running his thumb over the tallies on his hammers. He gave them a final twirl. It was time.

He sunk into himself, concentrating. His past prodded his defenses, seeking to suffocate the moment with a mass grave brimming with unwanted memories. He ignored it, all too familiar with its pesky claws. He emptied himself, shaking off a lifetime of blood and stubborn choices until the ocean roar of nothingness filled his ears.

Mar fired. The leviathan stopped mid-step as a bullet greeted muscle and bone. His massive club slipped from his grip as he sputtered dark blood. The man looked surprised. Magnus smiled.

By then, a second bullet was dragging bone and brain from one of the archers. Magnus only registered the second shot peripherally, his eyes still fixed on the big man. The gasping was too distant to hear but he reckoned the mountain man was drowning. It would drag out another few moments. As much as he wanted to watch, he couldn't pause the world. He moved.

The other archer had him sighted and loosed an arrow. It tore a chunk of flesh from Mag's left arm. He didn't bother to look at his wound, feeling the hammer still tight in his grip. Mar's third bullet left the armored archer gutshot and clutching his stomach.

Then, they were on him.

IMPATIENCE HARRIED the Boy as he waited for the opening salvo. After his mother cleaned Beckett's daughter's wounds, Magnus' son had bandaged them and left her to rest on the chesterfield. She was unconscious, her breathing slow but steady.

He gripped his saber as he paced, swinging the blade in slow, small lines across the empty air. He didn't hear a sound from above, his mother a silent shadow of ill-fated doom. Returning his saber home, he sat beside Beckett's daughter for a few quick breaths before pushing himself up again. He went back to pacing.

It was the right choice, staying. That much he knew. They had given up too much already. Something had to be saved. Some things were supposed to be saved. But he couldn't just hide away and wait. That was only making things worse. Worry knotted his thoughts, burrowing into the fragile caverns of his mind. There, it planted seeds of doubt and fear and other bastard concoctions. Keeping focus was taxing.

Drawing his saber again, he stopped to listen. He chewed the dry skin on his bottom lip until he tasted blood. When the first gunshot rang, he startled.

After two quick breaths, he ran to the door. When another shot came, his hand was on the door knob. Trembling. Another shot. Deaf to the world, his hand didn't register the handle in its grip, didn't seek to turn it, to enter the chaos beyond.

The snappy whip-crack of another bullet brought him to his senses. He turned the handle and threw open the door, sword drawn and ready for violence. To keep his jaw from quivering, he screamed.

IT HAD BEEN years since Mariam had set foot on the roof, something she regretted immediately as she shimmied out the narrow attic window. Looking over the water, she had forgotten just how lovely the view was. Tracing the shoreline to the smoke-rising ruins of Hope, she admired the fragile landscape. Its stunted copses and butchered fields; the eroded coast, its rocky edges jutting out like exposed bone.

She was barefoot, her right foot resting on the wooden frame of the attic window for balance. She settled into the dry grasses and speckled weeds that layered themselves over the buried wood and clay of the rooftop.

A balcony would have been nice, she thought as she pumped the carbine. "Maybe next time..."

She dropped the big man first. She debated shooting him twice—a single bullet might not do the trick—but she decided against it when she saw the round took him in the chest. He'd die there, in the grass. Not fast, but fast enough.

Mariam pumped the carbine and took aim at one of the archers. The man got an arrow off but she took him down immediately after. He was on the ground before the rifle's empty casing hit the grass and weeds at her feet. He died fast.

Swinging her focus, a second archer was taking aim. His arrow flew wide. Her bullet didn't. It punched him in the gut. The archer folded over, dropping his bow.

Mariam continued her hunt, grinding the lever to chamber another round. Her husband was in the thick of it now and she dared not risk hitting him. Glancing back to the big man, she saw the bruiser had pushed himself to his feet, leaning on his club.

"Tough son of a bitch," she muttered. She sent a second bullet into his chest. Just to be safe.

She was chambering another round when she saw movement out of the corner of her eye. The wounded archer in armor had taken a knee, firing off another arrow. She steadied herself and put a bullet through his chin this time.

As she eyed her next target, the archer's belated arrow dropped through her shoulder and stabbed deep. The force of the blow thrust her off balance. She fell against the roof and rolled down its slope, clinging to her weapon as she tumbled. It was still in her hands when she careened off the edge, falling some twenty feet before hitting the dirt hard. She tasted blood

for a moment. But only a moment. After that, the world was
dark.

A WILD SWING forced Magnus to duck and lunge right, folding
under the swooping arc of an axe. It was an old tool, the thick
head heavy with rust. He slipped beneath the two-handed
swing, backhanding his hammer claws along the man's stomach, freeing skin and fat from their proper home. The paunchy
brigand, whose neck was scarred with rope burn, recoiled.
Magnus pressed, his left hammer striking the man's temple.
The brigand went slack, his eyes rolling backward as he
dropped.

Before the blow was finished, Magnus was moving. A spear
lunged at his exposed flank, guided by a bony-limbed boy who
couldn't have been much past twenty. The young man's eyes
were tainted yellow where they weren't brown, his spidery
limbs gangly and fast. He was a good few inches taller than
Magnus too.

A spear was a good choice, Magnus thought to himself,
batting the metal tip wide. He stepped in to close the distance
and punched forward with a hammer, shattering teeth and
splitting the young man's lips. He followed up with a hit to the
skull next, dropping him. Before he could take a step, a
machete slashed in. It was set to sever his face from his form
but he parried while leaning back, curling a hammer in a
sweeping circle that knocked the machete into the air. Two
quick blows to the head cured his attacker of life.

He hadn't had time to blink before a ripping heat seared his
guts. He couldn't help but shout, more in rage than surprise. He
pivoted to face his attacker, hammers raised. A second arrow
punched him in chest. It didn't go all the way through, but it
went deep enough. He could feel it bumping against bone. The

resistance of it. The familiar wetness of blood. He stumbled a half pace from the force. A hammer was in the air before he recovered, his fingers tingling phantom spasms.

The shortest of the band was a boy—a child, really. Fourteen, maybe fifteen. He had picked up one of the bows and was staring at Magnus when the flying hammer bludgeoned his arm. The kid was still staring when the second hammer smashed him in the face. The teen's nose shattered, gushing a fountain of blood. Magnus pulled his knife before the kid hit the dirt, stalking the distance with a dogged determination to see the job through.

He wasted no time, grabbing the teen by the scruff of his greasy hair and jabbing his knife into the young boy's eye socket. The effort winded him; pulling his knife free was exhausting. Looking back toward the house, he spied his son struggling with one of the raiders. He sprung forward but his legs gave out after a single step. He collapsed into the blood-fed grass, the world a distant and darkening blur.

THE BOY CHARGED out the door saber first. He blinked against the light, his long legs launching him into the fray. Two steps off the porch, he heard movement behind him. He spun, sword arm half-cocked as his mother crashed into the dirt.

"Ma!"

He ran to her, taking a knee at her side. Her neck was lathered red, an arrow protruding from her collar like a broken bone. He started to roll her over when a rush of footsteps cornered him. A gruesome club careened in, swung by a heavyset brigand with a sagging grimace. The man's face was a mural of bruises and freshly sown scars, bits of thread dangling from his wounds like thin maggots. Magnus' son leaned back and rolled, pressing himself to his feet as he spun away. The blow clipped his arm but managed little more than a bruise. The scar-faced outlaw followed up with a two-handed backswing that battered the saber from his grip. Seeing an opening, the brigand charged.

The pair tripped over Mariam's body, losing their footing as they grappled. When they hit the dirt a few feet away, his attacker was atop of him, fighting to land a haymaker. With his left hand, the Boy reached for his knife but his arm was pinned so he fired a flurry of punches upward instead, hoping something connected. The man, his wide jaw braced for the blows, took them in good measure.

The scar-faced man cursed and shouted, hocking a mouthful of spit into the Boy's eye. Magnus' son flinched. The distraction gave the ruffian a moment to pull his own knife which came pressing down with both hands. The Boy struggled to slow it. He grabbed at the man's wrists, bucked and kicked his legs, working to squirm free.

But the blade inched closer.

Murder lit the man's eyes, his bloodied lips a red slit among purple and blue contusions. Fear diluted the Boy's rage. He screamed fury at the man, digging his nails into the outlaw's arms, drawing blood as he shifted his weight, hoping to let the blade sink into his shoulder instead of his heart. Shimmying in the dirt, he worked his body away from the blade as best he could. He felt the tip of it against him, pressing through his shirt, the virgin skin unbroken but willing to part.

With his father's stubborn refusal, the Boy screamed. His final breath was a deep and guttural growl that dragged the bile from his gut. The knife slid in. It parted a centimeter of flesh before stopping, an explosion drowning out his death cry. The maggot-faced ruffian went limp before toppling into the dirt.

On the ground a few feet away, his mother gripped her rifle. Her eyes were vacant and unmoving, staring at nothing and everything. She was smiling.

Magnus rolled himself over, gazing into the blue and white above him. The air was warm but not sweltering.

A perfect day.

He reached for his tools, fingering the dirt as he groped for them. His vision narrowed, the dark edges of the unknown creeping forward. He tongued the blood in his mouth, smiling. The Boy would be safe. Mar would see to that. They'd manage as best they could without him. He could see his baby girl now. He could rest.

He had hardly closed his eyes when someone pawed at him. Hands pressed on the wound that soaked his chest. They were guided by the blurry outline of his son phasing in and out of focus. The Boy was shouting but the words were muffled. Magnus tried to reply, to say his farewell. To tell him he was proud as any father could be. Despite everything.

Lips trembling, his muscles sought out the unfamiliar shapes, tripping over themselves in the attempt. Then, his arm was moving. Being moved. His hands were wrapped around something. A hammer. His hammer. The handle was slick with blood. He squeezed it.

Eyes heavy as dark water, Magnus fumbled the tool, letting it slip from his numbing fingers. He pushed the tool into his son's hands. He held it there. Skin and blood and wood together. It was all he could gift his only son before the darkness and its demons welcomed him home.

35

He placed their bodies side by side when it was over. Together, the family grew cold, stillness their final bond as the bright blue sky dimmed to a silkier hue.

"We should have run," Magnus' son whimpered, coming undone. "We should have run..."

The burden of failure kept him in the dirt until a grey-black sky devoured the horizon. Until his stiff muscles shivered in the evening air. Until his eyes finally had nothing left to shed.

Pushing himself up, the Boy plucked his mother's carbine from the earth and saw it loaded. He stalked the yard to gather his father's tools, carefully wiping the blood and dirt from each. He unclipped the tool belt and tightened it around his waist, slipping the clean hammers home.

Home.

It was all his, now. The run-down house. The dying garden. Sarris and the hens. Hope was his to carry, and it was a burden he could feel with every tired step as he shuffled inside. Beckett's daughter was still unconscious on the sofa. He left her there, her breathing shallow.

Armed and exhausted, he went about looting the outlaws,

digging into their pockets and packs, seizing their weapons and valuables. Then he stripped them naked. He dragged their bodies down the lane. Some he grabbed by the feet, others by their arms or hands. He didn't bother crossing the field to get Ax's sled nor did he walk back to the barn to get a cart. He just dragged their naked corpses through the dirt and rock and grass. They were rubble to be cast aside, their flesh and blood smearing the uneven earth.

He left the bodies in the road, heaving their empty frames into a mound of limbs. They would not be buried or burned. Instead, their tanned and unwashed skin would be left to rot on the road. As a warning.

As he stood entranced by his totem of flesh, a solitary noise creaked in from the distance. Ducking under the rifle's sling, he peeled the weapon from his sweaty back, absent-mindedly pumping the juddering lever. Blood still leaking down his chest, he peered down the road, rifle level. Someone was coming.

Rolling along the compact dirt was a man on a bi-cycle. It was Joao, the herbalist. His clothes were burnt and recently weatherworn. They had been fancy clothes, once. Clothes that betrayed a life comfortably lived. The woolen suit and matching trousers had several tears, including a ripped knee that exposed red-scraped flesh. His olive skin was unwashed and, like the Boy's, bloodied.

A three-legged dog hopped along behind him, struggling to keep up. In its mouth was a broken horn, half crushed and blackened. The crippled mutt dropped the instrument every dozen feet, falling over itself to pick it back up before hobbling on.

The bi-cycle squeaked as it neared. Its rusted-out wheels, lined with padded cloth, came to a halt just shy of the bodies. The apothecary's face was sunken and masked by a few days' worth of dirt and stubble. A bandage covered his right hand, dried stains of blood splotching through the fabric. The Boy stared him down, waiting for an excuse to summon bloodshed. Not longing for it. Just expecting it. In another life, he would have greeted the man as a friend.

"What happened in the village?" he demanded. His voice cracked as he spoke. He was thirsty. Dehydrated, even. Exhaustion hit him as soon as he opened his mouth.

Leaning off the seat onto one leg, Joao shifted his weight before answering. "Raiders. And the sh-ship," he stuttered. "They took everything. Folks...they fought. Some of us hid." Joao paused to breathe, as if the memories were hard pressed upon his lungs. "The rest were captured. They're down at the quarry. And in the mine, being forced to work. Some went to *The Ark*. The women, anyway..."

The Boy looked northeast toward the quarry. It was just east of Hope, home to a dwindling supply of limestone and a mostly depleted shaft of iron ore. He wasn't surprised someone had seized it—it was priceless. With its stone and iron you could make a fortune trading with the other settlements. Glass from Fort Bastion, tin from Cardinal, flour from Huron Mills. Trade wasn't just survival. It was power.

Joao's gaze lowered to the mess of bodies that blocked the way. "What happened here?"

It wasn't a question the Boy wanted to answer. It wasn't a question he could answer.

"Are you going to shoot me?" Joao eventually followed up, looking down to his furry friend who had finally caught up with him. "Please don't eat us if you do."

The Boy looked the man in the eyes, holding his stare before he turned to the ratty mongrel panting at his side. He looked back to Joao and lowered his rifle.

Nodding his thanks, Young Joao stepped from the bi-cycle and walked it past the Boy and the bodies. The dog followed a few steps behind.

"There's some cans in one of the packs," the Boy said. His voice was hoarse, distant. "Take them."

Joao nodded, wincing as he stooped to examine the nearby packs. "Your parents?"

Magnus' son shook his head.

Suddenly Joao took a quick step toward him. The abruptness was unexpected; he raised the rifle to block the man but Joao was quicker, wrapping his hands around him, squeezing him. Holding him.

"Don't give in," the young man whispered, his own voice gritty and fragile. "Whatever you do, don't give in."

Magnus' son shuddered, standing immobile in the man's unexpected embrace. And then the flood came, pried from his eyes by juddering shoulders and open wounds and the fresh pit of cancerous grief that eroded his every breath. Joao held him through it all. Until the Boy had stopped crying. Until silence and the stench of the dead reclaimed the road around them.

With a nod, Joao picked up his bi-cycle and dusted off the seat. He waved goodbye with an exaggerated salute before hopping back on the metal seat. The dog, still carrying its trumpet, followed.

As the battered young apothecary disappeared down the road, the man shouted his final farewell. "Don't give in!"

PART III

BEFORE

The bottle shattered as soon as it hit the hot brick. Shards of glass shot onto the floor, scattering from the hearth. Tom didn't bother to clean them up, leaving the pieces to shimmer in the fading firelight. The glittering pinpricks of glass crunched under his boots as he shuffled to the kitchen. He could smell his own breath as he walked; it was stale and touched with vomit. The caustic aroma spurred a dry heave though the spasm hardly slowed him. He needed another drink.

None to be found in the kitchen, he hobbled out into the night. The village was quiet. Peaceful, almost. The council—and much of the folk who called Hope home—were in the hall debating some trifle problem not worth his time. He had other priorities.

While the past haunted his steps, it was the present that drove him to drink. He had taken another loan, a small portion of which was well wasted on the burning concoction he had just consumed. The harvest was shit yet again, though that was hardly a surprise. The summer burned hot enough to scorch the ground, dragging on for months without a drop of rain. His crops weren't much more than compost now, feed for whatever few rodents and birds were still among the living. The quarry, too, provided no help. It was over worked and in no need of his labor.

But, regardless of his ill fortune, loans needed to be repaid.

He fumbled his way along the dirt lane, his glossy vision strained in the dim. After stumbling across the square he wheeled down a narrow alley, sticking to the shadows. Ahead, a wedge of firelight leaked through a window and cut across his path. It took him a moment to recognize where he was, to see whose house it was.

"The kids..." he mumbled, staggering closer. They were gathered in Ax's hut, a two-story hovel hardly visible in the darkness. He inched closer. No voices stirred, just the gentle rising and falling of a dozen sleeping children. He slipped into the house, feeling his way toward the kitchen. Rummaging through the pantry, he uncorked a few random bottles but smelled nothing that would suit his purpose. He checked again to be sure, cursing under his breath as he came up empty handed.

"Fuckin'...fuck," he slurred, lurching back toward the front door. Halfway through the den, he stopped. His stomach tightened and he retched. Chunks of bile and spittle spewed from his mouth, splattering the room that he was so mutely navigating. He leaned against the wall, reaching into his pocket for a handkerchief to wipe his face, catching his breath as his vision blurred. When his stomach settled he continued toward the door, tossing his puke-stained cloth into the den as he passed.

The disgruntled man slammed the door behind him before wandering off. The force knocked something over inside but he paid it no mind. He was thirsty.

When the fire spit a trio of embers into the room he was long gone. He wasn't around to watch two of those glowing specks land on the lone square of cloth he tossed near the fire.

He didn't see their hot weight consume the booze-stained rag. By the time he found a bottle down the lane, the items he knocked from the mantel were alight. Within minutes, Ax's den was burning. The children in the loft above, fast asleep and dreaming, suffocated in peace by the bottle's end. The unlucky few downstairs, those curled up close to the flames, were consumed as the fire fed on cloth and wood and the flesh of hope. By that time, Tom had passed out, dreaming dreams of more.

36

She stared at the corpse for some time, more disappointed than surprised.

"Another one dead," Beckett's daughter sighed. "Poor girl." Wiping the pooled sweat from her brow, she grabbed the stubby yellow legs and pulled the lifeless hen from the coop. It was still warm.

The summer had dug itself in, its arid grasp strangling what little life was left in their small corner of the world. Three hens had died in the past two weeks alone and none had laid an egg for almost a month. The creek was dry and the garden cracked and scorched, more dustbowl than anything else. It hadn't rained since she was bedridden, the premature birth of her child a bloody and taxing affair.

She shuddered at the thought of it. How she couldn't scream lest they attract unwanted attention. How she bit down so hard on a piece of leather she lost a tooth. Beckett's daughter tongued the gap in her smile, poking her gums before pushing away the memories. She had survived. Her daughter was small but healthy. These days, that was all one could hope for.

Strolling through the garden, she looked over the crops,

checking for signs of its imminent demise. The harvest was overdue but without rain little had grown. They could only haul so many buckets from the lake.

Near the palisade, a few of their misshapen carrots had been dug up, likely by some desperate rodent. A bit of spinach, too. She made a mental note to discover what little critter was poaching from their fragile field. Maybe they could trap it.

She paused to listen for movement. She was safe behind the fence but it was a habit now, one the Boy made sure she embraced. But nothing stirred, not even a breeze. The world was busy cooking itself and those who ruined her. Those who lived.

HE GAVE up wiping the sweat from his face some time ago; there wasn't enough fabric on his sleeves to soak up his tidal perspiration anyway.

There hadn't been any movement on the road for weeks but the Boy made sure to scout each and every morning, stalking the parched landscape for warning signs. Leaving the rifle with Beckett's daughter, he'd reconnoiter the road for a good half hour in one direction or the other before walking the fields. Never at the same time. Never in the same order. He doubted anyone would be paying so close attention, but it was the wise thing to do. It's what his parents would have done.

Ahead, a stack of bones, arranged in neat crisscrossed piles, dotted the road. The smaller bones were scattered about like ivory stars in a sky of dry earth. The skulls were spaced along the width of the thoroughfare like a finish line to some ungodly race. A few times they had been knocked aside by stragglers running from this horror or that but none dared to walk up the lane to see who had built the open-air ossuary.

Satisfied all was in place, Magnus' son trudged up the lane, looking forward to the water and shade that would greet him. Before he had even made it to the porch, he heard the baby crying from inside the den. His baby girl.

"LET'S TRY IT AGAIN, a little faster," he wheezed. The air clung to his lungs like honey. Talking was like wading through mud, the heat wave a daily onslaught.

The couple had slipped out to train. Sweltering in the fleeting shade of the homestead, the Boy had his tools out and his shirt off. His torso was slick and taut from a life of labor and a year of blood. The rifle was not far from reach, leaning against the house. It was never more than a few feet away.

"Ready?" Beckett's daughter asked. She looked significantly less winded.

He looked over to the baby, whose tiny body was sprawled on a blanket beside the rifle. He took a moment to listen too, pausing to peer out across the field. The Girl did the same, looking the opposite direction, prey ever vigilant. Then, they fought.

He let her attack, leading with her knife as she charged. She was quick and agile and accurate. Her blade cut the air on an angle, crossing along his body but missing by a good foot as he slipped back.

As practiced, she followed up with an opposite sweeping arc, completing the cross that forced him back another step. That's when she lunged, blade lowered to his gut. Her footwork was perfect, her movements elegant and smooth, unimpeded by oafish feet and the crippling hesitations of self-doubt.

His hammer swooped down to bat the blade away as the Girl extended her reach in an attack that would have gutted him otherwise. She followed up with an upward jab to the neck, which the Boy slipped under, the blade far closer than he would have liked.

Without a beat, she hopped back, legs bent and knife up, ready to defend herself. Her face was glistening but plastered with a smile. Even she knew she was good. Fluid and nimble, like—as he had read in one of the books she gave him—an elven warrior.

He nodded his approval, saving himself the winded breath. They both looked about, eyeing the horizon once more before collapsing in the grass, their daily session over. He missed their longer training sessions but there wasn't enough food for them to be overworked beyond what was necessary. Every calorie mattered.

Settled in the grass, Beckett's daughter rested her head in his lap. Strands of hair stuck to his sweaty stomach, tickling him as she scraped them aside. He could feel her talking, the sound reverberating against his hand that rested on her chest. But he wasn't listening. He wasn't there. He was months away, in the past, reliving training sessions with his father. Stumbling through the motions and hating the world for its selfish dedication to idiocy. All he ever wanted was to read and write and water the last few seeds of knowledge the world had to offer. To learn, maybe even teach, and illuminate the best of mankind.

He felt her finger jabbing into his ribs, which brought him back to the remnants of the moment. "Where were you this time?" she asked, curious and kind.

"I..." he stopped before he even started, changing gears as he looked to her. "What would you want to be doing now if there was never a Year? If all this was different?"

She paused, staring up at the cloudless sky, pondering. "Well, truth be told, I wanted to be a painter when I was a kid," she replied. "I never painted much—it was hard to get paints this far north—but I did it a few times and it was absolutely lovely. I'd love to travel and paint all the new things I see. I had a map my pop gave me that I'd always daydream about. It's silly. But it was something, you know? You?"

He shrugged. "I thought about working at the school for a while. Help write more books, improve the curriculum. Maybe even write my own book someday. I don't know," he sighed. "I mostly just wanted to be left alone."

"Is that why you kept skipping the exams?" she asked bluntly.

Magnus' son tensed, his mouth suddenly dry. "How did..."

"My aunt knew everything that went on in town," she shrugged. "Especially the goings-on of people she wasn't fond of. She mentioned every time your father added your name to the exam register...and every time it was removed when you didn't show up."

"He was always disappointed when I backed out," Magnus' son admitted. "Never said as much, but I could tell. He wanted me to move on. I get it—it was six years ago. But I'm not sure I want to move on. I'm not sure I can."

Beckett's daughter squeezed his hand. "I'm sure he just wanted you to get back out there. Enjoy life. You kinda fell off the face of the earth for a while after..."

He shrugged, hoping to avoid a conversation. "It was quieter that way."

The Girl nodded, interlocking their sweaty fingers. "Look, it's not my place to say anything so I'll just say this: the only way out is through. I know you enjoy being a loner but you can't hold yourself back forever. When we cling to the past..."

"Next year," the Boy insisted, stroking her greasy hair from her reddened face. "It'll be a fresh start.

Sensing a change in direction was necessary, the Girl brought his scarred digits to her lips and kissed them one at a time. "Realistically?" she added with a sigh, "If all were normal, I'd be keeping the books for my aunt. Hiring farmhands, arranging caravans, and doing whatever else she told me to do. You know, all that fun stuff you like."

"We'll do your traveling one day," the Boy vowed. "Maybe

not beyond the Faroff like you wanted, but at least as far as New Gamling. Maybe even Ranger Lake. And hey, there's nothing wrong with being organized," he mocked. "It's what separates us from the beasts."

"*Separated* us," she corrected.

Magnus' son clicked his tongue in agreement, their conversation wilting to a halt. Staring into the distance, he retreated once more into the past, painting better days with brighter colors.

———————

THE MAN WATCHED the couple from the tree line. He couldn't see what they were up to—they were in the fenced-in yard and mostly out of sight—but he kept watch anyway. That was all he could do. Day in, day out. Occasionally he'd head off to hunt or scavenge, but for the most part he just watched. Waiting.

A part of him wanted to kill them and loot the house. A roof over his head was a tempting notion. Yet he also wanted to apologize and make amends. To go back to life before the Year. Best as he could, anyway.

Help them or kill them. That was his dilemma. He leaned a different direction every day, though he'd long since lost track of the actual days. He supposed it didn't matter. All that mattered was staying alive.

37

It wasn't long before the remnants of the garden succumbed to the elements. Another month of cracking heat dragged in storm clouds and thunder but never more than a few drops were shed. An uncommon muggy tension brewed, leaving the Boy and his new family clinging to life on the outskirts of nowhere.

As supplies danced along the margins of scarcity, training sessions were cut back to just once a week. Sarris and the remaining hens were moved to the cellar, free to enjoy the cooler temperature of the basement. As the flock dwindled, Beckett's daughter plucked and prepared the corpses each time a bird passed, scavenging what she could from the carcasses. Magnus' son could never bring himself to eat them though. He'd try, poking and prodding the fleshy morsels, but he never managed more than a bite before pushing the bowl aside. Meat was rare, even to one brought up with the luxuries of wealth, but the Girl was not a fan of it either. He would watch as she made faces, choking it down with a dedication only mothers can conjure. Responsible for feeding their child, she needed the calories.

Magnus' son felt bad every time he watched her gag down chunks of bird, knowing her discomfort, seeing it in her face as she reluctantly swallowed what had essentially been their pets. It didn't seem right.

As they sat eating one of their former companions, he tried to lighten the mood.

"Do you think chickens used to be able to fly? Seems strange they can't, doesn't it?"

The Girl shrugged. "Maybe they were normal birds before the End? I dunno."

"Think there are many left? Chickens, I mean."

"In the entire world?" The Girl set her spoon down, happy to postpone the inevitable next bite. "Hmm. I don't know. I know there weren't even a dozen left in the whole village before the Year so there likely aren't many. We only had seven before Viktoria left."

"Only," the Boy scoffed, sailing his spoon around the dark broth.

Beckett's daughter rolled her eyes, continuing. "We tried to breed more but they would never live longer than a few weeks." She paused, frowning into her bowl. "If you think this is unappetizing, try eating dead chicks. Nothing went to waste at our house."

Looking at his mangled reflection in the broth, Magnus' son realized how foolish he was being. He pulled the bowl back and scooped up a hunk of meat, the uneven edges of its tender surface filling his utensil. The dark soup dribbled off the wooden spoon, rippling the seasoned water. He wanted to tell the Girl that he was only eating it for them. So he would have the strength to protect them. So he would be ready when the worst came. He wanted to tell her that he would do anything for her and their daughter. But he couldn't find the words.

Like a growing number of thoughts, they remained entangled in the weeds of his mind. Instead, he brought the meat to his lips and scraped the dead bird off the spoon with his teeth and chewed it to bits.

"We're not eating Sarris if he dies," he insisted after he swallowed. The Girl nodded.

They finished the rest of the meal without speaking, an impromptu vigil for the dead and dying. Thunder seeped into the growing gap of conversation as it rolled in toward the shore, teasing the wasted earth. It was a daily occurrence now, the air tense and thick and wanting.

Brewing clouds stirred and the Boy watched them through a gap in the boarded-up window. Estranged pings echoed on the porch roof as thin droplets trickled down. It was slow, almost imperceptible. A flickering spit was all it ever amounted to, the thunder and lightning more rage than substance.

Beckett's daughter broke the silence as she gently rocked their daughter. "That's my favorite color." She nodded with her head toward the nearest clouds that had yet to darken, the swirling tufts foaming at the edge of the storm.

"Grey?"

"Not just grey. A white-grey. Like a rain cloud on a foggy day." She gestured to the outskirts of the storm, where the black clouds had yet to touch. "Wintergrey, my pop called it."

The Boy drifted off to the few proper winters he had seen, his memory dancing through shades of snow and rain and wintergrey. In the background, the wind bucked, blowing billowing storm clouds over the coast as far as he could see. Within the hour there would be waterspouts twirling over the lake, whipping the waves into a frenzy.

The Girl rested her head against him. He reached out and wrapped an arm around her. They stood there until the weather was upon them, until wintergrey turned haggard black. Until lightning stabbed the sky with flamboyant forks of pale. Until the rain fell—a proper rain. The kind that smothers the backdrop, that blurs your vision.

Outside, the starving earth drank what it could but it was cracked and baked and most of the water rolled off toward the creek. Soon the torrent frothed. The deluge surged over the rounded stones in the creek bed, drowning the grass and garden as the sky bled clear its purpose.

In silence, the couple watched the whims of their fate through wood and dappled glass.

THE STORM WAS SHORT-LIVED. The matte black canopy blew over the coast in a matter of hours, dragging its fury onward toward whatever life could be found further inland. Its damage, however, would last. Branches and stones and twisted clumps of dead grass formed a makeshift dam in the creek, swelling the stream and flooding the front field. They let the tangled mess be. Tedious labors were a problem for another day. Their focus was on the garden and field crops.

Beyond the fenced garden, the fields had taken a slick battering. The tenuous strands of half-dead flora that would see them through the winter were fragile at the best of times. As the couple paced about the mucky field, the Boy couldn't help but notice he had taken on his late father's grim countenance. Things were not looking promising.

As he puttered and pouted around the field, Beckett's daughter rescued busted carrots and drowned onions from the muck. She took the time to watch her steps, salvaging what she could from the soupy field, squatting over each row for a close examination. Her eyes were attentive, routinely darting from the crops to the distant grass and the dying trees that lined the field's edges.

It suddenly dawned on him that she was a survivor. He could see it now, just as he saw it in his parents when it all began. It was like looking beyond a shadow to see the life that cast it. To see new depth, new colors. They had been there all along, of course. He just hadn't seen them. For the most fleeting of moments, he felt hopeful.

Out of nowhere, something slammed into his chest. Mud, warm and wet, splattered stringy chunks across his shirt, splashing up his neck.

"You need to pay better attention, Magnus' son," Beckett's daughter giggled.

After walking his gaze from the mud to the Girl, he slowly shook his head in mock anger.

"Tsk tsk tsk. You're lucky bullets are scarce, young lady," he teased, scraping the muck from his shirt. He bent down and scooped up his own clump, threatening retribution. He feinted a few throws, laughing as she flinched. Rushing in, he chased her around the garden, leaping over the remaining crops as she ducked and dodged in anticipation.

"Okay! Okay!" she begged, throwing her hands in the air. "I surrender!"

The Boy narrowed his vision, arm held high, drops of muddy water leaking to his elbow. She peeked between her fingers, hands held out as a shield, her face red from laughter.

"You're lucky I don't want to be stuck doing laundry," he conceded, flinging the mud to his feet. Looking back up to the Girl, he expected to see a smiling face awash with relief. But she wasn't smiling any more. She was pale.

"What? I said I wouldn't—"

The rifle was off his back in no time, his slippery digits working through the motions his mother taught him. Spinning, rifle raised, the Boy eyed the field. Someone was there.

A distant silhouette loomed just shy of the tree line. The person wasn't hiding. They didn't move either. They just stood there, a ghost in plain sight, haunting their levity.

Eyes locked on his target, the Boy started backing away, closing the distance between himself and the Girl.

"Get behind me and look for others!" he snapped. He kept

his eyes on the shadow that tracked them, trusting the Girl to discern if there were others about.

He scolded himself for dropping his guard as they scurried to the nearest tree. It was an old elm off the edge of the field that crowned the windbreak with an umbrella of shade. It was also their burial tree. They stepped lightly to avoid the cairns that marked the graves—both old and all too new—that rested around the tree, keeping it nourished. Soggy and faded grass carpeted the past, feeding on inevitability.

From behind the broad trunk they spied into the distance, combing the wet and dying colors for movement. The shadow had disappeared, slipping back into the thick brush beyond the plowed land. They would have to make a break for the house soon, the Boy realized, his palms slick with muck and nervous sweat. They had left their daughter napping in the house, a decision he now regretted.

His guts twisted themselves into a knot. It was a long run across open field to get home. And they could be running into a trap.

"Shouldn't have let my guard down," he cursed to himself, looking about. "We'll wait a minute. If nothing stirs, we run."

The Girl nodded, keeping her eyes on the fields as she scanned for predators, knife in hand. She was standing on a stone. A grave marker. He watched out of the corner of his eye as she traced her glance over it.

Eventually, her eyes fell to his sister's grave. Rach's gravestones were round and colorful. Greys and pinks and browns piled a foot high at the head of her grave while smaller rocks outlined her resting place.

"Rachel."

It was hardly a whisper, just a gentle puff of warm air slipping over her dry lips. The very mention of the name, however soft and secret, sent him off kilter. It had been a long time since anyone had whispered those syllables. They sounded foreign, almost taboo.

His mind worked to picture her, scraping up memories. What images he conjured were mostly fiction now, dulled by the years. All he had was a cobbled-together revenant of fact and fantasy, one he clung to with despondent dedication.

"It was my mother's mother's name," he finally said, eyes glued to the landscape. "I was always jealous of it—of her having a name."

The Girl stepped in closer to him. He could feel her hand on his back. "She was always nice to me. Never gave me crap for having a shitty aunt. I was never jealous of her name but I was jealous of her hair. Remember how long it was? I bet she'd still be growing it to this day."

He forced a smile but didn't respond. Couldn't respond. He was back in the fire, waking up to the searing pressure of intimate heat, to the confused dizziness of a sudden jolt to life. To the heavy punch of black smoke.

He felt her arm slide up to his shoulder, the gentle squeeze calling him home.

The Boy dragged his eyes from the field. They were red and lost but desperate for safe harbor.

"Okay," he finally said. "Let's run."

Beckett's daughter grabbed his hand and held it tight as they sprinted toward the house, hoping their world hadn't ended.

38

He was a whirlwind, tearing through their house, chest pounding from their mad dash to safety.

"We shouldn't have let our guard down!" he cursed, as much to himself as to the Girl. She was coddling their child at the table, her face equally flush.

After checking—and then double checking—all the windows and doors, he darted around the house packing their bags. He filled one with food and another with clothes and supplies, haphazardly shoving everything into them. Dropping the rucksacks on the kitchen floor, he paused to comb over his thoughts. His leg was shaking, muscles shuddering sporadically.

Was it Tom? Someone else?

They waited an hour, armed and ready for attack. None came. By nightfall, they were still on edge and expecting.

As they braced for Tom or brigands or both to come crashing through the door, Magnus' son mulled over their options. As far as he could see, they only had two choices: stay where they were familiar, had water and food, but where they were being watched—*or hunted*—or pack up and go. Leave whatever danger had encircled them and hope that a better life could be made elsewhere.

The latter was a frightening choice. Until now, it had simply been their backup plan should days turn desperate. But desperate days were upon them.

He closed his eyes, taking a few deep breaths the way his mother had showed him. After a few moments, his leg stopped shaking, the quivering muscles lulled back to normal as he stood over their packs.

"Normal," he scoffed, massaging his thigh. If the world had stayed normal he'd be working in the village now. Teaching, writing. He had so many ideas. A better system for copying and sharing books. Improving the school curriculum. A new irrigation system for the common. Launching more trade caravans and expeditions. His brain had been a fountain of ideas his whole life. Ideas to make things better. For everyone.

He leaned against the wall, staring down at their packed bags, "Things could have been so much better."

"Understatement of the year," the Girl replied, forcing a smile.

"What do you think we should do?" he asked. He had made the choice once before and the outcome haunted his every waking hour. He knew leaving was the worse choice—they had shelter and water, even if they were being watched—but the idea that there was somewhere safe out there, that there was somewhere where they could be free, poked tempting holes in his reasoning.

"I think we should stay," the Girl stated. She was rocking their daughter as she shifted in the chair, chewing over their options. "I think it would be better for all of us here. And it's your home. You can't just give that up. It's worth fighting for."

"But is it worth dying for?" he asked.

Beckett's daughter didn't reply.

Magnus' son tapped the words against his leg, thinking. He

let his mind chase itself, pacing over the next steps of their continued existence. He felt like he did on that night, a lifetime ago. Surrounded by flames, desperate for fresh air.

Beckett's daughter extended her hand, her tanned skin almost as dark as his now. "You with me?" she asked.

After a long moment, he nodded.

"Good. Because we have a plan to make. We're survivors now; we have to be. So fuck whoever is out there. This is our home."

She was right. As always. There would be no escape to greener pastures. There would be no running. If they wanted a fresh start they would have to make it. Here. Now.

"We'll stay," he said, folding himself over to rest his head in the Girl's lap.

"We'll stay," she echoed. "And we'll survive."

A MONTH WENT by without another sighting of the man. Though whether the man had seen them was a mystery. Every urge the Boy had to relax was met twice over by the need to stay vigilant.

Vigilance is survival.

The words might as well have been his father's. He could hear their stubborn tone, austere and unwavering. He envisioned them tempered by his mother's warm embrace. Her hands on his shoulder, a kiss on the forehead. Ever as stubborn as his father, but kind and reassuring. He choked the thoughts before they blossomed further.

In the den, Beckett's daughter and their nameless daughter sat by a diminutive fire. Across the kitchen from where he was sprawled on the floor, Sarris poked and pecked. His entire world was within a few feet of him. Everything he had, everything he cherished. Together.

He struggled to use that togetherness to kindle the embers

of hope that had been ever so slowly suffocating since it all began. What was once a deep-seated dedication to better days had been uprooted. In its place blossomed grim necessity.

"I'm becoming my father," he sighed. The Boy twirled the sheriff's star he had taken from his father's shirt, poking the metal into his fingertips. Under the kitchen table, Sarris preened himself. There was bird shit smeared over the floor and on the chairs. He almost didn't notice the smell.

"You say it like it's a bad thing," the Girl replied. "Your father was a good man. My pop always spoke highly of him. And my aunt didn't like him, which I'd take as a compliment."

Flashes of his father's final moments imposed upon his thoughts. The weight of him in his arms. His mouth tracing silent, final shapes. The blood-soaked hammers in his grasp. The stillness.

Beckett's daughter interrupted his meandering thoughts. "Tell me a good memory you have about him."

Magnus' son thought for a moment, sifting through the past.

"When I...when my ma taught me to read, I caught on quick. She said I never stopped and would read the same couple books over and over again. They were the only ones we had and the pages were ripped and rotting." He shifted his weight, his right leg starting to tingle as he leaned into the wall. "I could read them from memory so my da' would always test me. He'd let me stay up late and watch the stars or tend to the fire if I could finish a whole book without a mistake. The books were only a few pages so it wasn't a lot. But he was always pleased when I got it right."

"So you've been a bookworm since the get-go, eh?" the Girl teased. "I'm not surprised."

"I was," he smiled, turning to watch Sarris. "I knew, later, that he wanted me to do something more practical with my life. Same as every parent, I suppose. But he knew how much I loved my books. So he let me study. Brought me as many books as he could get his hands on. I'd stay up late copying them all out until my hand cramped or I ran out of ink."

"It's nice that he supported you. I think most parents wouldn't let that stand. Plus, books aren't cheap."

"They eventually trickled to a halt. He started spending more and more time with Rach; they had a lot in common, so I get it. They'd train and wrestle or go tracking. We grew apart. But I grew closer with my ma after that. After the fire."

"Just because you grew apart doesn't mean he wasn't proud of you, though," Beckett's daughter replied. "I saw how he looked at you in the market, after those outsiders attacked. And I bet he was proud of you when you decided to stay. To protect me. You made a tough call but you put your foot down. That took guts. I bet your mom would be proud too. Your sister too."

As Sarris strutted past, climbing over his outstretched legs, the Boy realized he was crying. The tiny droplets trickled to his ears as they weaved their way over stubble and scars.

"Your sister...tell me what she looked like," the Girl asked, her voice easing in from the den. "I remember her from school —especially her hair—but it's been so long now. What do you remember? What do you think she'd look like now?"

He took a moment to wipe his eyes, coughing to clear his throat lest his voice crack. "Well. She'd look like my mother. Thin but strong. She had my ma's nose; long, but not too long. A little bony. But she had my father's eyes. Not their color, but their shape. Their watchfulness. She had long legs, like me, and she was fast. Boy, was she fast. And funny. Much funnier than I am."

"That's not saying much," Beckett's daughter teased.

Magnus' son smiled. "Her hair was long—you remember. She hated haircuts so it grew like wild grass. It'd get tangled and dirty and my ma would plead that she cut it but she said she never would. Stubborn as my father, that's for sure. It'd be past her waist by now, no doubt about it."

"I always wanted a sister," the Girl replied. "Sounds like she was a good one."

The Boy nodded, sitting up. "She was."

He looked at the scars that became her. Life and death together. Shared. He sat there, lost in thought for the better part of an hour, watching the metal sheriff's star flicker in his fingertips. Remembering.

The soft padding of Beckett's daughter on the floorboards brought him back. He didn't bother to stand as she neared.

"She'd be proud of you." The Girl handed him something. It was a piece of paper.

He looked at the parchment but there wasn't enough light so he dragged himself into the glow of the den. A face was staring back at him, one both familiar and foreign. It was his sister. Older, as she would be now. Not exact. But it was close. As close as ghosts can be. It was the greatest gift he had ever received.

39

It was scorching before sun up. Again. By the time he finished his rounds he was sweating though he poked around the Luddstow ruins one more time before stalking home. Just in case. Scanning the shades of dying green, he paused to watch for movement. He could feel something out there. Someone watching. It left him on edge, sent his skin into a shiver that eased into a serpentine chill. Tom—or whoever it was—was still out there. And there was nothing Magnus' son could do about it.

Maybe it was just his mind playing tricks. Maybe. But every morning it felt the same. There was an uneasiness to the air, a foreboding pallor prodding his defenses. It kept him awake at night, kept him ragged and on edge.

Which was exactly the point, he mused. It was a smart plan. A way to attack without attacking. To weaken your enemy. To distract them before the blade rushes in.

The torched ruins of the Luddstow home had long since been scavenged. Untamed weeds and grasses inched their way over the burnt-out home, spreading like a holy sickness. The world, as he listened, was silent. No birds or breeze made a sound in the warm air. All he heard was his footsteps atop the grass and dirt. The creek had once again dried to a trickle, a slow drip over indifferent stone, imperceptible unless you were standing in it.

The Girl opened the door when he was a few steps from the porch. Whenever he was out, the door remained barred.

"Morning," she said with a smile, kissing him on the cheek as he stepped into the shade. She looked as tired as he felt. Maybe it was just the weight loss. They had been rationing for a while now and were more bone bare than ever.

They paused on the porch to watch the soundless morning slip into its daylight. Nothing stirred, the cresting hill before them devoid of life. No sounds from the surrounding forest or the road that lay just out of sight either. The world was dead to them.

"Do you think there is anyone left in the village?" the Girl asked, leaning against the doorframe, hand resting on the pommel of her knife.

The Boy shrugged. "Maybe at the quarry, being forced to work? I reckon we'll hear some wagons pass sooner rather than later if so. Unless they leave by boat. After that, we'll be the world's end. There's nothing north of here now."

"We're the Faroff," the Girl exhaled, chewing her lip. "I suspect there's no coming back from that."

"Maybe that's a good thing," he replied, wrapping an arm around her. "Maybe we'll be left alone."

Beckett's daughter smiled and stepped back into the shade of the house. "Let's hope so."

His stomach rumbled so he followed, reaching to close the door. Out of the corner of his eye he saw something. His vision narrowed, stopping him in his tracks. Letters had been carved into the wood of the porch. They were fresh.

"What th—"

He dragged his fingers over them, taking on his father's

grim countenance. It said LEAVE.

———————

THEY DIDN'T STEP OUTSIDE for the next three days. No training. No patrols. No water runs. Tom was still out there—or someone like Tom—and he wanted them gone. Was the man alone? Did he have a posse? Would he torch the house if they stayed? The questions chewed at her day and night.

If she didn't have the child to care for she'd take the fight to them, no question. Some things were worth dying for. But she had a child now. That changed everything.

Yet leaving was incredibly risky. Heading north past Hope meant potentially running into whoever had claimed the village and quarry. South meant New Gamling and more people. East was a wasteland of ruined landscapes unfit for the living. All that left them was the lake. To find a boat and try to escape somewhere further afield, somewhere they could start fresh.

"As if a place like that even existed," she huffed, aimlessly spinning her knife on the table. Their choices were grim. It was a lose-lose and she knew it. They both did.

The knot in her gut tightened as she stewed over their dilemma. She gave her blade another spin, watching it twirl on the table. Before it slowed, she grabbed the whirling weapon and launched it across the kitchen. It stabbed into an ugly cupboard Magnus' son had built.

"You okay?" the Boy shouted from upstairs, his voice lined with concern.

"Yeah," she hollered back, staring at the knife. "I'm fine."

THE NEXT MORNING, she awoke with the sun in her eyes. She jumped out of bed, tasting worry. Magnus' son usually woke her for her shift on watch. The fact that he didn't sent her head spinning. She reached under her pillow and grabbed her knife, listening. When she smelled breakfast, she relaxed.

The Boy was at the kitchen table, humming to their daughter as he sewed some strips of leather into his jacket pocket. Sarris was on the floor, nestled into a filthy blanket, peering about the room with his beady little eyes. A feast of oats and dried fruits awaited her on the counter. Mint and nettle tea, still warm in the cauldron, steamed into the air, concealing the musty odors of their barricaded home and the bodies within.

"Mornin'," he smiled, pushing his project aside. She looked at him and wrinkled her nose. Something was up.

"Morning," she replied hesitantly, leaning into the counter as she cradled her breakfast. "Whatcha making? And why didn't you wake me?"

He was grinning. "I figured it out."

"Figured what out?" she asked, chewing on a leathered apple slice.

"What we need to do," he replied.

She raised an eyebrow, waiting.

"Tom—or whoever—left us a message. They could have torched the place or ambushed us. But they didn't. What does that mean?"

"That he doesn't want to lose the house and its supplies? Doesn't want to risk losing the food and garden and seeds and everything else?"

"Exactly. And?"

"And?"

"And he doesn't want to kill us," the Boy declared. "Not if he can get away with not killing us, I mean."

She set her bowl down and shuffled toward the table, pondering. "That seems like a stretch," she concluded.

"It is," the Boy admitted. "But I wager he could have killed us by now if he really wanted to. Instead, he's been waiting. Hoping that—"

"—that we just pack up and leave."

"Precisely. So, we invite him to talk. We send him a message and see if we can work something out. Maybe we buy him off with food or supplies."

Beckett's daughter tapped her knife. "And if he can't be bought?"

Killing Tom was easier said than done. But a hidden knife during some kind of parlay? That might work. She walked over and gave Sarris a pet. His feathers ruffled and shuddered in the dawn light. She didn't like the plan, but what else could they do?

"You don't like it?" the Boy probed as he shifted the baby up to his shoulder, bouncing her softly.

The Girl shrugged. "It's no worse than our other options," she conceded. "Do you think I can stay back? With the rifle?"

Magnus' son shook his head. "Tom would see that coming. He needs to feel safe. Like he has the upper hand."

"He does, though," she sighed.

The Boy nodded in agreement. "He does. But maybe with some knives we could take him? If worse comes to worst, that is."

Beckett's daughter rested her hand on the knife on her belt, giving it a reassuring squeeze. "Well, I suppose it's the best shot we have. So, how do we get Tom to talk? Do you want to just go, I don't know, yell around outside?"

The Boy smiled. "That was exactly what I was going to do."

She scooped up their daughter, kissing the drooling child until she cooed. Then she turned to the Boy. "Shall we?"

They went out every other hour, weapons sheathed. She brought their daughter along, refusing to leave the infant alone again. She also brought some extra knives. They took turns yelling from the front yard and the garden and from the ruins of Tom's old homestead. They didn't go further than a couple hundred feet from the house just to be safe.

"Tom! I know you're around so listen up. We want to parlay —to talk. Meet us in the lane tomorrow at noon. We don't want any trouble. Just wanna talk. Tomorrow at noon."

They shouted every rendition of the phrase they could think of, hollering until their throats were hoarse and dry. She suspected Tom heard him but there was really no way to be sure. They'd have to wait and see.

By nightfall, she had lost her voice. By morning, she was jittery and on edge. By noon, she was pacing in the kitchen, drowning in *what ifs* as Magnus' son fed Sarris. He seemed confident an agreement could be made. That a solution could be bartered. She felt less confident but kept her thoughts to herself lest she erode his brittle optimism.

Together they packed up some food as a peace offering, filling a small cloth bag with a few cans and jars of preserves. Waiting by the front door, hand on her knife, she drummed her fingers and hummed to herself. In the kitchen, the Boy waited by the back door, spying over the fields, scanning for trouble.

Out of the silence, a noise. The creaking of a wagon bouncing along the rutted road drifted over the homestead. Voices rolled into earshot next. They were coming from the north. From Hope.

"There's someone on the road!" she snapped.

"He's early," the Boy replied, shuffling into the den, peace offering in hand.

Her lips were quivering. "No. I heard a wagon. I heard people."

The Boy's face soured, his fragile shield of hopefulness shattered. He glared out the front window, waiting. Listening.

"He betrayed us," she murmured. Her heart was sinking.

"We're leaving," Magnus' son stated, the fury in his voice palpable. He stormed into the kitchen and hauled up the emergency bags they had kept packed. He gave them a quick once over before slinging one onto his back and the other over his chest. Picking up the carbine, he stomped back to the window, scouring the day.

Beckett's daughter chased Sarris down and shoved him into a sack. After checking her knives once more, she slipped their daughter into a wrap, bouncing her calm.

"To the Luddstows'?" she asked. Adrenaline was kicking it. She could taste it.

The Boy nodded, his face red with anger. "We'll watch from there. If they turn up the lane, we retreat to the woods. If they pass by, we'll run back here. Watch the trees for others. It could be a trap."

She reached out and squeezed his hand. After a moment, he squeezed back.

"Ready?" she asked.

He raised the rifle, unsmiling. Once again, they were running. Together.

They dashed alongside the house, angling their way toward the creek and the ruins of the Luddstow home. Slightly higher on the hill, it gave the couple a better vantage point from which to watch their fate unfold. They could see the posse, now. Wagons, animals—at least a goat or two by the bleating—and a handful of people. She heard voices, conversations pitching over the distance. Whoever it was, they weren't afraid.

The group rolled into view from the north. The carts were loaded up with metals and supplies, including the goat she had heard moments before. There were empty cages on the third wagon.

Neither she nor the Boy moved a muscle as the group rolled past. The Girl was grateful her daughter wasn't fussing. Luck would see them through.

As she watched the posse muddle their way along the abandoned road, she couldn't help but second guess their choice to stay. Living so close to the road and the remnants of a village was always going to be dangerous. Luck would only get them so far.

Working over her worried thoughts, she took her eyes from the posse to look back over the fields and garden. To their home. A man was there, standing on the porch. It was the ghost that had been haunting them. It was Tom.

"Well, fuck," Tom muttered, shuffling back to the edge of the house. He could hear the wagons closing in from down the road. It was just about noon. "Shitty timing."

He watched the couple slink away to safety, sprinting to the burnt-out remnants of his old house. No doubt they'd be blaming him for whatever was coming down the road. He wagered it was the whoresons from the quarry. They'd have bigger fish to fry and would likely just pass by. But with the house empty, he could raid it 'til his heart's content. No more getting by on dead rats and squirrels. He could have real food. His stomach grumbled at the mere thought of a proper meal.

Just take what you want and be gone.

It was a reasonable notion. And fair, all things considered. Mag owed him that much at the very least. There was still a part of him that wanted to kill the Boy and be done with it. That was the safe choice. The smart choice. But Tom pushed the thought aside. The kid had been family, once. He'd raid the house and be on his way.

Tom sprung from the bushes beside the homestead and leapt through the garden, hopping over the side of the porch. He kept low, skulking toward the front door. He looked to the pair as soon as he had his hand on the doorknob. The Boy was looking back.

40

Tom had betrayed them. Now he was trying to rob them.

"Bastard!" the Boy growled. He leapt to his feet and fired. The bullet ripped into the door inches from where Tom had stood a moment prior, splintering the wood. Tom jolted, stumbling backward before scrambling behind the house.

"What are you doing?!" Beckett's daughter snapped. The wagons had stopped. He heard shouting in the distance.

"Fuck!" His brain was catching up to his stupidity. He searched for Tom among the garden of weeds near the palisade, trigger finger itching for attention. His heart stuttered, the familiar vice around his chest tightening.

Come on...

But Tom was gone. After a handful of seconds he lowered the gun. "FUCK!"

"They're coming!" the Girl cried.

He turned to the road, raising the rifle. "You need to run!" he insisted, eyes locked down the barrel.

"No!" Beckett's daughter pleaded, grabbing at him. "I'm not leavin—"

"You need to run, NOW!" His face was flushed by his own foolishness. His eyes darted from the road back to the house. Flustered, he dumped his packs in the dirt, double checking his tools and weapons. "I'll hold them off. Make it to the clearing and wait for me. Take the bags."

He knew she didn't have a choice, not with their daughter at stake. Someone had to run.

Beckett's daughter grabbed the packs with one hand and Sarris' sack with the other. The unwieldy collection encumbered her, stooping her over. Rage and worry tattooed her face.

"I'm sorry," he whispered.

She kissed him on the forehead. "I love you." Her words were short and honest and painted with loss. His throat tensed, his lungs a sinking ship of short breaths. Drowning in the space between words, he leaned down to give his daughter a kiss. "I'll see you pretty ladies soon."

He couldn't manage another breath of them so he turned away, letting them disappear into the brush. He clawed them from thought, scraping his chest empty. His world—the only world—was that which stood before him.

Through hardship is the journey. From less there will be more. Through hardship is the journey. From less there will be more.

He repeated the mantra as the wagon crew crested over the knoll of corn and wheat by the orchard. He let his brain work over the situation. Didn't force it—he trusted himself and his training. He just let his mind devour the facts before him.

He counted thirteen. The carbine had seven bullets before a reload but he'd likely miss for half. That would leave nine or ten invaders. Even if he hammered two and knifed one he'd be left with at least six to fight with his saber. Bleak odds. These were practiced men, too. They had to be. Because, this far into the

Year, the weakest had already been culled. If he fired too soon the group would scatter. He couldn't have that, not with the Girl about. He couldn't run either—they'd track him. Or Tom would find him. Yet if he waited too long he would be surrounded.

It was his parents' death all over again. The sound of his mother falling from the roof poked at his defenses. The smell of his father's final breath taunted him.

"There's no way to win," he whimpered.

Through hardship is the journey. From less there will be more. Through hardship is the journey. From less there will be more. Through hardship is the journey. From less there will be more.

He let his mind free again, hoping to corral a solution he had missed. Nothing came but memories of death. His mind flashed to Ax. To Fort. To Patt. To his sister. He followed the trail of bodies until they led to Tom's brother dying alone, surrounded by a handful of brigands as he bled out on the road.

"He took the pricks with him and we're all better for it."

The Boy plucked a single cartridge from his pocket and slipped it into the rifle's port, a realization dawning.

"I don't have to win...I just have to kill them all."

He bolted to the house. Inside, the air was stale and familiar, the warm perfume of unwashed bodies layered over the stench of Sarris' makeshift coop. In the kitchen, embers from the morning's breakfast had faded. Ripping open cupboards, he snatched a few rags and soaked them in lantern oil. As they absorbed the dark pitch, he picked up one of the kitchen chairs and shattered it against the floor until its legs broke off.

Scooping up the four pieces of wood, he tied a rag around each. Leaning down over the woodstove, he blew life back into the fire, feeding it oxygen. He blew a few more times but it was slow to catch. The torches struggled to light. The fire needed proper food.

He hunted for something to burn, something that would

catch easily. He rummaged through the pantry, through draw-
ers. He couldn't find anything.

"Fuckfuckfuck!"

His battle calm was fraying, his mind choking on its stalled
momentum. He needed something flammable, like paper, but
there was no time to get a book from upstairs.

Then, he remembered.

He pulled Beckett's daughter's sketch from his pocket.
Unfolding it, he took one last look at the picture of his sister
before setting it against the embers. Once more, she burned.
Magnus' son wasted no time lighting his torches. The rags
blazed hot and bright but they wouldn't burn long. He rushed
back out the front door and leapt off the porch toward those
that would do him harm. He closed half the distance before
stopping to check the wind. Then, he launched the flaming
chair legs into the dry wheat and corn and grass of the dead
orchard.

The men were close now, just a couple hundred feet away.
They stopped spreading out when he launched the torches. An
archer lined up a shot but didn't shoot. They were cautious.

The fires didn't take long to catch. The whole world was
tinder and smoke rose from the field by the time Magnus' son
eyed his first target. It wasn't the biggest man, nor the man who
looked to be the leader. It was the archer. The lone archer. He
would be the first to go.

The Boy walked himself backward, looking over his
shoulder for Tom every few paces as the fire consumed the
field. Mindful of the growing flames, the posse merged in the
lane, funneled by the flames as they stalked closer. The air grew
gloomy and opaque, the smell and heat gamboling together.

A gunshot cracked.

One of the brigands, a shirtless bald man wielding a
hatchet, stumbled and fell. His screams battled the blaze as he
clutched his leg, rolling in the dirt. He had stepped on one of

the Boy's traps. It was a new design, but a simple one. When the small pressure plate was stepped on, a bullet shot up through the man's foot, shattering bones in the process. One of the other men slowed to help him up but the bald man shoved him away, cursing.

"Careful boys! We got a clever fucker 'ere!" another raider shouted, poking his weapon into the dirt as he moved forward.

By the looks of it, the man couldn't have been more than twenty-five. Lanky and dirt-stained, he had a makeshift bandage over his right eye. He slowed their pace as he prodded the earth. It was an imprecise gesture, though, and one of the Boy's pits went undetected. A two-foot hole riddled with wooden spikes devoured the one-eyed man's foot and calf. The stakes stabbed and flayed, impaling and trapping him.

Squirming and shouting, the young man keeled to the side. His knee snapped. The Boy didn't hear the break, but he felt it as he watched, the joint folding at a curious angle.

The rest of the men stepped off the lane immediately.

"Lockes! You good?" one of the brigands shouted, sidestepping into the grass.

"Kill the fucker!" the injured man spat, cradling his leg.

The fire inched closer.

Dead center in the lane, the Boy held his ground. He looked back once more to make sure Tom wasn't around before pushing the man from his thoughts. These men had to die first.

Bringing the rifle to bear, he sent his first round into the archer. He hit him again, just to be certain.

"Fuckin' archers."

The raiders charged. They spread out as much as they could though the fire pressed closer, overwhelming the grass and crops with a frenzy of heat.

The Boy dropped another outlaw and grazed a third but missed his remaining rounds as the men ducked and dodged. Not bothering to reload, he left the weapon in the lane, slipping into the black smoke of the burning field. The shroud of fume smothered the landscape. He waited, squinting through the haze.

A few seconds later, a brigand appeared. He wore a floppy leather cap with a slight brim, his face gaunt and blushed by ginger stubble, a small wooden buckler in one hand. The wood was blackened and chipped and used. In his other hand, a long dagger led the charge.

The Boy launched his knife.

It hit the brigand in the chest but didn't stop him. The man slowed, confused, looking down to the metal embedded in him. By the time he looked up from his wound the Boy was spilling his guts with his saber. The brigand didn't scream or shout. Didn't even groan. He just stared at the Boy, lost, before sitting down in the dirt, poking at his insides as they oozed into the afternoon. The smell of blood was brief.

Darkness wreathed the yard in its entirety now, the wind-blown grey and black stinging his eyes, filling his nostrils. Ducking low near the gaunt-faced ginger, the Boy waited. Voices sounded everywhere, inching toward him. Creeping like the flames. They were searching in a line now, their ragged coughs heard between the crackle and strains of the growing blaze.

Movement.

Magnus' son lashed out with the saber, splitting the air with its grace. The steel blade bit into a man's ankle, taking his foot clear off. The raider stumbled, shouting in surprise as he collapsed. He was large and thick boned, the kind of man who was born big and stayed that way. He fell into the Boy, knocking him backward. Magnus' son struggled against his wounded attacker as they hit the ground together, the raider's writhing weight pressing the air from his lungs. He could feel the hot sting of ashy grass on his neck, tonguing his exposed flesh.

Limbs entangled, the big man groaned and flailed, jabbing

at the Boy with a rage of fists. Magnus' son took the punches in good measure. He could feel the man's blood soaking his pants, dripping into his boot. He bucked and thrashed, fighting back against the weight atop him. Working his wrist, he struggled to find purchase with the sword. Sitting up as best he could, he spat in the man's eyes before leaning in and biting the big man's face. He tore off a wedge of dirt-stained flesh, beard hairs and all, adding another scar to the mess. The big man growled, lashing out with a frantic head-butt. It rippled the Boy's vision but the shift in weight freed his hand.

Dazed, Magnus' son angled his arm, finding a soft spot for his sword. The big man, his torn flap of his cheek sagging like damp laundry, gasped as the blade touched skin. He felt it coming, eyes white and wide. His gasp limped into a whimper as the Boy pushed, slipping the saber between the man's ribs. Wetness leaked from the sudden corpse, piss and blood alike.

Before he could sit up the next bandit was on him, raining down blows with a barbed cudgel. Saber lodged in the big man, Magnus' son was forced to shield himself beneath the slack torso that pinned him down. He could feel the blows vibrating against the corpse, hunting for him. He looked to his attacker but the smoke was everything now. He couldn't even see the man's face.

Yanking a hammer from his belt, the Boy attacked, taking a hit from the cudgel on his left shoulder in return. His arm went limp, fingers tingling, but it bought him time. He cracked the raider's elbow with a hammer, sending the cudgel tumbling. Even so close, his attacker remained invisible in the smoke. But the Boy trusted his instinct so he let the tool fly. The grunt and crush of skin told him it connected. He tore free his saber, his left arm pounding pins and needles, and sprung after the injured bandit.

Launching blindly into the smoke, he made it two steps before bumping into the man, who was bent over and spitting blood. They fell together, Magnus' son tumbling saber-first. The weapon skidded up the man's neck as they hit the dirt. It split the raider's jaw, cleaving his palate and severing his tongue and nose from his face. The gurgle and choke of the bandit's last gasp was brief as the Boy watched the inner workings of the bandit's throat slow to nothingness.

Struggling to a knee, he leaned on the sword, stifling a cough. His whole left side was numb.

"He's 'ere!" a shout echoed from behind him. The Boy turned, side-stepping over the body at his feet. A bolt split the air where he had been standing a moment later, its metal tip dragging across his cheek. It tore off a chunk of his ear before flying onward.

"Fuccckaahhhhh!"

His father's rage bellowed in his chest. Without missing a beat, he charged the crossbowman, running into the smoke. He heard the metal lock of a second bolt being loaded and leapt aside before it passed. When he saw the man, he lunged.

The saber ripped into the crossbowman's belly with hardly any effort, poking a hole through the outlaw's guts like a pencil piercing paper. He thrashed the blade around, screaming, whipping it side to side with enough force to rattle the outlaw's teeth. Inches away from their face, he realized it was actually a woman he had skewered. Her hair was long, braided down to her stomach. Her mouth drooped slack, exposing missing teeth and the brown-black shades of rotted gums. She was branded on her forehead with words he couldn't decipher. Her eyes were summer blue and bright as July. But only briefly. They soon rolled back into her head, her lifeless weight sudden on his sword. He held her there, a bloody puppet of his own making, until his arm quivered. When he pulled his blade free, she collapsed into the grass.

With a grunt, he bent down and plucked up the crossbow. Bracing it against his legs, he forced the string back with his good arm. It was a heavy bow built for stronger arms but he managed, huffing exhaustion into the smoke. Blood leaked down his face, hot and warm.

As he turned away from the fire, a shadow appeared. He didn't wait for the attacker to reveal himself. Didn't wait to see their face. He just fired.

The bolt hit flesh with a groan. A second later he heard the body drop. Tossing the crossbow into the fire, he pressed forward. The feeling was starting to return to his left hand, though his shoulder was slow to move and tender.

After a lopsided shrug to test his mobility, he stumbled down the lane, squinting through the grey, choking on its airlessness. Saber in his good hand, he stalked the fiery field for his next victim. Fatigue seeped in from his wounds. His footsteps dragged. He needed a foe soon, before the dregs of adrenaline that nourished him dissipated.

After a few paces, he found one. And another. And another. And another. Four men waited near his front porch. They blocked his way into the house, the building yet untouched by the fire. Enveloped in a smoldering garland, they were hardly more than a handful of feet away, shadows outlined in smoke.

"Fack off, boy!" one yelled. His voice was hoarse and dry as he waved a cruel looking machete. "Go'on!"

Another man spat profanity, the words more cough than language. The Boy didn't move. He let them approach, let them shuffle their way toward him. His heart and hands were primed for violence.

He lunged.

A man with an axe reacted first, tree-trunk arms swinging the tool wide and high. Too high. The Boy sailed under the weapon as it arced, dragging his saber over the man's thighs with enough force to part muscle and greet bone. He continued the motion as he rose, the man crumpling on the spot.

His saber crashed into an oncoming machete, preventing

the rusted steel from peeling off his face. He kicked the machete-wielding man in the groin, keeling him over before a pommel to the head sent him down.

Sensing movement, the Boy flipped his grip and stabbed backward with his sword. His quick thrust slowed the attacker, but not before the man plunged a knife into the meat of his back. He felt it slide in, grating on his shoulder blade.

"Fuckkkkk!" he roared, twisting his saber deeper. The impaled man sputtered blood and stumbled into the grass, taking the saber with him as he fell.

The last raider carried a scythe and kept his distance. He was a solid foot shorter than the Boy but built like a boulder. He was round and hard, beardless and hairless and tanned like dry earth. His curved tool stood a solid six feet tall, a grim mix of smooth wood and stained metal that far outstretched his lone hammer.

Magnus' son held the tool in his good arm, shifting his stance. He could feel the knife in his back, the metal poking into meat and muscle. He pawed at it but his arm was too sore, his busted shoulder refusing the motion. Around them, the fire burned hot and high, orange waves peeking through the haze. He hungered for clean air, his heart wavering. He began to doubt his ability to see it through. His body was tired. So tired. His feet hardened to iron, his legs cumbersome and shaky. The fog of war was clearing and all he wanted to do was flee. Questions nudged their way into his mind, distracting him.

Where is Beckett's daughter? Is the baby safe? Is Tom watching?

They pummeled his resolve, eroding his fragile confidence. He waved his hand, hoping the man would take the opportunity to leave.

"Go!" the Boy coughed, his eyes red and white and shining. "JUST GO! Please!"

He was nearly in tears, the world spinning as the loss of blood took its toll. The brigand didn't move. Didn't say a word.

Maybe he didn't even blink, the Boy couldn't tell, his own vision leaking focus. Staring at the boulder man, he drifted back to a world where none of this was possible. To a world where he was reading a book on the porch, listening to the distant waves and the grass blowing in the warm wind. To a world of more.

He threw the hammer.

The tool beat the air with practiced speed, hours of discipline forged to the moment. It battered the hot wind, the hum of it his anthem. The raider shifted, letting the tool slam against the wide blade of his scythe. The blow rang metallic as the hammer fell to the dirt.

Defeat snaked itself from his throat, whimpering into the bushy air. He could taste blood on his lips as it leaked from the gash along his cheek. He spat red into the embers.

You don't have to win.

He charged.

The scythe-wielding raider didn't hesitate. He swept his weapon low, kicking up dust as it scraped across the lane. The low slice prevented the Boy from sliding under it. It sought to remove his legs at the knee, the dark metal curving to greet him with its nightmarish embrace.

The Boy leapt instead. He cleared the blade and slammed into the big man. They tumbled into the burning grass together. Into the fire. Home.

41

The darkness was cold and slippery. Like wet, mossy stones or slick muck over trampled grass. It was a shallow darkness, inevitably and regrettably brief.

The Boy coughed himself awake. The spasm hurt every muscle, every bone. It was forced; liquid had filled his throat and his lungs were desperate for air. He hacked up the warm water before collapsing. The knife wound in his back pulsated; the blade was gone and he could feel the gash bleeding.

As his vision cleared, he turned his head to look around. He was in the creek bed—what was left of it. Water dribbled through his hair and down his neck. His clothes were damp. With heavy eyes, he blinked away the confusion, his brain a muddled mess. And then he saw her.

She was light and the world. Her hair swayed above him, sheltering him like the canopy of a willow tree. He reached toward her, his hand making it half the distance before she grabbed it.

"Not this time," he coughed. He did his best to hold a smile, his mouth somehow dry again.

"No," the Girl replied, blinking back a tear. "Not this time." Her smile was as bright as all the fires the Boy had ever seen.

"Where is—"

"She's here. She's safe. Sarris too."

Letting her go, the Boy fumbled for his tools. His movements were clumsy and disjointed, his arms heavy as stone.

"I have them," Beckett's daughter whispered. She placed the hammers on his chest. He wrapped his good arm around both, holding them close.

"Drink this," the Girl insisted, tipping her waterskin against his lips. "Then we'll go home."

Home.

He wrestled his exhaustion enough to sit up as Beckett's daughter poured water into his mouth. He swallowed a few sips before coughing, spitting up on his shirt and tools.

"Let's get you inside, okay?"

Before he could reply she was pulling him up. Pricks of light dazzled and spun as he rose. His left shoulder ached, the arm slow to move. His right forearm was tender, his sleeve blackened. No doubt the skin underneath was freshly burnt. The skin on the back of his neck felt tender too. Whether it was another burn or some unknown wound didn't matter. It was a problem for another day.

There would be another day.

Standing in front of him, Beckett's daughter pulled him close, holding him upright. Beaten and drained, he couldn't help but cling to her, kissing her cheek with bloody lips. She was the only thing holding his broken body together.

Pressing his arms out, the Boy leaned back to look her in the eyes. "I love y—"

His words were cut off by a gasp of surprise. His gasp.

Somehow, he was stumbling. Falling. His legs buckled under the surprised weight of himself as the ashen sky slid into view. The Girl was moving, her knife a silver haze. She was off kilter but managed to launch the weapon out of sight as the grass disappeared from his periphery. All he could see was sky. Sky and her. Sky and her and the blur of a crossbow bolt. It knocked her backward and out of view.

He hit the ground. His skull smacked off the hard dirt, the creek's pebbles and stones rounding into his skin. The stars were back, flashing madness over the upside down. Frantically, he flailed for his tools but they were scattered and out of reach. His throat was too dry to scream, though he managed to turn his head to see a wounded outlaw failing to pull a knife from his throat. He let the man die unseen.

A long moment passed as his senses steadied, his brain bucking at the darkness. Then, a voice.

"I'm okay," Beckett's daughter rasped, rolling over in the creek bed. The bolt had pierced straight through her left bicep, shredding her arm. Magnus' son crawled to her, dragging himself forward as she wrapped the wound tight with fabric torn from her other sleeve. It soaked through within a few breaths.

"I'm okay," she insisted, squeezing his hand as he neared. They embraced, bloody and sweat-soaked, collapsing into one another.

The Boy whimpered, his eyes half-glazed, blinking off the smoke. "We're okay. We're—"

Hands fumbled over his mouth, smothering him silent. He coughed and froze. Beckett's daughter paled. He could feel her blood dripping onto his face as her voice curdled to a whisper.

"There are more people coming."

Craning his neck, Magnus' son looked north to the tree line but his eyes were clouded by smoke and exhaustion. "How many?"

"Four. Maybe five?" the Girl counted.

"We need to hide. We can run."

Beckett's daughter cut him off, her tone firm and final. "We can't. They're coming this way and you can barely move. They'll find us."

The Boy fought back a tightness in his throat. He knew what was coming.

"I'll lead them off." She was already rummaging in her pack for another knife. "When the coast is clear, get inside." She pulled her daughter and Sarris, who was still in a sack, closer so the Boy could reach them. "The rifle is in the lane. Grab it if you can."

She kissed him on the head, holding him in her lap. He squeezed her hand, refusing to let go.

"I love you, Magnus' son. Keep our daughter safe."

He buried a scream, sobbing into her lap before he steadied himself. The world was still spinning, albeit slower. "I love you too," he wheezed.

"You need to let go now. You need to save our baby girl. Crawl if you have to, but you get her safe, okay?" She handed him a hammer.

He wiped his eyes before grabbing the tool.

"I'll see you soon." She kissed him hard on his bloodied lips. And then she was gone.

42

Her arm was numb. She could feel something dangling where her bicep was torn. Maybe skin, maybe muscle. Blood had already soaked through her shirt, dripping off her fingertips as she raced toward the road. She banked south at the end of the lane, leading the men away from the house. She looked back to make sure they followed. They did.

Dizziness kept pace as she pushed along the coast, the wide grey of the lake visible between the sparse scruff of trees that lazily hugged the last road.

When her vision began to dance and dazzle she slowed, breaking into the brush behind a mess of dying shrubs and thorns. A matted carpet of dead leaves crunched under the tired weight of her. Her lungs heaved, unhappy with the suddenness of being used. She exhaled into the crook of her good arm to stay quiet as she waited. Her left arm hung immobile at her side. For half a heartbeat, she worried it would need to be amputated.

You've got to survive first...

The thought nipped at her courage so she smothered it,

waiting for her moment to strike. When she heard footsteps, she pounced.

Side-stepping back onto the road, Beckett's daughter launched her knife. It took her assailant square in the chest. His dirty-blonde hair whipped from the lash, the wind forced from his lungs. His eager grin shattered into a contorted grimace as he stumbled and fell, his long legs jellied. Beckett's daughter rushed his body as he died, stealing back her knife and wrestling another free from his belt. She hadn't even stood up when someone barreled into her.

The collision sent her somersaulting across the dirt. She tasted blood, the packed earth scraping skin off both knees as she rolled. Before her eyes regained focus, a thickset woman with muscle-knotted calves and long red hair charged. The woman's two-handed axe chomped at her torso, biting into the lane not a finger-width from where the Girl had landed.

Beckett's daughter replied with her knife; it was in the woman's thigh before the axe swung back around. She gripped the handle and pulled herself up, the blade splitting meat and carving bone. Back on her feet, she twisted the weapon free and jabbed it into the red head's temple. The knife and the woman fell together. Beckett's daughter ran.

Shouts hounded her, the remaining three outlaws closing the distance. One stopped to check the bodies before sprinting onward. These three were younger. Faster. She could only hope they weren't smarter. She took the chase off-road, banking left into the woods opposite the water. It would be slow going but she was at least somewhat familiar with the area. Maybe that would give her an advantage.

For the better part of an hour she weaved through the dying woodland, pushing into denser brush. She didn't hide her grunts or wheezing, keeping her trail easy to follow. She had to stop twice to tie more cloth around her arm, the tourniquet so tight her fingers were numb. Only then, when she was still, did her mind drift to Magnus' son and her daughter. She hoped they were safe.

"They are," she insisted, kissing the hilt of her father's knife. "They have to be."

Squatting under a crisscrossed pair of fallen fir trees, the Girl groped for rocks or wood, launching what bits she found in opposite directions. She needed to get her attackers to separate. With just two knives, that was her only hope.

Peeking between the rotting logs, she waited for the trio to approach. They were less than a hundred feet away and slowed to a prowl. Staying low, she tossed another hunk of wood deeper into the brush. That got their attention.

"We ain't gonna hurt ya, missy!" one of the young men yelled, chuckling between rasps. "Well, we ain't gonna hurt you *too* much!"

"Speak fer yerself!" another spat. "That bitch made me run. I hate runnin'!"

As two of the raiders weaved toward a thicket, the third circled around, thinking to cut her off. She waited for him, fatigue and rage grappling for dominance in her gut. At ten feet, she could hear him huffing. His wheezing was heavy, as if his lungs had been dipped in sand. She let him get close; she couldn't waste another knife.

When he finally crept by, she lashed out and severed his Achilles tendon. He screamed as he fell, a gravelly mix of pain and surprise. By the time the raider hit the ground she had opened him up with both blades half a dozen times. Lifeless green eyes stared back at her from the forest floor. They were pretty eyes; little emeralds wrapped in a cloud. She could hear the other bandits rushing toward her but she stayed with the young man until his eyelids swallowed the gems.

She made a break back toward the road. Dodging between trees, jumping over shrubs and broken stones. Eventually, the forest thinned as the coast neared. Exhaustion pawed at her, harrying her every action. Her thoughts were growing sluggish too. Bounding back onto the road, she didn't even see the loose rocks. Her ankle rolled.

"Fuckkkk!" Pins and needles stabbed her foot and ankle as she tumbled into the dirt. The pain lanced up her leg, an electric jolt. "Get up!" she scolded. "Come on!"

She rose, testing her foot. She could walk. Barely. Behind her, the men neared; they were crashing through the forest, hooting and hollering like rabid animals. They'd flank her soon if she let them. She pushed on.

Limping across the road, she aimed for the coastline. A couple hundred paces away, the forest gave way to a rocky drop that crashed down to the water. It wasn't super high—maybe fifty or sixty feet—but the water below was shallow and riddled with boulders. But at least there, with her back to the grey, they wouldn't be able to surround her. That was her only chance. The two outlaws must have sensed her plan because they slowed. They knew she had nowhere to go.

Eventually, as her breathing settled, the pair sauntered into view. They oozed confidence, the hunger in their eyes something physical. The tallest of the duo led the way. He twirled a hatchet, bobbing his head as he neared like he was listening to music she couldn't hear. His eyes were too close together and large, even as he squinted. He waved when he was just twenty feet off.

"Bit of a mess back there, eh?" he grinned. "You owe us an apology, I reckon."

Beckett's daughter stayed silent. She could take two. She had to. They were in the way of her getting back to her daughter. To her family.

The pair shuffled closer.

"Just a quick apology? We'll be gentle, I promise."

This time, she didn't freeze. She didn't hesitate. Her knife took the big-eyed man in shoulder, embedding itself in meat.

"Ahhhooohhhh! You little bitch!" he cussed, dancing off the pain. "Fuck! That don't tickle." He poked at the knife protruding from his shoulder. "Helluva throw!" he muttered through gritted teeth, genuinely impressed. "Quicker than lightnin'. Damn."

"Think she's got some other talents too?" his friend winked.

The big-eyed outlaw slowly teased the knife free, testing his arm. He kept the weapon, stepping in with a hatchet and her knife raised. Beckett's daughter pulled her last knife—her father's knife—and kissed the handle.

"Another knife?" the big-eyed man snorted. "What else you hidin' under those clothes?"

"Why don't you come and find out?" she quipped. Her heart was a cannon, thumping explosions. Her throat was tight and dry. Her right hand was slick with sweat, her left slick with blood. They were just under ten feet away.

"If you insist," the outlaw bowed. He attacked.

Beckett's daughter let him come, ducking under his hatchet as it sailed over her. She poked him hard in the guts but he slashed her across the back at the same time. Her father's knife slipped from her grip as they stumbled apart. A fresh wave of blood flooded down her shirt. The big-eyed man looked pale as he took a knee, breathing heavy. "Finish the bitch off!" he barked at his friend.

Her knife was just three feet away, laying atop the wind-blown weeds. It might as well have been a mile. Her ankle throbbed. Moving was a grueling affair. Keeping focus was taxing, her blinks getting slower by the minute. She needed a solution but her thoughts abandoned her, leaving her fate to the flat-nosed brigand in front of her. In his hand, a foot-long dagger glinted in the sun.

"It's yer lucky day, girl," the bandit grinned, "Sharpened it this mornin' fer a shave. Be nice now, or I'll fuck ya with it."

Beckett's daughter took a step backward. She'd need to lure

him in close. Get him off balance. That was her only chance. Send the fucker over the edge.

"Bring that needledick of yours here and let's see what you got," she taunted. She took another hobbled step back before faking a lunge for her knife. The outlaw sprung forward, hoping to beat her to the blade. She let him come.

When the man was two feet away, he faltered and screamed, tripping into her at the knees. His eyes were wide in surprise as he pawed at her. There was an arrow in his back. Beckett's daughter stared at it as they toppled over the edge. It was the last thing she saw before the grey-glass lake swallowed her whole.

43

His nightmares broke to the sound of his daughter crying. Mouth dry and head pounding, he sat up quick. Too quick. His vision careened into a lopsided dance that left him woozy. He reached out with his hand to steady himself, the familiar trickle of drool fresh on his face. He wiped it on his bare forearm before pushing himself to his feet and padded over to the child, scooping up the fragile infant with his good arm. Even so small, she felt heavy.

"Shhhh. I'm here now," he coughed. "I'm here." He pressed the child against him, bouncing her as best he could, his body still stiff and tired. "It's okay."

He doubted the words as soon as they were given shape, feeling their hollowness. When the child refused to calm, he set her down on the threadbare sofa, pressing pillows around her before getting a fire going. As light gave birth to sight, he noticed it wasn't drool but blood that had flooded his face. It was all over his neck and smeared along his daughter's face. It was everywhere. He remembered, now, stitching the crossbow wound on his cheek before passing out. He must have done a crude job of it as the threads were already loose. He poked at the gash as his daughter continued fretting in the glow. She was hungry, that much he knew. But what could he do about it?

"Hello?" he called out. The house felt empty but he called out again before walking upstairs.

Maybe she came home and passed out like I did.

Beckett's daughter wasn't upstairs. He didn't see her in the backyard or the front field either.

"She'll be back," he whispered to his daughter as he checked the kitchen again for signs of her. "Once it's safe, mamma will be back..."

He took a moment to collect himself, poking and prodding his ear to feel the damage from the bolt. His earlobe was gone, the wound sealed with a hot blade. He had been in no shape or mood to play surgeon in such an awkward place. He had done the same with the knife wound in his back, burning it clean and closed before blacking out. It still throbbed, sore and itchy from the inside out. Further triage would have to wait. His daughter needed food and he was utterly unprepared to deal with that.

Checking the front door to make sure it was bolted, he took a candle into the cellar to inspect his options. Until Beckett's daughter returned, he'd need something to feed their child.

He found Sarris relaxing in the cool dark of the basement, pecking at some oats on the floor with a lazy indifference.

"Did I give you those?" He kept his jaw tight to avoid stretching his torn cheek. While the rooster snacked, he held up his light to look over the shelves.

"Canned pears...pickled cabbage...canned tomatoes... dried...?" He picked up a bag and smelled it before setting it back on the grubby shelf. "Thyme. Not helpful." He rested on the stairs, out of breath and aching. "Okay, think. How did they used to feed babies without a parent?" he asked the bird, his throat scratchy and sore.

"They used a wet nurse," he replied to himself

"But how did they feed babies without a wet nurse?"

"They used animal milk."

"Okay, but how did they feed babies *without* animals...?"

It was a question he didn't have an answer to. He hoped that it was merely due to his exhaustion, though he didn't have the luxury of waiting. The baby needed to eat. Setting the candle on the ground to wipe his eyes, he took a moment to settle himself. No ideas came. Without the Girl, their daughter would starve.

"I can't do this Sarris," he sobbed, feeling the walls of the cellar close in around him. "I can't do this alone."

He let the tears come, giving in to despair as it ensnared him with violent memories. The Luddstow boy bleeding out in his arms. The echo of his mother's last bullet. The cold whisper of his father's dying breath. And now, added to the heap was the smoky silhouette of Beckett's daughter sprinting into the distance, hounded by violence. It was an avalanche of misery, a toxic swamp sucking him deeper and deeper into its murkiness.

"No," he whimpered, balling his fists. "She'll be back." He chased her down in his mind, corralling pieces of her. Her smile, her laugh. How she whispered lullabies to her daughter by the dancing light of the fire. He held onto the flotsam of her. He hoarded it. "She'll be back."

When his hands stopped shaking, Magnus' son reached down and picked up the spilled oats and wheat. He pressed a fistful between his fingers, grinding them together and watching the powder fall to the floor as he contemplated his options. As he stared, head hung low, a drop of blood rolled off his chin into the oat dust. A tear followed, mixing into the paste. In the corner, Sarris scurried after a bug.

"Wait a second..."

Leaving the candle, he limped into the kitchen and scoured the pantry for an open sack of oats. Emptying them into a stone bowl, he ground them into powder with his good arm before dumping the bits into a pot. He added some ground wheat, some water, and set it over the woodstove to boil, whisking the mixture while it heated. Once boiled, he strained it into his canteen, sealing the mouth with a nub of bunched cloth the baby could suck on. When it was room temperature, he walked back down into the cellar and grabbed the candle.

"Thanks for listening, Sarris. I'd be lost without you, buddy."

He shambled upstairs and muddled his way through feeding the baby his cooled oat and wheat water. It wasn't particularly tasty—and likely not particularly suitable for an infant—but he hoped it would suffice. The two fell asleep together in the den shortly after, his daughter curled in his arms. For the first time in a long time, he slept soundly.

THE ENTIRE NEXT day was spent resting and waiting. Tending to his wounds, making batches of oat water for his daughter. His shoulder was a rainbow of purples and blues and browns, swollen and sling-bound. It hurt to move; hurt to talk, the tear along his cheek resewn too tight for comfort. His ear pulsated like a sunburn. Movement was exhausting. Thinking was exhausting. But he couldn't risk waiting any longer. He needed to find her.

Armed with his mother's rifle, he limped out into the dawn, leaving Sarris and the baby barred in the cool cellar. Outside, smoke lingered over the homestead, thick in his nostrils. The field before him, once a gentle wave of tall grass and rows of wheat and corn, was dark burnt and dead. Scorch marks cut along the edge of the porch, the house itself saved by its wide garden that had kept the worst of the flames at bay. Rifle level, he eyeballed the horizon. When nothing stirred he made his way down the lane, checking for fresh tracks in the soot and ash. The scattered bodies were mostly burnt up. He didn't bother with them. Not yet.

As he dragged himself to the road, he conjured dreams of her. Pictured her breaking through the trees, bloodied but alive. Pictured them together, living out their days at the end of the world. He played back her voice, basking in her tones and tempo. The way her words could be pressing but warm. How she spoke when she was tired versus how she spoke when she was annoyed. How she would braid and unbraid her hair when she was in a mood. They were going to build a life together. He was excited for it.

He returned to the present when he heard a noise. Down by the wagons on the road, a goat was bleating. He wasn't particularly interested in it at first, his eyes scanning the tree line for the Girl or danger. But then his brain took over.

"Milk!" he exclaimed, picking up his pace. As he crested the hill, he saw the goat. There was a man on the road too. It was Tom.

"Bastard!" Magnus' son cursed.

Gripping the rifle, he hurried toward his unsuspecting nemesis. He needed to get close. Close enough to guarantee his bullet would taste blood.

He limp-sprinted over the scorched earth, rifle raised, pushing his beaten body onward. His shoulder ached from the weight of the gun. Revenge tasted acrid on his tongue. He welcomed the flavor.

As the distance narrowed, he slowed his pace, letting himself catch his breath as he crouched. Tom still hadn't seen him. After a dozen more paces he started crawling, snaking across the razed field. Soot and dirt powdered his clothing and smudged his face. He could taste the fire in the earth as it brushed his lips. His left hand tingled, his shoulder a throbbing bolt of pain. On the road, the bleating continued, repetitive cries concealing his approach. He closed the gap as Tom tugged the reluctant goat forward, struggling to lead the animal away from the posse's abandoned wagons.

Greedy for vengeance, Magnus' son took aim. He waited a few breaths to steady himself. Prostrate on the ground, he pushed the air out from his lungs, ever so slowly squeezing the trigger. Tom staggered.

The Boy leapt up, an ecstatic fury pressing him forward. He readied another bullet, pushing aside the tidal wave of pain that was engulfing him. Tom squirmed on the ground near the edge of the road. The Boy stopped, aimed, and shot him again. The second bullet tore a hole through the man's thigh.

"TOMMM!" he roared, slinging the rifle across his back. In its place, he drew a hammer. He funneled his budding rage into the tool as he neared, strangling the handle white-knuckle tight. He devoured the man with ravenous eyes, smiling as Tom writhed and twisted on the road. Blood smeared over the packed earth, spilling into its dark cracks.

Towering over the soon-to-be-dead man, Magnus' son brought his hammer to his lips, kissed the metal, and slammed it against Tom's spine. The man's cry of pain was met by another primal shout from the Boy, who brought the tool down again, this time against Tom's tailbone.

"I'LL KILL YOU!" he screamed, his voice ragged and dry.

Using his good arm, he grabbed the scruff of Tom's tunic and flipped him over. He wanted to look the man in the eyes when he killed him. He wanted to see it. To see justice.

But it wasn't Tom. Staring back at him was a dying man, bearded and pale and wheezing bloodied breath. The man's eyes were frantic and wide, blue-green orbs clinging to their final moments. He raised a shaky hand to the Boy, pressing up from the dust to gasp for mercy.

"Fuck!" Magnus' son snapped, whipping his hammer into the dirt. He ignored the man's outstretched arm, stomping off toward the wagon. He kicked one of its wheels, startling the sickly horses still attached to its yoke. "FUCK!"

The dull pain from his shoulder evolved into a sharp pinching of nerves. The sewn skin on his cheek felt like a hand smothering him. Blood leaked from the wound and curved over his lips. He was winded. He thought about kicking the wagon again but was too tired. The lone wanderer fidgeted a few feet away, clinging to a diminishing life. The Boy left him be, pulling the blinders off the horses before cutting them free. Their reluctance to move kept them standing more or less in place as he marched back to the dying man.

"Ple-ple-please," came a stuttering whisper, "I have a so—"

The Boy plunged his knife into the man's chest. Steel grated on bone before pressing through the thickness of muscle. He felt the heart contract, the suction tugging at the weapon as he held it there. The dying man stopped twitching.

Upon closer inspection, the man looked quite dissimilar to Tom save the shirt and the hair. Magnus' son stared into the man's lifeless eyes for a long moment before wiping his blade clean on the dead man's sleeve. He could hear this father's chiding heckles of disappointment rattle in the back of his mind.

Collecting his weapons, and leaving the corpse to bake in the sun, he looked over the wagons. There was food to be had —canned goods and jars of various vegetables, as well as some weary-looking brassicas and wormy seed potatoes—but more importantly, there was a goat, which had plodded back to the second wagon. It started bleating again as he approached.

"Hey goat," he whistled. "Are you a...?" He bent down to see if it was a doe. It was.

Ripping some grass from the edge of the lane, he tempted the doe with a fistful of greenery. It chomped at it briefly before bleating once more, ignoring the gift. He gave the animal a scratch behind the ear and continued his inspection.

He found bodies in the back of the second wagon. Three tiny, furry kids laid motionless in a cramped pen. They were still small, no more than a week or two old. Flies swarmed the corpses, a buzzing cloud of black feasting on the remains.

The doe ambled over, bleating as she looked up at him. The dead baby goats stifled the growing bloodlust that had beset him moments prior, the grim reality of unexpected consequences sitting heavy on his shoulders.

If I had died yesterday, they'd likely still be alive, he realized. Guilt trickled in with its natural and practiced subtly. "No. No. That's not on me," he insisted. "That's on them. That's on Tom."

Merely saying his name sewed threads of anger in the foreground of his thoughts. But it also reminded him he might not be alone. It was time to get back to the house and check on his daughter. He'd have to look for Beckett's daughter tomorrow; what little energy he had was spent, his body longing for respite.

Emptying a bushel basket of rotten food, he placed the dead baby goats inside. They would be buried. He grabbed the doe's lead and pulled the fussing goat home, death and hope in his hands.

44

After three days of searching he found her knife. It was laying atop a trampled patch of weeds on an overhang near the lake. A body was there too but it wasn't hers. Below, slender wavelets met their fate against snaggletooth rocks. He set his daughter, who had been wrapped against his back, in the grass and shimmied to the edge. He didn't see any bodies in the shallows. Walking back to the road, he followed the tracks, searching for more clues.

Did they take her? Did she jump?

Not knowing chewed at him, worming its way through his already overwhelmed defenses. He hunted for a path down to the water but it was too treacherous for him in his state. Back on the clifftop, he followed the footprints again.

"If she jumped and survived she might need help. She might come home. But if she was captured..." If she was captured, he'd need to chase down whoever took her. But that would mean leaving the farm. That would mean going south.

And what if I leave and she comes back?

He squeezed the rifle in his grip, frustration coiling around him like some ancient serpent. He nudged a stone off the edge before resting beside his daughter in the weeds.

What would my father do? No, not him. What would Beckett's daughter do? What would she do if the situation was reversed?

"She would look for me," he nodded. "She wouldn't give up."

He scooped up his daughter so she was wrapped across his chest, kissing her tiny hands as she grasped at the fabric. "So we won't give up."

Hiking into the brush, he searched for a viable path to the water. When he found one, he doubled back toward the cliff. It was slow going along the shore until he reached the grey waves, thin and soft against his ankles. Setting his daughter—and the carbine—in a rocky nook of loose stone, he waded into the lake. It wasn't deep but there were jagged, algae-covered boulders scattered on the lakebed. Most were enveloped by brown mussels, their hard shells drawing red from his hands and feet as he pushed deeper.

Eventually, he was swimming though the water wasn't more than six or seven feet deep. He craned his neck up to the clifftop. With all these rocks, surviving the drop would be a coin toss at best.

The thought capsized him. His muscles started to waiver and he gulped a mouthful of water, sputtering in the shallows. He panicked, flailing at the realization that she might actually be gone. Then he saw the body.

It was drawn against the base of the cliff, beaten and battered and misshapen. Strings of seaweed clung to the corpse like straw poking out of a scarecrow. He swam to it, the rocks and mollusks cutting up his knees and toes. His heart was drowning.

It was a man. His face was waterlogged and half bowed from the fall, his skin nibbled at by small things. In his hand, looped around his rigored fist, was a piece of fabric. It was from the Girl's shirt.

"No..."

Around him, the lake water tinted red as he sank. He became a boulder, cold and unbreathing. He stayed on the lakebed until his lungs burned. Until his muscles convulsed and blackness hummed in his ears. Only when the ending neared did he push himself up for air. He was weeping by then, blood and salt spilled amongst the waves.

Pitter-patter.

MAGNUS' son brooded for weeks. He searched the road and nearby woods every few days but found nothing, souring his mood further. He hadn't the strength to work or train so he simply drifted the days away with his family—past and present. Sometimes he waited up in the attic on lookout for Beckett's daughter but deep down he knew she must have went over the edge. That she was gone.

Yet he hoped nonetheless, conjuring daydreams and fantasies of her return. Of their future. Of anything that would drag him from the septic reality around him.

He never bothered with the bodies in the yard, leaving them to the sun and bugs. Their rancid balm spilled like the overripe bounty of some corpulent fruit but he grew indifferent to the stench. Some afternoons, when the air sizzled, he would watch the bodies decompose. Ants came in droves, feasting in single file. Flies swarmed. Maggots wiggled. As days became weeks, the bodies dried and shrunk in the continuous heat, their leathery skin thinning like wet cloth pulled taut. Sometimes they would shift, from the wind or the rain.

Fearing Tom, he stayed inside for days at a time. He even stopped using the outhouse, relieving himself in a makeshift chamber pot instead.

At night, he would bring Sarris and the goat—which he named Gamling—up into his room, bolting the door. He slept with the rifle on one side of the bed and his daughter on the other. The animals shared Rachel's bed. She would have gotten a kick out of that, he suspected. His parents, too, though his father would by no means tolerate the mess.

"Get this cleaned up by noon, son, or there'll be trouble," his father would have barked, his face a contorted mix of displeasure and amusement. His brow would be cross though his mouth would be curved in the beginnings of a smile. The words would be firm, but not angry or surprised. Nothing ever really surprised his father. It was something the Boy, floundering in calamity, was beginning to understand. As he curled into bed, the Boy made himself a promise.

"I'm never going to be surprised again."

A MONTH PASSED before he finally ventured back to the cliff. The air was dry with a slight breeze, the grey lake almost blue in the brightness. In an ugly world, it was beautiful.

"I miss you," he whispered, crossing his legs in the weeds. His daughter was with him, curled in his arms. "I hope you're okay...wherever you are."

He ripped out a handful of weeds and stepped lightly to the edge, his daughter in his arms. He cast the greenery into the air and watched it tumble in the breeze. It would be so easy to follow. To take another step. To let it all go.

Pitter-patter.

The wind tickled his ears, urging him on. He shifted his weight.

His nameless daughter cooed. She was staring at him, smiling.

"I shouldn't have fired at Tom. It's my fault," he sobbed,

collapsing into the scraggly weeds. He pulled her knife and kissed the handle like she always did.

Tom's treachery flashed in his mind. How he must have sold them out to the posse, how he sought to raid their home and leave them for dead. It was enraging.

"No...it's Tom's fault. Tom did this to us." He stabbed the knife into the shallow dirt. "Tom did this."

He stabbed it again and again and again, his father's temper brewing. He wanted to scream but his voice was shot, his throat stealing away even his whispers.

Instead, he let himself dream of vengeance. He gorged on it like some bountiful feast, binging in the grass as he listened to the lullaby of blue-grey waves. A thousand plans came and went, a thousand ways to kill Tom teased and tempted him. Most were impractical—or impossible—but there was one idea that could work. One plan that could balance the scales.

"I think I've got it," the Boy whispered to his daughter. "It will take some time to prepare, but I think I know how we'll kill Tom Luddstow."

45

It took a week to organize. Collecting the firewood, making birch oil, packing supplies. He had to be subtle in case Tom was spying. To tempt the man into action, he started eating all his meals on the porch. If Tom wanted food, he'd have to come and get it.

Once everything was ready he waited an extra week just in case Beckett's daughter returned. In his heart he knew she wouldn't. But somewhere inside of him, threads of optimism clung to life like stubborn grass on weathered stone. He went out each day searching, walking the shore and the road and the woods. But he found nothing.

"I guess it's time," he whispered to his daughter, tapping the letters against her tiny hand.

With everything packed, Magnus' son filled the den with firewood and dry grass, dousing it with his most recent batch of oil. The tarry substance coated the wood, pooling onto the floor like black blood. All the food had been shoved into bags and crates and piled in a makeshift pushcart. Gamling was leashed and Sarris was safe in a small wooden cage. His knife and sword had been sharpened and he had even done laundry and dressed himself in clean clothing. He wanted it to be perfect.

After checking the fields from the attic, he crept out into the blackness of night and stashed the trio in the ditch by the road. Skulking from shadow to shadow, he scurried back into the house and lit the fire that would inaugurate his vengeance.

The blaze spread in a matter of seconds, lapping up the oil as the grass sizzled and ashed. He didn't wait for the wood to catch, fleeing into the phantom night.

Magnus' son shouted his invitation to the night. "HELP! FIRE!"

He hid near the creek, obscured by a few tufts of grass and an outcropping of stone, keeping his eyes on the Luddstow ruins and the forest opposite. Tom would likely come from one of those directions. He would need to be quick, too, knowing full well that all the goods inside would soon go up in flames. Once Tom was in sight and rushing to the house, the Boy would strike.

He squeezed his rifle's forestock in anticipation, wiping the sweat from his palms onto his clean trousers. For the first time in weeks, he felt awake, his shoulder sore but ready. He pressed his toes into the ground, swallowing hard. It was a risky plan, but he knew it would pay off. Tom would be desperate by now. And that would be the man's downfall.

The fire grew. As it came of age, the Boy slinked further into the shadow to evade the bright of the budding inferno. He avoided staring at the light too, protecting his night vision as he scanned for Tom. Waiting. Watching. Hungry. He kept his finger on the trigger, eyeing into the abyss, combing it for motion. The hot pitch of burnt wood huddled over him, a canopy of smoke and familiar heat.

He'll come. He's just cautious.

After five minutes the house was awash in heat and light

though the Boy had seen no sign of his quarry. After another five, doubt trickled in. He crawled closer to the Luddstow ruins, snaking through the grass. Shadows bred shadows as the crackling heat and splintering of wood filled the broiling air around him as. Shimmying over the creek bed, he took a closer look among the ruins. There was no one to be seen.

As the fire crested, the Boy stood up. He would have his vengeance. "TOM! I KNOW YOU'RE HERE!" he screamed over the rising inferno. "FACE ME!"

His words lurched across the heavy, hot air. He stepped out into the light. "TOM! TOM!?!"

The night gave no reply, save the rolling din of his home ablaze. As he paced the field, panic crept into his mind, the reality of his actions taking hold.

"Nonononono!"

The fire peaked, its yellow aura consuming itself. It wouldn't be long before it was more coals and embers than raging flame. His house—his home—would soon be nothing.

"Tom! Fight me!" he quivered. "Fight me!"

Night swallowed his words. No answer came. Smoke claimed his lungs as his mind fractured in a thousand directions, each one arriving at the same terminus.

What have I done?

FROM THE HALF-COLLAPSED attic where he took refuge in the raided village, Tom watched the hazy outline of a fire far in the distance. It didn't last long, the orange hue rising only to be swallowed by the starless night.

Naturally, his mind wandered to the fire that took his own home, to the night Magnus and his bastard son ruined his life. But the thoughts loitered for only a few moments. He dug into his coat and pulled out a dented flask, opening it and bringing it to his nose. It had been empty for weeks but the smell was all he needed to cool his temper, closing his eyes to the ruins of Hope and the place he now called home.

46

There was nothing to salvage. Save the stone foundation, the entire homestead had been gutted by the blaze. Blackened timbers leaned upon one another like ashen flagpoles, fragile fingers of burnt wood stabbing out of the roofless heap. Everything was sooty and coated in smoky snow. The air was noxious and thick. It was a miserable place and Magnus' son had no one to blame but himself.

They lived in the torched remnants of the homestead for a few days while the Boy drowned himself in pity, happy to postpone his return to the village. Then, when his lungs couldn't take another breath of failure, they packed up and left. It was a paltry shelter and no place for a child, its existence a permanent reminder of his foolishness.

Before he left, he collected a handful of stones and spelled out HOPE on the lane. Just in case she came back. He then dragged a small pushcart from the barn and loaded it with supplies. There was too much for him to carry by himself and the cart was hard on his shoulder so he jury-rigged a rope harness for Gamling, allowing the goat to pull the load. The stubborn animal would have none of it.

"Stop—just stop chewing it!" he snapped, tugging the rope from Gamling's mouth. When he pulled it free, the doe stopped in her tracks. Again.

"For fuck's sake!" he groaned, pushing the animal with his good arm. After half an hour of butting heads with Gamling, he gave up. He unharnessed the animal and tied her to the back of a wagon on a long lead. Hoisting the handles of the cart, he did his best to pull the wagon himself.

"Don't blame me if you all get eaten," he barked as they limped toward Hope, rifle slung helplessly across his back.

A flimsy roof of clouds rolled in, cooling the air in a rare act of charity. The morning had been spent waiting in the ditch for signs of movement on the road. Watching. Preparing. Tom never came though, and the Boy had come to grips with the full dimensions of his stupidity. He was ashamed, and for the first time in a long time, he was happy he was alone. He couldn't bear to be scolded or chastened now. Not after what he did.

He looked back to Gamling, the goat already trailing behind. She had stopped to eat a bunch of thistles that sprouted at the edge of the road, chomping the purple flowers and sharp needles with her usual indifference.

"No, don't eat that!" he nagged. "There's grass right here!" He waved his hands toward the weeds near his feet but the goat didn't budge, content to munch the thistles.

Magnus' son stared, his mind unraveling like a ball of twine in the wind. He set the cart down. Gamling continued to grind the thistles into mush. Small thorns poked from her chin. The Boy pulled them free and flicked them into the brush when the doe meandered by, giving her a scratch behind the ears.

"Don't eat those things, dummy," he huffed, patience fraying. "Just because you can stomach them doesn't mean you should." He bent down and yanked a thick handful of grass and dandelions, holding them aloft for the doe.

"Here." He offered the goat the grass, which she eventually took, giving her another scratch behind the ear.

They set up camp in the bush just off the road, making sure he was far enough away should anyone pass in the night. He uncoiled a spool of barbed wire and set a perimeter. There would be no fire, but the night was warm enough and he had a quilt should it get cool. Rifle in hand, he tucked himself between Gamling, who had sprawled in the dirt, and his daughter. He read them whispered pages from a book before it got too dark. They fell asleep to the delicate whisper of the wounded forest and the hopeful thoughts of those who lived.

Pitter-patter. Pitter-patter.

It was a dream. *The* dream. Of bones and endings. Of white oceans and their violent tides. It jarred him awake with its familiarity. Its inevitability.

Sitting up in the wood, the Boy scanned the scene in every direction. Something felt off. Like a déjà vu of déjà vu. It was just a feeling, a discomfort below the skin that left him ill at ease. But it lingered. Gamling sensed it too, her ears perked.

"My thoughts exactly," he whispered, grabbing the carbine.

Breathing in the new day, he could almost taste the pine and dry bark in the mulchy air. The dirt on his hands, more dust than loam, was feeble and windblown. Nothing stirred as he waited so he waited longer, crouched behind the wagon, every sense urging alertness.

But the world showed him nothing.

Begrudgingly, he eased his senses and broke camp. He fought the cart back to the road, stirring up a racket as he bounced and tripped over dried roots and ratty shrubs.

"Well, they know where we are," he grumbled to the group, not bothering to look back as he continued toward Hope. Sarris crowed in his cage as the wagon rolled, bucking against his small pen.

"Hey, I didn't get breakfast either, so don't blame me," he replied, turning to Gamling. "He's grumpy in the morning. Takes after my da' in that regard."

As they rolled along, Magnus' son combed the scrawny wood that straddled the road. A troublesome sense of ill-defined unease hounded him. He was confident something was amiss. Yet that confidence was fragile and lined with doubt. He had felt that same confidence about Tom and his plan to lure him to the fire...a feeling that proved disastrously misguided.

He stopped anyway. Standing in the middle of the road, he slipped the rifle from his back and waited. Maybe it was nothing. Maybe it was her. Maybe it was something worse. He'd wait and see, remembering his new-found vow.

"No surprises," he whispered.

A handful of minutes passed. Then a handful more. Then, noise.

Three people sauntered into view. He could tell by their voices they were young. They crossed from the woods onto the road some fifty feet ahead. He kept the gun ready but didn't raise it. He was changing tack.

From less there will be more...

"Mornin'," he waved. "That's far enough, please."

They flinched, weapons drawn, as they looked around. For a second, they hesitated. But then, seeing he was alone, the trio plodded closer.

"I said that's far enough," he hollered, raising the weapon to his shoulder. That's when he recognized them. The McKelsies.

The tallest of the trio, and likely the oldest now that Fort was gone, was a gangly kid. He looked sixteen or so, with long limbs that dangled past his belt and a mouth that was all gums. He was taller than the Boy, but thin. Rooted along his jawline was a shabby beard the color of a bird's nest. A heavy head of brown hair topped him like a helmet. At his side, his brother held a short bow. It was homemade and crude but the Boy didn't doubt its effectiveness. Like his brother, he too was a mess of lanky joints that looked like they were pieced together in haste. Maybe they were twins, the Boy didn't recall.

It was clear that they had seen trouble. The youngest McKelsie's busted nose was crooked and recently bloodied. It sat at an unseemly angle, like a jigsaw piece forced into the wrong spot. One of the eldest's hands was bruised and skinned, dry blood tracing lines down his neck in dirt-stained streaks.

"It's...yer the fucker who killed our brother!" the tallest McKelsie cussed.

Magnus' son didn't reply.

"It's him!" said the twin, his curved short bow slack in his grip.

"The b-burnt boy," the youngest mocked. He was shorter than his brothers, a couple years their junior. His hair was just as bulbous and dark, though his face lacked their skeletal gauntness, his limbs more rounded and proportionate.

"I don't want any trouble," Magnus' son replied, eyeing the trio. "Have....have you seen a girl recently?"

The trio exchanged glances, chuckling to one another.

"You can have some food if you answer," he added.

"You got food?" the tall boy grinned, moseying forward. "Lucky us!"

The Boy leveled his gun. "Don't."

"Pfff. Like fuck ya got bullets I bet. Yer just—"

He pulled the trigger. An avalanche of noise buried McKelsie's words as a bullet slammed into the dirt at their feet.

"I've got bullets," he confirmed, priming the weapon for a second shot. "But I don't want to waste them."

He lowered the rifle, setting it in the wagon. His eyes stayed on the group as he fumbled in his pack for a peace offering. He tossed two cans toward them.

"Take them and go. Just tell me if you've seen anyone recently."

The McKelsies eyeballed the cans as they rolled to stop in the road.

"We ain't leavin'," the twin spat. "And we ain't sayin' shit. You killed our brother so we're gonna kill you. Fair's fair."

"I don't want any trouble," the Boy reiterated, letting his arms drop to his sides in anticipation of a foregone conclusion. He held his ground, refusing to make the first move. "Just take the food," he implored. "Please."

The twin reached for an arrow. The Boy was faster. A hammer chugged its way into the archer's face, beating teeth from home and watering the morning with a dew of blood.

So much for changing tack...

The tall McKelsie charged, forcing the Boy to side step under a sweeping cut from a knife. As he slipped under the attack he drew his saber, flicking the blade upward to remove a few fingers from McKelsie's hand as it soared past. The Boy followed up with the guard of his sword, sending tall McKelsie into unconsciousness.

The sole remaining brother was behind him now, chopping down with a hatchet. He let the attack come, not even bothering to turn and face it. Dropping to a knee, he caught the wood of the axe with his saber. The force of the blow shook him but he held the weapon at bay. As the youngest McKelsie pulled back for another chop, the Boy elbowed him in the groin, slipping his blade between the kid's legs but pausing before he did any irreparable damage.

Catching a hint of movement from the corner of his eye, he looked up to see the archer, still on the ground, aiming a shot. He side-stepped as the missile flew. The arrow punched into the guts of the youngest McKelsie. The kid shrieked and stumbled back, clutching the wound and the wood that filled it.

"What did I fucking tell you!" the Boy shouted as he stalked toward the archer. "I said I didn't want trouble!"

He grabbed the twin by the quiver, shaking the arrows free and battering them with his saber until they broke.

"Did I stutter?" He kicked the kid in the chest. "Were my intentions unclear?" He kicked the kid again before severing the bow string and hurling the weapon into the woods. The young McKelsie was groaning in the road, his stomach leaking blood. Magnus' son stomped back to him and cut open the kid's shirt. The wound was low, well into the intestines. There was nothing he could do. "And now your brother's gonna die. All because you wouldn't answer a simple question!"

"You can...you can stitch..." young McKelsie whimpered, his voice cracking. The kid's brown gums were in a dark state of rot, a boggy gulf walled in by yellowed teeth.

"I could stitch it up, but it's in your guts. Your intestines are punctured and there will be bits of cloth and wood in the wound so it will fester. I'm no surgeon."

His words were tempered, though on the inside he was seething. He had tried to do the right thing and this was his reward. A part of him wanted to scream at the injustice. Another part wanted to bash the kid's face in.

"You can...try...please..." young McKelsie groaned. The kid's wet hands were smeared red and slippery against his forearm.

"Okay," the Boy conceded. "I'll try."

Kneeling beside the wounded McKelsie, he wiped away the blood that pooled on the kid's stomach. "This is going to hurt so close your eyes. On the count of three I'll pull it out."

Young McKelsie nodded.

"One. Two..."

The young McKelsie winced, jaw tense as he waited for the sudden jolt of pain. It never came. Instead, the Boy slid his knife into the kid's skull, ending his suffering.

"I told you," he whispered, holding onto the kid, fighting back a sudden onslaught of tears. "Why wouldn't you listen?"

After a silent moment, Magnus' son shuffled over to the ditch and ripped out a handful of weeds. The nettles and this-tles stung but he ignored the pinching itch, scattering them on the dead boy's chest. Just like his sister used to do in their mock battles. He didn't bother with a prayer. No one was listening.

He picked up the two cans he had thrown and set them beside the surviving McKelsies, adding two more to the pile. As he slung the rifle back over this shoulder and grabbed the handles of the cart, the Boy turned to the duo.

"It doesn't have to be like this, you know. And I'm sorry for your brother." He looked to the dead McKelsie in the road. "Brothers."

He walked off without looking back, leaving the past where it fell.

47

He watched the village from the outskirts for over an hour. Nothing moved. No sounds, no life. Just a tableau of destruction, the fired ruins more rubble than remnant. Grass had crept its way into the settlement, untrimmed and untrampled. What houses were salvageable had long since been ransacked. Black scorch marks sketched permanent shadows over the uneven stone of the village hall, its centuries-old colored glass either smashed or missing. High on the bluff, the torched frame of the Beckett house sat watch. If there were people forced to labor in the quarry, they had long since left. Across the square, the schoolhouse—where his parents had hoped he would write the exams—was gutted and torched.

"I never liked the noise...but this..."

With weary and wary footsteps, Magnus' son left the brush and entered the village. He pulled the cart to the main hall as quietly as he could. Not a sound rivaled him. He parked the cart by the hall door, walking the hall's exterior, checking for traps and signs of life. Finding none, he checked again. He would not be surprised. Not this close to the end.

A few shards of stained glass crunched underfoot as he explored. He stopped, picking up one of the larger pieces and holding it toward the sun. How nice it must have been to live in a world with the luxury of making beautiful things. No motive. No practical excuse. Just art for the sake of it.

"It must have been special," he sighed, turning to the wagon-bound trio. Sarris was preening himself in his cage while Gamling gazed around the square with her usual indifference. His daughter fidgeted, irritated from the pressing heat. An eerie silence hovered over them. He'd never seen Hope so lifeless. The familiar smells—of people, of food—were gone. No nebulous din shaped the background. It was unfilled; a fresh nothingness carved into the coast.

After checking the building over, he lifted the heavy latch and opened the iron-bound door. Standing in the threshold of the hall, his senses tested the space before him. The air was murky and dust-laden. Rot tickled his nostrils. Something—or someone—had died inside. He tip-toed forward, pausing every other step to listen. When he saw no signs of life he dragged his cart inside and barricaded the door behind him.

"Keep an eye on them, Sarr," he whispered, creeping down the hall. He found nothing in the main chamber save a few birds nesting in the rafters. No fire pits or bedrolls, no food or bodies. The room had been ransacked, its chairs and benches strewn about. Shattered glass sparkled on the stone floor.

He moved on to the first office, finding it looted save for a couple dozen books buried under a fallen shelf.

"Jackpot!"

He scanned the titles. Most he had read, though a few were new to him. There was even a leatherbound collection of essays and questions from the exam.

"I'll be back for you."

The second office was empty and, seeing there were no books to be found, he didn't bother to search further. Halfway to the third and final office, he stopped. Someone was near; he could smell them. And, as he waited, he could hear them. Someone was hiding in the office ahead.

His mind flashed tempting thoughts as he aimed the rifle forward.

Tom.

It was an all-encompassing notion, enticing him to play along. He conjured up the violence he would unleash. Pictured Tom's gaunt face and desperate pleas as he begged for mercy.

"That you, Tom?" he shouted, aiming down the hallway. His finger teased the trigger. When no reply came, he tried again. "Whoever's in there...I don't want any trouble. I have food. Just come out peacefully and you can have some."

"Go away!" a voice screeched. The words were coarse and unhinged. It wasn't Tom, as far as he could tell. The disappointment stung.

"I've got food an—"

"GO AWAY!!" the voice screamed again.

No more eating thistles. "Listen," he sighed. "I don't want any trouble and I don't want to hurt you. Just come out and I'll give you some food," the Boy pleaded. "The Year's almost over."

"Gooooo Away!"

The Boy pulled the trigger. His bullet chewed into the bottom of the wooden door. He didn't want to hurt the man, but he didn't want to waste time either.

"Okay! Okay! Don't shoot!" the man begged. "I'll come out!"

Keeping the rifle raised, Magnus' son sidestepped across the hallway to improve his vantage. As the door creaked open it swept a mess of clothing and blankets inward. A horrific smell fanned from the space, assaulting his senses with a putrid concoction of human aromas.

"Stop there," the Boy coughed, keeping his distance. "Show me your hands."

A skeletal man raised his arms. They were thin—the man

was thin all around—but his hands were empty and the Boy spied no knives or other weapons. He doubted the man would have had strength to lift a weapon anyway. He was emaciated and stooped, his grey hair dreaded in mismatched clumps. Splotches of weathered skin poked out from the layer of dirt that covered him. He looked familiar.

"Pete...?" the Boy whispered, lowering his rife. "Horse Pete? Is that you?"

The man before him blinked a vacant reply. His mouth quivered around each cluttered syllable. "Please...I...I'm just so hungry...please..."

Horse Pete's once round face had caved in upon itself, a greasy beard rounding out its sharp edges. His feet were bare and black from dirt, his toenails green-brown and curled. Hollow eyes blinked away the light. His mouth, which once flashed a toothy grin, was a dark and battered void edged by open sores.

"I'll get you some food, Pete. We've got plenty and you're welcome to share. I just need you to give me your word you won't try anything."

Horse Pete nodded.

"Alright," the Boy smiled, shouldering the rifle. "Come meet the family."

He turned back toward the hall, letting Pete follow a few paces behind. He buttoned down the myriad questions that bubbled up, choking on the man's stench. When they passed the second office, he gave in and spoke.

"Have you seen anyone else around?" the Boy asked over his shoulder. "I've been looking for someone and—"

Sudden movement. Acting on impulse, Magnus' son ducked, sweeping his torso down and to the side as a fist-sized stone careened overhead. He slipped the rifle off his shoulder as Pete lunged. Magnus' son fired. The bullet took Horse Pete square in the face, dropping him hard and fast.

"Fucking fuck!" the Boy cursed, tripping backward. The man wasn't moving but Magnus' son kept his guard up for a long minute, heart tripping over itself.

When the moment settled, he wiped his sweaty palms on his thighs, shaking off the shock.

"Shit!"

Blinking back the stench, the Boy buried his face in the crook of his elbow as he neared but Pete's putrid stink still managed to weasel its way into his nostrils. Stepping over the body, he padded to Pete's hideout. It reeked of death but there were no immediate signs anyone else had been there recently.

I'll deal with that tomorrow, he thought, mood soured. Twice now he had failed to find a peaceful solution. Twice he had been forced to eat thistles.

"Am I crazy?" he said to Sarris, who had wandered out into the hallway. He set his rifle down and picked up his daughter. "What do you think, my dear? Am I crazy?"

The fragile child looked him in the eyes and smiled, drooling down her tiny chin as he held her aloft.

"Hm. That's what I thought."

After setting a perimeter of barbed wire in the hallway, Magnus' son got a small fire going in the corner of the room, well away from the high windows that might give away his presence. Having fed his daughter and his two companions, he sat himself down to do something he hadn't done in a long time: he was going to read a new book. The sliver of normalcy wrapped him in a quilt of familiarity. For the first time in a long time, he felt like himself. A part of him knew, sitting there in the firelight, that the calm was an illusion—the corpse of Horse Pete was just down the hall, Beckett's daughter was gone, and his parents were buried—but sometimes, he conceded, a hint of a pleasant lie was better than a fistful of the hard truth.

He stretched out on a blanket, folding open the collection of exam essays. Its cursive font was smooth and dark, its text hardly faded or smudged. The pages were soft brown and gently used, save a crumpled dent in the right corner. His eyes feasted on the paper, his brain ravenous for an escape without real consequences, one imbued with poetic beauty and heroic characters and all the trappings of adventure.

But as he fingered his way over the text, the hard truth of his own experience bowled over the story he so desperately sought out. Adventure wasn't heroic; it was necessity. It was gut-wrenching violence and the dreadful smells of dying. It was the rise and crash of adrenaline. How it kicks in hard and, over time, leaves you almost craving more.

No, not almost, the Boy thought. *Always.*

Magnus' son folded the book in his lap. He rubbed his eyes, realizing then just how heavy they were. Walking to the threshold, he listened into the hallway. Miniscule flecks of snow, few and far between, blew in from outside, tumbling from the yawning dark. They were hardly perceptible unless you stared. He watched them for long moments. Then he was pummeled to the floor.

The force of the surprise blow dropped him to all fours. He tasted blood as his teeth dug into his tongue. He could hear screaming but he didn't have time to process it, collapsing further as a weight heaved onto his back. The smell made it apparent who was upon him, though he had hardly a breath of the stench before an arm was around his throat, choking him. He collapsed onto the stone floor, his arms pinned. He couldn't reach his weapons as he bucked and kicked. Horse Pete yelled gibberish warnings, cackling in his ear. The man's knee pressed into his side, forcing air from his lungs as the flow of blood to his brain trickled to a halt.

In a panic, the Boy threw blind punches. He knew had only a few seconds before the blackness stole the world from him, seconds he couldn't waste.

Stretching out his fingers, he felt for Pete's head and traced along his face until he reached the man's eyes. Twisting his wrist, he jabbed a thumb into one socket, forcing it inward. No slow testing of the senses. No steady increase in pressure. He simply forced it in, fingernail first, pushing with all his might. His left thumb fumbled for the other socket but missed, finding the gunshot wound that had torn open Pete's face. He pressed his thumb into the split skin, stretching it, spreading it as he burrowed.

The wound gushed anew. He could feel the man's cheekbone against his fingertip, the inside of his face warm and wet. After a forceful second, liquid splashed his other finger, Pete's eye giving way to blood and ooze. The vagabond was still screaming, though it was a different kind of scream now.

Pete's grip loosened as he failed, allowing the Boy a breath before he bucked the man over his shoulder and onto the hard floor. In the flickering darkness, dazed and dizzy, Magnus' son groped for what was nearest. He found the book of essays. He slammed the hardcover into Pete's throat. He did it again. And a few times more, until he felt the larynx snap under the force. Until Pete's spine unbuckled and the man went limp. Until stillness reclaimed the night.

Collapsing beside the body, he caught his breath as best he could, gulping mouthfuls of soiled air. Eventually he rolled over, staring up at the rafters beside a dead man he had now killed twice. He vomited. The thin juice of chunky liquid spilled down his chin and onto his shirt and sleeve. It didn't smell half as bad as Pete.

Shuddering into the dank chill, he watched his breath dissipate and float into nothingness as it settled, the caustic tang of the unwashed drifting over him. Near the fire, Gamling stood idle, staring at him for a few seconds before curling back up against the wall.

"So much for no surprises," Magnus' son coughed.

Wiping his face, he checked Horse Pete's pulse. The man was dead.

Rising to his feet, the Boy scooped up the bloodied essays and walked back toward the light of the small fire. He tossed the ruined exam manuscript into the flames and watched it transform into ash and air.

48

The next day, as thin splinters of autumn snow tumbled from the empty sky, Magnus' son dragged Pete's corpse outside, leaving it by the front door as a warning. He spent the rest of his morning in the bell tower, watching for signs of life, poking the bruise of false hope. When nothing unexpected stirred, he climbed down and grabbed his handkerchief.

"I guess there is no excuse now, is there?" he asked Sarris, tying the bandana around his face. He rummaged around his backpack for gloves. Finding none, he poked around their makeshift camp.

"No, I'm not stalling," he grumbled to the animals. "It just smells terrible and I don't want to waste our water on washing. And, no, I don't want to go down to the lake either," he confessed. The thought of the chill water sent a shiver down his spine.

"Well, I'll be back. Unless anyone volunteers to go for me?" He stood, gloveless, in the middle of the room, hands on his tools. "Fine," he sighed. "Sarr, you're in charge. Don't make a mess."

Adjusting his mask, he unbarred the chamber's wide double doors and stepped into the drafty hallway. The stink of Pete's hideaway swelled in the open space, peppering each breath with nausea. Reaching the end of the corridor, the Boy could see why the smell had spread: the door to Pete's room was ajar. Magnus' son pulled his knife.

"No surprises."

He leaned into the small space. The pungent fumes were asphyxiating. A bucket brimming with piss and shit sat idle in the corner, the floor sullied by its overflow. Across the room, a small fire pit had scorched the stone walls black. With no ventilation, the Boy could only guess how smokey the room would get. Beside the fire was a collection of odds and ends. Including bones. They had been boiled and picked clean. Having dealt death and displayed its aftermath, Magnus' son had become gruesomely familiar with how the body connects. How it breaks and rips and bends. These were human bones.

While there was a part of him revolted by the horror, there was a part of him, some new appendage of his mind, that was not even remotely shocked. He had seen what people do to one another to survive. This was just another color on that canvas.

Tucking his knife away, he scooped up the bones. He closed the door behind him and made a note to cover the bottom of the door with mud or fabric to keep the smell at bay. But that would wait. He needed to take the bones outside. Not to bury them; these bones were for the living. These bones would stand guard, as a warning.

HE SPENT the next month on watch, wandering the village and searching for life. Searching for her, in truth. But there was nothing to see but bodies and bones and the pillaged carcass of Hope. The Beckett house was torched and empty, the village shanties blackened and left to weather. He looted what he could, though most things of value had already been snatched away. He never saw any people, not even a solitary footprint in the dirt. One day he caught an old tabby tussling with a pair of crows, the trio clawing and biting themselves into a stalemate, but that was the only life left. For all intents and purposes, Hope was dead.

To distract himself from his soured reality, he spent hours collecting bits of stained glass. He piled them in the village square so they would catch the light when he was on lookout in the bell tower. As the sun danced over the colored glass, he chased daydreams of the future. New buildings sprouted over the derelict remnants of Hope. A bigger school. A new library, where books could be copied and stored. Instead of stones and lumber, knowledge and art would be their exports. Hope would bloom anew, a place free from the Year with its own laws—just laws. Merciful laws. From the ashes of less, a new world would be seeded. Out of misery, there would be more. That would be his mission. It was something he knew his parents would be proud of. That she would be proud of. But it was something necessary too. No more sacrifice for selfish gain. No more fighting for table scraps.

Staring out over the ransacked village, he let his voice carry over the wind-blown ruins.

"Through hardship is the journey. From less there will be more..."

49

With a week before the end, the Boy looked more and more toward the future. It was a comforting reprieve from the past, which often dragged him into darkness. There had been no sign of Beckett's daughter and the loneliness was paralyzing. If he wasn't so busy keeping everyone alive he might have even succumbed to it. His daughter was barely keeping down his makeshift formula of milk and wheat powder, her sleep irregular and fitful, and the exhaustion of looking after her full-time—along with Gamling and Sarris—was all-consuming.

Yet even the future, with its promise of purpose, stood daunting before him. Life would continue after the Year—he would make sure of it—but he had no one to share it with. Sure, there was Sarris and Gamling and his daughter. He loved them to death and knew, in all honesty, that without them to care for he would not have survived the Year. But without Beckett's daughter, without his parents, survival felt hollow. He also knew that if he didn't find a wet nurse soon, his daughter might not survive.

He rubbed his tired eyes, shrugging off the weighty thoughts. "Let's get some air."

He shuffled up the stairs toward the bell tower to reconnoiter the ruins. He spied over the remnants of Hope for the better part of an hour before he was satisfied. Then, he kept watch for another handful of minutes, just to be certain. It was too close to the end to take any risks. It was too close to the end for surprises.

Committed to his plan, the Boy removed the barricade from the front door and stepped into the day. The light was warm, bordering on hot, but the December air was fresh. He patrolled the building, rifle at the ready, before bringing his family out.

After laying his daughter in the shade, he hammered a stake into the dirt and tied Gamling to it lest she wander. He slipped a small rope around Sarris too. There was grass nearby that the two would be more than happy to pick at it.

Reclining against the stone wall of the village hall, Magnus' son laid his rifle down and armed himself with a thick book, ready to lounge away the morning. He made sure to keep his guard up, scanning the scene regularly. Within a handful of minutes he was warm but he kept his jacket on, letting the heat envelope him. He wanted to warm up enough so he could leap into the lake and not shiver himself to bits. The child would need a bath too, and probably some clean clothes as well.

"You're coming too you lazy brute," he nodded to Gamling, who was chomping at the weeds near the hall's foundation. "You too, bird brain."

The Boy glanced to Sarris but didn't see the rooster. Squinting in the light, he scanned the shade for Sarris. The rope was empty.

"Sarris?" he called out, looking over the open space. He spotted the bird's prints in the dust leading beyond the edge of the building. He followed them, tucking the leather-bound book into his jacket. He pulled out his hammers just in case.

No surprises.

He found Sarris around the corner. "There you are, you little sneak." The bird was pecking in the dirt, chasing bugs and ignoring him. "Come here."

And then he stopped. A man stood a dozen paces beyond the bird, face twisted in surprise.

"Tom...?"

The Boy's fingers tingled. His mind numbed. A black hole gnawed at him, sucking life from day, draining color and hope. He left the rifle by the door with his daughter. Tom already had his bow out. There was nothing to be done.

He didn't move as the arrow came. Didn't even flinch. He just looked toward his best friend, soon to be his former neighbor's next meal. "I'm sorry."

The arrow cracked bone, stabbing through skin and muscle. It knocked him back a full step, his lungs pushed empty as his legs wobbled. The hammers slipped from his sweaty palms, falling to the barren earth. The pain surprised him. It sounded different too, so close in his ears. His vision flickered as he buckled, crumbling to his knees. A stream of warm blood tickled its way down his torso, pooling where his shirt had been tucked into his trousers. Helpless, he watched the blackness approach. No farewell tears. No consolation smile. Just the cold acceptance of bitter circumstance. He was his father's son after all. He was ready.

50

The arrow was in the air before he realized what he had done. It was reflex. Habit. A lifetime of being quicker than the dead. He didn't regret the action—he was a survivor after all—but he wished it didn't have to be so.

"I'm sorry, Boy," he hollered. The words were gruff and unwieldy. It had been a while since he had spoken to anyone and he found the sound of his own voice unfamiliar.

He approached Magnus' son, who had fallen to his knees. "I am, truly. We were even, you and me. For the most part, anyway."

He pulled out his knife. "For what it's worth, kid, I am sorry."

Magnus's boy was folded over, his chest rising and falling with slow, shallow movements. He wouldn't survive long but Tom wanted to see that it was quick. The Boy had earned that much.

"I'll look after the child, don't worry," he said. "She'll be in good hands. Ya've my word on that."

He squatted down to look his friend-turned-foe in the eye.

For a dragging moment, he debated telling the Boy about what happened to Beckett's daughter but the kid looked tired. He looked broken. So he decided against it. That was another burden he'd have to carry alone.

"You were a fighter, Boy," he finally spoke. "Played the game well. I admire that. Yer old man and I, we were one trick ponies. A hammer, a bow—that's all we got. But you?" he paused, gesturing to the kid with his knife, "You were something else. Not at first, I admit. At first you were a clumsy oaf and I chided Magnus for even bothering. 'Leave 'em to his books,' I told him. But he musta saw somethin' I didn't because you became a survivor. And you almost won too."

Pushing himself back to full height, Tom loomed over the Boy. He gave the kid a pat on the head before pressing his fingertips in, holding Magnus' son steady.

"You've earned a name, kid. I'm proud of you." Tom squeezed the knife, severing the few threads of hesitation that ensnared him.

He stabbed the blade forward. To kill his past and break the scales he once thought balanced.

"Tell Mag I'll be seein' him."

51

He had been waiting for the end for some time. It had come at a heavy cost but he was ready for it. Longed for it, as much as it pained him to admit it. He was ready to start anew.

"Tell Mag I'll be seein' him."

Distantly, he felt Tom's hand on his head. The man's fingertips were pressed against his skull. Not hard. Just firm enough to keep the weight of him steady. He felt the shift in pressure, watched Tom's feet pivot as the knife moved. The blow was aimed at his temple; a quick finale to a life half lived and poorly spent.

A finale he expected.

As the blade stabbed in, the Boy slipped his right hand down and pulled his own knife, jerking his head aside. Tom's knife careened by, cutting nothing but air. Lightning quick, Magnus' son stabbed down through Tom's boot, punishing skin and breaking bone. A scream shattered the morning. Tom jerked his knife back, jabbing a second strike. Just as anyone would do. Just as the Boy expected. Magnus' son dodged the attack and pried Tom's knife from his grip. He stabbed it into the man's other foot.

"YOU TELL HIM YOURSELF!"

He shoved Tom backward. As the man fell, Magnus' son slammed his hands down onto the knives buried in Tom's feet to keep them steady. Tom flailed, falling flat and hard as the blades gashed flesh. The man's scream was a guttural burst of pain and surprise, the weapons splitting a multitude of bones.

The Boy ignored the cries, pushing himself up, winded. Slowly, he twisted the shaft out from his chest, feeling the metal tip grate on bone as he teased it free.

Tom stared, bewildered and red-faced. Magnus' son forced a weary smile, pulling a book from the hard leather pocket in his jacket. It was pierced straight through.

"Tolkien," he coughed, blinking off the dizziness. He tapped his chest. "Always take the heart."

He reached down and tore his knife from Tom's foot, igniting the man's unrestrained ire. As Tom scowled and groaned, the Boy limped over to Sarris. Adrenaline left his hands shaking but he did his best to smooth out the bird's ruffled feathers. His mind drifted back to when his parents had surprised him with the bird, smuggling the rooster into his bed while he slept. He remembered how hard they laughed, how his heart raced in surprise. He didn't realize it at the time, but that was one of the happiest days of his life.

Feeling drained, Magnus' son sat down in the dirt beside his old neighbor, whose busted feet watered the earth red. The man was shaking, his pale face on the verge of weeping or raging.

Resting in the dirt just beyond Tom's reach, he let Sarris go, watching the bird waddle back toward the grass. Above him, tufts of white listlessly roamed. Beside him, Tom seethed.

The Boy didn't expect an apology; he wasn't looking for answers or explanations. He knew, now, that the world rarely granted them. He just looked at his former neighbor—his former friend—and extended his arms upward, holding out his hands for the world to see. The scarred skin reflected the light, its ruinous patterns cross-crossing their way from his fingertips to his elbows.

"From less there will be more..." he quoted.

"Piss on more, Boy," Tom growled. "Just be grateful yer still on the board."

"Grateful?" Magnus' son choked. He fought back the condescending laughter that brewed in his belly, tightening his cheeks. "Grateful?! Is that the kind of world you want to live in, where we're grateful to just get by? To cling to the precipice and hope we can somehow limp to the finish line. Is that what I should be grateful for?"

He glared at his old neighbor. It would be so easy to smash his face in right now. So easy. To crack open his ribs and make a mess of his organs. To set fire to his flesh and watch him ash to dust. It would be music. It would be art.

Magnus' son pondered what his parents would do. His father would kill the man, no question. He'd beat Tom to pulp here and now without so much as a word. And his mother? She'd put a bullet in him without thinking twice. That was how they solved problems. That was how the world solved problems.

Catching his breath, the Boy scanned the village and the encroaching grass nearby. A weedy patch of parched thistles danced in the stale breeze, long stalks capped by dead off-purple seedheads.

Just because we can stomach something doesn't mean we should.

The realization was a punch in the gut.

For too long, he had been blindly following the rules, playing the game. But the game wasn't meant to be won. It was rigged from the get-go, a see-saw tossing them back and forth until they inevitably fell off. And it wasn't a game the Boy was good at anyway. That much was abundantly clear.

"We've been eating thistles..." He bit his tongue until he tasted iron. It was so obvious now, the world coming into unblemished focus. "Not anymore," he whispered. "I don't want to live in your world, Tom. I don't want to play your game. It's a mess of blood and shit and all I'm left to clean it with is rags. No wonder the world is a fucking cesspool."

"Yer a survivor, Boy, same as me. Same as yer old man."

"No," the Boy insisted, shaking his head. "No. You think that winning and surviving proves we are strong, that competition hones us. But it breaks us, Tom. Divides us. Rots us. Then the few that remain —us *winners*—are actually the worst of us. Not the best. Because the best of us don't sacrifice what matters for a shot at another sunrise. The best of us don't care about *surviving*. They care about *living*. About *helping*. And I'm not like my father."

Tom coughed, coaxing a smile as he rolled his head over to face the Boy, squinting against the light. "Then what are ya, Boy?" he rasped. "Fuckin' enlighten me."

The Boy said nothing, keeping his thoughts hidden.

"Figured as much," Tom scoffed. "Alright. Make 'er quick," he wheezed. "I deserve that much at least." Tom looked up into the blue, eyes open as he waited for his ending.

He turned to Tom, still gasping for a proper breath. "You really don't get it, do you?" the Boy exhaled, looking down to the helpless pale-faced man he had pinned to the earth. Tom blinked but didn't look his way. "We can't just keep killing our problems. That doesn't fix anything. It just spins the wheel again and again and again. You know where that gets us? Right the fuck back here," he shouted, "with blood in the dirt and bodies on the ground. Good grief, has no one read a fucking book!?"

He paused to look at his wound, peeking under his shirt to

watch the blood stream from the open sore. He'd live. Not just out of stubbornness, like Tom, but out of a desire to build a new world. A world where you didn't have to stab your neighbor before they stabbed you. A world of more.

But it had to start somewhere. There had to be a first step.

Through hardship is the journey. From less there will be more.

"I'm not going to kill you, Tom Luddstow," the Boy sighed. "I should—my parents would. But I won't." He looked the man in the eyes, a wellspring of sadness splintering the façade of rage that kept him standing. The words, as an idea, made sense to him. It was a meaningful gesture.

But as they entered the world he felt the weight that they carried, felt their substance in every vessel of his body.

"But I can't forget. Not what you've done. And not what you've taken from me."

He paused to wipe away a tear, the liquid smudging the dirt on the back of his hand. He drew his saber, dragging it from its scabbard, listening to the metal sing as it emerged, polished and sharp and hungry. Without a word, he chopped Tom's bow until it broke.

"You're never going to shoot another arrow again."

He stepped forward. Tom tensed. Pressing his foot down on the man's wrist, he pinned Tom's right hand against the ground. A flick of his sword sent two and a half fingers tumbling into the dirt. Tom growled through clenched teeth, his bloodshot eyes and pallid face glaring.

"Never again," Magnus' son insisted. "Not. Another. Single. Arrow."

Tearing a piece of cloth from his own ruined shirt, he threw the strip to Tom, letting the man wrap his wound. Sheathing his saber, Magnus' son scooped up Sarris and dusted his friend off before turning back to his old neighbor. He brought his face —and Sarris' face—close. Close enough to smell the man's breath, to see the red in his eyes and the venom in his twisted sneer. Tom was thinner than he looked, his beard hiding the lost weight.

"If I ever see you again Tom Luddstow I am going to flay the skin from your body. Do you hear me?" His voice didn't waver. His mind didn't wander. "Nod if you understand me."

Tom nodded.

"I will break every bone in your body with my hammers and scrape the muscle from every which where I can. I will drag your guts from your belly and hang them from your neck so you can smell your own insides. I will pry out your teeth, batter them to pieces, and blind you with them. There is no limit to the suffering I will cause you should I even sense that you are near. Do you understand me, Tom?"

Again, Tom nodded.

"This is your fire, Tom. You have a second chance now, if you want it. A chance at living. Or, you can take your knife and end it. I don't care. But the game is over."

On wobbly legs, he rose, his unblinking eyes locked on his defeated foe. Satisfied his point was taken—and knowing full well he meant each and every word—the Boy slammed his foot forward and ushered the man into unconsciousness.

His family safe from harm, he let down his guard. And then he screamed. With every ounce of rage, he screamed.

52

Magnus' son stayed inside the hall until the end. Safe behind stone walls, and with a barrel of water to ration from, the family stayed put. Most days were spent healing and reading and cobbling together elaborate barriers to keep Gamling and Sarris away from the grass and shrubs he had stored in the corner. A good many hours were spent looking out over Hope, dreaming. It would start with movement in the distance. Then, she would appear. She'd break the tree line at a sprint and he'd call out to her. She would wave and spring to the door where they would embrace. Then, everything would be okay.

It was a fool's dream, but he basked in it as often as he could. Escape was addicting. And maybe, at times, necessary.

But then the end arrived. The last day of the Year.

As a clear day cast spacious light over the ruins of Hope, the Boy waited in the bell tower with Sarris and his daughter. He wasn't sure anybody would come but he waited anyway, longing for the bells' liberating echo. He pictured people trickling in from the surrounds in anticipation, survivors ready to recover, to unite and rebuild.

Maybe that's what she was waiting for...for Hope to be safe before she comes back...

But as the day dragged on, nobody came. No carts approached from down the road, no boats rowed into the harbor.

"I finally got my wish," he realized, rocking his daughter with tired arms. "I wanted to be left alone..."

Before him, his dream-turned-nightmare sprawled into the distance. Miserly forests and unkempt fields layered themselves atop the world, a jumble of fragile geography. Snaking east, his eyes followed the lane out to the quarry, the pit hidden from view though the gap it left in the trees was apparent enough. He continued east, out to where he figured the McKelsie homestead was. Beyond that, far beyond what his eyes could see, was the Faroff. Scorched and poisoned and solitary.

As his eyes traced their way back to Hope, he spied movement. Someone approached from the south. Elation rose in his throat, his chest ripping itself a new wound.

But it wasn't her. The realization pushed back against his excitement and he kicked himself for embracing a fool's hope. That's when he finally saw who it was.

"A ranger," he gasped, the truth dawning on him. "A ranger!"

Below, the weathered guardian hopped off his mount and sauntered into the village square. The man had a long-barreled pistol in his grip as he pressed forward. He was cautious, moving slowly as he scanned the market. When he reached the center of the square, the Boy whistled. Instinctively, the ranger ducked, bringing his gun to bear.

"Whoa!" the Boy shouted from the tower, waving. "It's okay. It's just us," he hollered.

The ranger slowly lowered his weapon, eyes darting about, continuing toward the hall. Heart racing, the Boy tucked the

baby into a wrap and scurried down the ladder. He exchanged
his daughter for the carbine before stepping over his tripwires
and removing the barricade, opening the door to the world for
the first time in days.

The ranger was waiting near the door, pistol raised. He
looked weatherworn. Smelled it too. His leather was bloodied,
his face etched with a grim and sinewy countenance. The man's
resting scowl reminded him of his father.

"Welcome to Hope," the Boy stuttered, pushing the door
open wide.

The ranger nodded, slipping into the building, horse in tow.
Magnus' son sealed the door behind them, barricading it once
more. By the time he finished, the man had navigated the tripwires and made his way into the hall without a sound.

"Um, excuse me? Sir?"

The ranger didn't stop. He walked into the main chamber
and grabbed the Boy's canteen, gorging on the water that
poured from its slender spout. The man drank until he
coughed and sputtered out a mouthful onto the floor, sucking
in air to wash it all down. He was shorter than the Boy and at
least twice his age. A tangled beard outlined a grimy, hawkish
face. It was dark like the man's eyes. He had a lean frame to
him. Not underfed. Just light. Like he could run for days and
never break a sweat.

"You're here to end the Year?" the Boy asked. It was a stupid
question but he wanted to hear that it was over. He needed to.
The ranger simply looked up, the crease in his eyebrows
serving answer enough. "Have you been through any other
villages?" the Boy continued. "How is it in New Gamling? Rockmantle? Is it this bad everywhere?"

The ranger didn't reply. He made no mention of the empty
village, no mention of the destruction, of the bones piled by the
entrance. The Boy could only assume such horrors weren't
uncommon.

"Do you know when the caravan is supposed to be here?" the Boy pried. "And did you see anyone nearby? I'm looking fo—"

The ranger cut him off with the shake of his head and a distant shrug. "Look, kid. I gotta sleep. It's been a long time since I had a roof over my head."

The man got up and stalked back to the hall, removing the wires and obstacles before walking his horse into the room. He didn't bother to set the tripwires back up, leading the animal into the main chamber before grabbing his bedroll and cozying up against the wall, pistol resting on his chest.

Having had to wild camp for a few nights, Magnus' son was only slightly familiar with its discomfort. Yet he knew full-well how taxing it was to the body and mind. He let the man settle, setting up his tripwires up once more. It was probably unnecessary. After all, the Year would be over come midnight. But, as he had learned, worlds can end in far less time.

"No surprises."

He had planned to sleep but his eyes never grew tired. Sitting by the fire, the Boy read and counted the hours, conjuring new lives and better worlds. His chest was healing and free from infection, which was something he had worried about after he stitched it closed. The stitches were crooked and he wished he had taken the time to learn when his parents were around. He wished they were there to see him, so close to the end. Beckett's daughter too. So close to a fresh start.

But what would that fresh start entail? Would he rebuild in Hope? Would the ranger take them somewhere? Could they look for Beckett's daughter together? There were so many questions.

He grappled with them into the dark of night, twirling his father's sheriff star, until the ranger stirred. Out of the corner of his eye, the Boy watched the man check his pistol before slipping it back into his holster. Without a word, the ranger walked over to the fire, drinking once again from the Boy's canteen. He emptied it this time. There was still no one outside. No voices in the night, no survivors gathering to bid the Year farewell.

"It's just me," the Boy spoke, the words falling from his mouth before his brain could stop them. "I'm the only one." He looked down to his daughter, who was sleeping in the cart. "We're the only ones."

The man looked at him for a long moment. It made him uncomfortable but he held the stare.

"What's your name, kid?"

"My name? Oh. I, uh, don't have one," he confessed. "Besides, what's the point of a name if no one's around to say it?"

The ranger finally smiled, his lips thin and honest. "Well, I reckon you've earned one. But, the question you have to ask yerself now, *sheriff*, is what's the point of any of this?"

Without waiting for a reply, the ranger walked away from the light of the fire, slipping into the shadows. He padded up the stairs and then up the ladder, creaking his way to the alcove below the bells. There was no announcement. No warning. Just an ending.

The bells began to toll.

Twelve round and hollow sounds, one for every month of the Year, were the finale. The echo reverberated through the building, washing over them. Cleansing them. The relief was all-consuming; tears warmed the Boy's skin, sliding from his cheeks onto the blanket he had wrapped around his daughter. It was over. They had made it.

Parts of them, anyway. Not the best parts. The best parts were buried under earth and stone. They were the pedestals stood upon to keep above the waves.

The bells stopped ringing.

"We made it," he whispered again, kissing his daughter. He'd have to name her now, he realized. She—like him—had earned it. "It's finally over."

He almost didn't believe the words. They felt foreign. Too delicate to be brought to life. They had survived. They could rebuild. He didn't know how, didn't even know where to begin...but he would see it through. That was his purpose now.

To make things better.

To build the world he and the Girl had dreamt about.

He owed it to her. To them all. It was a new world now.

Springing up the stairs, he craned his neck toward the bell tower. He wanted to thank the ranger. He still had a million questions too. It had been a while since he had talked to anyone who could talk back. It would be nice to have a conversation.

As he stared into the dark of the bell tower, waiting for the man to come down, he noticed movement. It was subtle; a gentle wavering of the thick strand of rope that drooped from the bell tower. Like a ripple in a shallow pool. By the time he blinked it was too late. The bells were ringing.

"What?"

No. No!

"No!"

The bells continued, battering the sullied air.

"Nonononono! What are you doing?" he shouted. "What are you doing?"

It sang a chorus in his bones. The sound was everything, a cavernous melee compressing him. When it faded, the Boy lashed out, flustered and confused, his world collapsing in on itself.

"It was over!" he screamed. "It was over! You can't do this to us!" His voice betrayed him and he could hear himself quivering, cracking and straining like the world around him.

"You don't get it, kid," the ranger sighed, backing down the ladder. "It ain't never over. Not here. Don't you see?"

He dashed after the man, bounding down the stairs and into the main chamber. He was shaking, his mind fragmented and unable to process the death sentence he had been handed. The balls of his feet pressed into the ground. His fists clenched. Words were jumbled on his tongue.

"I...we..."

The world was spinning. The ground kicked out from under him. He wanted to vomit but nothing came, his stomach grasping at bile and air. He tried to speak but choked on the words. The scaffolding that kept his mind collected turned to dust. Unmoving, he watched with mottled vision as the man gave his horse a scratch.

"Take good care of her, eh?" the man said, looking to his horse. Then with a deftness that made the Boy feel oafish in comparison, the ranger whipped out his beat-up pistol. The Boy didn't move—he didn't have time to. Before he could flinch, the gun was in the ranger's mouth.

The shot coughed a sonic punch that hung in the air for long moments, a familiar thunder slow to fade.

Wide-eyed and frozen, the Boy choked, breathing in the mist of former life. He felt its speckled warmth against his face. He tasted liquid on his tongue and lips. Bits of foreign substance were swallowed as he chased another breath. The body, suspended in the air for half a heartbeat, tumbled over, hitting the stone floor with a sticky thud.

The ringing in his ears blocked out his crying daughter, sending him into a light-headed spin. He collapsed against the wall.

Magnus' son wanted to speak, to curse, to question. But he could only muster ragged breaths of balled nonsense as he spat out chunks of man. He was breathless, chest compressed vice-tight, his mouth almost too dry to swallow. All he could hear, kicking at his brain with a downtrodden obsession, were the bells.

It was the sound of his lungs filling, the sound of his heart beating hard and furious.

It was the sound of his child, screaming alone in a pile of furs and blankets.

The bells were everything. They smothered him, ringing infinite.

He watched them take his parents. Watched the bells take Fort and the Luddstows too. He watched the bells pry his love from life, painting wintergrey days a milky and ruinous red.

Crumpled on the uneven stone, he listened to the blood pour from the body beside him, noting it slow from a fresh gush to a slight trickle. The smell of stale piss and unwashed horse and human insides crafted a perfumed concoction that lingered in the stagnant air. He swallowed it.

He stayed on the floor until it hurt. Until his limbs were stiff and numb. Until his bones were sore and tender. Immobile, he eyed the motes of dust that floated in the firelight, pointlessly drifting through the invisible above him. The baby had stopped crying. So did he, he realized.

After a time, he wiped his eyes, clearing the salt and blood and dirt from his face. He didn't bother to get up. He couldn't if he tried. Not yet. He needed to think. To breathe. His chest ached. His heart ached too. His guts felt twisted and wrong. The pool of blood that leaked from the ranger had weaved amongst the rivulets of stone. He could feel it against his shoulders and the back of his neck. It was thick and sticky and lukewarm.

Retreating, he slipped away from the present. He let his eyes embrace their heaviness, burying himself in the coarse sands of thought, adrift between nowhere and everywhere. He stayed there until the blood that pooled around him turned cold. Until his back was stiff and itchy. Until his daughter had cried herself to sleep again, hungry and lonely. Laying on the floor, the Boy listened to her breathe gentle breaths of life. Determined, tenuous life.

She had earned a name. So, he realized, had he.

As if on cue, his eyes drifted toward his father's tools. Gate-keepers between worlds, they were home and hope made tangi-ble. He brought the hammers to his face, resting the metal of each tool against his skin. His eyes traced down the handles to the hands that held them. To his scars and the guilty skin he once worked hard to hide.

Pitter-patter.

Once again, he was in the fire. Chewing thistles. He wasted no thoughts on why. It didn't matter. He didn't feed the blos-soming questions or water the reluctance that stowed away in the backbone of his mind. He just buried them. He made them a home, tucked away in a place so deep and hidden it would never be more than a grave to carry.

He buried his name there too. Those syllables could wait. Because there was work to be done.

Through hardship is the journey. From less there will be more.

For a Less Year had begun.

THANK YOU

Thank you so much for reading this book. It's been an absolute labor of love putting this story together over the past decade and to see it finally out there in the world is something I'm immensely proud of. I hope you enjoyed reading this adventure as much as I enjoyed writing it.

If you did enjoy the book, I'd love to hear from you. Reviews are vital for indie authors like me and help ensure our work gets seen (and we get paid). But they're also just really nice to get too.

If you could leave a review on Amazon or Goodreads I'd be incredibly grateful. They really do mean a lot and make a difference.

You can also reach me at info@ckoldfield.com. I'd love to hear from you!

ACKNOWLEDGMENTS

This book would not have been possible without the help of my good friends Mitch Arend and Evan Wise, two gents I've known for over twenty years who helped me shape the story and provided valuable feedback and insights. I could not have finished the book without their help and support.

I also want to thank everyone who messaged me over the years checking in about the book. Your interest and enthusiasm kept me excited and engaged. I'm grateful for your love and support.

Of course, I need to thank my beta readers, who helped spot problems and typos. Because there are always typos.

Finally, a huge thanks goes to my partner Christine. She tolerated me spending countless hours, day in and day out, hunched over my laptop while she picked up the slack around the house. She is my best friend and I love her to death.

ABOUT THE AUTHOR

Born in Canada and based in Sweden, Chris spent his formative years toiling away on a sprawling organic farm in rural Ontario before spending over a decade backpacking around the world. After dabbling in travel writing with his debut travelogue THE DOGS OF NAM, Chris is now stumbling through the world of fiction.

Vegan, straight edge, Buddhist, and bald, when he is not writing, he can usually be found tinkering with his prepper gear or wasting time playing video games. He reads a lot too.

He currently lives on a small island in rural Sweden with his partner, rescue dog, blind cat, and son.

To learn more about Chris and his ongoing projects, visit ckoldfield.com and follow him on social media:

- Facebook: /ckoldfield
- Instagram: /ckoldfield
- Twitter: @learnedabroad

The Less Year